Duplicity

A NOVEL BY

Nanette M. Buchanan

Acknowledgments

I was challenged to write this third part of "The Mince Family Saga". For various reasons I took on the challenge and anxiously await your comments. The Mince Family started my literary journey and now, twelve years later this is the beginning of yet another personal chapter for me. I prepared for this moment ten years ago and I can honestly say I have mixed emotions. I'm excited about the new and anxiously awaiting the unknown.

To my family…we made it! Eleven years of published works, without you it wouldn't have been possible. This is the beginning of a new. Retirement, the big move and so much more to come. I'm ready for the next step on this journey. I'm blessed you're sharing these steps with me.

To my readers, reviewers, book clubs, stores, and distributors…ten years and I hope you've enjoyed my work and shared it with others. Thank you for being in the midst. I've learned so much over the past eleven years. I chose this path to share my writing. I now believe it was meant to be. Thank you…and continue to read, relax and enjoy…as I pen.

Forward

***Duplicity** is the third book in what is now "The Mince Family Saga". What was meant to be one novel, my first, eleven years ago took on a life of its own. **Family Secrets Lies and Alibis** is a story that so many of us live. We live among and with family and relatives that have held secrets. Secrets about health, relationships, and the lies told for generations to keep the secrets. These secrets continue to be passed on as truths.*

When the secrets are revealed there is the initial shock, this we learn to suppress in time. The hurt, the pain and sometimes the shame often takes a lifetime to overcome. We question ourselves, we question who we are, and we question those we've trusted. We ask one simple question...why?

I write the "realities" that we live. I ask the questions that we ask in private. I answer the questions that we dare not ask. I allow my pen to take me deep and find a resolution. I research the methods of those who have evolved and overcome. I pen not just for the entertainment but for the lessons. Lessons I, as well as my readers, may find rewarding, refreshing, and sometimes a way of our healing.

***Family Secrets Lies and Alibis** birthed **A Different Kind of Love.** A part of the story that we often can't find in our reality is the answer from those who have passed on with the secrets. Those who are here with us don't feel obligated to tell, to inform, or to share. They too are hiding the good, the bad, and the ugly. We can't fully understand who we are without knowing those who came before us. D.Q. Mince left his family to live under a cloud of secrets. Upon his death, the secrets began to unravel and the lies that followed* created questions. The untold truths seemed to be overwhelming but his son 'Rell, with the help of his lawyer, uncovered D.Q.'s answers.

This story is endless and picking up the pieces of his father's past brings challenges. **A Different Kind of Love** tells the reasons behind the secrets and the lies. There is no excuse for the lies and the secrets of the untold past. There is the story, the reality lived by D.Q. and his reasons to live with the secrets.

When I wrote this novel that became my first two books, I wanted people to understand what could happen when untold secrets unfold. I wanted my readers and others to understand that our past is important to our present and our future. I wanted to preach and teach a lesson.

We left 'Rell and Shai in a happy place, married and successful. One might say they got their "Happily Ever After". There are those in the story who see a different reality in this fiction. Those that would say... "It ain't over." I invite you to read, as the saga continues...

Duplicity

One

The plans to sleep in changed quickly when the phone rang. Tonya reached for the phone blindly. She promised Karlton she'd stay home while he was out of town. She answered the call hoping he wasn't checking on her again.

"Karlton, I'm fine darling. Say you're on your way home."

"Ms. Mince, this is Mr. Monroe, good morning."

Tonya sat up in the bed and pulled off her satin eye mask. Mr. Monroe, her lawyer, was the only one aware of her intentions. Now that she was medically cleared, Karlton and Shai resumed their regular routines. Without them watching her every move she contacted her lawyer to handle her unfinished business.

"Good morning, I didn't expect to hear from you this soon."

"As I told you, I would look at your assets and what you acquired from your ex-husband. I do see you have stocks that were sold…."

"Yes, without my knowledge!" Tonya firmly interjected.

"Ms. Mince, stay calm, please. Those stocks are doing very well. It may be an advantage."

"It is no advantage to me if it is not connected to D.Q. Enterprises."

"Ms. Mince. You have no claims to D.Q. Enterprises. Your agreement before the separation clearly stated you would not receive any other payments or be connected financially to D.Q. Enterprises after your husband's death."

"And was that told to me by you, or did you simply say it would be best if I signed the papers? Let's not play games. You talked me into giving up what could have been mine today."

Disgusted, Tonya threw back the covers on her bed. The clock read ten thirty. There was enough time to get dressed and meet the lawyer for lunch if necessary.

"Mr. Monroe, I'll need to understand fully what I have. I also need to know what I gave to that bastard son and his mother."

"Ms. Mince you didn't give them anything. What was left to Darrell, Derek and Dershai is in D.Q's will. There is really no need to dispute it." The lawyer paused waiting for her to respond. "What I'm simply saying Ms. Mince is, D.Q's will was written years before his death. It seems he may have done this at the same time as your separation. There is nothing to argue. He wasn't sick or dying then. I'm sorry, there's nothing to dispute."

"I want what's mine. After thirty years of marriage, and I get nothing? I know you don't think that sits well with me."

"Ms. Mince, why don't you read the email I've sent you? It explains what those stocks have done over the years and what you have in assets. I believe D.Q. gave you the best without giving you the business. You'll see you are gaining more than you anticipated."

Tonya opened her closet door. She took a step back from her clothes hoping she heard his response correctly.

"Did you say I'm gaining?" The thought of beating D.Q. at his own game gave her a smile but stock in another company wasn't what she wanted. "I'm sure D.Q. didn't think there would be any assets. Why would he sell them for me to profit? It can't be much."

"Yes, you're sitting in a good position. If you'd like to come into the office we can talk about the dividends and other stock options. I've got to say it again, D.Q. sold the stock to a great company and they've been very attentive to your shares."

"I haven't gained enough Mr. Monroe. I will get my foot in the door of D.Q. Enterprises one way or another."

She hung up the phone without a goodbye. Her rudeness wouldn't upset Mr. Monroe. He had been her lawyer for more than fifteen years. She was a difficult client but she paid well. There was a time when she thought he was working for D.Q.

She smiled as she remembered the conversation they had. D.Q. questioned why she needed a lawyer. She smirked as she told him every woman needed more than one man to be on their side. Mr. Monroe stood by her even when she knew she was wrong. Over the years she didn't explain her actions and he knew not to ask.

There were those who would label her bitter and others who would agree with her anger. They didn't need to know her story, the reasons D.Q. left her bed and their marriage. They didn't need to know she groomed him for success, or so she thought. Even if he would have accomplished all he had without her, he married her with nothing. Tonya believed they were in love at one time. Tonya believed D.Q. Enterprises was a result of that love.

D.Q. Enterprises became his new love. One where he found friends, now partners, to invest in. It was his dream. Tonya held on tightly hoping he wouldn't fall for a secretary, a client or the wife of another executive. She watched as he lived his separate life, away from home, away from her.

There were many overnight trips, meetings, and out of town presentations. In the beginning, he would invite her only to leave her alone in the hotel room. She didn't consider it fair to be the wife at the table that knew nothing about the business or the plans. She declined his invitation twice and he never asked again.

Over the years she wondered where he met Nikki Robbins, the woman he loved even after death. They had a child together who now sat as President, of D.Q. Enterprises. Tonya didn't see that thirty years of love lasting. *What kind of woman would be sloppy seconds for years?* It was obvious now that D.Q. was gone. He promised Nikki and her son everything. He kept his promise.

When she found out Nikki was pregnant she had to plan her own pregnancy. She too had "others" who wanted to play. Karlton Harris was her choice. He became her target and scored twice. Derrick and Shai were Karlton's children but no one needed to know that.

Karlton had no idea he was a father. He loved her and the extramarital affair would be their secret as long as Tonya paid him. Somehow D.Q. found out and after his death, the secret was exposed. It explained D.Q.'s reason for leaving Tonya out of the will. Tonya's attempts to destroy what he left caused her to attempt suicide. Now that she was better she needed those who found comfort in D.Q's death to feel her pain.

She hadn't said enough to anyone about Shai marrying Darrell. Nor had she found what part of Brazil Derek called home. The family was scattered, divided by secrets and lies. She promised them she had changed since her near death experience. The start of another lie that she wouldn't deny. It fell right behind the first lie when she said she wouldn't take another drink.

Karlton came to her rescue and hadn't left her side. Tonya loved him and he professed his love to her. During her recovery Shai, Derek and the rest of the Mince family were told the truth. Shai and 'Rell married and had twins. Shai had become easier to deal with, but Tonya refused to bond with D.Q's bastard son. She still held on to an in-depth conversation she would have with Derek and Shai once she took back what was hers.

Mr. Monroe may have helped her without knowing it. Tonya let her thoughts continue to play on. As she added facts and her vision of the future she knew what her pitch would be. She was sure Mr. Monroe would give her insight on the rules regarding stocks and trade. She would walk in the back door of D.Q. Enterprises.

"D.Q. by now the fires of hell have warmed up around you, my dear. But baby as they say, 'Hell hath no fury as a woman scorned'. I'm coming for what is mine D.Q. I'm taking it back from that winch and her son."

Two

Derek handed the letter to Leeza. She could tell by the look on his face it was serious. The couple made their home in Rio de Janeiro, Brazil near her family and childhood friends. The thought of returning to the United States was no longer a part of their discussions or vision.

Leeza was hired as an RN at the local hospital in the city of Resende. Derek had two more surgeries after leaving his home in the States. Now three years after his near-fatal accident he was learning to walk again. His family knew nothing about the extensive surgeries or the therapy that had him up and walking. His use of a walker or crutches would soon be a memory.

Derek worked from home, sending designs and contracts to his uncle, Darryl Mince through the internet. Quintech Designs was up and running full time. The company opened after its construction while Derek was recovering. Darryl kept his promise and relocated to start what was now a full-time operation. Derek was fired from Carson's Web but continued with his vision of having a graphic designs business. After D.Q.'s death, 'Rell funded the construction and staffing of Quintech Designs. The company was under the umbrella of D.Q. Enterprises. Quintech Designs handled startup companies, from construction designs and layouts, both interior and exterior, to graphics, logos and websites. The business was growing rapidly.

The letter was a dark cloud for both Derek and his uncle. Since his separation from Carson's Web, there had been various lawsuits filed against Derek. Most were handled by Stanley Simpson, the lawyer for both D.Q. Enterprises and Quintech Designs. The letter indicated this hearing was the beginning phase for an indictment against Derek for trade infringement. The thought of Derek's past stirred the memories of bad decisions and his misfortunes. There had been no evidence of who ran him into oncoming traffic the night of his accident. It certainly was connected to either his business or his pleasure.

Derek and Darryl paid all but one of their gambling debts. The two promised they would make good on the debt once Quintech was up and running. The creditor remained silent but Derek wondered if the accident was to be taken as a subliminal message. Neither Derek nor Darryl told anyone about the last amount owed. It was more than they could borrow and it certainly was enough to be killed for.

Leeza handed the letter back to Derek. "When are we leaving?" She left the kitchen table where they sat. "Do you want coffee this morning?"

"Yes. We're not leaving, I am."

"Derek you can't go alone. I can't stay here and wonder if you're okay. You don't know if there are people looking for you. No, you tell me when and I'll be ready to go."

"And your job Leeza? I can't expect you to give up your job again."

Leeza poured herself a cup of coffee.

"No thanks," Derek responded to her gesture to pour a cup for him.

"I want you here. You'll be safe here. If you return with me whoever is after me may come after you. I can't allow that Leeza. I can't jeopardize your safety or your life."

"Is it that serious Derek? It sounds like you know who it is."

She returned to the table with her plate and her coffee. Derek buttered another biscuit and passed it to her. Neither spoke, determined to avoid what needed to be said.

"I don't know who it is. I've been eliminating people since my accident. I've added a few to the list only to find they weren't even in town the night I got ran off the road. Leeza it may not be connected to the infringement. I just don't want you hurt."

"I can't stay here and worry. What if we didn't travel together? If they thought you were coming home to satisfy the court order they would keep an eye on you." Leeza hesitated before continuing her thought.

"What? What were you going to say?" Derek looked up from his plate. Leeza allowed her tears to flow freely.

"Derek what if they're watching you here? Leaving me home could be just as dangerous."

He hadn't given any thought to someone being able to trace his whereabouts. She was right. Derek didn't know if they were safe in Brazil. She had family in Brazil, but nothing would compare to the security 'Rell could provide for them in the States.

"Pack for both of us. I'll call Mr. Simpson."

Three

Marci packed her overnight bag. She promised Mitchell she wouldn't forget to pack before she left the house. It seemed everything was going too fast. 'Rell and Shai were supposed to be married and settled before she and Mitch took their place as Godparents or parents. Marci accepted Mitchell's marriage proposal and in the midst of a whirlwind of emotions they were surprised to find out she was carrying his child. They decided on an intimate wedding with close friends and a few family members. By the time 'Rell and Shai walked down the aisle, she and Mitch had been married a month and she was three months along in the pregnancy. It was a rough time for the couple. During the first trimester, she lost the child.

Mitch and Marci went away after the wedding. They were determined not to be around a family who would grieve and point fingers. Their love and faith kept them together. Coupled with Shai and 'Rell consoling them, they became parents in waiting again. Now that the excitement of the Mince wedding was dying down all eyes were on her and Mitch as they awaited their loving bundle.

Mia, her sister, was excited about becoming an aunt. If anyone asked Mia she would describe her sister as pleasantly annoying. The two of them adored Shai and 'Rell's children, Bryce and Brianna, but the thought of a little one to call their own brought on anticipated excitement.

Mitch purchased a home on the outskirts of town. It was a compromise. He showed Marci properties for more than a month without a nod of approval. Marci wanted to stay close to her mother and sister, but living closer to her job and having space for family and company to visit changed her mind.

Mia thought the house was too big for the newlyweds, but when they announced there would be an addition to the family she fell in love with it. She and her mother picked their rooms knowing they would be selected for babysitting.

Marci and Shai decorated the four-bedroom home with help from 'Rell's mother, Nikki. Now with three months left in the pregnancy, they were beginning to buy for the joyful bundle. Mitch nor Marci wanted to know the sex of the baby, so soft pastel colors would be the color for the room and any gifts. Mia and Darlene, their mother, promised to take her shopping but first, she had to pack the overnight bag.

Marci placed the bag near her bedroom door. She smiled to herself when the doorbell rang. Shai promised to stop by before her mother and sister arrived.

"Hey Girl!"

Marci heard the voice but stood in shock. She questioned herself stunned that Monique Davis was at her door. *What could she possibly want?* The last time she saw 'Rell's ex was at his wedding.

"Don't be so shocked girl. I saw Mia yesterday and she told me you and Mitch were married. I thought you were pregnant at the wedding. Another Mince family secret or what? Girl I just had to come by and congratulate you. After all, if I was still with 'Rell I would have known all about this."

She waved her hand in the air as she stepped into the grand room. Monique took her time looking around as the fake smile returned to her face.

"Girl, this is nice. So how are you? You don't return my calls, that's what I told Mia. I lost my man and a friend?"

"Not at all. If you considered me a friend you would have known that. I think you stopped talking to me to spite me and 'Rell. I simply wasn't beat and I'm not beat now. The last I heard you were still with Craig. Was that before you and 'Rell broke up or what?"

"Does it matter? He married his so-called sister right?"

"They're not brother and sister; you know that and yes, it does matter."

"I came to talk about us. I miss your friendship and I want you to know that I'm sorry if it was because of me that it ended."

"Listen, I'm on my way out. Shai, my sister, and mother are on their way here. I don't want the drama. You miss getting the inside information on 'Rell. No need now, he's married."

"Willingly is the question."

"Willingly?"

"Let that simmer girlfriend. There are questions about that convenient marriage."

"Monique, stop. Take that BS somewhere else."

"Really? I'm not about the drama either but I'm being labeled in all of this. I don't want to make a stink but before I do there's some things I think need to be exposed. Listen, I understand this is a bad time. Here, take my card and call me."

Marci took the card and opened the front door for Monique's exit.

"I just want answers. I'm sure you do too. So call me before the weekend. No need to take this to 'Rell's mother or Nana. I'll talk to you first or maybe Shai's mother would be best. But I do respect the Mince family, that's so much more than they showed me."

"I don't think they owe you anything if that's what you're getting at. You and Craig seem to be able to get what you want even if it's not yours."

Marci didn't wait for Monique to answer. She closed the door. Glancing at the card, she noticed Monique's number hadn't changed. She would call her for Shai's sake. Monique could and would start trouble if she had any dirt on 'Rell or D.Q. Enterprises. The thought of calling Mitch crossed her mind, but the doorbell interrupted the thought.

Shai stood with her back to the door admiring the curbside appeal she and Marci created. The green foliage would last longer than the flowers that were in full bloom. She turned around at the sound of the door opening. Stepping into the grand room she knew trouble was brewing.

Four

"So assuming she knows something, whatever it is, she thinks it will be the end of our marriage?"

"Shai, she said the marriage was one of convenience. I guess she thinks whatever she knows will dissolve the marriage. What could she be threatening to expose? Do you think Craig knows something about 'Rell?"

"What could he possibly know that would dissolve our marriage? 'Rell had him fired from their prior employment, but he was stealing customers or something like that."

"Maybe Craig thought 'Rell owed him a new start like he did for Mitch and the others."

"Girl be glad Mitch is not a Mince. There's always something going on with them and it's never small. Derek called this morning. He and Leeza are on their way here."

"Really? I thought he was settled in Brazil. Are they coming to visit?"

"He's answering an indictment. They're still suing him for that trade stuff. Marci, he doesn't know if he or Leeza is safe."

"Safe in court? What does he mean?"

"He's not sure people aren't still looking for him or Uncle Darryl."

"Oh. Well, they haven't bothered Uncle Darryl. Maybe the accident was just that, an accident."

"We can speculate about that but even Darryl admits there's a possibility that someone was sending him a message. Anyway, they're coming here to meet the court demands and I guess they'll find out if someone is truly after Derek."

"Do you think Monique knows something about the infringement?"

"Going after Derek wouldn't hurt 'Rell. It's got to be closer to 'Rell and D.Q. Enterprises. Maybe Craig did know more than he should have. I just don't see how whatever it is tied into our marriage. Monique may be just fishing. Maybe she thinks we are related. I don't know. Enough about her, whatever she knows I'm sure Mr. Simpson and 'Rell have discussed it. So what about you, Mitch and that angel you're carrying?"

"We're good, no more than good. Shai I'm as happy as you. I truly believe that although it was a rush. You know, us getting married because of the pregnancy…"

Shai's frown caused Marci to raise her brow questioning her reaction.

"You married because of the pregnancy? Really? Marci the two of you were and are in love. Why would you think the baby is the reason for your marriage? It may have changed the date but not the fact that you would be married."

"I don't know why I said it that way. You're right, we do love each other and that's why I am as happy as you."

"That's the second time you've said that, or maybe just said it to me. Your happiness is yours. You can't possibly compare you and Mitch to me and 'Rell. Why would you?"

"Oh, so you are in a different kind of love because it's 'Rell?"

"No, but love is not the same for everyone. With the ups and downs of love and marriage, I don't expect you and Mitch to follow our pattern or lifestyle. Create your happiness without comparing it to anyone else."

"I just don't want the family to think that our happiness is any different from yours. You know, you had a grand wedding compared to ours. Everything fell in place for you and we had to rush through everything."

"Marci you chose to get married when you did. You could have had any type of wedding you wanted, been situated in your home and then had the baby. No one thinks of you as anything other than happy. The two of you are in love and that's all that matters. 'Rell and I waited for many reasons. That was our choice."

"I guess. We are in love but I'm sure there have been whispers. Maybe Monique heard something. You can't tell me there hasn't been any talk."

"About you? I doubt it. About Mitch and 'Rell? Maybe, but like I said they'll handle it. We don't need to worry."

"How do you do it Shai? How do you believe it will all work out? I mean, thinking the man you loved was your brother and you still loved him. Derek being attacked and now new dirt being dug up by Monique, how do you stay strong?"

"Prayer and the belief that we will make it past the nonsense. I can't live regretting the past or regretting my love for 'Rell. It is what it is, Aunt Darlene's words."

It wasn't long before Darlene and Mia arrived. The weather brought on showers with the threat of a downpour. The ladies decided to stay with Marci and just visit. It had been a while since the four of them got together.

Shai didn't hesitate to make the tuna fish salad they all loved. The impromptu lunch gave them the time to catch up on the recent family matters. Marci and Mia looked through the baby magazines Darlene brought with her.

"You've done so much with the house since the last time I was here. I love your new paintings."

Darlene examined the pictures closely as she moved on into the dining room.

"Marci, did Mitch have trouble with this chandelier?"

"No, it was his mother's. I think he put it up for her when she had it. I loved it so we kept it," Marcia responded raising her voice so her mother could hear her.

Darlene continued her self-guided tour. Every time she visited her daughter's homes there was something new. She loved their taste in art as well as their choice of décor'.

"I'm sorry I didn't ask. How has Mitch and his family been since his mother passed?"

"Mia, he hasn't really talked about it. They were raised by their grandmother. They didn't live with their mother until they were in high school. I think Mitch was in college before he lived there and that was brief. It's three of them and they're not really close. I think his younger brother lived with their father. Another family with drama."

"Ladies, you will learn that all families have drama. Your Nana says it all the time. Secrets and lies you live through them holding on to what you know is true. It's hard to believe sometimes but there's not a family that has not had drama or secrets."

"You're right Aunt Darlene. If they say they haven't had any they're living with the lies." Shai responded as she began to prepare the trays with the impromptu lunch.

Darlene and Shai brought out the trays with the salad, crackers, pickles and a pitcher of ice tea. The afternoon would be filled with sharing updates, laughter and family bonding.

Five

Darryl Mince slammed the phone into the receiver. It seemed as though every call brought on more frustration. He agreed to "handle things" until Derek returned to the States. Darryl had to admit the business grew faster than they planned. 'Rell suggested they hire an office manager, but neither Derek nor Darryl could trust anyone to handle the books. They needed to be able to access the accounts without questions. 'Rell even suggested his accountants could eliminate some of the overflow. Darryl didn't want 'Rell to ask any other questions. They agreed to have the payroll handled through D.Q. Enterprises. All other funding or monies would be handled in house.

Quintech Designs was the second company that had the name of Darryl Mince tied to it. After leaving his wife, Francine, he found himself in a court battle for his construction company in Detroit. Francine filed for a divorce, the company assets, and alimony; she won. Darryl didn't protest. They had years of an off and on marriage. If asked about his love during the years, other than his love for his children, he didn't know when he stopped loving Francine.

There were affairs over the years that birthed children that bore his name. The toddler they raised was proof Francine had endured it all in spite of his desire to risk it all. He was a true gambler. He gambled with the cash they acquired from the business they owned. He gambled with the women in the street and those he thought he loved. The Mince family bailed him out of his financial problems over the years or so they thought. Francine knew different. She refused to stand on the stern of the sinking ship again.

Darryl's attraction to other women caused him to "flirt" and get into trouble. Nana told him that was the lie he packaged nicely whenever he got caught. His mother and wife knew it was more than flirtatious comments or gestures that pulled him out of his home again.

Simone Marshall, Nikki's cousin, became his target.

"One more time," he told himself as he spent time in New York and New Jersey. If anyone asked he would deny she showed him a new way to love a woman and love himself. Simone didn't tolerate his excuses. Immediately she would point out his wrongdoings and lies. She didn't accept his irrational behavior or empty promises. Their lovemaking sessions left him wanting more in and out of the bed.

He couldn't compare the two. Francine was a homemaker, Simone was what he wanted as a life mate. They talked about their families, their childhood, and the years before they met. Simone explained clearly what she expected from him and their relationship. Darryl didn't want to lose what he hadn't felt for years. Francine deserved to finally know the truth. He needed to admit to the truth.

Moving from Detroit to Virginia would raise more than eyebrows from his family. No one bothered to ask until he introduced them to Simone. She was no stranger to his mother. Nana knew Nikki's cousin and of the months they spent together. The choices Darryl made never pleased her and she feared it was too late for him to change. Leaving Francine with their children and the business they built was a bit much but for once her son seemed committed. Nana asked the family to keep him in prayer. No one asked his reason for leaving his wife or family.

Darryl looked at the pictures on his desk, his children and Simone. He kept them there as a reminder of his loss as well as his gain. Francine didn't argue and neither did he. Their relationship was better since the divorce and the children all in their teens didn't seem to miss their father. Now that he and Simone lived together, he knew his loving her was different, a mature love. He realized now the years he missed while playing with love as Francine tolerated it all. Maybe he did love her now. He loved her enough not to put her through living the lie.

The intercom interrupted his thoughts. "Mr. Mince, Mr. Washington is here to see you."

Darryl forgot 'Rell told him Byron would be stopping in to offer his assistance. Darryl tried to deny being frustrated but his nephew smiled and assured him everything would be fine. After talking with Derek, Darryl wasn't sure how they would balance the books without questions arising about the deficit. Byron entered the office and closed the glass door behind him.

"What's good Uncle?" Byron greeted Darryl as most of 'Rell's friends did. Byron Washington, Mitchell Carter, Keith Larson, and Craig Masters were like brothers. D.Q. Enterprises was a part of their brotherhood although Craig had not been invited to work in the business D.Q. Mince left his son. Darryl envied their friendship. They were closer than the relationship he had with his brother, D.Q. They were strong-willed and professionals that were on a rise.

"You tell me, young man. My nephew sent you here to clean up our books?"

"Something like that. It's probably a missed entry or bad calculation somewhere. I brought the payroll figures as well." Byron walked over to the conference table. Preparing the table he glanced at Darryl. He hadn't moved.

"Hey, listen, 'Rell told me to fix this. Believe me, Uncle, I will. What I find is between you and me. Now if you want to talk to Derek or tell him about it, it's okay. 'Rell is not looking for problems and we want to make sure there's nothing the court can search for."

"Most of the books, since the start of the business is here." Darryl got up and went to the wall files. "Do you think they would include the files from Quintech? I mean, this indictment doesn't mean we have to disclose information about our financial status now, do we?"

"I don't know, we'll find out. Mr. Simpson suggested we take a look at it and if anything looked too out of sorts….well you know. He's the lawyer and I'm the CPA we don't ask too many questions unless it's a notable violation. It's my job to make sure Quintech is protected financially. So let's look at what you got, what's coming in, what's going out and what you may still owe."

"First the phone calls and now what could be an audit from hell." Darryl's thoughts were racing. A liquid lunch would be his order at noon. He needed to talk to Derek. He would need to know that their financial secret was about to be exposed.

Byron worked in silence. Darryl left the table answering calls and preparing blueprints. After leaving the drawing room on the opposite side of his office, Darryl returned to the conference table and waited for Byron to look up.

"Yeah Uncle, what's up?"

"Thought you'd want to break for lunch. Have you found anything?"

"No nothing really. There is one fund that I don't see. I'm assuming these figures here are donations of some sort. Each month it seems there's a deduction for the same amount but it's not noted."

"Uh, it may be something Derek is doing with the hospital Leeza works for." Darryl knew what it was. He and Derek thought it wouldn't be noticed. They were peeling off one to two thousand dollars monthly. They wouldn't let the sum get too large before they would change it under another account name. It would be a charity contribution. Now that Byron was asking about it, Darryl didn't remember the names they made up to cover the withdrawals.

"There were a few organizations that asked for donations. I guess being new and a part of D.Q. Enterprises it put us on a list of donors."

"Hmm could be, maybe not," Byron replied without looking up. "Are any of these books your invoices? I'll need them and pending transactions as well."

"Hey what about that break? I know I could use one."

"Okay. Just tell me Uncle, who is JWL and Company?"

It was then that Darryl remembered the letters. It was the name to cover the withdrawals. *"Just Want to Live"*, it was what the payment would secure, their lives.

Six

Darlene left Marci's house with her own secret. She wasn't ready to answer the questions they would ask about her new interest or what she had been doing. Her daughter and niece joked about her leaving her salon early the past few weekends. Darlene smiled as she got into her car. They had no idea she had been leaving early for more than the past few weekends.

Darlene was sure she would lose Warren Stykes' friendship once their relationship went beyond business. He was a salesman for Haircare Solutions, one of the companies where she purchased her hair care products. She started her car with the thoughts of when he first walked into her salon.

Darlene had only one salon then with no intentions of becoming a manager with a staff and two other locations. She had her own customers and three beauticians who paid for their chair space and products monthly. Salespersons came and went. Most didn't have the products any of their clientele used or wanted to sample. Darlene purchased products online and it didn't bother her that she was paying higher for some of the items.

D.Q. argued with her often regarding how she structured her business. He explained she could be successful if she came from behind the chair and took a seat in the office. Darlene loved the hair business. Her salon often competed in hair shows and did well. They were booked for fashion shows, proms, and weddings. Her decision to change the name from Darlene's to Diva Hair Designs prompted another meeting with D.Q. His offer to fund another salon in her name took her from behind her chair. It wasn't long before she added a third salon, a full-time staff, and enough business to sustain her dream.

Managing the salons left little room in her schedule for free time. Warren Stykes caught her attention when he approached her office door with his leather display case. As she turned the key in the ignition the radio blasted "Damn Baby" by Janet Jackson. Exactly her thought as the six foot four, dark chocolate, smooth-skinned, well groom man asked, "Ms. Mince?"

His pearly white teeth returned a smile after she asked, "Are you looking for me?"

"Yes, I'm Mr. Stykes from Haircare Solutions. I believe we have an appointment with you today."

Darlene was still enchanted by his stance. His voice was a notch above baritone but the melodic sound caused her to feel a bit giddy. She hadn't felt that way since college when she accepted a date with Marci and Mia's father. She tried to collect herself but stumbled again as she spoke.

"Uh, uh, yes, I remember now. Won't you come in and sit. I mean have a seat." She knew where she wanted him to sit but she didn't want to give him the wrong impression.

She could hear Nana's voice about checking his clothes and shoes. *"From head to toe, you can tell a well-groomed man."* Nana would say. Darlene watched as he entered the office and unbuttoned his suit jacket to take the seat in front of her desk. She couldn't help but notice his choice in color coordination and accessories. The grey suit and shirt accented by the black, grey and white diamond patterned tie had her mesmerized. She hoped he didn't notice her staring at his physique or that she could tell him that the details of his belt and the buckle were unique.

As she approached her home she remembered Warren's icebreaker. "Maybe I should have offered you our best-selling product."

His statement brought her attention to the business he obviously was there for.

"I'm sorry. Are you here to tell me about this month's best seller?"

"Ms. Mince I'm here to tell you about any of our products you're willing to add to your inventory. I reviewed your file and you've been a customer with us for more than five years. Haircare Solutions appreciates your business so they sent me to talk to you about supplying you with our new line. Also, we'd love to show you a few things that will help promote your business and our products."

It was three years later when Warren asked if she would join him at the Haircare Solutions Christmas party. A few months later he was chosen for a salesmen award. Again Warren asked Darlene to be with him for the occasion. Soon it was periodic lunches, dinners and a few trips to the west coast for hair care shows. It all seemed to fit as "just business" for those that didn't know who Warren and Darlene were to each other.

An invitation for an impromptu trip to New York prompted Darlene to invite Warren to her home. Until that night there had been no effort on Warren's part to cross the borders of their friendship. Each trip they took came with separate rooms and respected hours. Darlene was eager to know his feelings. She knew she was falling in love.

Warren arrived about seven. He explained he would be leaving his office late that day. He wanted to stop at his home to shower. Darlene made dinner, nothing special after he insisted whatever she prepared would be fine.

The bell rang and Darlene tried to control her emotions. She had that schoolgirl feeling again. She opened the door and as he passed her, he kissed her cheek presenting her with a bouquet of flowers. His cologne sent a message and as the recipient, she responded with her hands clutched around the flowers. She loved the roses and baby breath. The colorful mixture was beautiful.

"Aww, thank you. Let me get a vase. Make yourself comfortable. I made a vegetable lasagna since you wouldn't tell me what you liked."

"Whatever you cooked will be fine. It is a break from my cooking."

"I'm glad you accepted my invitation." Darlene returned with two glasses of iced tea. "Is tea fine?"

"Yes, don't go through any fuss, whatever you have in this glass is fine."

"Warren, we need to talk." His facial expression showed concern. "I'm just going to say it. I don't want to lose a friend."

"I don't quite understand. You think you'll lose my friendship? Why?"

"I mean where are we going with this relationship? I don't want to rely on my feelings without knowing yours."

Darlene smiled as she pulled into her driveway. She parked her car behind Warren's. He got out of his BMW and waited for her to get out of her vehicle. She let her thoughts continue before turning off the ignition.

"I've had feelings for you a few months after being assigned to your account. Totally against my company's policy. I asked you to accompany me to various outings and events so the people I work with would meet you. I didn't want them to think our relationship should be confused with the nonsense they often do with their clients. I feel you Darlene and I know you feel me. We've known each other for a few years now. I think I'm ready to commit to a relationship that's more than a mere friendship. We will always remain friends, at least I hope so."

The memory always gave Darlene a sense of security. Warren walked to her car and opened the door for her.

"Good afternoon my lady. How was the visit with the girls?"

"The rain stopped us from shopping. We had lunch and sat around reminiscing. I really want you to meet them. I know they thought it was strange when I left. The rain let up and I didn't give them a chance to say the obvious."

"The obvious?"

Darlene ignored his question but smiled as she commented, "I bet they're shopping. A late start but they live to go to the mall. Marci's pregnancy gives them an excuse."

The couple walked into her home without discussing it further. Warren made himself comfortable on the couch. Darlene went into the kitchen a routine she had whenever she entered her home.

Warren could hear her movement in the other room. Memories of their last year together teased his emotions. Their relationship was a change for him. Until he met Darlene he had been dating women who thought romance began in the bedroom. The bedroom was his playground. He soon would tire of the disconnected romps and the next player would be chosen. The meeting with Darlene was pure chance.

Haircare Solutions promoted Warren to an executive position in sales. He decided to meet with the business owners that were in his territory. A face to face meeting with the owners would spike sales and increase profits. His relationship with Darlene was where he found love. He thanked God for her.

"Warren, I want to have a dinner and invite my family and friends. I want them to meet you."

She kicked off her shoes and sat next to him waiting for his response.

"Whatever, whenever. That's up to you. I hoped to meet them sooner. I mean we've been together for a while. I thought maybe I hadn't passed your rate of approval."

"Warren, really? If you hadn't passed my approval do you think I would have traveled around with you? You wouldn't be sitting here."

"Okay, I told you I'm moving at your pace. I don't want to rush this."

"This?"

"Yes us. I've made a mess of relationships before, on purpose I might add. I want this. I want us."

Warren leaned into Darlene, their lips met. The kiss was passionate and again Darlene felt like she was floating. She stood and led him, for the first time, into her bedroom.

Seven

Nikki put on the water to boil. Simone agreed to stay for dinner. They needed a few extra hours to complete the design presentation for their first interior franchise project. Niki wasn't pleased when Simone presented it to her. Darryl and Derek finished the graphic design and interior construction for a new restaurant. They gave the owner Simone's number for the interior decorating.

Nikki and Simone were partners in Nikki's business, "Interior Dreams". They traveled often when the business started and now five years later, they had a profitable endeavor. Referrals had become the prosperous link, but Nikki didn't care for Darryl giving Simone inside jobs. She preferred the customer calling on their own. She had to admit this job with the restaurant could open new doors, so she remained silent.

Simone hoped Darryl's referrals would be the olive branch between them. Nikki was upset that her cousin had an affair with a married man, especially since it broke up his family and home. Simone wanted to share her happiness, the love she and Darryl had and invite her cousin to visit their new home. There was nothing she could say that would change Nikki's thoughts. So relationships weren't a part of their conversations. It was uneasy at the beginning of the relationship but if Darryl's ex-wife could get over it, Simone thought Nikki would be fine. The business was business and Darryl's referrals proved profitable each time. That was enough for Simone to have a comeback if Nikki ever complained.

"Do you need me to do anything?" Simone shouted from the makeshift workspace in the grand room.

Nikki's home was beautiful. D.Q. made sure she had more than enough space for her after the birth of Darrell. Simone stayed with her whenever she visited from New York. Now that she lived in Virginia she could go home in less than twenty minutes. Simone was in awe when Nikki opened the door for her first visit. So much had happened since that day.

Nikki had rearranged, changed and decorated since Darrell left home for college and D.Q's death. Although she often spoke of moving into a smaller home, Simone knew it was hard for Nikki to let go. Nikki often referred to the home as still having D.Q.'s presence. Simone smiled to herself as she thought of what D.Q. would say about Nikki's new love interest.

"Is the Deacon joining us for dinner?"

"Girl, please! Why would I have him come over knowing this presentation needed to be done?" Nikki shouted from the kitchen. The clanging of pots was the next sound.

"You sure you don't want me to help you?"

"Simone, look over the proposal. Make sure we totaled everything. The presentation's PowerPoint should be complete by tomorrow. Derek is coming home so I hope he sent it before boarding the plane."

Simone wasn't sure she heard her correctly. She walked into the kitchen with her pen and pad in hand. The aroma of the sauce distracted her.

"What seasoning do you use? It smells like, girl that sauce has to be better than most at the market."

"It's all fresh, homemade sauce is just better overall."

"Since when have you been making homemade spaghetti sauce?"

"It's a recipe Samuel had. I loved it so much I cooked it for him. He loved it more than his. So I made some and stored it."

"The Deacon cooks?"

"Simone you don't have to call him the Deacon. Yes, he cooks often and he can throw down in the kitchen."

"Damn, do you ever get one with something wrong with them? First, you get the top businessman, now a chef."

Simone took a seat at the island waiting for what she knew would be Nikki's response. When her cousin didn't respond she slammed the pad and pen on the granite surface.

"I know damn well you're not letting me get away with that comment?"

"What? Was that supposed to be some kind of dig? Girl, you got what you wanted. Darryl isn't a bad catch if you can hold on to him. Francine held on as long as she could. So you've got a Mince and he cooks."

"Darryl don't cook girl. He burns and I mean that literally. Breakfast is his forte'. There's not another Simone out there that can put it on him like I do. So with that said, I ain't worried about him going nowhere."

"I hope you're right. You both are too old for that B.S."

"And you know it. It's different though. I mean Darryl has a lot of baggage to clear up but he's making an effort."

"Well, I guess more will be cleared up when Derek gets here. He's got to meet with Mr. Simpson. 'Rell called to say he was picking him up at the airport."

"Nikki, how much trouble is he in? I mean this could cause problems for Quintech if he's facing jail."

"Whatever it is, Mr. Simpson wants 'Rell to bring him to the office first thing in the morning. Darryl is involved, Simone. I'm sure of it."

"I thought this had to do with Derek's old job. That thing he did with the logos and designs for his clients at Carson right?"

"I don't know but it may be tied up in some other mess. I don't think Carson's Web would have people that would try to kill him. Derek and Darryl were heavy gamblers. I mean owing people thousands. Nana, Darlene, and D.Q. have given them money to cover the debts owed. 'Rell thinks they may have someone they still owe. Simpson was trying to dig up the background dirt when Derek left. Darryl never returned his calls and until he moved back here no one knew where he was."

"Nikki, he was with Francine during that time, in Detroit. Who didn't know that?"

"Francine for one. He wasn't with her. She had no idea where he was. Simone, I know you think you've struck gold but believe me, Darryl has baggage."

Simone sat in silence listening to Nikki's revelation of Darryl's past. Darryl hadn't mentioned much about his relationship with Derek. He told her about his past affairs, Francine, his children, and his business.

"Why wouldn't he tell me about this mess?"

"He's a Mince baby. Everyone thought D.Q. and I had the best thing going. Simone, I thought so too until I found out he had children and no intentions to leave Tonya."

"Damn you were together thirty years and you didn't know he was married with children?"

"Listen, Simone, with both ears. I didn't know he had children. He didn't leave his home because of them. After his death, everyone found out Shai and Derek weren't his kids. So even though he found the proof they weren't his children, he stayed in that marriage."

"Shit. When did he find out? Nikki, maybe he didn't know until he left her."

"He knew and I still loved him. The secrets, the lies, the excuses; girl, it was too much. Like I said, Darryl is a Mince. Proceed with caution."

"Nikki you loved D.Q. and he damn sure loved you. That's what matters right?"

"Some will say I was dumb, others will say I wrecked his home, but love did matter. He loved me and proved it from the time we met. He showered me with his love and I gave him love in return. But you know what Simone? He wasn't mine to love. He was tied to his baggage. I can't imagine how we would be living, yes living today if he had dropped his baggage. It killed him. He couldn't break away."

"He knew those kids weren't his when he met you?"

"Damn near but no. Darrell is the oldest than Shai and Derek. D.Q. didn't tell me about them, Simone because they were born after 'Rell. He didn't know they weren't his. I believe he found out after I broke up with him. He had his suspicions. I cried right here in this kitchen for weeks after I found out those kids were born after I had 'Rell. I thought he had been using me and screwing Tonya whenever she threw a fit."

"Did she know about you?"

"Yes, he made damn sure he told her about me and 'Rell."

Eight

'Rell waited for Derek's call saying the delayed flight from Brazil had landed. He fiddled with his phone in obvious frustration while his grandmother ignored his annoyance.

"Nanna, do you think it's possible that Derek and Darryl are still gambling or even owe money?"

"Baby, how would I know? I always found out whenever it was time for them to pay off before trouble arose. Month after month, the same thing. That's what made your Aunt Francine so mad. That and those women he would lay around with, not Derek, I'm talkin' 'bout your uncle. Seemed like he was younger in the mind then Derek. They'd bet on any and everything or that's what they led us to believe."

Rell put his phone on the kitchen table. Nanna continued to wash the morning dishes. She knew Rell would have more questions; before he asked she went on.

"You see, your uncle would come this way and swoop up Derek. They'd go out with the story that they'd pair up and win a few rounds of pool down at the community hall. It wasn't until they asked for the first few thousands from your father that we knew that was the covering lie. They went to the race track, the casino, anywhere they could throw away the money they worked for. Then it was a few of the stocks they owned. D.Q. put a stop to that. You know your father didn't speak to your uncle for almost six months after that. Gave me and Darlene strict orders not to get involved and don't give them any large sums of money."

"So when did you and Aunt Darlene have to give in?"

"Darryl went to some club not far from here and acted like he was the man with the fat pockets. They emptied his pockets and Derek's too. Well, the fools wanted their money back and I suppose real gamblers know a fool when they see one."

"They had to fight to get out of the place?" Nanna turned around laughing.

"No chile. If they had fought they would have stood a better chance. Some of those men was police, officials in the town they was in, people they didn't even imagine was there. Right here in Virginia, gambling right long side those that would lock them up for years on false charges. Mr. Simpson told D.Q. pay the money and be done with the charges. Your father would have let Darryl rot right there, but not Derek. He wouldn't pay for Darryl. So me and your Aunt Darlene paid a hefty bill to get him out of that mess. We told him that was it."

Nanna wiped her hands with the dish towel and took a seat across the table from her eldest grand. She couldn't help but see her eldest son D.Q. She loved them all but D.Q. and 'Rell were her favorites. It was something about their spirit, their character and they were so much alike. All she could pray for was that 'Rell would carry out his father's vision.

D.Q. Enterprises was his dream and he left it in the hands of his son to build and complete that vision. 'Rell had been obedient to his wishes, Mr. Simpson's instructions and advice. Often he would talk with Julia Mince to connect with his father, after all, she was D.Q's mother and knew him well.

"I know you hate when I say you look like your dad, but I believe you're going to get that receding hairline he had too."

'Rell gave her a smirk as she giggled, a sound of her sweetness.

"Nanna, I had to bail them out again before opening Quintech Designs. I told Mr. Simpson not to tell them. Francine called to say how their books in Chicago were in shambles and if we didn't watch over

Quintech they'd run through the profits there too. They were about to lose the business and their home when he left."

"Rell, no! He left that woman with that burden?"

"I'm afraid so. I sent Byron to Chicago to find the problem or if there really was one. Uncle Darryl didn't know we left the company in the clear. Well you know Derek ran to Brazil after the accident. Mr. Simpson advised him it would be best. We can't figure out who it is they owe but it's a lot of money."

"Lord have mercy. Is that why they tried to kill Derek?"

"We don't really know yet. Byron went to Quintech today and found some of the same errors in the books. Something is going on but we need to know the truth from the start."

"Baby, I wish I could help you. I know we all put in our savings to get that boy out of trouble. Your dad paid a lot to cover Derek's debt too. So it could be, nah, after that mess I know they ain't still involved in that."

"Listen, Nanna, they questioned both of them for this indictment. Uncle Darryl didn't work at Carson's Web Designs so why question him? The money is tied up in this one account that Byron is focusing on."

"How much money?"

'Rell's phone rang before he could answer. He got up from the table whispering, "Excuse me, Nanna" and proceeded into the living room.

"Is my uncle there? Okay, I'm on my way. Thank you, Mr. Simpson. Yes, I'll call Mitch and Byron. We'll meet you at the office."

"What's going on?" Nanna asked coming into the room.

"Derek is with Uncle Darryl. He picked him up at the airport. They knew I was waiting for Derek. Leeza is being dropped off by our company driver to my house to be with Shai. Mr. Simpson tried calling them, there was no answer. He wants to meet with us before he tells us what Derek and Uncle Darryl are facing."

"Lord, you think they looking at jail time?"

"I don't know but you always say the dirt comes out…."

"Yea, baby in the wash."

Nine

"So how's your family?"

Shai didn't know what to say. Leeza had been her brother's nurse, then lover for what seemed to be less than six months before they left for Brazil. International calls were few and between so they wouldn't be traced by whoever they thought tried to kill Derek. Shai would call at least once a month, but most of the time Leeza was working at the hospital.

Leeza was beautiful from her God-given features to her spirit; she was meant to be a nurse or caregiver. Shai still wasn't sure she could be a Mince. Derek told Shai he loved her and he didn't think there was another woman he could love like her. Shai listened without responding each time he expressed his love. Loving the nurse who stayed by his side through his near-death ordeal seemed normal. She just didn't believe Derek would be in a committed relationship long. Now sitting with Leeza, Shai was at a loss for words.

"They are all well. My mother was worried when we left. I didn't tell her about, you know, what has been going on with Derek. I didn't even tell her when we would be back. My mother is one to worry herself to sickness. I did tell my brother I would let Derek explain it. I don't want to worry them you know?"

"That's best. Derek would want it that way. I've never been to Brazil. Were you born there?"

"No. I'm the only child of five that wasn't born there. We have family in Mexico and during a visit there I was born. Tell me why my mother was even in Mexico if she was nine months pregnant?"

Shai shared the laughter. Leeza's accent was as funny as her question. Shai liked her. She could see how easy it would be to fall in love with her. She had a comforting personality.

"Are you staying with us? 'Rell didn't tell me you guys were coming here to stay during this mess or not. It's not a problem if you are, that's not what I meant."

"Oh, no, no. You know as much as I do. I don't ask questions I wait and let him tell me what's up. Now when it comes to anything other than this mess….."

"Girl I was just about to say!"

The two laughed again. Shai had misjudged the nurse. She had spunk and that would even the playing field when she had to deal with Mince family madness. Shai could only hope that the mess with Derek and her Uncle Darryl, the stir that Monique thought she would cause, and whatever the queen, Tonya Mince would set fire to would miss Leeza and Derek's love.

"Do you know if Derek called our mother?"

"I don't think so. He did call Nana. We both spoke with her last night. I'm not sure that he spoke with any family today."

"I sure hope he didn't call her. All our mother would need is to know Derek is in town."

"I didn't know that they were having problems. Derek calls her, well not as often as he speaks to your Uncle but…"

"Believe me I understand. We each have our reasons to be careful with her. You should know there's been issues in the past. I don't think we'll ever really trust her or her actions."

"Derek did talk about what happened. We talked a lot while he was healing, us moving to Brazil, his therapy and deciding to come back together. Shai, I'm not in the dark."

Shai smiled understanding there was more, more that wouldn't be discussed until it was necessary.

"So how long will you be here? Are you guys thinking about staying?"

"I doubt it. Derek didn't say. Shai we don't want to be in anyone's way. I think I know what you're trying to say."

"I'm not saying or implying anything. Leeza if you are staying you'll need to be able to deal with my mother. She's a trip and the queen of the Mince family bullshit."

Leeza smiled softly, remembering the nights Derek would talk about his hurt. The pain he shared with Shai once they found out D.Q. Mince wasn't their father. They were a comfort to each other, support. They prayed together hoping their love for each other would keep them from hating their mother. They agreed to distance themselves from her once she was back on her feet.

Derek got the call three months ago that Tonya was able to go to and from therapy on her own. Karlton explained she was getting more independent each day. It seemed she was striving to be better and feel better. Leeza listened as Derek took a deep breath and said he was done with Tonya Mince regardless of her recovery.

"Shai, I don't know if your brother told you, he doesn't want anything from anyone here. I think it's safe to say that includes your mother. We won't be staying near here if we stay and otherwise we'll be returning to Brazil."

"Wow, I guess he really meant what he said. He told me once that she wasn't what a mother should have been. I took it that he was just angry. You know, I thought his anger would pass. Like time, he'd live through it. We said we would stay close, you know, not abandon her if she needed help."

"Shai, your mother doesn't even know what he went through. As a mother, she created so many problems during his recovery; I couldn't believe some of the things she said and did."

"Really?"

"Really."

Shai needed to know her brother's secret. She still had a love for her mother. How was he able to walk away from the woman who birthed him? 'Rell told her it was because she was a mother now and saw motherhood differently. After listening to Leeza she understood 'Rell's point.

Ten

'Rell, Mitch and Byron sat at the table in Mr. Simpson's conference room. They understood it had to be a matter of importance if he summoned the three of them to meet. Byron sat with files stacked in front of him and at the end of the table, Stanley Simpson had three separate piles of paperwork.

"Do you think it's about their bookkeeping or ours?" Byron was prepared for either but didn't understand the impromptu meeting.

"I think it's whether or not that account you found is connected in any way to the indictment. It's about prepping for the trial." Rell checked his watch. "I want to know where the two idiots are. They should be at this so-called meeting."

"Our driver called. They were told to get here after we leave." Mitch checked his phone before he finished. "I spoke to him about thirty minutes ago."

"Which driver? I was waiting for Derek to call me."

"Simpson called me for a driver, I told Eric to call him and go from there. I didn't know it was for Derek and your uncle until he called me back. I didn't think anything of it."

"Look, from what Byron found or is questioning on these finance reports, I think there may be a connection to this trial. We need to keep the communication tight."

Byron and Mitch understood. The three waited as the lawyer finished his call. Mr. Simpson seemed to always be a step or two ahead of the trio that headed D.Q. Enterprises. If he called to make any changes there was a reason.

"Mr. Monroe, as you've said, we've been through this over and over again. I'm not taking time to appease Tonya Mince. Tell her what you want. You have all the paperwork from the separation, the divorce, and the will. D.Q. had all of this done a few years before he got sick or even knew he was sick."

"Mr. Simpson I'm just reviewing a few things as I prepare to meet with her again. She seems to think we've missed something here. You know you get those types of clients every now and then."

"There's nothing now and then about Tonya Mince. She always wants the now. I just don't have the time to waste. I've submitted all that was needed to your office. If that doesn't provide any satisfaction for your client, I don't know what to tell you. Listen, the stock he sold is lucrative. If it's more money she's looking for it's in the stocks. He didn't leave her high and dry. The home is paid for as well as the taxes being paid quarterly. She's got enough for her to start a new life. D.Q.'s been dead over five years and so has the case. But as always feel free to call me if anything new arises. I doubt it, you know how D.Q. was. Man, he knew Tonya and he was legally prepared for her fight."

"Well, I've taken up enough of your time. Thanks for your tolerance. She's a lot easier to deal with when I can give her concrete proof of what I'm saying."

"She cemented her fate before they separated. What you have in paperwork is proof. There's nothing else for her to claim."

"Simpson, she wants part of D.Q. Enterprises."

"Not going to happen. She has no legal right to any of it. He made sure of that when the company's worth began to grow. I can send you the paperwork she signed and agreed to. I'll have my secretary pull it up for you. Listen, I've got some other business to deal with, thanks for the call and the heads-up."

"Heads-up?" Tonya's lawyer asked knowing the answer.

"C'mon man, you know Tonya Mince. This is her fury re-fueling. I think this paperwork will put out her fire."

The lawyers agreed to another call if necessary. Stanley Simpson had been dealing with Tonya Mince for years. He knew her next step would be to question the roots of the company. He emailed his secretary detailing what paperwork to send to Mr. Monroe's office. He smiled as he told her to put copies in the closure file for D.Q. Mince. Satisfied, he grabbed his suit jacket before walking into the conference room.

"Good morning gentlemen." The elder of the men entered the room and they all stood to greet him with a handshake. 'Rell rounded the table to give Stanley Simpson the greeting they had grown accustomed to. Over the years, after the death of D.Q., Stanley Simpson had become more than the lawyer for D.Q. Enterprises. He and Rell had formed a bond of respect and understanding. 'Rell left everyone in place as was suggested by his father. Although he had the opportunity and right to replace anyone working for his father, he followed the directions his father left with Mr. Simpson. It all proved profitable and still growing. 'Rell's vision of a million dollar business was on the horizon.

"Let's sit down and get this mess out of the way. I called you here for two reasons. One being this JWL LLC and the other Ms. Tonya Mince."

Stanley waited for their reaction. Their non-verbal response and 'Rell's sigh was noted.

"We can't duck either topic and we need to be ahead of any problems that may arise. Now, Darryl and Derek have been asked to come to talk with the lawyers and judge in chambers. I believe they've found some kind of connection between Carson's Web and this JWL LLC. We have not found any information on this account other than it being a part of Quintech's business accounts. I would imagine with the merging of the two companies, Quintech and your uncle's construction company, there would be some unknown companies in books for record keeping. This JWL is set up only on the account books. There are no other files on this company. If there needs to be a ghost company created, we need to build a prior connection to Darryl's construction company of at least ten years, if not more. It's clear what they did."

"Stan, wait. Are you saying they created an account to gamble with the profits?"

"Mitch, I'm not sure yet. I wanted to talk with you before telling Darryl and Derek what Byron and I have found. I think they've been doing this for a while. It may even be why Derek got this indictment from Carson's Web. It's more than a trademark problem. It's the money made when he was doing the trademarks. The money for those accounts don't match any of the records they've provided. Causing suspicion, Carson's Web investigated and found that same account on their books and Derek was their contact for that account. Money came in for the account but there is a question about deductions and deposits made."

Each of them was given a copy of the paperwork the lawyer held in his hand.

"Byron suggested this approach and I agree."

They took a moment to review the paperwork. Mitch and 'Rell made sideline notes agreeing to discuss them later at the office.

"Okay, so we create this account but if the courts are questioning it, doesn't that mean they know the account doesn't exist?" 'Rell wanted to be sure of the legal aspects.

"There has been no subpoena for any paperwork from your brother or uncle. We present it as a hidden account that Derek kept from Carson's Web's files. It's on his books for them, they just didn't reap any of the benefits. He'll be held liable per the company policy, whatever that is and they'll have to negotiate about the infringement. It also clears up the bookkeeping for Quintech Designs. The account will close in another six months or a year. They will have to understand they can't do business this way."

"I'll check how far back Uncle Darryl's books carry this. We're going to have to make sure the dates coincide."

"Byron, that's a good point. Stan, I want to know exactly what they're doing. This could be the reason Derek was in that so-called accident."

"I thought about that Rell. I'll meet with them once you guys leave."

"Stanley, you said that was one subject and the other?"

"She hasn't given up. She wants part of D.Q. Enterprises. I wanted you to be aware of it. Mr. Monroe will be checking for any loopholes he can find. Mitch go over the older books. I know we did this when you first came aboard but check when the company was established. If you find her name on any documents let me know. I believe I have all the legal documents. I'm looking for accounts like this JWL ghost account."

"Stan, my father would have caught that."

"Your father may have created them. How do you think your uncle learned how to sneak one in?"

The meeting ended with each of them questioning their conscious. It was obvious, D.Q. Enterprises may have not started on a level playing field.

Eleven

Darryl listened to Derek as he tried to reason with Mr. Simpson. The more he explained why JWL LLC had been created, the more trouble, the lawyer emphasized, they would be in. He remained silent until Mr. Simpson mention 'Rell wanting to know where the money was being spent.

"What does D.Q.'s business have to do with ours? I thought we agreed and signed that Quintech Designs didn't answer to D.Q. Enterprises." Darryl waited for the lawyer to explain 'Rell's questions.

"The money. It's just that simple Darryl. It's got to be clean money and the only way for the account to be reputable may be for it to have some connections with D.Q. Enterprises."

"Stanley, connected how? It was a company that worked with my construction company. Now that we've merged…."

"Uncle Darryl, just listen to him. Go ahead Simpson, what do you mean the money has to be with a reputable business? My Uncle's construction company was reputable."

"Did the two of you forget it's still operating? Francine owns it and has not changed the name. The company has no records of a merger between it and Quintech Designs. Darryl, you left Francine with the same account, the same unbalanced books, and the same deficit. So how do we take that company and merge it without her signing paperwork to show the merge? A merger would mean Francine would become a partner in this mess the two of you created. Darryl this is the same mess D.Q. had to bail you out of a few years back."

"That was different."

"Are you talking about him paying to bail me out and leaving Uncle Darryl in jail?"

"That was a part of it." Stanley sat back in his executive chair. Darryl couldn't argue the point.

"What he's saying is true. I don't need Francine in our business. Hell, she just stopped calling and nagging me about the mess she's had to take on. Tell me this is why no one mention Byron had been to Chicago."

Derek was lost. He had no idea that his uncle had left his aunt with the finances in a turmoil. When he asked about a partnership he spoke about starting over on his own.

"So how does all this fit into this court case?"

"Derek you owe someone, it's obvious. I've been a lawyer just about as long as you've been living. The two of you can shun this off if you want to but understand you could be looking at some serious time. Infringement is the least of your worries. Where are the tax records for this "so-called" account? It doesn't add up. It caught someone's attention. What I'm afraid of son is that Carson's Web shook a bear with this indictment."

"Huh?" Derek's scowl showed he was confused.

"Someone knows you owe money. They also know you're keeping it in your business. They've done just what Byron did. They asked for your accounts to be part of the evidence. They found JWL LLC, an account that had deposits and deductions that never made the front office. They traced and put a search out for a few of the connections and found your uncle's company did business with this same company. Money is missing and it shows in the books of both companies."

"Rell told you to make a ghost account?" Darryl had a few words for his nephew.

"No, I told Byron what I thought they were looking for and he found it. Now if he's an accountant and found it without a blink of the eye..."

"Okay, so if we need this ghost account what does D.Q. Enterprises have to do with it?"

"Nothing Darryl. But you need to understand. It was D.Q. Enterprises that gave Derek the money for Quintech and bailed your construction company out of debt. If they can't get the money back from you they'll freeze Quintech's money. Frozen money ain't no good to anyone, especially D.Q. Enterprises. 'Rell doesn't need records or accounts checked because he's dished out over a million to help you and Derek get up and running."

"We need to change this so-called power that 'Rell has over us. That's what needs to be done."

"What are you talking about Uncle Darryl? 'Rell don't have no power over our operations."

"Derek, ask Mr. Simpson here. He who has the money has the power."

There was an uncomfortable silence in the room.

Twelve

Karlton pulled into the driveway while pushing the remote for the powered garage door to open. He turned off the ignition and sat wondering why Tonya's car was not parked in the empty spot next to his. He entered their home praying she had not wandered off as she had done quite often during her recovery. She promised she would be fine without him for the week he was away. Dershai assured him she would check on her mother without giving a hint that they planned it that way. He'd have to call Shai before assuming that Tonya was back to playing games.

Before he left for D.C. he offered to take Tonya with him. He thought it would be a great get-away since they hadn't vacationed since her attempt on her life. The doctor's agreed time away from home may help with her depression. Tonya disagreed and before they argued about it, Karlton began to pack his clothes. He didn't think he left with bad feelings lingering but the silence in the house made him think twice.

As thoughts of where she may have gone toyed with his mind, he searched the house. There was no note left on the kitchen counter or the erase board they kept on the refrigerator. Tonya had been forgetful during her recovery and the board helped her keep appointments and return messages. If Karlton left home before she got up he'd put on the coffee and leave a note where he would be if she needed him. Tonya had not left home alone in almost a year, or so he thought.

As he went through the home hoping to find an explanation for her leaving, he didn't notice any signs of urgency. She took the time to straighten the bedroom, putting her nightgown and slippers neatly in the closet. He returned to the kitchen to check the sink. There he found her coffee cup with her lipstick stain and a plate. He assumed she made herself breakfast before leaving. She was alone, that was evident.

Karlton picked up the phone to call Shai. He pressed the re-dial and disconnected the call before the dialer completed its command. Mr. Monroe's number on the phones ID screen answered his questions. Tonya was headed to stir up an issue that Karlton thought had died with her spirit for revenge. It was obvious that Tonya was who she had always been, Mrs. D.Q. Mince. Karlton hoped once she recovered fully from her close to death experience she would forget the idea of owning part of D.Q. Enterprises. A visit to her lawyer's office would mean she hadn't given up and she was no longer sick.

Tonya didn't need the money. The stocks left to her by D.Q. were more than enough to sustain the lifestyle she was accustomed to. Karlton offered her all he had saved over the years as well. He explained their past to Shai and Derek during the months of her recovery. He loved Tonya and tried to show her the difference between the man he was and the man he came to be. He saw no reason to cause a problem for 'Rell or D.Q. Enterprises. That topic had become a continuous argument.

Shai agreed with Karlton while Derek refused to discuss his mother or her antics. The three talked often and although Derek wouldn't admit it, they wanted the best for her. Tonya's mental state was fragile and revenge seemed to be the only thing holding it together. She skipped therapy claiming it wasn't helping but took the prescribed medication with her favorite drink. She hid bottles and stayed to herself whenever company would stop by. Karlton thought she was regressing. Now he realized she had no intention of letting go of her past and building a future. He didn't know if there was a place for him in her plans.

Shai answered after three rings, Karlton almost hung up but he heard her voice as he was returning the phone to the cradle.

"Hey, hello?"

"Hey, Shai it's me, Karlton."

"Oh, I thought I missed the call. Trying to get your grands to eat lunch. How are you?"

"I'm good honey. How's Rell?"

"He's fine. Things are going well. How's my mother treating you? I know she's a handful these days. She says she's ready to get away from the house and do some shopping. She must be better now."

"Shai, I think she's been putting on a show for us. She's not here. The car is gone and the last number on the phone is Mr. Monroe's. Do you think she went to his office? Please tell me I'm wrong."

"Wow, she drove to the city? I didn't know she was ready to drive. She mentioned shopping a week ago. Maybe that's where she went."

"I would think shopping would be a bit much. She fired the housekeeper a few weeks ago. She said cleaning and keeping the house up would help her with her exercise. She's been really distant with me, that's why I took the trip to Washington. I thought maybe I was smothering her. Plus I had some business to wrap up."

"I stopped by there, Aunt Darlene, Marci, and Mia have been there. She seemed the same as when you left. She was out of bed, and the house was clean but she was still out of it. I don't want to think ill-willed of her but do you think she was faking, I mean really?"

"Well, I called her to tell her I was on my way home. She didn't say she was leaving."

"Karlton, did she know the time you were leaving. Maybe she planned on being back before you got there."

"Something is going on I just don't know what."

"Why would she go to Mr. Monroe's office? Is he still her lawyer? She swore after losing the battle with D.Q. Enterprises twice she was searching for a new firm to deal with."

"I don't know Shai. She doesn't talk to me about that stuff. I don't ask. But after this stunt of leaving home without anyone knowing where she is, well she can't do that in her condition."

"Well, she's Tonya Mince, what you gonna do?"

"I got your point. I'll call you back."

Thirteen

Tonya had the paperwork she thought she needed to stump Darrell Mince. According to her paperwork the stocks D.Q. gave to her could not be sold without her signature or her declaration she was surrendering the stocks to D.Q. Enterprises. She had done neither and she knew there was no proof in any file that said she had.

"Morons, every last one of them. Alright, Mr. Monroe come right or be prepared for a fight I know you can't win." Tonya continued to mumble to herself as she entered the law offices. She ignored the security guard's afternoon acknowledgment and stood waiting for the elevator doors to open.

Getting off on the fifth floor she noted the décor in the waiting area had changed. "My money for this mess and he can't seem to find simple documents."

"Ms. Mince, how are you?" The receptionist smiled as she greeted the woman she knew had at least ten different personalities.

"Good afternoon dear, how have you been? I love that necklace and the matching bracelet. I see Mr. Monroe decided to pay you what you were worth huh. Just teasing sweetie, is he ready for me? I called earlier."

There was no need to exchange sarcastic remarks. The receptionist announced the arrival of Ms. Tonya Mince. She returned to the paperwork on her desk without giving any further attention to the client who walked past her desk with a smirk on her face.

"Good afternoon Ms. Mince, please take a seat." Mr. Monroe, a man Tonya always thought was handsome walked to his conference table to retrieve a stack of papers.

She nodded her head giving him a nod of approval at his apparel while she took her seat. She snickered at the thought that he probably wasn't with his last catch. Tonya and Karlton had been to dinner engagements with them and he never could coordinate his colors. The matching tie, the handkerchief, and socks were a style completely opposite of his normal black suit, white shirt attire. She leaned over a little further than she meant to; she was trying to see his shoes.

"Is there something wrong?"

"Oh, no. At least not from what I see. How's your lady friend? What's her name?"

Mr. Monroe dared not to relax. Her questions weren't how their conversations often started. Although, he had agreed to go to a few of the functions she sent invites for him to attend.

"Well, we're not really together. You know I've been single for years after my divorce. She and I dated a few times but nothing serious came of it."

"Really? So, who is dressing you these days? You look like new money. My money, the money you should have recouped from 'Rell and his Mama."

"Ms. Mince! I don't think that's called for."

Tonya threw the two envelopes across the table at the stunned lawyer. "Cut the bullshit and read this. Why wasn't this mentioned or at least found before now? Do you have copies of this paperwork?"

Monroe opened the envelopes and read each document. He then searched through the pile he had. It was obvious they were in an order that made it easy for him to retrieve any document in the pile.

"Ms. Mince. I'm going to allow you to read this document that explains that the stock you own was transferred during the agreement for your legal separation. When you agreed to the terms of the separation; payments of outstanding bills, transfers of stock, property and future monies to be paid to you, this stock was included. You signed for it all. Here, let me show…."

"Give me this damn paper. What do you mean this stock was included? That was what I agreed I wanted to keep and would not give back to D.Q."

"Yes, you didn't give it back. It was transferred immediately and has been handled by Dickerson & Jackson LLC since then. In the agreement, you said you would not surrender stocks or sell them to D.Q. Enterprises, but you agreed to any transfers. Your stock was immediately transferred."

"Monroe, I was a part of the properties and stocks when we were married. My signature was for any of those properties. I didn't own them. I worked with the clients and companies that owned them. I couldn't agree or disagree to transfer something I didn't own."

"Ms. Mince, it was all D.Q. Enterprises stock. They didn't sell your stock they transferred it as they did and still do others each year. This was nothing new for your husband's company. Each year they list the stocks and properties that will be sold or transferred."

Mr. Monroe pulled out the listing for the year in question and handed it to her. "If you check the third listing from the bottom you'll see your stocks are on the list."

Tonya sat quietly reviewing each of the papers carefully. She couldn't believe D.Q. had slipped out of another knot she thought she tied.

"Mr. Monroe, so if I'm understanding you correctly all my dealings with this stock are with who?"

"Dickerson & Jackson Holding LLC. Their information is on the paper you have there. I took the time to give you a summary of each month they've had your stock. There has been no loss and your value has increased over the years. I had them send me updated records and a copy of your owner's paperwork. Ms. Mince, I might add, that too has your signature. Is there any other information you need from them?"

"No, I guess not. Monroe, there has to be something you're missing. No one helps a man build a business to lose it after thirty years of marriage to another woman and a bastard son!"

"Ms. Mince, I understand, but your name is on nothing nor has it ever been as far as ownership of D.Q. Enterprises. I have that documentation as you should have it too. It was presented…."

"I know, at the legal separation!"

"Yes. D.Q. and his team were thorough. The paperwork was not done overnight. There is nothing that hasn't been questioned gone over or even doubted. That's how D.Q. operated."

"He left it all to a boy he didn't even give his name. He's not a Mince."

"Not a Mince? What makes you think he's not a Mince."

"There was no DNA test taken. He was sleeping with a woman that had no attachment legally to him. How do we know she didn't have something to do with his decision or someone else?"

"I'm sure if he had proof of Dershai and Derek, he checked Derrell as well."

"No, he did what she wanted him to do. Strip me of everything when it was all over because she couldn't get it as long as I was his wife."

"Ms. Mince divorce papers were filed. You were legally separated. Also, Ms. Robbins has and had property owned by D.Q Enterprises and her own home."

"Suppose he wasn't D.Q.'s son. Would that make a difference?"

"You could fight it, but Ms. Mince you won't win. D.Q. was not obligated to leave his business to you or any of the children. He could have given it to the partners."

"Monroe do I have grounds to question it?"

Mr. Monroe sighed knowing she wasn't willing to give up.

"I'll check into it for you. Let's see how far we can push it."

"Monroe, push it and when you get tired find a way to put it in front of a judge."

As usual, she stood retrieved the paperwork and left without another word. Monroe tapped the intercom, "Lena, I'm done for the day."

Fourteen

'Rell opened the door to his home hoping to have a quiet evening. At the sound of voices coming from the dining room, he remembered, Derek and Leeza were guests. There had been no conversation regarding the length of their stay. As he closed the door he heard his Uncle Darryl's voice. Instant annoyance caused him to take his time walking to the crowded room.

Simone was with Darryl and they all seemed to be having a great time.

"Hey, I didn't know the boss man worked the entire day? You still overseeing operations or what?" Darryl teased waiting for his nephew to respond with a laugh or sarcastic comment.

"It takes a lot to keep the windows, doors, nameplates, and reputation of the companies and business clean when those within keep slinging shit on the table."

'Rell's comment silenced the room. The women grabbed their drinks and a plate of chips as they tipped out to the grand room. 'Rell continued to the refrigerator and grabbed a beer.

"So what's up Derek, how was your flight? You called to say it was coming in late, and nothing after that. I wondered most of the afternoon what was up, or do I send a car? Whatever, you're here, so I'm assuming you went to visit your mom or Nana."

"C'mon man, I know Mr. Simpson told you we were at his office."

"Yeah, with my driver who I sent to bring you to my office first. Enough of the shit man. If you're gonna do your own thing don't tie up my guys. You've got drivers, get one of yours to take you around."

"Really, you mad about that?"

"Not mad, just annoyed. It happens when shit gets done around you, has nothing to do with you, but you and your company get involved. You know me by now and if you rode around with Uncle Darryl all day he probably said I would be pissed. I don't play with my money or my family."

"Oh, I thought I was in the other room with the women," Darryl replied trying to ease the rise of his nephew's tension.

"You can go in the other room if you want. They'll listen to your lies and glorified past. I got problems with what the two of you are mixed up in. It's costing your company and mine money and we don't even know if spending this money will make the problem go away."

"Listen, this is the second time today that it sounds like we work for you. Maybe I'm confused but Quintech is our company and we run it."

'Rell nodded his head as he listened to what he knew would be the beginning of his uncle's rant.

"When we agreed for Quintech to be monitored until we got on our feet, hell, there's an end to that shit. It begins now. I'm tired of hearing about D.Q. Enterprises making financial decisions for us."

"I'm glad you understand my concerns. How much money do you think you owe D.Q. Enterprises?"

Neither Derek nor Darryl answered. Darryl opened another can of beer. Derek starred at 'Rell.

"Man are you serious?"

"Yeah, this is business. Love you and Uncle Darryl but he's right. We balanced everything for you to start out over two years ago and suddenly between sales, payments and some damn made up account it's gonna cost more than what we agreed upon. So, I agree. D.Q. Enterprises needs to cut the support string and you and Uncle Darryl clean up the shit and balance your books and continue business as usual. But I'm sure Mr. Simpson told you that these books are now a part of your court case. That ties in Uncle Darryl's construction company he had and my company. To untie those that know nothing about your gambling, womanizing, trips or whatever it's gonna cost. I'm excited that we can stop managing things and let the chips fall where they may."

'Rell left Darryl and Derek at the kitchen island.

"So now what! You know we need D.Q. Enterprises, especially now."

"Derek, we have a company. It's running."

"Barely, if we have to pay for a lawyer. A drawn-out court case could cost us a good penny. Man, have you looked at the books?"

"Yeah, but there's another way around that court case."

"Really, okay Unc, I'm listening."

"Do the time. We keep the company. The lawyer gets you a slap on your hand. You'll be out before you know it. We won't owe anyone because I'll run a couple of contracts and make the payments to those we owe."

Derek stood to his feet. "What the hell are you thinking?"

His voice was so loud, the conversation in the grand room ceased. Everyone tuned in to what was being said in the other room. 'Rell smiled hoping the argument would bring some light to the truth.

"Sit your stupid ass down!" Darryl said whispering through his clenched teeth. "You listen to me, you can do this!"

"Are you forgetting they tried to kill me? Going to jail ain't a safety net. What's to stop them from killing both of us?" Derek sat down and sighed. "Listen Unc, we need to come clean with 'Rell. I'm looking over my shoulder everywhere I go. Just being here is jeopardizing family and business. Hell, Stanley Simpson ain't stupid. We disconnect from D.Q. Enterprises now ain't gonna stop him from searching for what was going on. Right now we got a chance. Your idea, throw me to the pen and you run the company? Man the dream was mine, you left yours when you left your wife."

Neither spoke for minutes. They drank their beers in silence. 'Rell saw the chance he needed to step in and talk with them.

"Ladies can I refill glasses, bring you something from the kitchen," Rell asked as he pretended his beer was empty. He stepped into the kitchen. "You guys good? Need refills?"

"No man, once you get the ladies straight, uh come back we need to talk."

Derek looked at his uncle knowing he didn't approve of his next step. Suddenly thoughts of the truck coming at him became a vivid memory. He shook his head as the tears rolled down his cheeks. He remembered trying to turn off the road but the car that was bumping him wouldn't give him room. He wiped the tears before 'Rell returned, but not before Darryl saw them.

Darryl got up out of his seat and reached out to comfort his nephew.

"Don't touch me. You want me to go to jail? I'm just returning from hell and your solution in all this is for me to go to jail? You don't give a damn. When the tables turn and they will; let's see where you stand."

"What does that mean?" Darryl stepped back standing over Derek.

"Whoa, what's up?" 'Rell asked knowing they were now at odds about what was to be done. Just what he and Simpson knew it would take for them to reveal the truth.

Fifteen

"Tonya, baby you promised. I'm not trying to keep you caged, but why can't you let me know what's going on? What are you doing, where are you going, why? Why are you hiding?"

"Karlton it's been a difficult day for me. I tried to get a few things done by myself. It's hard for me to wait for everyone to drop what they're doing to do for me. What's wrong with me that I can't try to do for myself? I agree, it's tiring but I'll eat, shower and relax."

"You didn't answer my question. What, where and why? If you don't want me to know, say so. You should have called and said hey I'm going to go out for a few hours. I would have felt better."

"Karlton you would have had questions, just like you do now. Questions that I don't feel I need to answer. I went into a few stores, ate at the café downtown and breathed a little. I have been in this house, back and forth to the hospital and doctors for what, two years now? I was getting sick of depending on others. I tested myself. So now I know. Today was a bit long for me but I can build up to it."

Karlton listened as he felt the heat rise around his collar. He was angry, but he knew she was right. They would never have the relationship he dreamed of if he didn't allow her to "do" for herself.

"Okay, so where did your day take you?"

Tonya didn't want to blurt out her frustrations. It would be obvious why she was angry if she told him she visited Mr. Monroe's office. She did need him to know, but he didn't need to know she was still pursuing taking over D.Q. Enterprises.

"I drove around until I got hungry, went to eat, went in a few shops and drove back here. I didn't leave the house until after twelve."

"Honey, it's past eight." Karlton waited for her to give a reason for the time.

"I'm grown, Karlton. The malls don't close at eight."

"I see. So is this the new Tonya. You see, the old Tonya never walked the mall for hours. If you don't want to tell me fine. But if the living with me thing is changing don't have me hanging around until you've done whatever it is you're setting up. Tonya, I know you."

He left Tonya standing at the bottom of the stairs.

"Are you saying we're done with the conversation?" She hoped he would simply say yes.

"It will come up again, I'm sure. I'm going to unpack and shower.

Tonya wanted to answer "Fine." She decided she wouldn't start that habit with Karlton. She often said that to D.Q. and he wouldn't speak until she did. Sometimes it would last for a few days unless some household matters caused him to talk to her.

She and Karlton had been living together since her breakdown. She had no intention for him to leave her or smother her. She wanted the relationship to be mutual love. She had experienced thirty plus years of unrequited love. She'd have to give him bits and pieces of her thoughts and reasons for getting her revenge. D.Q. planned for her to be without any inheritance. She decided she'd just have to get it back. Karlton would have to accept her obsession.

Tonya left the envelope that Mr. Monroe gave her on the bookcase in the hall. She'd be sure to put them in her office before going upstairs. There was no smell of food coming from the kitchen. It was evident Karlton had arrived home shortly before she did. There would be more questions as they ate "a little something".

Tonya looked in the refrigerator and pulled out the salad and remainder of the chicken she baked the night before. She didn't cook every day. Karlton would alternate with her as they did with most of the household duties. She was getting better and the doctor was impressed with her progress. She promised she wouldn't overdo any of the prescribed medicine or exercises. No one knew she no longer took the medication that kept her dazed or in the bed. She slowly weaned herself off the valiums and sleep aids. Her herbal teas, oils, and natural vitamins gave her what she needed.

Revenge was also a prescription with a refill. The memory of D.Q. stating his love for Nikki and his disdain for her, gave her a jolt of new life. Her therapist constantly reminded her she would never be able to hurt D.Q. as he had her. Tonya accepted the reality her therapist repeated at each session. She no longer cried about it, nor did she try to tell anyone her reasons for how she felt. She made up her mind that they just didn't understand. She couldn't continue living if D.Q. Enterprises made life easy for D.Q.'s lover and her legacy.

The destruction of the Mince family, public humiliation and the fall of the business was her reality. It didn't matter if D.Q. didn't live to see her take it all back. Tonya's satisfaction would be twofold, his death and their loss.

She was in deep thought, warming up the chicken and preparing two plates. She'd call Karlton down, telling him she wanted to hear about his trip. Although he went out of town for business, he visited old friends and family. She was sure they asked about her.

Karlton entered the kitchen with the envelope from Mr. Monroe's office in his hand. He watched Tonya as she prepared their plates in silence. He wasn't amazed that she had no weakened movements, no fatigue after a full day. He was certain she had an excuse for the envelope that didn't come through the mail.

Sixteen

"Mr. Monroe stopped by?" Karlton stood at the kitchen door with the envelope in his hand. He knew the envelope wasn't mailed as it had no postage or their home address.

"No, actually I asked him for those papers from the stocks I owned. You know the ones D.Q. left for me."

"Tonya you have a copy of the papers in the vault. So you went to his office and picked these up?"

"He updated the information and after speaking with him on the phone I wanted the information explained. It seems he thinks the stock is actually benefitting me more than what being part owner of D.Q. Enterprises would. I can't see that being possible."

"Did he drop these off or did you go to his office?"

"Don't get stuck on the small details baby, yes I went to his office."

"Small details? His office is an hour away. A two-hour drive and you're on meds. Let's just say I'm a little concerned, no disappointed. You promised not to do anything that would put you in danger."

"I haven't had those meds in almost two weeks. That's what was keeping me in the bed. I weaned myself off that medicine. I'm functional now and I'm not depressed. I'm determined."

"I see." Karlton nodded his head and placed the envelope on the counter. "So you're determined to leave me in the dark about your intentions? What are they, Tonya? I thought we agreed to let that mess go. What changed that?"

"You were down with seeking what should have been mine. You tell me what changed."

"Tonya, you damn near died, no killed yourself over this mess. Am I not enough? Haven't I shown you commitment? You don't need the ghost of D.Q. or his Enterprises to keep you happy. Why do you insist on this revenge? He's dead Tonya!

"I know that! He's been dead for most of the years we lived together. For thirty years of marriage, there was no life in our love. I shouldn't have to beg to get what I helped him build."

"Tonya, for the first time be truthful with me and yourself. Even in his death, you are still in love with D.Q. aren't you? This pain, the thought of killing yourself, this rage you won't let go of, and the determination to conquer his business from his son, is proof of your love for him."

"That's just it Karlton. If we can prove 'Rell is not his…"

"Tonya, answer me. Are you still in love with D.Q? Would having D.Q. Enterprises fulfill the pain of him loving Nikki?"

"They don't deserve it. I do!"

"What does it matter Tonya? He's dead, he's gone. We've been through this over and over and you still won't let it go. I can't compete with a dead man Tonya. I've given you the children you needed to get his love back. I tried to blackmail his business so you could get his love back. I held our secrets for those same thirty years, so you could get his love back. He chose Nikki Robbins and his son 'Rell and you still fought to get his love back. Tonya this, this is what drove you to try to take your own life and you went to get this damn envelope of poisonous information for what? He's dead and you're consumed by revenge. When does this end?"

"Karlton, don't tell me I don't have a right to what was left to that home wrecking winch and her bastard son."

"Do you still love D.Q.? What's the reason for this madness?"

"It's mine!"

"We're not going to start this again. Have you thought about Shai or Derek in all of this?"

"Why would I? He left them theirs and I want what's mine."

Karlton was mad but he knew he had to try to be there for her. She would break soon and another attempt on her life might be successful. He wouldn't give his opinion or argue with her. She'd have to lose to D.Q. totally. Then they could continue to live. He knew she loved him as well. He thought after D.Q.'s death, she'd realize they were free to love each other for the rest of their lives.

"So what's different in this envelope? What did you find that was different."

"Karlton, how can we be sure he's D.Q.'s son? No one ever questioned it. It was just assumed."

"So, if he's not. What does that prove? There is a will in place Tonya. Your name was not mentioned for inheritance. His birthright has nothing to do with it."

"There's something strange about D.Q.'s intentions. I asked for what was in the paperwork from our separation, the sale of the stock and the will. I'll review it and decide the next move."

Karlton lost his appetite and the will to argue. "Well, let me know what you find and if you need my help I'll be in the den."

"You're not eating?"

"No, you eat. I've got some thinking to do."

$\mathcal{S}$*eventeen*

Nana packed the Reverend's "snack pack", as he called it. Once she became the First Lady she told him he wouldn't have any need to eat the meals brought to him by other women in the church. So the days she knew he would be at the church later than dinner she packed his food, fruit, and snacks. Reverend Wilcox didn't dare forget his pack, Jewels as he affectionately called her, would be at the church with his food and a scolding.

"So has Darryl or Derek been by to see you yet?"

"Rev. it's that Derek that I want to see. I see Darryl all the time. It's been a week. He's called but with the court case starting on Monday, I think he's been tied up with Mr. Simpson."

"Jewels, that ain't no excuse. He and his girlfriend, what's her name again?"

"Leeza," Nana replied shaking her head. Her husband could remember scriptures and anything on the church calendars. He just couldn't remember names.

"Yes, Leeza. They traveled across the country and don't visit the eldest in the family?"

"I didn't think of it like that. You know how young folks do. They don't think the way we do."

"I guess you're right. It's a generational thing. I heard you say on the phone, Derek was able to walk?"

"Rev. God blessed him. Spared his life, put Leeza by his side as he healed, took him out of danger and allowed him to walk again. God blessed him. I hope he knows that. He's got more to go through and he needs to understand it is only by God's will that he made it."

"Jewels, he also needs to humble himself. There's no love like the love of a mother, grandmother or family. You all created a shield of protection with your prayers for him. He needs to stop by before his court date. Tell him that when he calls again. There is a reason for each relationship. He needs to know that his life means a lot to you and everyone in the family. Hiding from those who love him is not the way."

"Rev. we ain't who he's hiding from; him and Darryl are in some kinda trouble. 'Rell is sure of it and I would imagine Mr. Simpson is gonna do everything to keep them out of jail."

"Wait, I thought this was about the job he was fired from."

"I thought so too. Honey, I think they bit off more than they could chew, gambling and not realizing who they were dealing with. I think that mess with the job may be crossed in their accounts. 'Rell tried to explain it to me but it's another mess. I'm kinda glad he didn't stop by to lie around the truth. Darryl knows better that's why he hasn't come here. It's almost three, you better be getting out of here. I'll see you when you get in."

"I'm hoping that the Trustee meeting won't be long. I want to start Bible Study on time."

"I understand but you got to get there on time."

The two walked to the door and kissed a soft farewell.

"Jewels, don't get yourself worked up. It will all work itself out."

"It's the last thing on my mind. Darryl and Derek are grown men. D.Q. warned them. They need to remember his warning."

Nana stood at the door waiting for him to back down the driveway. They waved at each other and she blew a kiss. After a year of marriage and over fifteen years of friendship she loved him dearly. She understood his devotion to God and the church would keep him late some nights. She offered to help him console parishioners that would come by their home with problems. Nana wanted everyone to understand she was perfect for him and his ministry. The whispers started after D.Q.'s death. The rumor was Reverend Wallace Wilcox married Julia Mince out of pity for her family crisis. Every now and then there would be whispers about his marrying her for the money her son left her.

"Church folks!" Nana would tell the family every Sunday a new rumor was whispered and overheard. Nothing changed as the time went on and Nana didn't trust any of the women that smiled and complimented her on Sunday morning.

Nikki called earlier and told her she would stop by if she was free. Nana looked at the clock knowing that the visit would be within the next hour, if at all. She enjoyed Nikki's company and since she hadn't seen her at church the last few weeks she was excited to see her.

The phone rang, interrupting her thoughts and her preparation for the visit. She put on her reading glasses to read the caller ID. *"Tonya"* appeared on the screen and Nana shook her head as she prepared for what she knew would be drama.

"Hello," Nana answered trying not to sound annoyed by the disturbance.

"Well hello, Mama Mince. I hope I didn't disturb you."

Tonya tried not to sound phony. She knew how keen Nana was. She had been trying to rebuild their severed relationship for years. Nana tolerated her because of Shai and Derek nothing more mattered.

"No, you didn't. How are you coming along? Are you following the doctor's orders?"

"Yes, ma'am. I'm actually doing a lot better. I'm driving a bit now and getting around by myself. Karlton and Shai are still helping of course, but nothing like it was. Thanks for asking. How are you and the rest of the family?"

"Fine, just fine. I haven't seen you at church. I hope you'll be able to return in time." Nana took a deep breath holding the phone away from her face waiting for the expected excuse.

"Yes, Women's Day is in a few weeks. I really don't want to miss that. I heard the guest speaker is great in her work for women who struggle with depression and other issues."

"Yes, Grace Patterson is one of the best. We've been to a few of her conferences."

"Well Mama Mince, I called to ask about some papers you may have or Mr. Simpson may have given you."

"Just what papers would that be? Why didn't you call him or your lawyer? You know I didn't handle none of those final papers concerning D.Q., the business or the two of you."

"Well, this is not about any of that. I can't seem to find my copy of the birth records for Shai or Derek. I'm thinking about getting my stocks in order and I need to show their records when I sign the papers. I thought maybe D.Q. had a copy of all that since 'Rell discovered D.Q. was his father and not theirs. I don't know if Mr. Simpson would have kept that in his office."

Nana paused before speaking. Tonya was fishing, she just didn't know what she really wanted.

"I can't help you with that child. 'Rell and Mr. Simpson took all that paperwork away from here. I think whatever was pertaining to personal records 'Rell kept and gave Mr. Simpson a copy. I wouldn't need it. Everyone is grown and should keep their own paperwork. Did you ask your children?"

"No, I didn't think of that. I guess I was thinking on the legal side of things. My lawyer suggested I check with family members so I thought I'd check with you. I mean, you being the head of the Mince family and all."

"No sweetheart, once I was told by Mr. Simpson that 'Rell was who D.Q. chose to fill his shoes, I let him. I would think Derek would have his papers and Shai would have hers."

"I was thinking all three of the records would be together."

"Three? What do you mean three?"

"Well if D.Q. had the records 'Rell's would be with Shai's and Derek's right?"

"Tonya, get off my phone."

The conversation ended as many between the two women had in the past. Nana hung up and continued to her chair in the den without giving Tonya's call another thought.

Eighteen

"Sam is meeting me at my house at seven, so we have a few hours of sitting time together."

Nikki walked into the home where she always felt love and comfort.

"I'm so happy you decided to come by. I guess Deacon Smalls, I just can't get used to calling him Sam, is there with the Reverend. He's wishing on that seven o'clock time. You know it will be later than that."

"Yes, ma'am. I told him to call when he's leaving the church. I'll leave when he calls."

"Well come on in baby. I'm glad you're here."

The two women hugged and giggled on the way to the den. Nana took her seat in her favorite chair and Nikki kicked off her heels.

"I meant to kick these things off at the door. Oooowee, that feels better."

"Girl, I don't know how y'all do it. I did it in my day too, so it must just be what we women do. We complain our feet hurt and we stuff them in those pointed toe heels daily. I'm glad I'm down to once a week, two if the church has a function."

They both laughed knowing it was true. Nana had shoes of all colors and heels of all sizes. Shoes and handbags were her weakness. D.Q. would buy her a gift almost every week. Jewelry, clothes, cars, furniture whatever she wanted she had. She tried to stop him, reminding him he had a wife and a home. It was then that she found out he had another woman and her home as well. She stopped telling him what she liked knowing he would buy it. Nana loved her son and who he became as the President and CEO of D.Q. Enterprises. She didn't realize his total wealth until his death.

"You're right we are our worst enemy. Even with our clothes. I can't wait to take off all that mess underneath after wearing it all day."

"Well, I know you're glad you have your own business. Going into an office everyday wears the body down for sure."

"Yes, I do love my business and its picking up too. Simone and I have to split our trips now. We still do the projects together though."

"How is Simone doing? I know it's a big difference living in the south compared to living in New York."

"She hasn't mentioned it. Nana, you know with Simone there's no telling the mess she left in New York. The move probably did her good."

"Nikki, now I know why she and Darryl get along so well."

The two women laughed again. They caught up on the church gossip, the news in the community, and the family matters.

"So what is Tonya fishing for?"

"I don't know child. I thought she was still in the bed with Karlton and Shai waiting on her hand and foot. She's after something, something that ain't gonna benefit nobody but her."

"Why didn't she just ask her lawyer to obtain what she wants?"

"Well, Mr. Simpson has no time to entertain her. I guess Mr. Monroe puts up with her because she pays him to. The court case for Derek starts on Monday. Don't nobody have time for Tonya digging up mess."

"Well, what would birth certificates prove? I'm assuming she's looking to prove something or digging up something. Maybe she doesn't believe that D.Q. had paperwork that proved Shai and Derek weren't his."

"She knows that. That's a fact that rose between her and D.Q. years ago. Karlton was the one left in the dark. She threw in 'Rell. I think she wants to see his birth certificate. Maybe she doesn't believe he's a Mince."

"Nana, she can look into that without anyone else knowing. He owns a company that has public records."

"She ain't gonna trust what they put on record."

"Well hell, I can mail her his birth certificate with D.Q.'s name on it. It still won't prove anything. D.Q. signed it but they didn't do DNA testing. What is she after? Always something with her."

"We'll have to watch her next move. I'll talk to Derek and Shai. You talk to 'Rell. Once again we'll have to be a step ahead of her."

"Nana, she can't step nowhere near you or me."

"And nowhere near D.Q. Enterprises. That's what she's after. Tonya knows what those birth certificates say. I think I'll call Mr. Simpson too."

Nineteen

Derek hadn't spoken much about the problem between him and his uncle. Everyone suspected that Darryl had pulled on the wrong nerve and it would pass after a few days. After two weeks and the court case set to begin on Monday, Shai was worried it was serious. 'Rell wouldn't give any details regarding the flare up the night of their return. Leeza told her she wouldn't question anything that Derek didn't bring up. Shai was there to support him, but he would have to explain what was going on.

'Rell left early for the office and as Shai left for work she reminded her house guests that they were to meet at Nana's house for dinner. It was Friday night and Nana called to say she'd be in church all day Sunday. She wanted to talk to Shai and her brother before the week of anticipated frustration began.

Nana's guidance and love never faltered. She still treated Shai and Derek as though they were her "babies". Shai thought it would be an awkward feeling between them and D.Q.'s family once it was revealed that they were not his children. Nana's dinner invites still included a request for them to visit and be seated with her at church on Sunday's, nothing changed.

"Y'all ain't never had to live without me and until God takes me home to be with Him you never will. I've been there for the two of you

72

when you didn't know you needed someone. That's my place in your life. I'm your Nana and that ain't gonna change. Your dad raised you as his, understand he loved you as his. He's known about Karlton Harris for years. It was your mother's secret. For whatever reason she had she kept that secret. I guess she thought she was hiding it from D.Q. She thought he didn't know, but he did. So don't y'all think you're abandoned, Shai ain't no reason for you to be ashamed of your love for 'Rell. He's a Mince, you're a Harris. Love him, love him like you were loved by his father."

Tears fell as Shai remembered that night and their conversation. It was then that Derek decided he was not returning home. He and Leeza would be leaving that weekend. Derek asked questions about their mother. Nana couldn't give him any reason for her actions or make excuses for her denials.

"Shai you can forgive her, take care of her or whatever. I can't say I hate Karlton, she did him just like us. I can't forgive her. Nana, I don't think I ever will."

Nana's response was all they needed to be reassured of her love. "It doesn't matter right now. You have to go through times of pain before you realize the reason for it. Once you've healed you will be able to forgive. Forgiveness is not condoning her actions, it's knowing the truth, accepting it and moving on. You're loved by the Mince family no matter who your father is and to us, you are a Mince. We are still a family and I want you to understand your uncle, aunt, cousins, and me have no intention for things to change between us."

Shai sighed. It had changed. Her mother had tried to end it all. She couldn't face either of her children and she was no longer a Mince. Tonya Mince had cut all ties to the family with one lie. Even after the separation and the divorce she still had been respected. Once it was revealed that Shai nor Derek were the children of D.Q. Mince, whatever respect was left had quickly disappeared. Rumors and gossip were confirmed and right before Shai and 'Rell said their vows people wondered what type of family they would be.

It had to be announced and explained to Tonya's family, extended family and friends that Tonya had lied. Shai and 'Rell would be married and it wouldn't be incest. 'Rell often teased, that the children wouldn't be deformed and after it all, she would be a Mince. Shai smiled returning to the forms on her desk the Mince family drama hadn't stopped. She was sure Nana was going to prepare them for the next blow.

Derek was prepared for court. He spoke on the phone to Mr. Simpson while sending e-mails and faxing papers to his office. Shai thought he'd work at Quintech for a couple of days but he worked from 'Rell's office in their home. Leeza watched him during the day and sent text messages to Shai hoping to break his silence.

"He's scared Shai."

"Hell, he's facing possible time. The fear of someone seeking to harm him, protecting you and jail. Yeah, I've seen him withdraw from everything before, not me, but everything and everyone else. It's okay, Leeza he'll be okay."

She tapped send on the screen and said a prayer. She hoped it would all be okay. Returning to her work she thought of her Aunt Darlene and whispered to herself, *"Yes, Auntie. It is what it is."*

Twenty

Marci dialed Monique's number again. She decided to find out what she could possibly stir up. Monique's relationship with 'Rell seemed impossible compared to the love he had for 'Shai. Marci didn't meet Monique until it was over. It seemed men could forgive friends that dated their ex-girlfriends quicker than any woman would forgive a friend of theirs. Monique cheated on 'Rell with his friend Craig. Although 'Rell had begun talking to Shai he had no idea how long Monique and Craig were a couple. Although 'Rell knew they were dating he still considered Craig a friend; he just tolerated Monique. Marci wondered if it still bothered Monique as it would any woman who had been just steps away from being Mrs. Mince.

'Rell never told anyone other than Mitch about Shai when he and Monique were dating. Nana was his go to for advice about dating and he understood when she fell silent when discussing Monique. Marci tried to talk to Mitch about Monique. His response was simply she was looking for trouble.

The phone rang again and Marci decided she wouldn't leave a message. She hadn't walked away from the phone before its vibration indicated she had a call.

"Girl, I am so sorry. I left this damn phone in my gym bag and couldn't find it. I remembered where it was after I was searching in my bedroom for it, in the damn closet. I'm rambling, hey I'm glad you called." Monique paused giving Marci a chance to speak.

"Well, I wasn't going to leave a message. I figured you'd see I called."

"I'm glad you did. I thought about us after leaving your house. There was some kind of bond between us right? I mean not just because we'd hang out whenever the guys got together right? Some kind of connection, wouldn't you agree?"

Tracey, Mr. Simpson's secretary, was dating Byron, who often came out when the four men got together for dinner and drinks. Keith never brought anyone to their outings. The three women would make small talk between them. Marci always thought of it as being cordial no real connection. She had been warned about Monique and didn't communicate much with Tracey who was a few years younger.

Tracey didn't seem concerned with either of them clinging on Byron as though he was going to run off. Monique would spend most of the evening flirting but pretending it was all in fun. Shai would often put up with the antics and then convince 'Rell it was time to go. Their outings became less frequent as each relationship became serious. Marci and Shai were now married women, Tracey and Byron were talking of living together and Monique was still the girl Craig cheated with.

"I don't think it was a friendship. We talked before the monthly outings the guys would schedule. Not enough to really say we were or are close. If I remember correctly I shut you down once you wanted to know about 'Rell and Shai's relationship."

"Wow, I didn't know you felt that way. You sound like you're upset with me or the fact that everything has changed."

"Everything like what? Nothing has changed." Marci frowned in the mirror as she played with hairstyles.

"What are you doing?"

"Nothing, what has changed?"

"Marci, you're married and so is Shai. It's not the same, it can't be. I mean hanging out with you guys has changed. Did Byron pop the question yet?"

"Not that I know of, has Craig?"

"Is that supposed to be a dig or something?"

"No, just talking right? Isn't that what you wanted me to call for? You wanted to catch up right?"

There was a noticeable silence on the line. Marci looked at the phone almost certain Monique had hung up.

"Hello?"

"I'm here. Just pulling out this bag. I wanted to invite you over to talk. Seriously Marci, I've got questions about 'Rell and Shai. I tried asking you before but I guess you thought that I was looking to be a problem for their marriage. I just want to know how long they were dating before he asked her. We had been together for close to five years. He never once mentioned marriage, I want to know why? I think he married her for the money. He knew what his father had and he wanted to be sure it wouldn't go beyond the family. You know, royalty will marry within the family to keep the money in the family."

"They're not related. I'm sure you've been on top of that story. It was printed in the society section of the paper that week. Didn't you get your copy?"

"Oh yeah, my Prince Charming comment made the paper. I meant it as a joke but the reporter printed it anyway."

"So what's really on your mind Monique?"

"I just think that when you invest your time into a relationship you're due something in return. You don't know, I mean I don't know what Shai may have shared with you or what 'Rell may have said about us. We were.....well, I thought we were on our way to the altar."

"Monique, what does this have to do with today? You can't still be chasing that dream. You got caught cheating with 'Rell's friend. I don't need to know much else. If you want to know why 'Rell got with Shai or how they got together you'll have to talk with him."

Marci paused thinking about the unnecessary drama she would cause.

"Really Monique, for what? There's nothing wrong with his marrying Shai. They have two beautiful children and they're happy. You chose to be with Craig, remember?"

"Oh, I remember. I confided in him and it got, well, it got messy. I'll admit to that. Marci, 'Rell wasn't an angel through it all and I chose to stay with him through his tears, fears and like I said…"

Marci didn't want to hear it again. "Monique. It's done, now what did you want to talk with me about. You already know I'm not going to discuss them with you. You said you wanted to talk before going to my grandmother. What are you stirring up?"

"Shai wasn't the only one carry a child. I saved 'Rell the embarrassment and I think for the drama I saved his precious name, I should be compensated."

"What? You saved him? How? Really, Monique, you could have found something better than that. Did you tell him you were pregnant?"

"No! I went to the doctor for the test and he was sitting there with his so-called sister!"

"Okay, so you were pregnant. Did you deliver or abort?

Either way, how is he responsible. You never told him and how would anyone know it was his. It could have been Craig's child. Does he know you were pregnant?"

"I took care of it, that's all anyone needs to know."

"Monique who knows. None of the men have mentioned it. I don't remember you being pregnant. So if you got rid of the child what do you want from 'Rell?"

"He married Shai to save their name. He'll have to save it again."

"What?"

"I thought I'd be a little more considerate. I have the test result here. I was pregnant and the shock of him possibly dismissing me as he had after getting with Ms. Dershai….what is her maiden name since she wasn't a Mince? Anyway, that bitch stole the father of my child which caused me to have a miscarriage.

That's what he needs to know. I'm sure the Mince clan can't stand another article in the paper. I mean with the other brother, the uncle, the crazy mama-n-law; that's enough to drive 'Rell to drink. I think a hefty compensation is in order."

"You're crazy."

"Marci, your girl or cousin whichever lie you want to stand on is weak. 'Rell holds her up like I told that reporter. Prince Charming he ain't and their home ain't no castle when it's built on sinking sand. The child I carried was a Mince."

"Again, I don't know what you think this has to do with me or mine. It was good talking to you. Good luck with your bull. I'm sure 'Rell and Shai will see through it."

"You don't have to believe me, 'Rell will and that's what matters. Once that weak bitch he married knows he loved me just like he loved her, she'll squirm. Finding out I was pregnant at the same time tells her she was being played just like me."

"They weren't married. There's no baby or proof he was the father. There's no reason for the drama. I think this is more about you seeing that castle and missing what you threw away. You thought Craig would be a part of D.Q. Enterprises. Sloppy seconds but he'd have a solid career, benefits, and money. That plan failed too. No one likes losing out, I understand. Like I said, great talking to you."

Marci hung up the phone. Shai was right, she was glad she wasn't a Mince.

Twenty-One

Tonya got up early. She nor Karlton spoke about her new morning rituals. Although Karlton was glad to see her up and busy for the past week, he had to wonder what she was up to. There had been no mention of a call from Mr. Monroe, nor did she seem concerned. Karlton was tempted to call Shai or 'Rell and ask had Tonya been in touch with them.

As a grandmother, she spent little to no time showering her grands. The twins were more attached to Karlton. Shai told him it had been because the children were scared of Tonya. She had spent most of their younger years being sick. They were told to be quiet around her. Tonya was frail to them and now that they were about to enter kindergarten, they wanted to talk and play more. Karlton was the grandfather they needed although he spent his "playtime" with them in their home without Tonya. She refused to visit Shai or the children in what she considered was 'Rell's home.

There was so much she missed. Karlton wanted her to know each detail. The birthday parties, the dance recitals the children were in, the conversations he had with them that still made him laugh. He thought about Shai and Derek when they were young, he missed those years. Tonya would regret what she missed when the children became adults. They would wonder about their grandmother and why she wasn't interested in their lives.

Tonya was in the kitchen cooking breakfast as he stood at the entrance of the dining room. He watched her as she hummed, seemingly enjoying the morning aroma and the music from the radio in the background.

"Good morning."

"Hey, good morning to you. I thought you deserved a full breakfast since you didn't have to run out of here early this morning."

"Well, actually I did. I canceled the appointment."

"Why, don't you feel well?"

"Healthy as a horse. Worried about you though."

Karlton entered the kitchen and took a seat at the island. He fiddled with the utensils that were placed in front of him. Tonya didn't answer, another sign she wasn't willing to discuss her plans.

"So what do you have planned for today?"

"Not much. I ordered a few things in town. I didn't have to pick them up today so if you want us to go anywhere, we can."

"No, nothing planned. I can ride with you."

"Okay, that's a plan."

Karlton was shocked. He was sure she would try to convince him to stay home.

"I thought I would stop by Quintech to see Derek before the case starts on Monday. It seems like I'm being left out again. I was thinking though, maybe I was wrong. What do you think?"

Tonya's question and statement caused him to do just that, think.

"You may be right, I guess. Why do you think you may be wrong? What did you do or plan to do?"

"Karlton it has nothing to do with any plans. I was just thinking I haven't extended myself to either of my children in weeks. Hell, before that I was constantly in the bed too drugged up to know who came and went. Derek has been out of the country and returned and I haven't seen him once. I know, I didn't make an effort. So today, I thought I would."

"I see. Do you know that he'll be in the office today? He may be spending time with Mr. Simpson preparing for Monday. Call him, then you'll know. I don't want you to be disappointed."

"You're right. It's all happening so fast. Maybe I'll call Shai first, then Darryl."

"Why Darryl?"

"He and Derek are close. He'll know what's going on with him."

"Tonya, the relationship you had with Derek is going to take time to repair. Are you sure you're up for that? Especially since he's got so much to go through right now."

"I am his mother. I'm going through it too."

"Baby it's not the same."

Tonya turned to the sink and stared out the kitchen window. She allowed the tears to fall freely. Karlton was right. It wasn't the same. She couldn't save him, but he could save her. Quintech Designs was a part of D.Q. Enterprises. She'd be there to be sure it didn't fall.

Twenty-Two

Robert Franklin flipped through the pages again. "Alan I can't find any paperwork to support her claims"

"Okay so do I call her or 'Rell?'"

"Man he has enough on his plate without this mess. She won't back off, you know how Tonya is. We don't have a record of anything she's claiming."

Alan stood and gathered the folders. He and Robert were with D.Q. Enterprises when it began. They were friends of D.Q.'s and their dedication paid off time and time again. 'Rell was clear when he took over the CEO position. He wouldn't hesitate to fire anyone who was caught playing both sides when it came to Tonya Mince. It became a reality when Craig wasn't offered a position along with the others; betraying 'Rell had consequences.

"I'll talk with 'Rell and you call that woman back and tell her enough of the nonsense. Show her where we will catch her."

"Put the noose around my neck? Alan, you can't be serious. If I show her the loophole that can be what she slams us with."

"What loophole?"

"Quintech could be paying for her dividends."

"Robert, what are you talking about?"

"We sold her stock on paper only. The money she receives is an account we created, it's a stipend. Once Quintech was on the books we moved the money there. I don't see where it was picked up by Dickerson and Jackson Holding."

"Man, damn. You know they're sequestering all of the books for the court case. How will that be explained as an expense for Quintech? Are the checks cut to her from Quintech?"

"No, it's deposited in her account. The money has never been touched. It's an investment account. Byron knows about it and it can be explained. The company's name isn't on it, but showing her a spreadsheet from D.Q. Enterprises, she'll recognize the company that's on her paperwork. We still deal in stocks and other property with them. She has no right to see that paperwork man."

"Oh, okay. Rob man you still will be the one to call her. Sweet talk her into a date and break it to her over wine."

"Hey you know before that breakdown I may have had a chance. She's still crazy and Karlton can keep her. Ain't no night out worth dealing with her insane ass."

The two laughed until the phone chirped. They both looked at the phone suspiciously. "Ms. Tonya Mince; line one, Mr. Franklin."

"Call me after the cussin' you're about to receive." Alan paused for Robert to respond. Alan waved his hand, picked up the folder and left Robert to the call.

Robert took a moment to prepare himself. It was something about Tonya that turned him on. He respected her and D.Q.'s marriage until he found out D.Q. was in love with Nikki. It was one thing to cheat and another to fall in love. He talked long with his friend only to find out their marriage was in name only. D.Q. knew about her affair with Karlton. The divorce D.Q. sought would be difficult and then there were the children. No one was aware at that time that the two children he raised weren't his.

Everyone knew about 'Rell. There was no doubt that the boy was D.Q.'s son. Robert decided after the death of his friend he had a chance to approach Tonya. Once Karlton returned Tonya's calls and attention seemed to stop. Alan reminded Robert she had a plan and it wasn't to be his bedmate. Robert decided he would wait. He was sure she'd call again. Her call the week prior proved he was right. He had his own plan in mind. Karlton Harris had lost her before. Alan wouldn't understand, she was crazy but Robert had held on to what he called crazy love.

"Hey, Tonya, what's up dear?"

Tonya took the time to use the phone when Karlton got out of the car to go into the bank.

"I don't have long to talk Robert. I know I said I would stop by the office today but something has come up. Are you free around six this evening?"

"Sure, are you coming to the office then?

"No, we'll need to meet somewhere less obvious."

"I'd like that for once."

"Robert, you never change, do you. Meet me at the café on Main Street. They have a jazz set there on Fridays."

"Perfect, this must not be all business."

"Robert, that depends on what you have to tell me. Gotta go."

He hung up the phone wondering what he could tell her. Persuading her to let go of her revenge tactics would spark the cussing Alan teased him about. He'd call Byron. Byron would help him prepare a few reports she could chew on. Stanley would have to be notified. D.Q. prepared Robert, Alan and his lawyer for Tonya's days of questioning. He warned them she wouldn't back away or take no for an answer. She would have to be worn down.

Robert knew his friend was right. Her attempted suicide was the first indication she knew she was losing. Robert's hope was she would cry on his shoulder. She wanted D.Q.'s money and Robert wanted her.

Twenty-Three

'Rell held his head in his hands as he heard the intercom beep again. The day had been nerve wrenching. The phone hadn't stopped with calls from Byron and Mr. Simpson's office. Derek called to say he didn't want to be blindsided by Nana at dinner, while their uncle hadn't returned any calls. It was past four and 'Rell was still sitting at his desk trying to take a moment to gather his thoughts.

"Yes, Tracy what's up?"

"Are you staying late? I'm shutting down or should I be staying here with you?"

"No, you go ahead. I'm good. Did Mitch leave yet?"

"Nope and Byron is with Mr. Simpson and your uncle."

"Darryl is at Simpson's office?"

"The last call I got from them he was. They were looking for Derek. He hadn't got there yet or called."

"Tracy, what time was that?"

"Hmm, about two? Maybe one, yeah, it was closer to lunch. He was supposed to be there at twelve."

"So, they've been there all this time waiting for Derek?"

"I don't think they've waited 'Rell. Since then they've called and asked for e-mail correspondence, meeting notes and a few other things. I don't think Derek intended on showing up. He called you remember?"

"Yeah. Well, you go home and have a good weekend. I'll be in Monday before going to the court proceeding."

"Oh, okay. Do you think Byron will have to testify?"

"He may. Hope not but if it comes to that he's ready. We're ready. That's why I don't understand Derek or my uncle."

"Jail time will make one nervous."

"Tell me about it. Have a good evening."

'Rell fell back into his seat. Nana told him about his father and his uncle. His father was right. There was no reasoning with Darryl Mince. Derek and Darryl hadn't spoken, other than business, since Derek's arrival. Their heated discussion hadn't settled the problem they were facing. 'Rell tried to tell them they had to be on the same page before the court date. To hear that Derek hadn't shown up at Stanley Simpson's office wasn't a sign of agreement between the two.

Mitch entered the office and took the seat across from 'Rell's desk. He didn't say a word as though 'Rell would telepathically respond.

"My super powers ain't working today. What's up?"

"Tonya Mince."

"Not today man. I've got a headache that I can't wait to conquer with my pillow and meds."

"You have a family meeting at Nana's, or did you forget?"

"Shit! Okay, damn. I just want to go home."

"Well, Ms. Mince and Ms. Davis are causing a ripple."

"Ms. Davis. Ms. Davis who?"

"Wow, you don't remember Ms. Davis?"

"Monique Davis?"

Mitchell smiled.

"Are you serious man? What's…wait let's deal with Tonya first."

"Well, she's been calling Robert and maybe Alan too. Alan just left my office. She's supposed to meet Robert about those so-called stocks."

"Does she ever just go away?"

"No the only place I know she stays away from is your house."

"No bro, she would visit when I'm not home if Shai would allow it. After her stunts over Derek, Shai does only what's expected. I thought she was still sickly."

"Apparently not. She's been to her lawyer, he called too. She's digging up the stock thing again. I don't know 'Rell with your uncle and Derek on the warpath she may try to slip in the back door."

"What? What back door?"

"Quintech. If Derek is refusing to work with Darryl she may see it as an opportunity. Maybe not to work there or anything, but to get in to find the money or books. I just thought about the court proceedings and everything. With the two of them feuding she may find a soft spot with one of them."

"My uncle knows better and Derek won't even speak to her. I think we're safe from her antics for the moment. Hell, man, I'll talk to them."

"Does your uncle really think you wanted to control their business?"

"Mitch it doesn't matter. Neither of them had control of their habits and it would have been a major loss to their business as well as ours. Once Quintech has covered what D.Q. Enterprises paid to keep them afloat they can take over their own books and profits. I won't bail them out again."

"What about this case? Do you see them doing time?"

'Rell sighed. The thought had crossed his mind.

"I don't want that to become a reality, but it is what it is."

"You sound like your Aunt."

"So what about Monique."

Mitch told 'Rell about the conversation Monique had with Marci. He shared what Marci thought and waited for 'Rell to respond.

"When did she abort or have this baby? I'm trying to think of a timeline. I mean, man this can't be possible or could it be?"

"Could Shai and Monique have been pregnant at the same time?"

"Mitch, when I packed to come here….okay we had one night together but… Nah man it ain't possible."

"Okay, so no need to mention it to Shai right?"

"Wrong! Are you crazy? Monique will ride this thing like its fact, the truth. While we're explaining it, we'll have to find out the truth. If there is, or was a baby, it's got to be Craig's."

"So that means Craig doesn't know?"

"Maybe not. Man, you just added to this pain in my head."

"You're a Mince. You can handle it."

"Y'all seem to think this shit is easy. Damn. I wonder what Nana cooked."

"See your mind has settled it already."

"I wish."

Twenty-Four

It was close to six-thirty when Robert noticed Tonya's entrance. She seemed different, refreshed since he had seen her. As he sat waiting he wasn't sure what to expect. The gossip that spread throughout D.Q. Enterprises was she had let herself go since her ex-husband's death. Robert would never admit it but he hadn't noticed the difference until she stepped into the light as she approached him. She was a beauty and she knew it. Tonya smiled at a few of the men that spoke as she passed the bar.

Massie's was a popular café for the after five business crowd. There were meetings held there over lunch and dinner. Tonya had been there on occasion when she and D.Q. were married. The décor hadn't changed much but the clientele seemed to be a bit younger then she remembered. She hadn't given sitting for the first jazz set a thought, but as she approached Robert she hoped he would ask her to stay.

He wasn't like D.Q. or Karlton in any way but he aroused her curiosity. Tonya always wondered what his love life was about. He never brought a friend with him to any of the company outings. He left early and arrived just in time for the toast of the evening. Robert was a well-built man, and in good shape for his age. He was a tennis buff and invited Tonya a few times to the courts. She promised herself after D.Q. died she may have to take him up on his offers. Karlton turned her around after D.Q.'s will sent her into a catatonic state of mind.

"I am so sorry. Traffic was terrible and I couldn't find parking once I got here. They really should have a larger parking area for this part of town."

Robert stood and smiled, waiting for her to take her seat. He waved to the waitress the moment she adjusted herself.

"Order what you'd like, please."

Tonya thought about the rest of the evening. Karlton would be out until late. She wasn't sure why or with whom. Lately, she just needed to get out of the house. Tonight she didn't care to be smothered by him or Dershai.

"Gin and tonic please, uh on the rocks. Oh, and please don't use the cheap gin."

"Hennessy on the rocks, please. Do you want an appetizer or anything to eat?" Robert wasn't sure how to treat their impromptu meeting.

"No, just the drink is fine. Thank you."

"So Ms. Mince, how are you? How have you been?"

"A lot better, thank you. I guess there's been talk."

"I don't listen to office gossip. I asked your daughter whenever she came to the office. I've been praying for you."

"Well thank you, sir. I really needed it. How have you been? How's the new CEO treating you?"

"He's easy to work with. His mannerism and a lot of what he does reminds me of D.Q. I have to admit Tonya, I've known 'Rell for years. D.Q. brought him to the office when he was young. So working with him or should I say for him is easy."

"Really, I would think you and Alan would resent him being able to just come in and take over. I mean you were there at the start grinding side by side with D.Q. only to have someone with no experience come in and tell you what to do. Seems insulting to me."

"Not at all. 'Rell's not that type of man. D.Q. groomed him for the spot and he knows more than any of us thought he knew about the business."

Robert paused as the waitress put their glasses on the table.

"You mentioned you needed to talk. I hope it's not about 'Rell. I thought maybe, this time, it would be a little different."

"There are still a few loose ends. The stocks, I didn't realize I left the papers home. I thought they were in the car," she lied, "You did bring me an update, right?"

"I thought my luck had changed."

"It may have. I mean I'm no longer that married woman."

"Then there's Karlton Harris. Has he gone back to…where was he hiding all these years?"

"Does that really matter? He's still here, but I'm here. So tell me what is the problem with this stock? I think my money has to be a part of D.Q. Enterprises, no?"

Robert shook his head slowly. It wasn't a response to Tonya's question. It was his recognition that she thought being with him would be payment for the information he'd never give her.

"Unfortunately, it's not. Did Mr. Monroe explain it to you? D.Q. set you up with a company that is doing very well with their stock values. I don't think, over the years that we dealt with them directly, that they've had a bad year. So you've gained quite a bit of cushion money. You can re-invest, withdraw or buy more stock with them or any other company."

"Not true Robert. I can't buy into D.Q. Enterprises."

"No, you can't. Also, you can't buy into Quintech Designs or any other company D.Q. Enterprises put under the umbrella."

"How can that be? D.Q. didn't live to see Derek's company."

"Rell did. He put it in the contract for Quintech Designs. They can't sell or share profits or stocks with you or any other family members."

"Why would he do that?"

"Tonya, c'mon you know why. 'Rell doesn't want the same trouble for Derek as his father had with you. Derek can set up a trust for anyone with another company but not his. Money can grow without being attached to D.Q. Enterprises. Check out this report and you'll see."

"Robert I think 'Rell has taken this thing too far. He can't control both companies."

"It was a stipulation that Derek and Darryl agreed to. Quintech Designs is a subsidiary company and his rules are the rules."

"So you all fall in like soldiers and march to his beat."

"It works Tonya. For all of us, it works."

Twenty-Five

Monique put her phone down again. She checked the messages minutes prior, as she tried to pretend she wasn't aggravated. She thought about the time and sighed. Being bored another weekend wasn't her plan nor was waiting for Craig's call. It wasn't easy dating him since he refused to move to Virginia. His excuse was always the same, his job.

Monique didn't understand his devotion to 'Rell and the others. It certainly ranked higher than his love for her. Telling him she had planned on sinking 'Rell's ego didn't sit well with him and she wanted to explain. She had to admit that telling him her plan wasn't smart, even though she hadn't given him the details. His attitude seemed to change quickly. Craig was an outcast as far as she was concerned. 'Rell, Mitch, and Byron held prestigious titles at D.Q. Enterprises and Craig wasn't included although they all were still friends. Craig accepted 'Rell's reasons for not hiring him. He and Keith Larson were the only two who hadn't been a part of the transition from Maryland to Virginia.

Monique toyed between 'Rell and Craig for almost two years before 'Rell decided to move back to Virginia after his father's death. Once he told her their relationship was fading, she gave Craig her time and her undivided attention. Craig knew he broke the silent code between friends but he took his chances.

Over the five years, they had three years she would admit that were exclusive to them. She loved the differences between Craig and 'Rell. Craig hadn't hardened to her ways and had no family that would dabble in his affairs. 'Rell was protective and now that he had inherited his father's business she understood why. His worth was more than Craig could ever handle. Monique's plan, if she played it right, would get him a seat in the conference room.

Craig promised he would be arriving about six and they could talk about her scheme that would guarantee him being hired and 'Rell begging forgiveness. She kicked off her shoes again and grabbed the remote just as she heard Craig's voice on the other side of her front door. He turned the key and entered continuing his conversation on the phone.

"You want to do what? ... Man, listen, I'm in town for the week so let me know what you guys want to do…. Yeah, I spoke with Keith…. Yeah, yeah, he said he'd get here in the morning. I think he's flying in though. That brother stays in the air."

He paused long enough to lean over the couch and kiss Monique on the forehead.

"No man, I think its family stuff… You know how Keith is, the man with a million secrets… Byron, man look, I'm here now so hit me up with when and where… No, I didn't speak with 'Rell but Mitch said he'd let him know… I thought about what he said, you know, about the court thing… Yeah, I think we should too… No, I just took two weeks. I'm here for the week and if necessary I'm free the next week too. Man, I haven't had a break for a minute…Listen, my money ain't as long as yours."

Monique looked at him sitting in the wing chair across the room. Her look let him know she was upset with his late arrival and the conversation. She put on her shoes and went to get her purse that was on the kitchen counter.

"Man, let me go before I have to come and stay with you… Yeah, you know it. I'll give you a call tomorrow so we can hook up with Keith… Alright cool, so 'Rell doesn't know we're coming, got you. Later man."

"Craig, I see your phone is working. You couldn't call and say you would be late. It's after six."

"Six forty-five. The traffic was tight. Look I'm sorry. Aren't you glad to see me? I mean it's been a minute."

Monique purposely sashayed to meet him in the middle of the living room floor.

"I missed you but I don't think you missed me." She whispered as their bodies met.

"Baby, I wouldn't be here if I didn't miss you. You, your pretty smile, beautiful eyes, soft lips…"

Craig leaned in and kissed her gently. The kiss was more of what Monique expected. She pushed him back teasingly.

"Okay, okay. Well, I need to eat first and then we need to talk about how you're going to get your spot at D.Q. Enterprises."

"Baby, we can talk about all that later. Let's go get something to eat and come back and enjoy each other. That job ain't guaranteed this week anyway."

"Why would you say that?"

"The court case starts Monday. 'Rell will be too involved with that to talk to him about a position. It can wait a minute. I mean, I don't think it's the right time to stir up any misplaced feelings."

'Rell is at his weakest when chaos surrounds him."

Craig frowned. Monique tooted her lips and rolled her eyes.

"Just wait until we talk. I think him knowing some details about our relationship will have him right where we want him. I just want to make sure you're alright with how I deliver the truth to him. Believe me, sweetie, he won't see it coming."

Twenty-Six

The dinner at Nana's would be one they all would remember. Nana couldn't believe that when dinner was served everyone was seated at the same time. Darryl was there early a big surprise for everyone. Simone sat with Nikki after dinner hoping no one else could tell she was nervous. Leeza joined them in the den until Nana came and told them all to return to the dining room.

It became obvious to all that Darryl and Derek were not on speaking. They also had no response to most of the conversations around the dinner table. Nana made sure those who needed to be informed were invited. So the table included Simone, Leeza, Sam, and Reverend Wilcox along with the rest of the family. They were told there was no need to bring anything other than an open mind. Now seated at the table they all were a bit nervous.

"I'll start Mama Mince." Nikki stood at the head of the table. After holding on to a few things she wanted to finally talk to the family without her thoughts turning into anger.

"Okay, Nana and I talked about a few things. The court case and Tonya; Shai and Derek's mother." She looked in Shai and Derek's direction. There seemed to be no objection so Nikki continued.

"I must admit, I knew the court case would be our new gossip. You know people assuming what the case was about; our fear for Darryl and

Derek; and simply put what were they up against. For some of us, we also are faced with the repercussions of it all. I'll be the first to say that looking from my place within the family, I may not be affected as much as others. But I've lived long enough to know if we don't come together and agree on how to handle the scandals that may arise, we will fall. So I think we need to know what we face with this case and then we'll discuss the other issue."

Silence fell in the room. Darryl stood and Nikki returned to her seat giving him the head of the table.

"We don't really know what they will say. According to Mr. Simpson, they're looking for money. Money that Derek made from the trademarks he sold. They think he took the money and somehow it was deposited and used to start our company Quintech. We were told that after reviewing the paperwork, you know what they submitted as discovery, it may not be the same people who attempted to kill Derek. We may still have to deal with them."

"So what plans do you have to do that Darryl? You and Derek have had time to pay anybody you owe off. Y'all got caught up again with that gambling mess D.Q. told you to stay out of. This boy almost lost his life, had to travel and live clean cross the world and he still ain't able to rest here at home? What are the plans?"

Derek cut his eye at Darryl and then to Rell. Darryl didn't want to be put on the spot but Nana was waiting for an answer.

"We've been dealing with the matter at hand Mama. I didn't talk to Mr. Simpson about anything else. Maybe Derek did since they're after him."

"After me. Hold on! I was the target but we're both in over our heads with this. The court case, those that want to hurt me and maybe you, and Quintech." Derek's words faded into an inaudible mumble.

"What's wrong with Quintech or better yet what's wrong with the two of you?" Nana scolded. "Y'all can't get nothing done fighting and biting at each other. This is what I was talking about. That's why everyone that we care about not hurting is here at this table. Now y'all got to do better than this."

"What did Mr. Simpson tell you about Monday?" 'Rell questioned looking to his uncle for an answer.

Darryl sighed. Everyone had their eyes on him again.

"Listen this ain't for all of y'all to concern yourself with.

Me and Derek spoke with Mr. Simpson and its being handled. Now, 'Rell you made it known the last time we spoke that it was D.Q. Enterprises money that was tied up in all of this so if you want to know Simpson's plan to get us out of this, hey he's the company lawyer. You call him and ask."

Darryl ignored the stares and returned to his seat.

'Rell stood up to speak. Pausing to control his aggravation and walked slowly to the head of the table.

"My father, your brother, your son didn't start this business to lose it to some habit that either will break you or get you killed. Whoever it is that deliberately ran Derek off the road wants something and the two of you know what it is. I'm tired of trying to ask you the dollar amount or what it could be. So as I said, Quintech Designs can't afford the cost of a good lawyer and Mr. Simpson knows your books and any connections it may have to D.Q. Enterprises. My only interest is the safety of the family and that company. Now if you want to lose your company to a bunch of thugs or a "fly by night" company, like Carson's Web, hey, dissolve it and be done. But I know you Uncle Darryl, and the two of you have been stringing along with this debt for far too long. Long enough to anger someone into trying to kill Derek. What is it? Now that you know he's not a Mince you don't give a…."

Nikki slammed her hand on the table distracting everyone's attention.

"Rell!! Your mouth!!" Nikki shouted.

"I'm sorry, but hear me. If they attacked Derek they'll come for you or anyone else at this table. We're a family man, and that comes first. The only reason I was willing to give you and Derek the money to start the company was for that debt to be cleared, the court case to be settled and you both to have a foundation of your own. I don't want your company or the responsibility of running it. Ruin it like you did your construction company or leave it to Derek and move on. You won't even talk to him to get things straight. What the hell is wrong with you?"

"Alright, now listen all of you." Reverend Wallace spoke and his voice seemed to bring new attention to the tension filled room.

"There's no such thing as go to Mr. Simpson and find out. If there's something that can be done by the family, handle it here. If Mr. Simpson has a course of action then we as a family should allow him to handle it. Now, Derek, you and your uncle got some talking to do. Don't expect me or your grandmother to be idle while there is still a chance of you being hurt. We can't help much but we can't go through that type of pain again. You and Darrell know how deep you're in and what you owe. Right now you owe it to those who could be innocently hurt to pay that money and stop thinking you can gamble and win the pay-off amount."

Derek and Darryl's eyes met and they both exhaled.

"Is that what you've been doing?" Simone broke the silence at the table. "Darryl is this true?"

"Simone, this don't concern you. Just like it don't concern most of y'all sitting at this table. Mama, what was this to put me on the spot?"

"Darryl we all have something to lose if someone is planning danger to any of us. If we need to get you out of this we don't need any more secrets. Put it out there son. How much is this debt?"

"Close to one hundred thousand. They want interest too. Uncle Darryl was trying to pay it off but they want higher payments. The payments are monthly. I was doing the trademarks to get the money. I got paid and gave it to him but I guess he lost it at the tables. I had been doing the trademarks for more than six months. The ones they caught weren't the only ones. The money never went on the books at Carson's Web and the companies called to complain that they saw their logos and trademark designs elsewhere. I did it. I thought they'd never see them. I didn't think of international trades I just, well it doesn't matter. The money is gone. I don't know how much has been paid. Uncle Darryl was handling payments."

Another wave of silence fell over the table. Simone got up and went into the den. Darryl got up to follow her.

"No sir, no you won't. Stay right here so we can get a grasp on this. She'll be alright. Francine learned to deal with your lies, so will Simone. If she's foolish enough to love you then you can deal with her later. Right now, I need to clear up this mess so I can put it in prayer and sleep through these next few nights."

Darryl didn't have a response. His mother was right. He had lied and used Simone for her money as well. There wasn't much he could say that wouldn't wait until later.

Twenty-Seven

Simone could barely hear the conversation sitting in the sitting room. She sat back on the loveseat and closed her eyes. She couldn't believe Darryl would gamble away the money she had saved. He lied when she noticed the envelope she kept with her jewelry was empty. He told her there had been an emergency at one of the sites they were working on. The contractors would only take cash. He assured her the money would be replaced through Quintech once they were paid for the job. She hadn't given it a second thought. It had only been two months ago. Simone understood some accounts didn't make payments for ninety days.

Tears fell slowly as she realized Nikki's warnings weren't an attempt to keep her from the love she sought. Now she felt foolish in front of everyone. She opened her eyes and allowed herself to find comfort and peace in the smallest room in the house.

Nana's library sat across from where she sat. Simone stood and walked over to the curio which held various titles. Nana's collection was complete with novels, self-help guides, cookbooks, and the Bible. Simone smiled looking over familiar titles that she wouldn't expect the elder to read. She continued to look around the room. It was peaceful. The soft pastel colored walls and the knick-knacks that brought personal memories of her childhood caught her attention.

She walked over to a smaller curio which held memorabilia from other states and cities. Simone thought of Nikki's mother who collected shot glasses, spoons, and magnets of the places they traveled. It was Leeza's voice that broke through her memories.

"Those are really nice," Leeza spoke softly as she approached Simone.

"Yes. Are they finished talking?"

"No. They're still at it. I decided to come and sit with you. There's nothing I can do to help. It seems the past has caught up with them and they'll have to deal with it."

"Karma is a bitch. Oh, I'm sorry."

Leeza smiled and they both laughed.

"You've heard that before right?" Simone questioned her and laughed again.

"Yes, karma is everywhere. You do know though that Darryl and Derek are good men right?"

Simone stopped laughing and looked at the young woman seriously.

"Leeza? Did I say your name right?"

Leeza nodded.

"The one thing I do know is that they are good men. It's just, well that's why I'm sitting here. Gathering my thoughts, you know. Conversations we've had over the last few months that finally make sense. I had no idea they were thinking gambling with their lives was an answer."

"I thought it was about your money."

"No baby, money comes and goes. Now don't get me wrong. I'm gonna deal with Darryl about the money, but taking a chance that could hurt or kill someone. That's crazy."

"Karma and gambling. At least you had conversations. Derek won't talk. Between the issues at hand and his mother, I'm lost totally."

"Baby, I can't help you with his mother. She's Karma's best friend. I can tell you this though. After tonight, we should both be able to sleep better. Nana will make it all clear."

Darryl interrupted Leeza's response.

"C'mon babe. Let's go. I'm done here. They talking about other things that ain't got nothing to do with us. I ain't feeling welcomed so let's go!"

"Darryl I'll be there in a minute, I'm talking now."

"Meet me at the car."

Darryl left the women staring where he once stood.

"He's upset? I don't understand why?"

"Leeza he got caught. I'm learning more and more each day. It's about patience, understanding, and something that somehow equals the love you accept. Sometimes it don't all add up but it's still love. Listen you've got our number call me before the weekend is over. I'd love for us to talk longer or get together. I think we'll need each other to get through this."

Twenty-Eight

The decision to call Mr. Simpson was brought up by 'Rell. He assured the family that if there was any danger, he would alert them. Darryl didn't agree with his input or suggestion. Nana thanked 'Rell, and Darryl stood to leave. When no one objected to his departure, he stormed out. Once everyone said their good-byes to Simone, the conversation continued.

"How am I supposed to be in business with him? He wants me to go to jail or better yet, be the sacrificial lamb. I tried to tell him just pay Carson's Web what they want and the money we owe to the partners in the casino group."

"Casino group?" 'Rell hoped he misunderstood what Derek was implying. "The guys you owe work for a casino?"

"No, no man. We only know them from a few of the casinos. They have backroom gambling that goes on. Higher stakes, no overhead for them, it's probably all illegal."

"You think?!" Darlene snapped. "You and your uncle. Derek, what were the two of you thinking?"

"Does it matter now Aunt Darlene? I mean, yes I've learned a lesson. Uncle Darryl thought it was a fast way to make money. We were even until this trademark thing came up. He wanted to help me without anyone else in the family knowing what I had done. I thanked him. When we started to lose, well, all hell broke loose. It started with little threats and I guess whatever he told them, pissed them off enough to run me off the road. Listen I know y'all want to hold it over his head, but I'm just as guilty as he is. I just don't know where that leaves us after all this is said and done."

"Let Mr. Simpson do his job. That's all we can do. Thank you for letting us know what we're looking at. Did he say he could talk them out of pushing the issue further?"

"Seems like it, but I don't know. Then Uncle Darryl is trying to tie both cases together like Carson's Web is a part of the gambling debt. I told him Mr. Simpson won't be a part of any arrangements for that. Since I didn't agree with him, he's pissed. Excuse me, Nana."

"Darryl needs to wait for the lawyer to ask him to speak. He's always trying to get the best for himself. 'Rell, can you talk to Simpson as you said?"

"I will Nana. That's not a problem. Now, what about Tonya."

Nana told the group about the phone call. Mitch added the information he received from Alan earlier while at the office. Shai shook her head in disbelief. Derek remained silent.

"There's nothing really any of us can do. If we say something she'll only change her method. D.Q. Enterprises is her target and she won't give up about it." 'Rell's head began to hurt again. "Let's just let her play her game."

"But 'Rell, when is enough, enough?" Nikki looked at her son for the answer.

"I don't know. I don't know what she'll be satisfied with having. Dad did more than enough for her to live happily ever after. She doesn't have to worry about her home, her property, and she has stock that has a lucrative standing."

"Sounds like she wants to stir the pot. She's hoping something will come up. When she asked for papers, I just hung up the phone. What papers could she be looking for?"

"Nana, she has all the papers regarding anything her name is on. All of the other documents belong to the company. She's looking for a way in." 'Rell stepped away from the table. Shai followed him.

"Derek has your mother called you?" Nana continued with the conversation at hand.

"I don't talk to her. When she calls, she speaks with Leeza. She won't ask her anything. So I have no clue what she wants or what papers she's looking for. All my papers are with Shai."

"What papers are with Shai?" Darlene was curious.

"My personal papers and the papers between D.Q. Enterprises and Quintech Designs. Shai has all of them. My life insurance papers too. We, well Leeza, made sure Shai had a copy of all my documents before we left for Brazil."

"I see. So the only documents she really wants is 'Rell's. I think you're right Mama, she wants to know more about 'Rell. She was digging. Why didn't she call her own children for their documents? She wants the paperwork that 'Rell looked over when D.Q. died. Maybe she thinks something else was stated in those documents."

"Like what Darlene?" Nikki questioned.

"I don't know Nikki. It all seems strange to me. She waited all this time to dig?"

"Aunt Darlene she didn't wait. We're doing just what she wants. Including her in our thoughts, our conversation, she's a thrill seeker. I'm done with her antics. That's why Shai has my documents. I don't want her to have any part of what I own. She lost D.Q. Enterprises and she lost me. She'll lose it all and try to kill herself again."

"Now Derek, she is your mother. Don't talk like that. We're here as a family to try to resolve issues not cause more. So now we're aware of what was said and what she may be looking for. Can we agree to be careful what we give her in conversation? It's simple, we know how Tonya is." Nana began waving her hand in the air. "Anyone want dessert?"

Reverend Wilcox excused himself to answer his phone. Everyone else took interest in the dessert options that sat on the kitchen island. Nikki found 'Rell and Shai sitting in the living room.

"You guys okay?"

"Uh, yeah we're good. Another issue to work out but we're okay."

"Rell, you don't look okay, are you sure?"

"I will be Ma. I will be. Is everyone still in the dining room?" 'Rell wanted to tell Shai about Monique's scheme. He couldn't find the words.

"No the kitchen. Attacking Nana's pies and cake." Shai smiled and left them to talk.

"I have a headache. So I stepped away for a minute, but I think there's another issue.

"What? Did you want to talk about it privately?"

"I just found out. Marci and Monique talked. What was said, I'm sure, has not been said to Shai. I don't want her to feel some kind of way if it's aired to everyone."

"Monique? What did she say to Marci?"

"See Ma, there you go. I just said I don't know if Marci and Shai talked about it."

"Well that's easy, ask Marci."

"It ain't that easy."

'Rell told Nikki what Mitch told him could be a problem. Nikki rolled her eyes without saying a word.

"What? I don't know what this girl wants. I'm sure I'm not or was not the father but how do I explain this to Shai. She'll be like most women would be."

"And how is that?!" Nikki tried not to show her immediate anger. "This ain't about whether you did or didn't. It's about her trying you again. Why? What does she expect you to do even if it was true?"

"I don't know. But Shai should know from Marci first, I think right?"

"Yes, that's best. Why don't the four of you have this conversation before you include us? C'mon before they suspect there is something else to discuss. Nana has to have something for that head of yours."

Twenty-Nine

Time slipped by as Tonya and Robert ate and had a few drinks. The band was returning for the second set when she realized it was after ten. Robert had been the perfect gentleman, the company that she needed for the evening. It was the first time in months that she wasn't asked every hour or so, how she was feeling. She didn't drink heavily since she was driving and knew Karlton would be checking her behavior when she entered her home.

Robert gave her the papers he prepared for her. His promise was to keep in touch. Tonya expected him to ask to see her again. When he didn't, she had to admit she wished he had. They laughed about old times and situations where they both thought D.Q. noticed their flirtatious actions.

Tonya pulled into the garage and entered her home through the laundry room door, an entrance she rarely used. The first floor was dark with only the lights from the front porch peeking through the curtained windows. She checked the hall table for Karlton's keys. He was home.

Not knowing when he arrived she went to the kitchen to see if he had cooked dinner or ate. Seeing no evidence of either, Tonya headed for the bedroom. As she climbed the stairs she heard Karlton talking on the phone.

It wasn't an unusual conversation. It was normal for him to take calls or make calls late in the evening. Tonya went into the guest room to change her clothes not giving a thought to what Karlton would think. She returned to her bedroom after a comforting shower.

Karlton heard the shower running and immediately ended the call. "Hey man, I gotta go. Yeah, I'll see you on Monday."

Tonya entered the bedroom. The fragrance that introduced her caught Karlton's senses.

"Hmmm, something else new?"

"What do you mean?"

"Tonya, are you trying to drive me away? You don't have to go through a performance or stunts. Just tell me. You're still in love with a dead man or someone else. I'll go."

"Karlton, what are you talking about?"

"You leave after I leave at night and return to the shower. Perfumed down to cover what, his scent? I ain't no boy. What's going on? I don't intend on asking you this every time you leave this house."

"Then don't ask Karlton. I told you. It's the same business that was going on when you got here. D.Q. owed me more and I intend on getting it!"

"And just what are you giving up to get it?"

"What the hell does that mean?"

"No one in D.Q. Enterprises is going to give you any information without you giving them something in return. Who is he?"

"So you think I'll have to sleep with a man to get information that I should already have?"

"Well let me ask you this. Did you get what you wanted tonight? Did anyone give you a way in? Did someone say D.Q. left this loose end so you'd get what you think you deserve?"

"Karlton, well no. It's the same information. Just paperwork that explains the stocks and the payments. Nothing else."

"And what did you do to get that information?"

"Nothing, we ate and had drinks. Talked and listened to music."

"At his home? Who is it?"

"Robert Franklin. One of the partners."

"So what does he want now? When is the next meeting? Tonya this doesn't make sense."

"It doesn't have to make sense to you. You weren't married to D.Q., I was."

"And you are not married to D.Q. You're not living with anyone from D.Q. Enterprises and I won't stay around while you traipse around with anyone who works there. Do you really think flirting and blinking in his face will get you better stock? Are you looking to work there? Do you want a monthly stipend? What is it, Tonya?"

Tonya could feel her anger rising. Karlton didn't understand. D.Q. couldn't win and she wouldn't let him. She'd avenge his antics and anyone who stood in her way would reap her wrath.

"I owe this to me, Karlton. I helped build that Enterprise and I won't let it go. My children deserve to benefit from it. They shouldn't be waiting for a handout from that bastard son of his."

"Are you listening to yourself? Dershai and Derek belong to us! Not you and D.Q.! You and me! They got what they have because the man raised and loved two children that weren't his. Children you threw at him trying to keep him from loving Nikki! Face the reality, Tonya. D.Q. stopped loving you, when you started loving me! Can't you see that? You lost what you had when you and I got caught. It's the price you paid for our love."

"Keep that shit to yourself, that's your reality. 'Rell is older than Shai and Derek so who stopped loving who. He cheated on me and I caught him. You were my selection that set off my revenge. She had one child, I had two. Two he raised and took care of, but he owes me more. I sat and helped him build that company from paperwork thoughts to ledger realities. I want what's mine Karlton and you won't stop me."

"Well, Ms. Mince, I do know this. You'll have to come to Baltimore to get me the next time you want to take your life. I'm not going to stand by and watch you destroy yourself over what you can't have again. You can have all the play dates you want, but I'm not the man you need to stand by and watch. There's nothing in it for me if I can't have a loving relationship with you. The man is dead and you can't admit that you still love him."

"Think what you want. Do what you want. I'm going to do what I promised that ass I would do. I can't stand by and watch that boy be what Derek should have been."

"Tonya, Derek has what's his. Shai has what's hers and 'Rell has what's his. D.Q. left them secured. What will secure you? What do you want? What will you do when you find out you're defeated?"

"I'm doing what I think is right Karlton. It belongs to me, I know it!"

"You're delusional. I'm convinced. I'm leaving Monday morning and you can contact me on my phone if you get yourself together. Sleep well."

Tonya watched Karlton leave the room. For the first time since D.Q.'s death she realized, though she was scared to admit it, she was still in love with D.Q. Mince.

Thirty

Monique sat on the edge of her bed listening to Craig ranting about her plan. Once again his alliance to his friends was standing in the way of his understanding her motive.

"I want this for you Craig, for us. If you just let your childhood love for 'Rell go, you'd see this is a win-win."

"Win-win? What the hell is wrong with you? Don't you think this will cause him to question my friendship with him again? C'mon Monique. You never said you were pregnant. But I hooked up with you knowing you were carrying 'Rell's child? Are you fucking kidding me? No, you told me you weren't pregnant remember? Now you've had a miscarriage and doctor's reports to prove it? Whose kid was it, Monique?!"

"What difference does it make? I had a miscarriage! That's all anyone needs to know. The less you know the better. I don't want you gossiping like a bitch to Byron and Keith. If this is going to work it has to come from me. I told Marci and she'll plant the seed of doubt for 'Rell to contact me about it. When he does, I'll tell him that you stepped in like he did with Shai."

"Are you out of your mind? Shai was carrying their twins. How is your pregnancy like hers?"

"If you just listen. You stepped in prepared to pick up his responsibility. You doing that for him would leave him owing you. What better way to repay you and me for my lost than giving you a position at D.Q. Enterprises. We can conquer more of what he has once you're in place."

"Monique, 'Rell ain't no dummy and neither am I. I don't know what all of this is about. Is that why you threw yourself on me? To make 'Rell jealous? I lost a friendship over you, what else do you want me to lose?"

"Craig, for real? You lost your friendship when you tried to gain more crumbs from that last job you had. 'Rell had you and the rest of the assholes eating out of his hand and when you tried to eat somewhere else, he snatched it from you. What the hell is wrong with all of you dumb asses? 'Rell has some power over all of you, his family and anyone else in his reach. Well, I have what I need to take his ass down. If you follow my lead you'll be sitting pretty with him kneeling at your feet."

"Whose baby was it, if there was a baby? Let me see the papers. Monique, I hope to God you didn't do something stupid to prove a point."

"Stupid like what?"

"Falsifying documents for one. Lying would be second on the list and thinking I'm a dumb ass, as you put it, third. What damn proof are you going to show him?"

Monique got up and went to the dresser. She had forms she filled in that were marked for a pregnancy. The doctor's visits that followed and the hospital she went to for weeks were stamped with a doctor's signature. It hadn't been hard to get the appointment pad and duplicate it.

"When was this Monique? I teased you for weeks about your little pouch you had. Were you pregnant then?"

"No. It doesn't matter when. What matters is the child is gone and 'Rell needs to know what he lost. He needs to understand you were there after the miscarriage to console me. Something he should have been there to do. Once he knows that's why we were together, he'll have to repay you in some way. He'll feel guilty."

"Now how the fuck am I supposed to feel. You telling me this shit. Did we get together just to disrupt 'Rell's life? Do you give a shit about how I feel? This ain't right on all levels. I can't believe you want me to be involved in this shit."

"You're already involved baby, always have been."

"What?"

"You didn't think that I'd be with you and not try to make 'Rell jealous did you?"

Craig gave her questions some thought. It was the first time he thought about hitting a woman. He walked out of the bedroom and went to the door. He had nowhere else to go. He needed a drink. Monique didn't have anything strong enough to cloud his thoughts or calm his anger. He grabbed his jacket and decided to leave.

Sitting in his car he dialed 'Rell's number and hung up. He thought about calling Mitch but changed his mind again. Monique was wrong. Her plan was a win, win for her. She'd get 'Rell to do whatever she wanted. Craig was sure a part of her plan was to hold the pregnancy and miscarriage over his head. She'd threaten to tell Shai. 'Rell would give in until he found out she was lying. That was the question; was she lying? Craig needed to know before he told anyone.

He drove to the liquor store a few blocks away. He wandered through the store aimlessly. Surrounded by the different brands of alcohol and beer, he realized he needed to be sober. Monique had confused him enough for the night. He'd go back to her home and tell her it was a stupid idea.

Monique called Craig's name again. He answered slamming the front door. She shook her head, disgusted that he didn't see that the plan would benefit him more than her. After all, she would risk their relationship. 'Rell would want her to explain what happened and understand her grief as well as her actions. He'd question his marriage to Shai and regret rushing into the marriage. Craig needed only to play his part a little longer.

It was more than an hour before he returned. Monique was positioned where she was earlier, curled up on the couch with a pillow and blanket. The illumination from the television was the only light in the room. Craig leaned over the couch and kissed her on her forehead.

"Monique, we can't do it."

She smiled. He knew the look. It was one he fell for each time he was leaving to return to Maryland. He sat on the couch as Monique pulled the blanket below her bare breasts. Her hardened nipples welcomed the warmth of his breath and the softness of his kiss. They found each other's weakness as Monique repositioned herself on top of the blanket. Craig unbuckled his pants and slowly removed them and his boxers.

Their lovemaking wasn't what either would call the most exciting. There was no prolonged foreplay or teasing moments to be remembered. It had always been rushed. The flirting always led to dared satisfaction.

Craig would try to last until she was satisfied but somehow Monique's body would cause him to release too soon. They would go through three condoms before either was really pleased. The thought of having a condom crossed Craig's mind but he dared not lose the passion that he felt wouldn't last if he stopped to reach for his wallet.

Monique stroked his masculinity with the thought of how pleased she was whenever 'Rell would surprise her with his weekend visits. He'd wake her as she laid on the couch waiting for him to come to town. His gentle kisses would lead him to her navel and below. Gently he would touch her breast, stimulating her as he inserted himself slowly. The ride would be long and smooth as they rocked together. His pace would be steady until she was begging for more.

"Aww….. 'Rell go deeper," she moaned.

Craig paused. Ignoring his immediate thoughts he pumped harder. He was preparing to pull out but her sensual moan changed his mind. *"Rell, you want Rell…… yeah, yeah take it all."* His thoughts changed his reasons. He hoped she noticed the difference in his strokes. As he pumped harder Monique was reaching a peak he had never felt with her.

"Aww….aww…aww….damn," she whispered a little louder.

"Oh shit!" They let out a yell together. The satisfaction was obvious. They separated and Monique realized she was wet with his pleasure.

"Craig! Are you, did you? No! Bareback? Are you fucking kidding me?"

Monique jumped up. She looked at Craig who hadn't tried to defend himself or his actions. He held himself as he picked up his boxers. Pleased he smiled as she wrapped herself frantically with the blanket.

"This can't be happening. Craig what the hell!"

"Did you ever give a shit about me Monique?"

"What? Really. Is that all you have to say?"

"I want to see the proof of a baby before we do this. No baby, no deal. Maybe we'll be lucky and have two."

Thirty-One

Shai, Leeza and Marci had plans to spend the day shopping. Their plans included meeting Mia and together the ladies would spend the time pampering the mother to be. They were sure her due date was rapidly approaching. Mitch and 'Rell had plans to meet Keith, Craig, and Byron although 'Rell had no idea Craig was in town.

Breakfast was a surprise prepared by Leeza. She promised the meal would be a mixture of the American and Brazilian favorites. Fresh fruit, cheese, Brazilian sausage, and cake were the favorites from her home, but as she brought out the platter of scrambled eggs everyone laughed.

"What is the laughter about?" Leeza asked as she put the large platter on the dining room table. "These eggs are the only American food I truly love. I made them with my own touch of seasoning. Also, I've added spinach, onions, and tomatoes. You'll be surprised by the taste. Maybe the eggs aren't made so American after all." She laughed with her attentive audience. "Come and eat please."

"Your accent makes it good enough for me. I'm convinced." Shai waited for everyone to enter the dining room as she stood beside Leeza. She looked over the spread Leeza prepared and set up on the dining room table. "I really think you outdid yourself girl. How bad is the kitchen?"

Shai turned to look at her kitchen, teasing Leeza.

Derek laughed, "Shai, it's probably already cleaned. She's a freak for cleaning and cooking. You guys are in for a treat."

The group sat, blessed the food, and teased Marci about how much food she put on two plates.

"C'mon this is family, you know I'm eating for two."

Mitch shook his head as he helped her with her plates as she adjusted her seat. The group talked about cultures. The differences in food and what they once thought was strictly Brazilian traditions

"There are many people from different cultures that live in Brazil. We have the influence of the older Portuguese colonizers, Black Africans, Europeans, Arabs, and there's even Japanese immigration. Our traditions vary depending on the family background. Our culture like the American culture has grown to be that of many. I love cooking and Derek has not lost his appetite when trying our truly traditional meals. It is really a beautiful country. I'm glad Derek suggested we continue to live there. I would hope you all will visit us one day."

Everyone agreed they would love to visit but there was a noticeable silence between each response. Derek broke the ice.

"We're going back, people. I'll be working Quintech from Brazil. That's possible, ain't it big brother?"

He looked to 'Rell for help in explaining all would not be lost.

"Yeah, wherever Derek, you have enough staff to run it no matter where you live. Once you guys get this mess out of the way, it's all yours."

"What do you think our mother really wants?"

"Derek, don't worry about your mother. We're prepared for her and whatever she digs up. You and Uncle Darryl need to be on the alert too. She'll come at you eventually."

"Rell, really?" Shai was shocked by his comment. "You guys really think she's after the business? Maybe she's....well, you know, maybe she's trying to figure out what your father, our father, D.Q. did to find out about us. I know it shocked us. Maybe she needs proof. You know, before she just drops this. I don't know. I'm hoping it's not about D.Q. Enterprises."

"Shai, she feels she should have stock, investments, or something that connects her to the business. Quintech Designs is connected. Listen, Robert and Alan are the only two that have talked to her about it. Alan was sure she was on the prowl about the business."

"Mitch, could it be that she's not sure about the stock she was left? I mean is that on the up and up or something D.Q. threw her way to shut her mouth?"

"Shai, your mother, excuse me for saying this, is not to be trusted. If she just wanted someone to explain the stock or explain the business, she has a lawyer. I'm sure Mr. Monroe explained what she was left in the will."

"Not only that Mitch, has she had copies of all that paperwork. She has our birth certificates. She asked Nana about the paperwork that 'Rell looked at. 'Rell went through boxes of paperwork. She's looking for something else."

"Derek, what do you think it is?"

"Shai, I don't know. I'll say this though. She wants revenge." Derek looked around the table. "It will be up to us to shut her down."

"Or find out what she really wants," Leeza responded and noticed the look she got from everyone. "What? I mean, if no one really knows what she wants how do you know what not to say to her?"

"That's easy. Don't talk business with her. Let her go to the main man here, 'Rell. Right Mitch, 'Rell?" Derek nodded his head waiting for everyone to agree with him.

"Okay, we can agree to that. I like that lil' brother. If she asks questions send her our way. Let us deal with the business. But who answers her questions about me?" Rell looked around the table. The same looks that were given to Leeza were now glaring at him.

"Let Nana and your mother answer those questions. None of you were born when your father found out about Derek and Shai so how can you answer what or how D.Q. found out. I don't think my mother or Uncle Darryl know either. But I'm sure Aunt Tonya will back down once she knows she has to deal with Nana or Nikki."

Marci's logic made sense. She looked at Mitch who winked and nodded his head giving her a sign that she should discuss the phone conversation she had with Monique.

"Hey fam, we have another problem. I should have mentioned it to you Shai but with all that was going on….."

"Ah hell, what else?" Shai put her head in her hands teasingly. "Leeza pass the juice, please. Do I need something in this juice before you tell us?"

"You might. It's about a conversation I had with Monique Davis."

Derek began to cough. "Are you kidding?" He asked.

"Nope. Not only is she crazy, she's serious."

Marci repeated the phone conversations and reminded Shai of the visit Monique made to her home prior to the call. Shai sat quietly without any response. She looked across the table at 'Rell. Before she could speak, he did.

"She hasn't called me. I haven't seen her since our wedding day. I talked to Craig maybe twice, but he never mentioned a baby or her pregnancy."

"What the hell?" Shai stood up and retreated to the kitchen.

Everyone began to clear the table. Marci and 'Rell followed Shai into the kitchen hoping to calm her.

"Baby you know better than this. She's trying us and our love."

"It's too much. Derek and Uncle Darryl involved in this court mess with the possibility of someone trying to kill them, my mother trying to take part in the business, and Monique being pregnant? What the hell does she want? If she had a miscarriage why tell us now?"

Marci sat across the kitchen table and reached for Shai's hand.

"Shai, I think it's a bluff. You're right, why would she wait what three or four years? She said the day you guys saw her at the doctor's office she was there to confirm she was pregnant."

Shai frowned, "The doctor's office? When was she at the doctor's office?"

"The same day we went to talk to the doctor about me possibly being your brother. Remember we went to tell the doctor that I was the father of our children."

"You never mentioned you saw her."

"No, because it didn't matter to me. She mentioned it later to me in one of her heated rants. By then I wasn't dealing with her at all."

"Did you deal with her while you were dealing with me?"

"When I was living in Maryland, once I moved here it was over. I hadn't slept with her either. She's trying us, babe, believe me. You know how I am about being a father. I wouldn't want to admit it was mine but if I thought it was possible….hell, I'd say so."

"I know it's too much Shai. I just wanted you guys to know what she's claiming and she thinks 'Rell owes her something for her losing the baby. Something about the stress of him leaving her and then marrying you. She even mentioned that your courtship was shorter than the time they were together. I guess that mattered to her in some way."

"She said something like that to me when I told her it was over. Hell, she had been flirting with Craig for two or three years. I didn't pay any attention to it. It probably was his baby. Listen, you ladies go shop and have a good day. We'll clean up the kitchen and any other mess we make. Shai forget Monique. I am totally devoted to you, my children, and our lives together."

Shai didn't respond. She couldn't explain the numb feeling that took over her. She knew there would be a fight. Her weapon was the love she had for her husband but Monique was willing to use an unborn child. *"What proof did she have? How many questions would go unanswered?"*

Marci and Leeza convinced Shai they would have a great day in spite of the Mince family drama. For the first time, Shai couldn't shake the thought of the drama they were facing.

Thirty-Two

Karlton was packing his garment bag when Tonya entered the room. There was no further talk of him leaving. Tonya thought he would give her another chance to explain her actions.

He had been up since daybreak. She waited until his movement became still to enter the guest room. Karlton's belongings filled the closet and the armoire in the room. Tonya's clothes seemed to fill every other closet in her home. She stood at the door hoping he would recognize her presence. His suitcases were scattered on the floor. He hadn't begun to pack them. The dresser drawers were open as was the closet.

Tonya didn't know what to say. Karlton's attitude seemed to have changed. He tried to convince her that she was making a mistake. Karlton would always try to change her way of doing things. She would listen to him for hours and he'd eventually give in and allow her to have her way. It was apparent, as she looked around the room, she would have her way this time but she wouldn't have him.

"I've made breakfast and that coffee you like. I picked it up last week. I saw you hadn't tried it yet. They say it's as good as that other flavor you like at Starbucks. I didn't want your food to get cold. I thought after hearing you were up and moving around, you'd be downstairs shortly."

Karlton didn't respond. He went to the closet and retrieved two suits. Placing them in the garment bag he paused and glanced at Tonya. After securing them in the bag he returned to the closet for the next piece of clothing.

"Karlton, you've never been rude. We need to talk. I mean even if you have decided to leave, we shouldn't part as enemies."

Tonya stepped into the room and sat on the bed next to the bag he was packing. When Karlton placed more clothes in the bag she grabbed his wrist.

"Sit please." She asked looking directly into his eyes.

Tonya could feel his hurt, although she didn't understand why he was in pain.

"Karlton, please." She repeated softly. She gently pulled him toward the bed. He didn't resist. He sat next to her in silence.

"Understand me, please. For years you know I worked to help build D.Q. Enterprises. It's true D.Q. and I only had two or three years of a loving marriage. I didn't love him. I saw a future with him only when the business was headed toward success. I cheated early in our marriage before I got with you. I don't think he even knew about him. I just didn't love D.Q. I loved everything he gave me, the home he provided and yes I accepted the love he declared. The foundation of an enterprise was built in our home. We went to business seminars, sat with investors, and talked with prospective clients. During the early years, I helped develop the blueprint for the business that grew quickly. We secured funding and stock investments and yes the plan for the expansion. That's the problem. Karlton, I shared his vision, his dreams, and now I can't share in what it's become. That was my dream too!"

Tonya took a deep breath before continuing.

"I kept thinking he would be fair. I kept saying to myself that he wasn't the kind of man that would play a game of revenge. Karlton, I need to be sure that I'm not leaving what is mine on the table. I thought you understood that."

"Tonya, you seeking to get what you want is not the problem. If I am here with you I shouldn't have to wonder where you are at ten o'clock at night. I shouldn't have to wonder why you're out with another man at that time of night. If we're in this together I need to know what you're doing and why. I changed my life, my living, hell I'm driving to and from Maryland once a week to keep my business matters straight. You know when I go and where I go. I think you love the idea of being a victim of a dead man. He's gone and if he didn't leave you anything else, you have to let this idea of yours go."

"Karlton give me a chance to satisfy my suspicions."

Karlton tried to pull back his hand but Tonya held it tightly.

"Please Karlton, stay and give me time. Don't you understand? You did, remember you went to 'Rell about the stocks."

"Tonya, I told you what he said. You don't have to beg anyone at D.Q. Enterprises to include you. You are set with what you got at the time of your separation. I have money and I'm still making money. I don't understand why you insist that you need more."

"I don't think 'Rell or his mother should get more than his wife got. Why? How is that fair?"

"Tonya did you sign papers or anything dealing with D.Q. Enterprises? Were you on any boards or committees? Do any of the deals or properties have your signature on the paperwork? I'm sure his lawyer told you don't have any legal rights when it comes to the business. That my dear is where D.Q. beat you. This wasn't an overnight decision. Tonya, D.Q. found out about us when the children were young, maybe when they were babies. He's been preparing his final paperwork and will since then. Like I said, he's dead and so is the possibility of you having any part of that business."

Tonya didn't want to tell him she needed to rattle 'Rell and Nikki if nothing else. He needed to understand having 'Rell as a son-n-law was a constant reminder of D.Q.'s revenge. She needed to hit back.

"Just a few weeks of shaking things up and I should get some answers. I don't know how D.Q. found out about Shai and Derek not being his children. That's the basis of all of this. Someone gave him the information to destroy my future."

"Someone gave him the information that explained the lies you told. You kept me away from my children. What about Shai's love for 'Rell?

How would they have handled their children with the idea of them being siblings hanging over their heads? The truth needed to be told and you held it. Tonya, it seems like you've met Karma. Let it go."

"Help me, Karlton. I can't let it go without your help and I won't let you go. Please give it a few weeks. I promise I'll drop it once I see and read the papers D.Q. left. I just need to know what those papers told 'Rell."

Tears rolled down her face. Karlton didn't know what to do. Tonya wouldn't stop pursuing the matter until she had the answer. He knew she would never be satisfied. He couldn't stop loving her and he feared no one else would. Her attempt on her life replayed in his mind. He held her tight.

"Sssh, I love you, Tonya. We have to settle this mess finally. We have to move on."

He kissed her lips passionately. Tonya laid back on the bed inviting him to lay with her. Karlton followed her lead. Before the end of the day, she would change his mind. He needed to be reassured she loved him.

Thirty-Three

Bryon called to confirm the time and place where they would be meeting. Keith's flight landed at Norfolk International Airport at twelve and Byron was at the baggage terminal waiting for him to retrieve his bags. Mitch and 'Rell hadn't told Derek they were getting together for him. They were determined to keep his mind away from the thoughts that would invade his conscious on Monday.

Mitch attempted to call Darryl but there were no return calls or messages. Mitch simply left the details of the outing during the day and the group meeting at Mitchell's home later. He was sure 'Rell's uncle would stop through even if he didn't hang out with them during the day.

Mitch, Derek, and 'Rell left 'Rell's home and headed to Charley's, their favorite burger and beer spot. They could watch the NFL games, shoot pool or play darts there as well. The crowd wasn't bad which gave them a choice of what they wanted to do while they waited for Byron and Keith to arrive.

"Man I miss spots like this. You know, where there's a few people you know and you don't have to watch over your shoulder."

"Damn man, I didn't think about that. Sorry, Derek. Would you prefer to go somewhere else? I mean we can hang out at my house or go back to 'Rell's. I didn't even think about it when I spoke with Byron and Keith."

Mitch looked around the room. Everyone seemed to be in their own realm. There weren't many patrons and the plan wasn't to be there too long after they ate. It was close to one and the Saturday regulars didn't begin to fill the place until after five.

"If you want to leave Derek…"

Derek shook his head. "Mitch man, don't worry, I'm good. It's just different you know. Being away and coming back here. Things look and feel different. Besides, I don't think those guys know I'm back in town."

'Rell called the bartender over to order their beer. "Hey beer good for you guys or what?"

The trio ordered and once again Mitch looked around.

"Hell, you've got me wondering. I mean, with the case coming up and all."

"Mitch man, it's good. I ain't no profile criminal. I don't even know if they know about the case."

"Derek, I'm sure they do. They want their money and they know you're on the hook from the Carson's Web thing. I'm sure our uncle told them once or twice that he couldn't pay it all because you guys were starting a new business or didn't have any income. That's why they didn't attempt to tag his ass."

"Damn 'Rell, you think Uncle Darryl would be that cold."

"Man I think he'd do anything to save his ass. Didn't he tell you to just do the time? So let's just go with they know. We'll be at the courtroom on Monday. We'll be looking for anyone suspicious sitting in. Shouldn't be any persons of interest unless they work with Carson's Web, so we'll see. But I don't trust that he didn't use it as an excuse."

"Yeah, I guess you're right. He had to say something to keep them off his back for the past couple of years. You know what, now that you mention it, he did say he'd take care of letting them know what we could or couldn't pay."

"When was that?" Mitch joined in the questioning.

"Right before I left. He said he'd make sure that they wouldn't bother me while I was in rehab. Yeah, right before I left."

Mitch looked at 'Rell but didn't say what was on his mind.

"What? Mitch, what do you know?"

"Your uncle met with a few guys who he said wanted to see the progress that was made at Quintech. 'Rell, you remember when Kenny called the office about Darryl wanting a walkthrough for possible investors?"

"Yeah, I do. We had Kenny escort them through the project. The framing and outer walls were just being done then. I think they came back once it was finished. Uncle Darryl said they were going to be financing one of the upcoming projects. You know I never checked to see who or what project that was."

"I don't know that we had any around that time. Now that I'm thinking about it, Uncle Darryl didn't agree to be a part of Quintech until after it was complete. What investment was he talking about?"

"That clown had plans then. That's why he's so upset that we're watching the books. Derek, man you may have to cut ties with him."

"There's got to be an explanation. I don't think he'd double-cross me 'Rell. Really? I mean, the guy is family. Man, what the hell? He knows all the information about my company and behind my back, he's got his own deals going on?"

"Rell's right man, that's a good reason to have Byron in your books. 'Cause if it's off by half a cent that dude will find it."

"So did Byron find anything other than that account we set up?"

"Listen, let's handle one thing at a time. Go through this thing with Carson's Web and then we'll deal with our dear uncle."

An outburst of cheers came from the other end of the large mahogany bar. Everyone focused their attention on the screen where the game between the Ravens and the Bengals was airing. Baltimore kicked a tie breaking field goal and the fans responded.

"Do you miss going to the games?" Derek was sure Mitch and 'Rell favored the Ravens.

"Sometimes man, we travel to North Carolina too. Basketball games are really our thing. All of us meet up for those. It's usually only me and Mitch at the football games."

"So you guys have always been close?" Derek seemed to be making a point. Mitch noticed 'Rell's expression and answered before he did.

"We go back a bit. College man, we all met in college. We've been together like brothers ever since. Now we've got you. We want you to meet the others so you know the players."

'Rell gave his input. "And how they play. Your business matters are yours my brother, but your personal life, well… Our father, D.Q. had some unorthodox ways of keeping his family close. Too close if you ask me but after meeting your mother and our uncle I understand why. There wasn't much about anyone that was close to him that he didn't know. So, with that said, Mitch and the others that you will meet are the brothers I have known for most of my adult life. Craig is not an enemy or an outcast but just like our beloved uncle, he must be watched."

"Why keep him around if he can't be trusted?"

"Derek, what better way to watch one? Keeping him within my scope tells me a lot about him. He's there for a reason. Once there is no longer a reason he will leave willingly. No argument, no hard feelings, and no need to cause a disruption to my business or personal matters."

Derek listened as he thought about what way to handle Darryl's obvious need to betray him. 'Rell continued.

"With this mess that Monique intends on creating, I'm sure Craig has his side of the story."

"Does he even know? 'Rell something tells me she's got him strung out."

"You're right Mitch, but if she does and he doesn't know, he will. I plan on getting in touch with him."

"With who?" The baritone voice that joined them was Keith's. Mitch and 'Rell greeted him and Byron with handshakes and hugs. They introduced Derek and ordered another round of drinks. It was after the lunch hour and they all were ready to please their appetites. The men moved to the dining area which was large enough to have catered events.

There were more people in the bar area now that the game seemed to be a challenge for the Ravens. It left room for the group to relax. Derek no longer checked the door each time it opened. Mitch checked his phone. There were no messages from Darryl or Craig.

Thirty-Four

"Jewels, why didn't you tell me Sam and Nikki were going away for the weekend. I didn't know they were getting along so well."

Nana stopped walking to the bedroom confused at the statement made by Reverend Wallace.

"Wallace you told me they were getting along well. What do you mean? Just last week you thought Nikki was going to join that new group that was meeting at the church on Wednesday nights. Don't you remember us talking about that?"

"I was teasing. I know Sam and I just thought since he stayed late on Wednesday Nikki would join the group. She would catch, who is that woman, Diane asking after him. I know Nikki too but I sure had Sam checking who was at each meeting for the last couple of weeks. Young folks. Honey, seriously they getting along well huh?"

"Yes, they sure seem to be. Going to the harbor for the weekend, some type of concert. Nikki needs it though. She works long hours and doesn't travel unless it's pertaining to work. Now that the business is doing well she should be able to get on with her personal life."

Nana continued to the bedroom. "Wallace you made me forget what I was coming back here for. What in the world?"

"You was looking for the phone number you said you had for Deacon Jones. I thought we had the same number."

"Oh yes, I have the brochure they printed last month for the sick and shut in. They had contact numbers on it. See if the number is different than what you have. I think it is."

The phone rang before she could return to the living room. Nana sat on her bed and answered it. Glancing at the number she wasn't sure who it was.

"Hey Mama Mince, its Tonya."

Nana took the phone from her face and looked at it as though Tonya could see her displeasure.

"Mama Mince, are you there?"

"Yes, what can I do for you, Tonya?"

"Did I catch you at a bad time? I hope not. I was going through a few of D.Q.'s things earlier and I was wondering if you or 'Rell would want any of these pictures or things I have here. I was looking for the papers I was talking about. I just can't seem to find any vital papers. You know I really should have secured them better. I bet D.Q. had a copy of the originals of every document we had."

"I think I have my share of pictures here. You keep those for your memories or toss them if you like. Maybe the children would want them."

Nana ignored Tonya's comment regarding the papers. She hoped this would be the last time Tonya would ask about it. Nana couldn't keep her patience much longer, even with a prayer for strength.

"I don't know Mama Mince, you know neither of them has really said much about this whole thing. You know, with D.Q. not being their father I don't know if his pictures would be a reminder of…"

"A lie Tonya? Is that what you were about to say? His pictures would be a reminder of the lie you told and held on to all their lives. It hasn't changed any of the pictures in my photo album, on my walls and if I'm remembering correctly Shai has pictures of the two of them framed and on the walls in her home. You can't erase the memories by tossing the photos. You're reaching child, and I ain't the one to reach out to. What you want I don't have."

"What I want? I was asking if you wanted what I had."

"Tonya! When have I ever wanted what you had? Listen, don't call here with this mess. I told you to get in touch with Mr. Simpson about those papers you looking for. Now there won't be no exchanging of pictures or us sitting to discuss them like we shared the same feelings for my son. Time has passed Tonya and you need to catch up. Ain't nobody got time for your foolishness, the papers you looking for is legal papers. D.Q. left Mr. Simpson a folder for you just like he left one for me and 'Rell. Now I believe he gave you yours. If you think there's more, something that was left out, ask your lawyer or Mr. Simpson."

"Mama Mince, I didn't mean to upset you. I just want to be clear about the whole ordeal. I just need to know so I can move on. It seems everyone has moved on and I'm stuck wondering why?"

"Why what child? What is it you don't know? You told that lie about your children and got caught. I think that's enough of the why. I don't know why D.Q. didn't leave you then. Maybe if he had you wouldn't be questioning me or anyone else. You knew those children wasn't D.Q.'s but you were willing to live the life he provided holding them over his head. Tonya, you made this mess. Live with it and leave me out of it."

"Well, I surely didn't think you'd be trying to help me clear up any misunderstanding I had with 'Rell." Tonya waited for Nana to answer. When she didn't she continued. "I think he and I need to understand what D.Q. would want our relationship to be."

"Tonya anything D.Q. wanted he said from that t.v. screen at the reading of his will. I think he made it clear for all of us and to be honest with you, it seemed that he was right."

"What do you mean, he was right?"

"About you. You've been trying to dig up dirt ever since he's been buried under it. You can't get him back. He's not here to smooth it over for you just because or give you something else to keep the peace. Now if you don't want bad feelings between you and 'Rell, stop digging at that grave."

There was no sound on the other end. Nana said hello three times before hanging up. She smiled at the phone and grabbed the brochure from her nightstand.

"Here you go Wallace. Check this number with the one you have."

"So you think Tonya got the message this time." He replied reaching for the brochure.

"I'll feed it to her every time she calls if it will stop her from acting like a fool. Wallace, she don't have no ties with her family and I'm trying not to cut the frayed ties she has with us. She's got to live with what D.Q. gave her and that ain't a little. She can live and be comfortable. I just don't understand why she keeps pushing the issue."

"She's hurting Jewels. When D.Q. had his dreams so did she. It's just that her dreams didn't include loving him. She's just hurting."

"I believe that and I have prayed for her. You know, just for her to be at peace with all of this mess. A mess she created. D.Q. couldn't even leave her and he had more than a reason to do so. It wasn't about love Wallace. She was greedy and greed is going to kill her."

Nana returned to her chair and grabbed the magazine she had been reading. Her mind drifted to the call she received about Tonya's attempt on her life. She remembered Shai's question. Why? If only Nana could have answered Shai that night. She remembered her last visits with D.Q. Nana couldn't answer when he asked the same question from his hospital bed. Why? He realized that night as he took his last breath, he had waited too long to leave Tonya and continue his life with Nikki. Now Nana was asking why. She still didn't know the answer.

Thirty-Five

Craig left Monique's home after making reservations at the Double Tree. They argued most of the night and although he thought they resolved the problem. Monique told him if he couldn't understand what she was trying to do for their future, he should leave. She wouldn't answer any of his questions. Sitting in his car he turned off the ignition. He didn't know what to do. He understood clearly. Monique had betrayed him. Her plan was to destroy 'Rell, his marriage, and possibly his business. Craig spent a few minutes to clear his thoughts. Pieces of the argument defined the woman 'Rell no longer wanted in his life.

"Craig I don't have to prove anything to you and 'Rell won't ask questions because his guilt won't allow it."

"So when was the last time you and 'Rell had sex? How does it add up Monique? You went back to his bed after you told me it would be just us?"

"I'm doing this for us. 'Rell owes me that much. He had you fired because of his guilt. He married Shai to hurt me. If you can't see that, then just leave and let me do what I need to do. I don't owe you an explanation. Where does your loyalty lie? Your lack of loyalty to our relationship is like me having sex with him, right? So we're even!"

"What? So you did have sex with him after we were together? I need to know Monique! Was there a baby or not? Was the baby mine? How can I believe you right now?"

"Shut up! Just leave Craig, just go!"

'Rell would want proof, the same proof Craig needed. There was no doubt, they needed to put their differences aside. He used his cell. It wouldn't be their usual but he'd send the message. He needed a chance to explain the mess. He hoped 'Rell would understand.

'Rell received the text message. *"We need a minute to talk. I'm in town are you still at Charley's?"*

'Rell didn't hesitate to reply. *"No, meet me at Mitch's house. Do you have the address?"*

The reply confirmed he would be there within the hour. 'Rell stepped away from the group to read the message unaware it would be Craig. He motioned to Mitch to step away leaving Keith, Byron, and Derek in the den watching another football game.

"I just got a text from Craig. He said he's in town. I guess he was here to see Monique."

'Rell wanted to be sure there was no other reason for Craig's visit. Mitch invited him to sit at the kitchen table.

"He called earlier this week. He wanted to be around during the trial. I invited him and your uncle to join us. Craig said he'd meet us at the bar, I haven't heard from Uncle Darryl."

"Why did he want to be at the trial? Mitch you know I don't trust Craig."

"I don't think he's trying anything shady. What did he say?"

"He wants us to talk a minute."

"Rell, it's about Monique, it has to be. I don't think he knows anything else. He didn't even know what the trial was about."

"Well, he'll be here in a few. I didn't know he was invited, just wanted you to know he was coming here. I was wondering how he knew where you lived."

"I gave him the address, it's cool. Are you okay with it?"

"Yeah, it's time. If Monique told him that B.S. about a baby, maybe he's questioning it too."

"Hopefully it was his baby."

"Hopefully? What the hell? It just ought to be his, it ain't mine!"

The two returned to join the others laughing.

"Hey, Craig is on his way. Derek, you get to meet the problem child." Mitch tagged Craig with the nickname while they were in college.

"You mean it's someone else in the group with problems. I thought I would hold that title the rest of my life. My mother would tell my dad….. sorry 'Rell, I mean D.Q. I was the problem child growing up. Shai was you know, the one who did everything the right way. Until she met big brother here."

"Yeah and I'm glad that shit worked in our favor. Listen, man, my father raised you guys as his. You call him what your heart calls for, D.Q. or Dad, it's all good with me."

Derek looked at 'Rell and his friends. For the first time in years, he felt like he belonged. He didn't know how he would feel after court but he finally felt he had the support of friends.

"Thanks, man, thanks to Mitch for setting this up. Seems like I should have got with you guys before I left. 'Rell you've had a head start with some good brothers. I'm really glad you're letting me share their friendship."

"Man, that's what it's all about. Just watch what you say to Craig. He's dating Monique. Gotta see where he's coming from and why, before I can trust our 'problem child' again. I mean that guys, not to mix business with pleasure. You know how we do, Craig's got to come clean about this shit with Monique. There's no way he doesn't know what she's up to."

"Hold up, 'Rell. Does somebody want to school me on what's going on? I mean I know about him dating your girl."

"Ex girl!" Byron, Mitch, and 'Rell chimed in together causing laughter to fill the room. Keith was still in the dark and his confusion showed on his face.

"Okay, okay yeah. You know what I mean. You and Monique were inseparable before Shai did you….oh, sorry Derek."

"Man, hey they married now. She turned his head backward. I mean they thought they were related and still had it going on."

"Derek, no man. Listen, your sister…."

"No need to explain. It's all good now, we ain't related so no foul, fair play. Plus you were seriously whipped, babies made, pushed down to the altar. Bro, I understand."

"C'mon before Craig rings the bell. What's up with Monique now?"

'Rell and Mitch explained the dilemma to Keith with injections of humor and memories of Monique's deliberate flirtations.

"I got tired of her shit. Remember, I told you and Mitch about her checking out my Dad's company. Byron hipped me to how much I was worth after the inheritance. I had to get rid of her gold digging ass. Since I knew she was teasing Craig, I threw him a bone."

"Man I thought she was just playing around, you know, we all had females that would do anything for any of us. That shit went further than that for Craig? What was up with that? I mean that's breaking code."

"Keith, he's the one that may be coded. Once she found out he wasn't making that extra bank she really turned up the heat. He asked a few times if it was because he was dating her that I had him investigated and fired. I ignored his ass for months. Then of course when I offered jobs to you guys he asked again. I just told him I couldn't trust him."

"Rell, I know he didn't think you would offer him a job."

Derek couldn't believe what he heard. No one spoke up. "Really?"

"Really. I was as surprised as you are now. Anyway, I didn't cut him off as a friend. I invited both of them to the wedding. We've had a few outings with all of us and our dates, so no hard feelings. But if anyone knows what that gold digger is up to, I think it would be him. If he can't tell it all, he'll remain on the watch list."

"So you calling your ex the gold digger?"

Mitch smiled knowing how Keith and Byron would respond to the question he posed to 'Rell.

"Rell, you know she don't want no broke nigger!"

'Rell shook his head and laughed. Derek understood the brotherhood.

Thirty-Six

"So when Darryl? When does this mess end? Your nephew almost lost his life. You've admitted it ruined your business and your relationship with your family. When does it stop; when we're not together?"

"Simone, what does that mean? What, you're threatening me too?"

"Too? Darryl too? Do you expect me to allow you to take my money and gamble it away? Too? Who else is threatening you? Do you realize that you are jeopardizing more than you, your business and your relationships?"

"What the hell does that mean?"

"Darryl, I have a business too. I have a relationship with my family and I don't want them using our relationship to change things between me and them. My money is mine and I don't tell people what I have or don't have. I'm sure they know you and I share what we have. If you're gambling and losing money, how stupid do I look?"

"What?"

"Darryl, I don't always pay for the expenses for my trips and my food. Nikki pays out of the business account for that."

"As she should, it's business."

Darryl could feel his anger rising. He didn't know how long he could sit for the chastising Simone thought he needed. It was a repeat performance. His immediate family along with the reminder from 'Rell was enough.

"And being a business partner I should put a fair share of money in it don't you think? Well, I don't and it's because I tell my dear cousin that I have expenses here, with you. I thought it would prompt a raise but right now the business is covering costs and the expenses it incurs."

"So you don't get paid?"

"I do but I save it. I don't put it back into the business."

"Well, you need to address that. Shit, you can't be working for nothing."

"Do you and Derek get paid? Do you work for free?"

"Simone, how we run our business…"

"Cut the bullshit, Darryl. I could have said the same weak ass answer to you. The point is when is your gambling going to cease? More so, well let me say it this way. Don't use my money to gamble with. Don't ask me for money to gamble with. Don't expect me to stand by and risk what I have, I won't. I don't want to jeopardize what I have, what I will have or my life over gambling debts I don't owe."

"So you saying what?"

Simone and Darryl had been discussing, arguing, and disagreeing since breakfast. It was now mid-afternoon and Simone felt she hadn't said anything that Darryl wanted to understand.

"Darryl, Francine and whomever you dealt with didn't have a say in the relationship, that's obvious. Well, this relationship is a part of my living, my life and you won't have me home, depressed, and scared. So it's one way with me or we're done. Gamble with your life, your business, and your money!"

Simone paused for his response. Darryl opened his mouth but couldn't put the words together before she spoke again.

"Look around Darryl. We just started living together. Look around this place, don't you want more? I mean, there are things I want to make this our home. Check out your business plans, don't you want more? Being able to have your own home and business is special. I'm determined to change my life to fit my wants. I have needs as well and one of them is to live without fear for my life or the fear that someone is seeking to harm you. For the loss of money, Darryl? You can't be willing to lose your life because you didn't pay a gambling debt made in a back room somewhere. Listen, don't use me or mine that's all I'm saying and I mean that, ain't nothing worse than not being free to go and come without fear. No, I take it back, being scared in your own home or losing your own business is worse. I guess since you've done that it don't matter, huh?"

"Simone, I can't defend my past. I can tell you I've changed but I don't have any proof that I have. I only have my word. I borrowed the money from you and promised myself that would be the last time. I thought I could double it, pay the bill I had at the time and give you yours back. I lost, but I don't want to lose you and I realized that then. I'm done, you're right it has ruined my relationships."

"I hope we don't have to talk about this again Darryl. I love you but I've been in relationships that destroyed me and what I had. I can't do that again."

Simone left him sitting on the couch. He looked at the television that showed the results of the games that played earlier. Her words were repeating. She was right. His gambling had ruined too much of his life. His choice to leave his marriage and begin a new life with Simone and Quintech mattered.

"Hey babe, I'm going to catch up with Derek. He's at Mitch's house, I'll be there for a few."

He heard her respond, "Whatever" from the bedroom. Her anger would linger for a few hours. He'd bring her roses when he returned.

Thirty-Seven

Darlene looked at the clock. It confirmed her fear, *"It's getting late";* it was nearing four o'clock. She was sure she'd be finished with the last appointment by five and Ms. Clark was still under the dryer. There were no canceled appointments, not that she expected any, but she was short two stylists. The ad for a new stylist had not been answered and every Saturday she found herself running late. As frustrated as she was, she filled in knowing the absent "girls" were devoted to their work and wouldn't just call out on a Saturday.

The stylists in the three shops, a total of ten were like family. Each of them held an important role in the business of hair care and took pride in being Darlene's employees. They helped with promotions, hosted hair care events, and toured together for fashion and hair shows. They understood as their clientele increased as well as their individual heights. Darlene pushed each of them equally and encouraged them to take classes to improve their skills.

They also dealt with the drama that only a stylist would understand. The day began with the drama of confused schedules and now Darlene was the one who felt the pressure.

Ms. Clark was an elder from the church and made her appointments as she left. Canceling her appointment would cause a riff with all the elders that Nana associated with. Darlene assigned each of the stylist an elder's appointment. She tried not to burden one with the care needed for the slower deliberate moves of the older women. Ms. Clark had a head full of thick hair. She didn't believe in relaxers and loved deep conditioning. She preferred a hot comb pressing and always sat for more than an hour under the dryer. She'd didn't hear very well and often fell asleep causing her head to drop lower than the dryer's hood.

Darlene was handling her mother's elderly friend. After helping her in and out of the seat adjusting the height and waiting patiently for her hair to dry, Darlene was tried. Warren told her he'd meet her at the mall, they'd go to the movies and have something to eat. The plans were great when she made them the night before, but after six clients and one left to follow Ms. Clark, she was done. Reluctantly she would have to call Warren to cancel.

The noise of the dryers, the radio, and the conversations had become a bit much. Darlene stepped into her office to make the call. The soft jazz playing in the background gave her the minute she needed to relax. She closed the door and sighed. It had been months since she worked the salon chair all day. Ramona, one of her favorites, opened the door slowly and peeked in. She joined the Diva Hair Design Salon right out of high school. Darlene paid for her to go to cosmetology school. Now six years later, Ramona was one of the best stylists in the state and her rewards adorned the walls of the salon.

"You tired ain't ya", she drawled as she smiled. "Been a while boss lady. That floor will work every muscle in your body, that's why I go to the gym when I leave here. Y'all be talking 'bout me but my body can stand it."

Darlene rolled her eyes and shook her head slowly. Smiling she replied, "Take your happy butt out of here. Are you caught up honey?"

"Yes, ma'am. I'm not sure if Mama Clark is ready yet but I'll take the other girl and set her up for the dryer if you like. What you need me to do. You sure look tired. You still going out?"

"Baby, I'm too tired to even say so." The two of them laughed. "I came in here to call him. Maybe we'll just go and eat. Anything else would be a waste."

"You want me to ask Cee Cee if she's almost done. You know Mama Clark likes her. She can finish her up for you."

"Tell her to come here a minute. Is she done with those braids?"

"Just 'bout. Make your call and get out of here we got this."

Before Darlene could say anything else Ramona closed her office door. Cee Cee peeked in the door just as Darlene was dialing Warren's number.

"I got you, Boss Lady. Ms. Clark will be fine. My customer is done. Go on to bed before you fall out."

"You and Ramona need to respect your elders." Darlene smiled and mouthed, "thank you" as Cee Cee closed the door.

Darlene said a silent prayer of added thanks as Warren's phone began to ring. She stared at the paperwork on her desk. The accountant would be on Monday for the monthly report. Darlene sighed again as she realized she was behind in her own work. She hadn't prepared the folder to be picked up.

"Hey, do you think we can skip the movie and just do dinner?" Warren didn't have a chance to say hello.

"Okay, no problem. Do you still want to go there to eat or do you want me to pick up something and meet you at the house?"

His question provoked serious thought. They hadn't been out in more than a month. She really enjoyed his company, but she didn't want to entertain at her home again.

"I was looking forward to eating out. I think I can keep my eyes open long enough to order and eat."

"Sounds like a long day. What do you want to do about the cars or are we meeting there?"

"Warren, sugar?" She didn't think her explanation needed to be repeated. Warren had been in enough salons to understand a busy day.

"Okay, I'll meet you at the entrance of Stoney Point and we'll eat and do whatever you wish."

"Thank you, sweetie, I have a taste for P.F. Chang's. I'll be on my way once I hang up."

Darlene leaned back in her seat and took a deep breath. She'd clean up her office on Monday. The office was another one of D.Q.'s ideas and she couldn't thank him enough. On a normal day, she could visit each salon and go into the office area and work. Each employee had their own file cabinet and locker. The offices had two desks, computers, a television, and a phone. She thought the idea was crazy but after seeing her business grow, once again her brother had the better vision.

Darlene waved her good-byes and thanked the customers for coming in. Glad the weather wasn't cold, she wrapped her shawl around her shoulder and walked to her car. She felt better as she got in her car and allowed her thoughts of the day dissipate. She felt the tension release immediately. Turning the key in the ignition, the radio played 98.5 FM, her favorite jazz station. Brian Culbertson's latest pumped her mood for the thirty-minute drive.

Looking for a parking space became a chore. *"It's Saturday,"* Darlene thought to herself. She knew she shouldn't have expected anything less. After circling as close to the front entrance as she could, she gave in and parked further away than she would have liked. She got out the car certain that a glass of wine would be her nightcap.

"Ms. Mince, Ms. Mince."

Darlene heard her name called across the row of parked cars. She looked up and wished she could pretend she didn't see Monique waving at her. She waved back hoping that's all the troubled woman wanted. Monique's steps seemed to quicken as she approached Darlene's car.

"Hey lady, you shopping?" Darlene gave a weak attempt at being cordial.

"I'm done. I picked up a few things just because, you know. I really didn't have anything particular in mind. Just passing time I guess." Monique smiled waiting for Darlene to engage further.

"I see. Well, you're looking well. How's your family?"

"Everyone is well and yours?"

"Good, everyone is good."

"Ms. Mince, I know your family doesn't think much of me, but I want you to know that my relationship with 'Rell was quite different than he probably told you."

"Sweetie, we're just getting our relationships to be what they should be. Funny, through it all, there hasn't been any mention of you or your relationship with 'Rell. Just so you know though, he's doing well, as is Shai."

Monique was stunned and Darlene noticed the change in her demeanor. *"I hope this girl don't start her shit here."* Darlene canvassed the area hoping no one she knew could see them talking. She expected an explosive response.

"And the children? Are they okay too? I mean, I can't imagine 'Rell being a businessman, husband, and father. He walked away from one child already."

"He's groomed well for the role. I doubt very seriously if he walked away from a child that he knew was his. However, sweetie if you think that, continue with the rumors and gossip. As you said you can't imagine. The family is good and ready for whatever you think will ruin us."

"Not my gossip, I'm just saying that when a man won't own up to being a father, well I guess like father like son."

Before Darlene could answer Monique turned to return to her car.

"Bitch, you just don't know." As her temper rose Darlene mumbled her way to the entrance of the mall. Warren smiled and then frowned realizing she was not at all happy. Darlene kissed him and grinned. It would be the first time that Warren would hear about the Mince family drama.

Thirty-Eight

Craig stood at the door of Mitchell's home hoping the gathering wouldn't turn into an exchange of incensed words. Darrell pulled into the driveway and Craig waited to ring the bell. He took the time to look around the property. Mitchell was 'Rell's right-hand man. It wasn't odd for him to have acquired the position he held at D.Q. Enterprises. Although they all met during their college years, Mitchell and 'Rell were inseparable.

Mitchell's home was large, not what Craig would think he would have chosen. Monique would love the manicured lawn, bushes and trees; the property line met the street which was a good distance from the front door. Craig could tell from the large garage that both Mitchell and Marci loved the acres the property occupied. He'd ask to see the home in its entirety.

Monique's assumptions were true. Craig wanted what the others acquired since joining the staff at D.Q. Enterprises. Each had homes, vehicles and a taste of peaceful living. He knew he couldn't live with Monique in peace, nor could he work with 'Rell if he and Monique stayed together. The confusion was causing him to pace. He looked out over the porch banister. Darryl parked his car behind Craig's. Craig was pleased to see a familiar face.

He waved as Darryl got out of the car an approached the stairs. "Hey there fella, how are you?"

"As well as I can be, I guess Unc. What about you?"

"Livin' man, livin'. It takes adjusting when your life changes you know?"

Craig was unsure what Darryl was referring to but he knew from late night talks it was better to just listen.

"I moved you know from Detroit to Virginia. Whole different world. The people, being around family more often, trying to start a new life with a new lady, and then the business. It's a little much for this old guy, you know."

Darryl put his arm around Craig's shoulder as they approached the front door together.

"I think I know what you mean. Looking from the outside in Unc. I've been doing that for a minute now. They include me, you know invites, but it doesn't feel the same. Women, or maybe just that woman."

"Seems like you need to do just what I need to do."

"What's that?"

"Craig, you can't trade the love you have for these guys with the love you have for Monique. If you love…"

Craig separated himself shaking his head. "Uncle Darryl I can't love her. She's poison and I was under her spell. I'll admit I was wrong to even get involved this deep. She's incapable of loving someone. It's all about her. I'm here for you and Derek. That's what the purpose of this is, you know. For us to get together and support one another. I failed Uncle Darryl. The man code thing isn't just a joke, it's a bond and I broke it. No one will ever know how sorry I am for that. I'm here to apologize and maybe save myself from being a total fool."

"Yeah, me too. I think I broke some part of that code too."

The front door opened and Mitch threw his hands up.

"So were you guys going to ring the bell? I saw you when you pulled up. Is everything okay?"

"We were working up our courage. I think we're both on the shit list you know."

The three laughed as they entered the home. Craig didn't want to look surprised. The Mitchell Carter he knew from their college days had indeed matured into a new man. The home Craig stepped into was nothing like the apartment Mitch had during their younger years.

"I see Marci has you in check."

"What does that mean? Oh," Mitchell laughed, "You're right I can't toss my clothes around in here. Please, she didn't let me do that too often at the apartment I had here. She's sort of a neat freak. I love it though. You look good, man. Unc you okay?"

"Yeah, I'm with Craig. This is nice. You wouldn't think it was this spacious from the outside. It looks like a quaint home, you know."

"That's what I like. C'mon in the guys are in the den. What can I get you? Beer, water, what? The harder stuff is this way."

The two followed Mitch as he led them to the roar of voices who obviously were responding to the completion of the football play on the television.

"Hey, Craig found Uncle Darryl."

Everyone stood to greet the two additional guests. Drinks were filled and re-filled. Mitch brought out more chips and pretzels.

"We ordered pizza and wings. If you'd like some, rather, by all means, have some. Follow me, let me show you. We've got a lot to eat before Marci comes home."

Craig and Darryl followed Mitch through the living room to the kitchen.

"I left everything here. Help yourselves."

Mitch left them to fix their own plates. The kitchen was large with a breakfast nook on the far side of the room. The large deck could be seen from the sliding glass doors. Craig stood at the doors looking out at the huge yard.

"I wonder what Shai and 'Rell's home looks like."

Darryl joined him at the door.

"It's larger than this one. 'Rell had it built for Shai. They added to it when they found out they were having twins. I designed it for them. We didn't do much here other than the deck. Are you thinking about joining your boys here in Virginia?"

"I don't know. I'm still in Maryland that's where the job is, you know."

"Understood."

'Rell entered the room. Darryl and Craig fell silent.

"Don't stop the conversation for me that is unless it's about me."

"No man, nothing like that but I do need to talk if you have a minute. I don't want to talk over the guys or Uncle Darryl. Unc you don't mind do you?"

"No, let me grab my drink here and I'll be out of your way. 'Rell you'll be a busy man or listener 'cause I want to talk to you and Derek too."

'Rell was glad Darryl mentioned he wanted to talk. It was on his mind as well. They needed to mend whatever it was that was rapidly unraveling.

"No problem. Craig, what's up?"

Darryl left the two in the kitchen. His nephew seemed well prepared to hear what Craig had to say. Darryl knew 'Rell had questions of his own.

"First let me say you guys have really stepped into the business owner's role well. I guess this is the kind of life we talked about during our college years."

He carried his plate to the kitchen table. 'Rell joined him after refilling his glass.

"Did you want a beer man? I mean it's cool if you want something other than water."

"Man I had a bad night. I need this water right about now and a friend's ear. I think I can still consider you my friend right?"

"What's up, Craig? I'm sure it's not about our friendship."

"In a way it is. I know you would have stopped my dealing with Monique if you really cared about her. I think, though I could be wrong, you let it go down as it did to show me she wasn't shit. I mean we all talked about the problems we had with our ladies but I was stupid man. I thought since the two of you were on the outs I'd take her up on some of the bull she was shooting my way. 'Rell it was supposed to be a one-time thing."

"Man am I supposed to feel better about it. One time too many, that's how I feel about it, Craig. You knew how I felt when it was good between us and yeah we talked about the problems we had as men in relationships. You went too far brother. You took the bait from a shark and now you're here to say what?"

"She's after you man. You, your marriage, D.Q. Enterprises, whatever she can destroy in your world. It started with us. She destroyed us. I didn't understand how evil she was until last night. I mean she's said a few things about you and what you have gained in the past. 'Rell she's sick. She's more than vindictive. I mean I don't know, she's borderline crazy."

Craig paused taking a slow drink of water as though there was alcohol in the glass. He sat silent for a moment, spinning the glass in his hand.

"Rell she has this devious plot and I guess she thought I would be a part of it."

"Craig, why now? You didn't give a shit about whatever she tried to do to me in the past. What's the difference now?"

"It's a lie, more than a lie. She's claiming she had a miscarriage. I don't remember her being pregnant but she won't say when or if I may be the father or...."

"Hold up man. So is your reason is because it's a lie, or because you want her to tell you if you're the father? I'm not understanding, why now? What's your worry?"

"Rell, she's claiming it's your child that she lost, aborted or whatever. I asked had you and her, you know, had sex since we were together. She wouldn't answer. I can't get her to just tell the damn truth."

"So you want me to do what? My conscious is clear. She can't do anything about a baby that's what, alive in her mind?"

"I asked her how she was going to prove it. She said she had the medical records. So I wanted to know more details, you know. I mean she should know who the father is. I wanted to know was it me or you."

"Look it may matter to you because you're dealing with her. It is of no interest to me. I have two children and I'm married to their mother. I'm sure the baby wasn't mine and she can't prove it. I'm not worried about it. Look, Craig, I would say if I'm feeling some kind of way about all of this. We're good man. You and I have had our differences but it has nothing to do with Monique."

"Well, she thinks it does. Her idea was to hit you with this and you would be guilty enough to give in to her bullshit."

"If you agreed what was in it for you Craig?"

"According to her plan you'd give me a position at D.Q. Enterprises, she'd get paid and you'd lose Shai."

"Really? Listen let me talk to Simpson. Let's do some checking. Let me help you out here. We'll find out I'm sure that there was no baby. Then we'll get you set up if my uncle agrees at Quintech. If you want a position I can make that happen. I can't bring you in to D.Q. Enterprises until we get her out of the way. I mean I need to trust you so if you really want that position you're going to have to work for it."

"Rell I wasn't looking for a spot, really man."

A look of worry crossed Craig's face.

"She won't know unless you're still with that dumb bitch. Did she think you could talk to me and I'd instantly panic? Craig tell me the truth. You were down with her simple ass plan until you thought about the possibility there was a child. I'm telling you to wake up. You let ass obscure your vision. The plans we had as brothers became a blur for you. You stepped off and tried your hand and it got you fired. Craig, I did that because I wanted you to know you can't work with me and betray me. You didn't learn. You thought you'd get back at me with Monique. Now she shafted you as I knew she would, and you're sitting here thinking I'm going to believe you didn't go with it?"

Craig couldn't answer. He could feel his stomach turning. 'Rell was sharp, always had been. The others would often tell him not to push 'Rell into a corner. They'd argue and he always found himself apologizing to the group for his mistakes. He wanted to prove himself but again 'Rell was about to crush him.

"Craig man, you're my brother. Just like Mitch and the others. The difference is that damn nick-name Mitch gave you."

"Humph, problem child. I guess he's right huh?"

"We're brothers. Let's bury this problem and move on. I don't want Monique to think I know about her little plan. Did you tell her you were coming here?"

"No. She knows about me coming to see her. She knew I was going to the trial though. I decided I didn't want to deal with her anymore in the car. I told her I wouldn't be back."

"So she thinks you're done with her?"

"Yeah, that's it. I don't care what she thinks though. I'm done with her crazy ass."

"Let me talk to Simpson and my uncle. Craig, if I find out you're dealing with her, the position is off the table."

"It's not about the position man. I need to know if there was a kid, possibly my kid. I mean if you're saying you know it wasn't yours. It's bothering me, man. Suppose there was a baby and she just got rid of it."

"We'll find out. You let me know after we handle things about the position. Just keep in touch, Simpson will know what to do."

Craig stood and went to the glass doors again. Tears began to form and he didn't want 'Rell to know how hurt he was. Monique was playing a dangerous game. If Stanley Simpson revealed that there was a child 'Rell wouldn't have to worry about Monique bothering him again.

Thirty-Nine

Tonya got up early on Sunday morning. She hoped Karlton would join her and go to church. She needed to make a few appearances to ruffle the feathers of the Mince family. She was sure D.Q.'s mother told most of the family members about the phone calls and questions she wanted to be answered. Nikki was attending the church frequently. Tonya called a few friends who were a part of the congregation and they confirmed her attendance.

Karlton came down to the breakfast table dressed for service. She knew the romancing she did the night before gave him second thoughts about what he would be missing. They talked after their lovemaking about the changes that needed to be made in their relationships. Both agreed this would be the last time they would attempt to recoup what Tonya thought was rightfully hers. What Karlton didn't know was that Tonya was after more.

"Good morning sweetie. I thought you were going to tell me what dress you were wearing. I saw it though, hanging on the back of the closet door. The blue one right?"

"I am so sorry. Yes, I threw on my robe to cook us a little breakfast before we leave. Sit down I'll cook your eggs."

"I have to go over those papers Mr. Monroe sent you before we say anything else to the Mince family or their lawyer."

"Karlton, Monroe is really dragging his feet. I think that stock is the key. If D.Q. thought it would make money for me..? C'mon you and I both know he would have given me some shit he didn't want. Did you see the returns?"

"Yeah, the stock stays hot. I want to check out a few things. I agree with you. I think there's a kickback to the Enterprises."

"Karlton, what does that mean?"

Tonya passed his plate. The steam from the eggs caused them both to pause the conversation.

"I'm hungry too, this is right on time. Where's your plate?"

"I'm working on it. Now tell me what you mean."

"I want to check the sale of the stock to that company, Dickerson and Jackson. I've never heard of them, but I bowed out of the stocks years ago. I want to check a few things. If they sold the stock outright why would they still be the holding company or getting kickbacks is the question. I don't think they let it go."

"I'm not sure I understand, but you do and that's what matters. Would that put me in a good position to get part of the Enterprises? That's what I'm after Karlton. I want to dethrone that damn boy they think is a king."

Tonya put her eggs on her plate and sat at the table. She poured herself a cup of coffee from the coffee carafe and gestured to fill Karlton's cup.

"No baby, is there juice in the fridge?"

"Yes, you want juice? No coffee?"

"Don't move, I'll get it. I drank coffee all day yesterday and the day before. I'm trying to get the paperwork ready for that deal in Maryland I told you about. There's still work to be done before we pitch the contract."

"Karlton, you stretch yourself so thin between here and there. You know if I get what I am due from D.Q. Enterprises you can leave that job."

"Baby I'm thinking about expanding and getting an office here. The partners agree it will be a good move for us. We can turn over properties both commercial and residential here just as well as there. Maryland and Virginia we can make some real money without being attached to your husband's fortune."

Tonya didn't respond. Karlton had made that argument before. The problem was she wanted what was hers. He still didn't understand her reason for revenge. It didn't matter, he was willing to look into the stocks she owned.

"Karlton, if the stocks are what they are, then what? I mean if the stocks weren't worth much five years ago or whenever D.Q. sold them leaving my name on them, then what?"

"Hmm… I see what you're saying. They may be profitable now and they did sell them while they weren't flourishing. I don't know babe. We may not have a plugin. We'll have to search for something else."

They completed their meal hanging on to their own thoughts. Tonya would take a stab at Nikki and 'Rell. Karlton would go through the other company and Mr. Monroe.

"Hey did your son contact you? His case starts tomorrow. There was talk about it on the business network. The internet has no problem putting up the local news. They've been following D.Q.'s legacy or so they called it."

"Really? I haven't talked to him. I didn't know he was coming home for the case. I thought they would be doing a teleconference since he's still doing therapy."

"Shai didn't tell you. He's done with the therapy. I think he finished it about three months ago. She didn't mention him coming home though."

"Are they sure he's in town for it? I guess I should be in the courtroom and be a support of some sort. Also maybe that stock is tied to his company as well. It won't hurt to ask if he knows about the company that's holding the money that's mine."

"Why would he know?"

"I've been wondering who paid for his company expenses while he was out of town. It all seems to be a tangled mess. I just want to be untangled and holding the key to my wealth. Thanks, I guess I'll check with Shai today."

"Darryl Mince is his partner. Just be careful of saying anything about what we are planning to do. We can't trust either of them with any information we find out."

"It may be an angle we can use if they're being cheated out of their own profits because they're in with 'Rell."

"Tonya, I doubt 'Rell is that dumb. Believe me, if there is anything to be found, it's buried. He's D.Q.'s son."

"Don't remind me."

They got dressed and left their home in time for the eleven o'clock service at First Chapel Baptist Church. The parking lot had a line of cars filing in for the morning worship service. Karlton found a place to park.

"Whew, have you ever paid attention to the cars these good ole church folks are driving? Most of them are seniors too."

Tonya looked as he pointed to the cars. She spotted Mama Mince's car in the spot marked with the insignia written in gold, "First Lady". Her silver Audi A4 was the last car her son bought her before he was hospitalized. She got a car every two years just because. Tonya smiled, it had been five years. She thought, *"Mama Mince must be missing her gift giving son"*. His mother had been Tonya's competition. Karlton bought Tonya a car when she explained she couldn't drive the BMW, the last car D.Q. bought her that same year.

They got out of Karlton's Cadillac and Tonya smiled with pride as he opened her door. Parishioner's passed the couple with morning pleasantries as they joined the line that was filing in the church. The choir was filling the atrium as service was about to begin.

They found a seat in the middle of the center section of pews. Tonya looked over toward the seats where the "family" normally sat. The Mince family, as she suspected, was seated together. Shai, 'Rell, Mitch and Marci were seated in the row behind Mama Mince, Derek, and Leeza.

"Karlton isn't that Leeza, the nurse that Derek went to live with in Brazil?"

"Yes, that's her."

"Maybe he is in town for the case. She's still with him so he may still be handicapped."

"Babe let's get the word this morning. It's for us as well as them."

"I don't know. You know that's Mama Mince's man in the pulpit. I don't trust his word would be useful to us."

"He's preaching God's word."

Before she could answer the choir entered the sanctuary singing the first song of the morning. The church began to clap and sing with them. The congregation rose to their feet.

Forty

The church service was refreshing, at least Karlton thought so. He looked over at Tonya during the sermon but she kept her head buried in the Bible she held in her hand. He noticed she was reading a different scripture entirely. Reverend Wallace's preaching always brought the congregation to their feet. They were clapping and shouting as he told them there would always be obstacles and challenges.

"God will make a way for you when you make a way for God to touch your life. Is there anyone here today looking for a church home?"

Karlton glanced at Tonya again. "Hey babe," he whispered. "You okay?"

"Yes, yes. I just found an interesting scripture. It caught my attention. Sometimes you have to read it for yourself, you know."

Reverend Wallace asked the congregation to stand and join hands for prayer.

"Heavenly Father we come to you today as a broken people. We ask for a healing today Father. We need you to walk through this sanctuary, through our community, through our homes, through the hospitals, through our families and Lord, touch us. Each and every time we call your name Lord, each time we give you praise, each time we stumble fall and become confused, keep us close. Father without you we are not whole Lord……"

"How long is this going to be?!"

"Ssssh Tonya, be still baby."

Tonya didn't say another word. The woman next to her closed her eyes again, disturbed by Tonya's question. The prayer concluded with the Benediction and the choirs melodic "Amen".

Tonya held the woman's hand longer to apologize.

"I am so sorry. I have to run to the bathroom and didn't want to walk out while Reverend was praying. You know when we're as old as we are you can't always wait until the last minute."

The woman gave her a phony smile, gathered her things and exited the pew. Karlton shook his head slowly.

"Well hell, I tried to be better than telling her ass to mind her business. Listen let's get out the door before they do. I want to see what Derek has to say about not calling me. I don't understand them. The two of them, Shai and Derek, they act like I don't exist sometimes. It's not fair to me as their mother. Why would they take to that side of the family?"

The couple exited the church and waited on the lower level of the stairs for Shai and Derek. The crowd flooded out of the church yelling goodbyes and best wishes for the upcoming week. A few of them recognized Tonya. They nodded and waved but none stopped to engage in a conversation.

Karlton tapped her sleeve and pointed to the entrance of the church. At the door, she could see Shai making her way to the steps with the twins.

"Papa, Papa." Brianna was calling Karlton from the top of the stairs. Shai leaned over and her daughter pointed to Tonya and Karlton standing at the base of the stairway. Shai waved but turned Brianna and Bryce around and re-entered the church.

"What the hell was that about?"

"Tonya, maybe she forgot something."

"The hell she did. See this is the mess I'm talking about. Shai has no concept of devotion. I should have done something about her and that damn 'Rell before they married. There's no hope now Karlton. I have lost both my children to the hands of that damn D.Q. reaching from the grave."

"Tonya, Tonya hush they're coming out see."

Shai picked up Brianna and 'Rell lifted Bryce. The couple descended the stairs and walked over toward Tonya and Karlton.

"Papa I saw you. I told you it was Papa." Brianna shouted at Bryce. The two ran from their parents to greet their grandparents.

"Hi, Papa." Bryce walked over to his grandfather and shook his hand. Karlton picked him up and gave him a hug and kiss. He lifted Brianna in the air. Her laughter was all he wanted.

"Did you speak to Mimi?"

The children chose the name Mimi and no one knew why.

"They went over to Tonya with giggles, smiles, and hugs."

"Hey, you two. Did you enjoy church?"

They both sang their answer, "Yes."

"Why didn't your mother come over here?"

The children ran to the other side of the wide staircase where Shai and 'Rell stood watching them. Derek and Leeza stood at the top of the stairs with Mitch and Marci. Again Karlton tapped Tonya on her sleeve.

There weren't many parishioners left at the front of the church. Most had moved over to the parking lot or were still in the atrium. Tonya looked up at her son who was standing on his own.

"Karlton, Derek has no cane, walker or chair. No one told me my child was walking. Let's go. I've seen enough. I can't take this deliberate pain they keep giving me."

"You don't want to speak to him or Shai?"

"Shai has been standing there and hasn't moved. She must have told Derek I was out here and now he's standing at the top of the steps and won't move. They've made it obvious. They both will know when I choose to speak to them."

As they turned to go to the parking lot Derek called from the top of the stairs.

"Hey, Ma, Ms. Mince. Wait a minute I'm coming to down to you. Watch."

Tonya turned to face the stairs and tears rolled down her face as Derek slowly walked down the stairs. Leeza watched from the top of the stairs with Marci and Mitch while Shai walked over to meet Derek at the bottom of the stairs. She kissed her brother on the cheek and they both approached Tonya and Karlton.

"Good morning folks. How are you? I didn't expect to see you at church Ma. Change of heart?"

"What is that supposed to mean? I'm glad to see you and you're walking? When did this happen?"

"It doesn't really matter at this point. I'm speaking to appease my sister here. Hey Karlton, how are you?"

"I'm good Derek. When did you get in?"

"We landed a few days ago. Staying with Shai and 'Rell in that mansion of a home they have. It's really nice. How's the real estate market?"

"Good, good. I'm thinking about doing a few things here in Virginia. I'll call you and Darryl about it. There may be a few to flip here and there and the partners and I could use your company on a few projects."

"Yeah, speaking of using people….. Ma don't bother asking me about those papers you seem to be searching for. If Shai doesn't have them then I don't. I don't need to be a part of another problem."

"I have no idea what you're talking about that may be a problem. I just need to check over paperwork that I have and I can't find some of the other paperwork I may need."

"Well don't call me about it. I don't have it and if I did I wouldn't give it to you."

"Derek, don't be so hard on your mother. She's doing a lot better than she has been and she's trying to pick up the pieces and move on. We all want that right Shai?"

Shai stood quiet. She looked at Karlton and Derek and didn't respond.

"What have I done to her now? This is what I was saying, Karlton. I can't win. I haven't done a thing."

"Mother, I don't care to discuss what you have done. That's just it. We don't know if it's today, tomorrow or next week but you will be back looking for a way to dig up the past or create trouble. I'm tired of it. I came over here only because Derek said he wouldn't speak to you at all if I didn't. I do what I do for you only because you are my mother. I don't have to put up with the rest of your nonsense. Oh, and the minute you start your mess again….. I'm done too."

"So you nor Derek want a relationship at all with me?"

"I don't and since I'll be returning to Brazil I think that will be far enough. Whatever you do won't affect me."

"If you can't be civil, I can't have a relationship with you. Oh, and that would include my children as well. So I guess this is a warning. Please let the past fade and don't trample on the future."

"Derek you and I need to talk seriously. I think there are some things that you don't know and need to know. Please allow me that time at least. It can be after your court thing, whatever that is, but we do need to talk. Shai I can respect your wishes if your husband stays out of my way."

Shai walked away without a goodbye. Tonya turned her attention to Derek.

"Leeza and I will visit before we leave. I don't know how long the trial is, but right now that's my focus. I don't really want to hear your ghost stories about D.Q. and what you think is hidden for you and me. But I'll give you that moment and it will determine if we ever have another."

Derek walked away and met the others who were waiting for him. Brianna and Bryce shouted their goodbyes. Tonya looked at Karlton as she fought new tears. Derek reminded her of D.Q. as he packed the last box before moving out of their home.

"Are you okay?" Karlton asked as he opened the passenger door of the car.

"It's not easy being the mother that's hated you know. I have to convince Derek first. That damn Shai is lost."

Forty-One

Shai stood at the window in her kitchen. Her thoughts after leaving the church were still nagging her. She hoped she would find peace as she gazed through the glass at the meadow beyond their property line. The open land brought comfort to her. It was a habit D.Q. passed on as other family members would ask his reason for staring into the empty land behind Nana's home. D.Q. would smile and simply say, "It brings peace." Shai prayed for it when they returned home from church and now she waited for the feeling of peace to ease her spirit.

The children were down for an afternoon nap which usually followed Sunday service. The family ate as a group at a nearby diner. Leeza and Derek decided they would go to the mall and then keep their promise and visit Tonya. Mitch and Marci said their goodbyes as the group parted in the parking lot.

'Rell walked in the kitchen and recognized her stare immediately. He too followed D.Q.'s ritual. He walked behind her and held her waist. They stood for minutes in silence.

"I just want to know when 'Rell. When will my mother stop her madness? Did you see her body language, her stance? It was as though Derek and I owed her an explanation for our actions. I understand Derek's point now. She's after money and nothing else. I mean the father we knew is gone. Karlton is now a part of our lives and the family. He was her secret. She kept him away from what D.Q. knew was not his family at all. She ruined two men, two good men and a family. I mean, 'Rell what was she thinking? That we would somehow just love her because she holds the title mother? I just want to be left alone about the whole thing."

"Baby you can't let what she does bother you. She's done her best to destroy anything D.Q. lived for."

"That's my point 'Rell. Why? What made her so angry that she decided to ruin him and anything that reminded her of him? Why not just leave him and start her life over? Not that I'm judging your mother but she and D.Q. had you before Derek or I came into the world. She knew he loved your mother. Why would she hold on like that?"

"You know I have that same touch right?"

Shai turned to face her husband. His sexy grin broke through the anger that was building within her.

"Just what does that mean?"

"I can remember a certain person saying she didn't care if we were siblings. She said we could leave the country, no one would know who we were. Something about not being able to live without my love. I guess D.Q. had that effect on women. My mom, your mom, you know?"

"You are so, so cute when you're trying to be funny."

"Come sit with me. Better yet follow me I want to show you something."

'Rell led Shai to his study. The study was a complete office at home, a room she seldom entered. He pulled out his keys and opened the door. The room was totally out of order bringing a frown on her face.

"Rell what went on here? What were you looking for?"

Shai went to the desk that held an array of files in no particular order. Books had been pulled off the shelves and were stacked near the leather couch and chair. The brown executive high back chair that usually sat behind the desk was sitting at the head of the small conference table. The phone was on the couch as though it had been tossed there.

Shai came to the middle of the floor. She visually searched the library that she and 'Rell acquired. Books adorned one wall. The unit stood six feet tall and spanned across the sixteen foot wall. Spaces indicated where the books on the floor were housed. She had never seen the room is such disarray.

'Rell didn't volunteer an excuse. He brought files to the couch and gently tapped the leather upholstery. Shai followed his signal and sat. She was shocked and it was obvious.

"Shai, I'll straighten it all out this week. I don't want anyone to touch anything. That's why I had the door locked."

"That was my next question. I never knew you locked it. Can I ask why it looks this way before you show me whatever…."

"The trial, your mother and Monique."

"Okay, I know they can't be connected." Shai sat back on the couch prepared to hear what her husband was presenting.

"No, you're right they aren't. Although they have all come to haunt us at this time. Mitch and I have gone over a few of these files and Byron went over the financial reports. Your mother is seeking to destroy the business or be a part of it. One way or another she sees it as a win. Well she may think her way in is Derek. The stocks D.Q. sold, stock she held while attached to D.Q. Enterprises, is an investment through Quintech. We moved the stock so it wouldn't be a line item with us. For the last year it has been hidden within the investments owned by Quintech. There's one problem, it may be disclosed at the trial."

"Is the company an investor?"

"No but the profits from the stock held by us was used as an investment for your brother's company."

"So why would my mother gain from that?"

"It's the same stock that she holds. D.Q. didn't sell all of it. There was some left. It has grown over the past five years. We used it and invested the profits in Quintech. If she reviews the records she'll see it. We've done well to hide it since his death but if she looks or has her lawyer look deeper, the spreadsheets will tell."

"Rell, why would that come up at the trial?"

"They're looking at your brother's finances. Money he spent on the company that may have been tied with Carson's Web. He made money from those trademarks."

"Well if he says he gambled it away then what?"

"The question is how much? Where did he hide it? How was Quintech financed?"

"Have they subpoenaed financial records from D.Q. Enterprises?"

"No, but it may come to that. That's what this is. The past records. I found the sale but I haven't found the original purchase. I need to know about the original purchase. If Tonya can't find how much there was originally she'll assume the entire stock was turned over and sold. If she finds out that what she owned profited and bought into Quintech, we've got trouble."

"So are you saying that her stock is still a part of the company?"

"D.Q. didn't sell it all. He gave her part of what she owned and kept the rest. That's what I think happened. It seems that some of it was sold in her name and we still have the rest. I don't have records to show we bought it from her and paid her outright. When Byron was looking over the records for Quintech he found the error."

"So she has stock that tied up in D.Q. Enterprises and Quintech?"

"We sold it to Quintech on the books but it's all one and the same. We used the profits outright to establish Quintech."

"Did you change the name?"

"No, we just found it."

"Will she know?"

"If she or her lawyer shows up at the trial and it's read into evidence as I said. We've got trouble."

"Does Derek know?"

"Not yet."

"So what did you do?"

"What do we normally do?"

Shai picked up the paperwork from the table. She knew the answer. Mr. Simpson was called and they would have to wait for his instructions.

Forty-Two

Derek and Leeza stood at the door waiting for Tonya or Karlton to answer. The weather was threatening rain and the warmth that was evident throughout the day now had a noticeable chill. Derek pushed the bell again just as Karlton opened the garage door.

"Hey, you guys can come through here. Tonya must be upstairs in the bedroom still. I'm sorry, I was in the den playing music."

"Thanks, you remember Leeza right? Leeza, this is Karlton."

"Yes, of course, I remember her. We had many conversations when you were out of it. How are you dear?"

"Fine thank you."

"Wow, looks like bad weather is headed our way. Big change from this afternoon huh? C'mon through, let me tell your mother you guys are here. Derek, you know your way around. C'mon in and have a seat."

Derek led the way through the house to the sitting room. The house had changed a bit since his last visit. Wall colors and accents were changed. There were also a few new pieces of furniture.

"I remember telling my mother I wanted to rearrange her home for her. That was well before the accident or finding out what I know now."

"You have fond memories from your childhood?"

"Leeza, my father, I mean D.Q. would make sure she was showered in gifts. I mean new furniture, clothes, jewelry, trips, you name it. We were just beginning high school when I became aware of the problems they had. I don't know if Shai ever noticed but I did. My mother became bitter toward us and him. I never knew why. I had that accident and woke up to the man who should have been in my life all my life. I don't know what she wants but I can't give it to her."

"We are here to listen. That's what you said. Don't build a wall you may miss what you need to hear."

"Baby you are so right."

Leeza got up from the couch to look at a vase that sat on the end table across the room. She admired the design and picked it up to view it closely.

"Put that down child before you drop it. I'm sure a nursing salary can't replace it. I thought you had decided not to come to Derek. Please put that down!"

Leeza obeyed quickly and froze. It took her a moment to regain herself and return to her seat. Derek stood and beckoned for her to join him. She took her original seat on the couch and moved close to Derek.

"Would you like anything to drink, Leeza, Derek?" Karlton broke the silence with his offer.

"No offer to me dear?"

It was then that Derek knew Tonya had been drinking.

"I left my glass upstairs. Yes Derek, to see you at church with 'Rell and Shai, and walking I needed a drink."

Derek wanted to respond but Leeza squeezed his leg. She kept her hand near his knee. He took a deep sigh but remained silent.

"Leeza, Derek?" Karlton got their attention again.

"Uh, water, please. We don't really drink."

"What do you mean son? Really drink. Is there a prerequisite to drinking? Well not for me. I'll have another honey if you would please."

Karlton left the three hoping Tonya would forget she asked for anything.

"So I guess I'm in the shithouse with your sister again huh?"

"I don't know. We didn't really talk about you."

"What? You want me to believe that Derek?"

"Believe what you want. We talk about a lot more than you."

"So what are your plans? I mean after this bull at the courthouse."

"I plan to go home. I live in Brazil now."

"Oh? Is that so? Leeza, you take him to your home and he loves it so much he claims it as his home now?"

Leeza looked at Derek before answering.

"We've made a home there Ms. Mince. We have set up our own living arrangement there. My family lives near but we will no longer be living with them."

"So you took him away from family to live with your family? Derek, we weren't good enough for you to stay and heal here?"

"I don't know. My mind was racing between what had happened, your lies, Karlton and who he was. It was just too much. I also had Uncle Darryl and the mess we are in and this court case. I was stressed and couldn't focus on living like I should have. I think it was best for me."

"Really? Do you realize what that did to me?"

"No and to be honest… Thank you Karlton…I never gave it any thought."

"What's that Derek?" Karlton asked as he sat across from Derek and Leeza.

"Nothing Karlton. Where's my drink?"

"It is there Tonya, next to you."

Tonya took a drink from her glass which was on the end table next to her chair.

"You know the weaker you make it the more I'll drink right? So the next one should be better right?"

"Derek you were saying. I'm sorry I stopped you." Karlton spoke ignoring Tonya's rant.

"I was saying I didn't know what affect my leaving would have on my mother. You didn't give a damn what was going on. Whatever would help me you were against, so why be upset when I left?"

"What are you talking about?" Tonya leaned forward and then sat back reaching for her glass again.

"Leeza was my nurse and worked with the therapist. Believe me, I've been told some of your comments. Shai called me upset about the fight between the two of you. I wasn't dead Mama. Paralyzed but not dead."

"That was panic boy. I was worried if you would ever walk again, have children, you know. Can you even have children? After all, you were near death. I was trying to be strong."

Karlton's eyes met Derek's. There was an inaudible agreement that Derek wouldn't respond to his mother's comment.

"So you called this meeting. We're here. What is it?"

"We can't just have a visit?"

"No. I didn't come for just a visit. You said you had something to tell me."

"That so-called brother of yours is pulling a fast one. Yes, don't look surprised." Tonya paused hoping Derek would show some interest. "He's pulling it on you and me. He married that damn sister of yours. You do know that she's the only one that will make out. You do realize that, don't you? She gets it all. That's why she doesn't care about me or you."

"I'm not here to debate with you if that's what you're looking for. I am not on your side and what Shai has gained, I hope, is peace. She's found love and I have too. Karlton is here with you and has been here for you. That should be enough yet you're still reaching. What exactly are you talking about?"

"My stocks. I need the original paperwork to prove that D.Q. kept my stocks. That enterprise he gave to 'Rell has my stocks wrapped up in it somehow. I own part of that company, I know I do. When he sold the stock and presented the paperwork at our separation it wasn't complete.

I've called the company that bought that stock and they could only confirm what was sold to them. They said they were the holding company for what I owned. I'm telling you and Karlton, there was more."

"So you're saying you owned more shares?"

"You damn right I did."

"Okay, so have your lawyer search the records. That's simple, have Robert or Alan check the books."

"Funny, they don't have access to the books. Mitch and Byron do. Why would that ass change their titles if he wasn't hiding anything?"

"Who, 'Rell? C'mon remember that stock was sold years before D.Q. died. Robert would know what was up. Mr. Simpson would know. Get your lawyer to find out. I don't care one way or the other. It has nothing to do with Quintech. Why tell me?"

"Well, we know your company is built on stolen money. It could be my money. I could own part of your damn company."

"Tonya! Stop it. I thought you wanted Derek to come by and talk not be insulted."

"He's covering for that ass-hole he calls his new brother. I know he is."

"You've had too much as usual. Karlton, thanks man we're going to leave this right here with you. You're a good man. Thanks for all you do. I know it's got to be near impossible."

Derek stood and helped Leeza to her feet.

"Oh, you done talking to me cause' I told you your company is built on false promises?"

"Mama please don't embarrass yourself or for that matter who you should be. Listen if you find out any legitimate grounds for concern call me. Karlton, you call me. If I need to talk to anyone about what you find, we'll handle it then. That good enough for you lady?"

"You and your sister will burn for this. You ain't so high and mighty that you won't fall too. Just like D.Q.'s ass. Karlton's your damn daddy and you ain't got an ounce of me or him in you."

Derek stopped at the door before Karlton opened it.

"Tonya, you've never been a mother and you stripped Karlton of the opportunity of being my father. D.Q. raised me, taught me and was there for me. If I am anything I am it's because of the man he was. You prove yourself holding a glass of poison. You wouldn't drown yourself in it if you didn't miss the man D.Q. was to you. Enjoy the rest of your evening. Karlton, I'm sorry. I'll see you before we leave I'm sure. Just not here man."

"I understand. Listen it's raining. Y'all be careful.

The couple exited the house and Karlton stood at the closed door looking at Tonya who was at the bar pouring another drink.

"Tonya, put the damn glass down!"

Forty-Three

Bryce and Brianna were bathed and ready for bed. They entered the study to say good-night to their father. 'Rell loved the moments they shared as a family. The evenings just after dinner, baths and bedtime stories belonged to the family. 'Rell followed the twins to their room where Shai was waiting patiently.

'Rell could see the fatigue in her face as she gave him a fragment of a smile. Bryce and Brianna chose a Dr. Seuss book, one of their favorites, and raced to their beds. Their parents agreed, they were still too young, to have separate rooms. At their age, they shared the same interests and were learning quickly how to share and understand their emotions.

"Okay, tell me what or who are we reading about tonight?"

Shai sat in the recliner and allowed 'Rell to give the animated version of the "Cat in the Hat". The mischievous character that 'Rell seemed to love the most. The children laughed and squealed as their mother watched. 'Rell told Shai that it was what he remembered most about D.Q. and his mother during his younger years. D.Q. would read to him just as he read to Shai and Derek whenever he was home with them.

Shai learned shortly after D.Q's death that he wasn't her father but she loved him for he was the only father she knew. Watching 'Rell she saw their father. The father that kissed her and tucked her in whenever he was home and not away on 'business trips'. Now she knew 'Rell and his mother Nikki were his "business". She appreciated D.Q. more and she loved her husband.

The story ended and the twins were tucked in for the night. 'Rell tapped Shai lightly as she had fallen asleep in the chair.

"C'mon Mama, kiss the babies."

Shai kissed her babies and followed him to their bedroom where she entered the bathroom. She turned on the water and called out to her husband.

"I was trying to stay with you Mister Cat. The children love your acting you know."

"You mean my bad acting. As many times as I read Dr. Seuss, I change every time and your son calls me on it."

"Really?"

'Rell stood at the bathroom door. "Yes, that's what takes so long. Repeating it and trying to get the acting exactly the same as before. Bryce is a critic. Good thing I'm not trying to get an award for acting or something."

"Will you join me?"

"A shower? Together? How can I refuse you, my dear?"

Shai led 'Rell into the master bath. 'Rell followed her stimulating walk to the shower door. She began to disrobe and he again shadowed her lead. They stepped in the shower and the heated water brought them together as they moved away from the showerhead.

'Rell adjusted the water as they eased under the showerhead and embraced each other. The water hitting his body raised his nature and Shai's nipples hardened as he kissed each of her breasts. She allowed him to explore her as he had done often. A pleasure neither of them would deny eased their nights and kept their romance alive.

Sponges became a part of their foreplay as they gently bathed the others back. 'Rell reached around Shai's waist and rubbed her stomach in a circular motion. As his hands caressed her hips and thighs, he moved her closer to him. He kissed her neck as he began to massage her inner thighs. He bathed her legs slowly and turned her to face him. He started from her neck and followed the path that led him to a familiar place. He deliberately teased her touching her buttocks softly and kissing her lips.

Shai took her sponge and rubbed 'Rell's chest. His abs were her next target as she squeezed the soap down the front of his sculpted body. His chocolate thighs and manhood gave her a chill as she fondled him with both hands. She gently turned his body and leaned into his back. Her nipples were still aroused as she pressed harder allowing herself to rub against his buttocks.

'Rell turned and held her face in his hands. They kissed passionately. He reached behind her and cut off the water. The wet steamy foreplay was a prelude to what they both knew would be another beautiful sexual encounter.

They wrapped each other in oversized matching bath towels. Their bed became their next erotic playground. Shai giggled as she plopped onto the bed allowing the towel to fall under her. 'Rell dropped his towel as he walked toward her.

Her libido was on the rise, a rise only 'Rell was able to satisfy. He began at her feet and kissed her slowly from her ankle to her inner thigh. As he kissed her thighs she opened her legs waiting for him to explore her at will. 'Rell used his tongue to tease her thighs as she anticipated him touching her erect clitoris.

'Rell pleased her. She thanked him with her juices and her moans for more. He took his time. It was his way, his way to be sure she would be satisfied each time he made love to her. He entered her slowly waiting to feel the heartbeat of her love for him between her legs.

She responded, "Deeper, ah oh yes. Deeper."

'Rell began his quest. The warmth caused him to speed up the pace as Shai wrapped her legs around him. The tighter she held him the harder he got. He moved methodically holding her butt up to meet his hardened rod. The juices between them were hot and 'Rell couldn't stop the flow that was mounting. He gave her all he had as they moaned together in ecstasy.

Shai moved her body back and forth quickly as she felt his manhood rising again. Once again he kept the pace until their expectations were filled with heat and passion. 'Rell rolled off his wife to his side of the bed.

"Shit, I'll meet you in the shower." They both laughed.

"Rell, we didn't finish our talk."

"What talk baby?"

"You said, my mother, the trial and Monique."

"Oh, girl in the morning babe. I like the way I feel right now. Please, in the morning. I promise I'll tell you everything in the morning."

Shai looked at 'Rell knowing he'd wait for her to come out of the bathroom. He would talk then. They often talked after making love. She left him on the bed and when she returned he was snoring. Their conversation would have to wait until the morning.

Forty-Four

Monique checked her phone for the awaited text message. There was none. It was Monday morning and Craig hadn't called since he stormed out her door on Saturday. She refused to call him before Monday arrived. She was sure the bait she dangled was enough for him to think twice about backing out of her plan.

Craig often spoke of the dream he shared with 'Rell and the others. They would finish college and work in a company where they would hold the top level positions. 'Rell provided that for all of them accept Keith and Craig.

Monique had done thorough checks regarding Keith. She didn't quite understand why he didn't accept 'Rell's offer. She hoped Craig was the only one that hadn't been offered a position. It would make it easier for her to portray Craig as the sole example of 'Rell's jealousy, and revenge.

Keith and Craig were as close as 'Rell and Mitchell. Byron joined them during their sophomore year of college. She had to admit she craved friendships that were that strong. She blamed 'Rell for that loss as well.

Her co-workers admired her work ethics, loved her choice in fashions, but rarely invited her to join them for lunch or any events outside of the office. Those she dealt with in college either moved on, were married or she thought they were jealous of her relationship with 'Rell. She prided herself in flaunting the anticipated success of her then-boyfriend, the young prospective accountant. They dated throughout their college years. They alternated weekend visits when 'Rell began his job in Maryland.

She waited for 'Rell to tell her he was leaving Maryland and seeking a permanent place for them to start their life in Virginia. She bragged about D.Q. Enterprises and emphasized one day it would be 'Rell's business. After his father's death, she took it a step further and researched the company and D.Q.'s assets.Mitchell and the others were offered jobs together. Monique knew it was D.Q. that put that in place. 'Rell gave them a seat at the conference table at the lucrative business he now owned. There were empty seats between D.Q. Enterprises and Quintech Designs. Head Hunters provided that information. She felt Craig deserved one of the positions before he fell from 'Rell's grace.

'Rell was an emotional man, one who cared what others thought of him. Her announcement of his abandoning her because of an unborn child would shatter his relationship with Shai and maybe his marriage. His grandmother and mother would drill him about what was the right thing to do. They would want to protect his image. His lawyer would tell him to settle with Monique to silence her. Craig would have a new position and she would be compensated financially for the embarrassment he caused.

Monique should have been the bride and proud mother of his children. The home should have been built with her in mind. She saw her future fade when the gynecologist said again, she was not pregnant.

Craig had failed her. She needed to be pregnant when 'Rell and Shai were dating. Her last attempt would have been easy to prove. She was seeing 'Rell and Craig during that time. The next visit shattered her dreams. 'Rell came home to announce there were two deaths, his father's and their relationship.

She knew there had been others. None like Dershai' Mince or whoever she really was. Everyone was in the dark about them dating. 'Rell was pretending to be the doting brother. Monique didn't believe it. He was to be the uncle to her unborn twins. The pretense lasted until D.Q.'s papers proved that Shai and Derek were not Mince children. Karlton Harris was their father. There no longer was a need to cover the love he had for Shai.

That bit of information found its way to the newspaper. Monique was sure it was the same reporter that was at their wedding. Once her plan was in place Monique would contact the reporter to announce Darrell Mince was the father of her unborn child. The loss was due to an emotionally stressed pregnancy. Her story was set. Monique took off time from her job that would coincide with her fabricated lies. She had steered instances that would be recalled and it left no proof she was lying. Craig was causing problems.

The timing was everything and the court proceeding would distract 'Rell. She planned on being in the courtroom with Craig to razzle the Mince family. Now she'd have to give in and call him. She needed to know if he was still upset.

She dialed the number and just as she was about to disconnect the call, Craig answered.

"Good morning." He snapped.

"Wow, you still pouting?"

"What's up? You're up early."

Monique looked at the phone. Craig's question confused her. *He's pretending. I know he's not okay with this call.*

"Ok, you're flipping back and forth early today, huh?"

"Monique, what do you want? I need to get dressed. I really don't have time to chit chat."

"So where are we with all of this Craig?"

"We? We? I'm good sweetie, there is no we."

"Oh, so you taking this on by yourself? You know damn well Mr. Mince ain't feeling you."

"I'm not looking for him to feel me. You seem to forget 'Rell and I are friends. You didn't change that. I'm here for Derek as is everyone else. That's it, I'm not taking on anything."

"Oh, so no need for me to mention your need for that position huh?"

"Right. No need for you to mention me at all. Do you sweetie, that's what you do best."

"What the hell does that mean?"

"Look I gotta go. You got a plan, go with it. Don't include me in it. If you do, I'll tell 'Rell the truth."

"What truth? You don't know the truth. Shit, you only know what I told your dumb ass."

"Girl you gonna get enough of rolling the dice. You gambling with the wrong people."

Who? You? 'Rell? Craig, you don't know! I get what I want one way or another."

"Yeah and that's why I'm done with your selfish ass. You want, you want …you want 'Rell. It ain't happening. He's married and lucky for him, he didn't marry your gold diggin' ass."

"What the hell….hello, hello?"

Monique held the phone until the dial tone confirmed Craig had hung up. She looked at the clock. It was almost eight thirty. She'd carry out the plans without Craig. D.Q. Enterprises opened at nine. Leaving a message at the office wouldn't do, she'd have a discussion with 'Rell's secretary in person. Mr. Mince would be at court and his employees would remember her name.

Forty-Five

"Shai, what time are you going in today?"

'Rell stood at the foot of the stairs waiting for her answer. He took on preparing the morning breakfast for the family while Shai got the twins ready for daycare.

The twins could be heard racing for the stairs as their mother yelled, "Careful, you'll fall."

"Morning monsters, what's up? You look like you're going somewhere?"

"School", they chimed as they dashed pass their father to the table.

It was the morning ritual. It changed whenever 'Rell or Shai decided to stay home. Shai followed the two down the stairs at a slower pace. She kissed her husband giving him a side eye.

"What didn't I do? They have their breakfast, your juice and breakfast is on the island. I have to call my mother before I leave."

"What was up with Craig and Monique? You fell asleep and I couldn't nag you about it."

"Wise man that I am." 'Rell teased. "Follow me into the dining room please."

Shai looked back at Bryce and Brianna who were deep into their own conversation. She decided she'd remain in the arched doorway to keep an eye on them.

"Craig came over Saturday."

"He came to Mitch's house?"

"Yes, he and Keith are here. I knew Keith was coming. I was surprised about Craig. Oh, and Uncle Darryl did show up."

"Okay, he talked about you hiring him again?"

"No, but I think with all that's going on we should fill the two seats at Quintech with people we know."

"Rell I thought the saying was know and trust. Can you trust Craig?"

"He isn't a bad guy. It's Monique, she's bad news and she used him. Our friendship held strong. He told me about her plan. She thinks portraying me as a deserter will ruin me personally as well as professionally. She told him he'd get a position with me and she'd be paid. You, my dear, would leave me. I'd be ruined. I guess she would offer me comfort when my world collapsed."

"Really. How is she going to prove this pregnancy or miscarriage?"

"I didn't ask. He did and she told him he didn't need to know. Shai, Craig thinks it may have been his child. So when she didn't tell him anything that made sense he left her. He's staying with Keith, I think. He was in a hotel downtown. She messed up. Craig was the only one on her side. So we'll see."

"So are you going to confront her with this mess?"

"No my pretty and neither are you. Let her make her move and then we'll ask for proof. Hey, you've got medical connections now, can you find out from your girl if she gave birth or whatever?"

"Maybe, I don't know. You know there's a confidentiality clause. Marci has the same GYN maybe we can just be curious about births the same year as the twins. I don't know, I'll see what we can dig up."

"Let me know. Maybe Mr. Simpson can make that call."

"Yeah, so what's up with the court? Are you going there today?"

"Got a staff meeting this morning. Keith is starting this week and Craig will be deciding over the next few days. Then we'll all go to court together."

"What is Derek and Uncle saying about the new additions to their staff?"

"They're okay with it. Uncle Darryl actually welcomed them on. Derek is definitely going back to Brazil. But Shai, we don't know yet how this case will be decided. It's a mess that can rattle Derek and the gambling can cause some other problems."

"So it wasn't paid in full? I thought Uncle Darryl handled it."

"Shai I don't know what he handled. We just have to be sure the business is secure. So Keith and Craig will make sure of that."

"Mommy, we done." Brianna sang from the kitchen.

"Go ahead, babe. I'm gonna call my mother from the car. She's been hanging out all weekend with the Deacon. I have to let her know she's not grown."

"I'm on the ten to six shift this week so I'll be dropping them off and hanging with Leeza most of the morning."

"She didn't go to court with Derek."

"Nope. He told her to stay out of that drama. Hey, I understand. It's enough that he has to worry about the case but not knowing who's in the audience is a problem too."

"You're right, love. You stay away from there too."

"Mommy!!"

'Rell kissed Shai and yelled his goodbyes to the children.

The morning forecast was rain but there was no mention of the downpour that 'Rell experienced as he drove to the office. The sudden change in the weather immediately slowed the anticipated traffic. 'Rell decided to use the delay to his advantage.

He dialed his lawyer's number hoping the morning muddle wasn't the sign of a hectic day.

"Rell, good morning. I expected a call from you earlier."

Mr. Simpson always gave 'Rell the impression that he knew more than he led one to believe.

"Morning chaos as usual. Are you close to the court?"

"Leaving the office in a few. Appearance is at ten as you know. This judge is known to be late so I expect we will start later than that. What's on your mind young man?"

Over the years 'Rell had come to know Stanley Simpson better than he knew any of the other employees that stayed with the company. He had been a confidant, more than the company lawyer. D.Q. trusted him with everything pertaining to the business and his personal life. 'Rell learned to rely on his expertise and wisdom.

"Monique and Tonya."

"Yes, they will present a problem. I've been in touch with Byron and your uncle regarding the stocks. We're ready for any request from her lawyers. Everything has been recorded and checked for both companies."

"And the company my dad sold her stock to?"

"They don't have any information about the sale. They only know what she owns currently. It's no problem. The stock was split and she got her share. The paperwork that was prepared when your father separated from her is clear. No need to worry. The stock that Quintech owns is not with the same company and shows no ties with Tonya's stocks."

"Okay great. You know about Monique. I sent you an email trying to explain her intent. Shai and I were talking and thought maybe we need to research her accusation. Was she pregnant at all? That's the question we have. Maybe as a lawyer, you could…

"No problem." Simpson cut him off before he could finish his thought. "You mentioned the GYN was the same doctor that handled Shai?"

"Yes. She said she was there when we went in to talk to the doctor. Supposedly that's when she found out she was pregnant."

"Okay, that's enough to go on. We'll make some calls. Now, Mr. Mince, I think we spoke about Craig Masters before."

"Yes, we did. Keith and Craig will possibly be starting at Quintech as we discussed."

"Rell, Keith is not the issue but Craig…."

"Simpson, I know, keep an eye on him."

"As you request. I will let Kenny and the team know."

"Kenny will be at the meeting this morning and I'll be talking to him separately. Do we know anything else about the people who tried to kill Derek?"

"We've got a few things that are being checked. Kenny is heading that as well. He'll brief you this morning with what we have. I'll have him get two men for Craig."

"Mr. Simpson, I'll see you in court."

"Yes, until then, young man."

Forty-Six

Simone woke up to an empty home. Darryl left for court without her as he said he would. She told him she'd sit with him to show her support. Without giving a good reason he told her it wasn't where she should be. She spent the early hours trying not to cry. Again, she was left to her own conclusions about their relationship and it seemed Darryl didn't care.

Nikki wouldn't understand her frustration, nor would Simone give her cousin the opportunity to say, "I told you so." She decided she'd simply go to Nikki's house and not mention the dilemma between her and Darryl. She picked up her briefcase and checked to be sure she had the folders containing their upcoming projects. She grabbed her laptop and looked for her car keys. Her phone rang and vibrated as she was leaving. It was Darryl, she let it ring. She went into the bedroom and found her keys laying on the bed. The phone vibrated again in her jeans pocket.

"Yes."

"Traffic is bad babe, be careful. Are you going to Nikki's?"

"I'm leaving now. It's a regular work day. So you drive careful too, I'll talk to you later."

"Wait, Simone. I need to tell you something. I didn't want you to worry or try to convince me not to come to court. I have to be here for

Derek, I know you understand that. There may be others, and you know what I mean, in the courtroom. I don't want them to know who you are to me. I can't worry about them trying to get back at me through you. You do understand, don't you?"

"Darryl, if they are watching you they know me. They know where you live, where you work and they know I am here. They know that we are together. So now I'm alone? Damn Darryl!"

"They'll be here. I'm sure of it. It's us first, me and Derek. We still owe money and that's what they want more than anything else."

"How much Darryl? How much more?"

"A few thousand."

"A few thousand? How much Darryl?"

"Sixty, sixty thousand. They want it by the end of the trial."

"You've been in touch with them?"

"Simone please. Just know that I'm handling it."

"Sixty thousand? How did it get to be that much?"

"I tried to get it back and I failed. It's on me. They know Derek is not a part of this. It's me."

"So now you're the target?"

"Not yet. I gotta go. I need to find parking. Listen, I love you and I'm going to get us out of this mess. I love you."

Simone didn't have anything to say. She was in shock as she listened to Darryl confess he put himself in harm's way. She took a seat on the couch. Tears fell from her eyes. There was a moment of fear that she had to let go before she drove to her cousin's home.

An hour passed before Simone attempted to get in her car and drive to Nikki's. She stopped to pick up coffee. Nikki's favorite, hazelnut, had become an addiction for her as well. She went through the drive-thru in a fog. Her thoughts drifted from the danger she and Darryl were facing to the money that was owed.

She entered Nikki's home using her key.

Simone yelled from the lower level. "I've got the coffee. Do you need help?"

"No, I'm just bringing down the drawings that we went over. I thought you were going to court with Darryl." Nikki carefully descended the stairs leading to the living room with a large portfolio.

"Girl, have you been rearranging things in here?"

"No just made some space for us to work in. I've got a carpenter and painter coming in this week to turn the garage and the extra room into a work area for us. I thought about what you said. I don't use that room as much as I did before. We can use this space here without paying for a studio. Darryl said he'd get someone to check the specs and these are the drawings we went over."

Nikki opened the portfolio. The penciled drawings took up a good portion of the space provided once they spread the pages out. She grabbed the coffee and noticed Simone hadn't moved.

"Hey, are you okay?"

"Uh, yeah. Let me go to the bathroom. Hang on a minute."

Simone returned after she freshened up. She hoped Nikki wouldn't notice the quick change in her behavior.

"It seems you're re-doing the entire first floor. Are you decorating the top and bottom levels too?"

"Just changing a few things, nothing much. Giving it a different look. I'm leaving that man cave thing on the lower level alone. Whenever 'Rell comes over with Mitch and the guys they hang out there. That's really just the entrance to the patio and pool, girl I ain't got time for re-doing that area. I have to give the upstairs a thought or two."

"So show me what you guys came up with."

"First tell me why you aren't in court. You pleaded your reasons to be there pretty strong on Friday."

"Darryl had thoughts against it. Nothing else to be said. I respected his opinion and now I'm here."

"And obviously shook. What's up?"

Nikki asked questions until her cousin opened up. Nikki eased her mind but not her fears. She let Simone know that 'Rell and Mr. Simpson were aware of the debt. She didn't know what else to say once Simone began to cry. So they sat on the floor drinking coffee and allowing the silence to control their thoughts.

"How's Sam?"

"We had a great weekend. I told him I'd call him around lunch to see if he made it to work. Simone, he's so different than what he appears to be. I mean my thoughts of a deacon, well I was wrong."

"So y'all sinning for real, for real?"

"Girl from my lips to God's ears only. We have had time to talk, get to know each other on another level. I mean he's been married and he's had a loss after the death of his wife. I, of course, have not been married, but I lost D.Q. He understands that kind of love. I appreciate that."

"So with that said, you sinning for real?"

"Can you tell?"

"Well don't go to church with that look on your face. I'm happy for you. Do you think there's a future between you two?"

"I don't know. Day by day, I'm not going to think about anything else."

"So you are sinning for real!"

Forty-Seven

'Rell gathered his notes as he waited in his office for the conference room to fill with the staff. The top-level staff were called and told to report to the mandatory meeting over the weekend. The regular monthly meeting would be in two weeks, so it was strange not to get a text or e-mail for the impromptu gathering of the minds. Ms. Berry, 'Rell's secretary would sit in and take notes. Kenny, who headed the security team was to be there as well. The buzz in the conference room increased as those who normally didn't attend meetings took a seat at the table.

Breakfast crepes, croissants, and fruit were on platters in the four corners of the room. Coffee, tea, juice, and water were the beverages available. 'Rell appreciated his staff and showed them what they meant to the business immediately when he became the owner of his father's empire. There were whispers when he first took over. There was a new silence when the rumors and gossip were dispelled regarding the young CEO. 'Rell followed the advice of the employees who matured with D.Q. Enterprises and his father's directives. Mr. Simpson warned him of a few and 'Rell fired a few. His expectation was loyalty, the same loyalty that had been an integral part of the company when his father was in charge.

'Rell's office door opened without a knock or phone announcement. As he turned from the large window that was behind his desk overlooking the city's busy streets, he saw the look of anger on Mitch's face.

"What's up?" 'Rell looked at his watch. It wasn't quite nine o'clock.

"Kenny is not going to be in the lobby? You pulled him for the meeting. Who's standing in his place?"

"Man, whoever Kenny puts in place will be fine. The trial starts at ten. This meeting is short and sweet. There's no need for questions. It is, what it is man. Those who don't conform to what I tell them this morning can turn in their ID."

"Okay, well, a call got bounced to me this morning by mistake. It was for Robert. It was Tonya Mince."

"Let it play out. She's picking him. After this meeting, I'm sure he'll tell her he can't give her any information. After all, he no longer handles current records, you do."

"I think there's more to it."

"What more? What else could it be Mitch?"

Mitch didn't answer causing 'Rell's eyebrows to raise.

"Man get the hell out of here. Rob and Tonya? Nah man, I can't believe that. Where'd you get that mess from? Let me find out you spying on the breakroom, getting the gossip."

"His partner told me. Alan thought something was up with them and brought his concerns to me. I didn't think much about it, but I did express your problem with it."

"I don't have a problem with who he deals with. Mitch that's not what the problem is. There's no reason for any of our business information to get to the media or any other source. Our information is to stay in house. Especially with this trial going on. If there's a leak people will be fired."

"Got you. So I'll check with Kenny. You ready boss?"

"Stop your shit man. You just as much a boss as I am. Are Craig and Keith here?"

"Yeah, I think everyone is here accept your brother and uncle. Oh will Ms. Berry be able to give us a copy of the minutes or are we waiting for the monthly report?"

"I'll have her prepare these separate. Go ahead I'm right behind you. I want to be sure someone's sitting in for her at her desk."

Mitch and 'Rell exited the office in separated directions. 'Rell walked into the main office to find Tonya sitting in the reception area.

"Well don't you clean up well for a Monday morning? I thought you'd be holding Derek's hand since his sister and girlfriend bowed out."

Tonya spoke from her seat. It was obvious from her dress she wanted most to know she was there for business. 'Rell's curiosity caused him to question her intent. He kept the thought to himself.

"Good morning Ms. Mince. How are you? Looks like I'm not the only one that cleans up well. I love that color on you."

"Rell you remind me of your father, full of shit." She winked not speaking loud enough for the receptionist to hear her.

She stood to give him a full view of her soft lavender classic dress and jacket. The embellished satin trim added to the simplicity of the design. She picked up her matching crocheted wrap and purse hoping to follow him to his office.

"Excuse me a moment." 'Rell walked over to the receptionist. "Can you have Mr. Franklin paged. I believe Ms. Mince is here to see him. I'm headed to the conference room, hold my calls. Ms. Berry will handle them when she returns from the meeting."

Tonya watched as he spoke. His demeanor and tone reminded her of the days when D.Q. would give directions to his secretary whenever she visited the office. 'Rell returned to where she stood with a smile.

"Robert will be right with you. We are having a brief meeting and as you know I will be leaving for court afterward. As usual, if you should need anything that Robert can't handle, call Mitchell and he'll be sure to assist you."

"Rell, you have a way of avoiding me. You aren't scared I'll find out your secret are you?"

"Now what secret would that be?"

"We all have our secrets you know?"

"Yes, my father kept them a lifetime. I don't intend on making the same mistake. If you haven't caught on, I'm more an in your face kinda guy. Oh, here's Robert, I've got to make this meeting."

Robert greeted 'Rell at the door. 'Rell pointed to Tonya and his words though inaudible to Tonya and the receptionist, it was obvious that Robert was not to spend too much time with her.

"Tonya now is not a good time. There's a management staff meeting that I have to get to. Can I meet you somewhere for lunch, after lunch, early dinner?"

"Robert, don't sound so desperate. I've got some information I need to share with you. Maybe it can clear up the mixed data I have about the stocks. I've got another stop I can make. I'm going to talk with Mr. Monroe sometime today, but we can meet around five. How's that sweetie?"

Tonya got closer to him hoping to increase his interest. Robert agreed, waved at the receptionist and escorted Tonya to the elevator. The meeting was just beginning when he tipped into the conference room and returned to his seat.

"There's a few things of importance that I want each of you to understand. This is not a new business however we've become a parent company to Quintech Designs. It is imperative at this time that no company information is released to any source that is not approved by top management. Any communications that may entail more than sales, schedules, or ongoing projects will be addressed by Mr. Keith Larson and Mr. Craig Masters. They will be handling all communications and approvals of all projects. This includes financial payments and receipts as well as quotes. Byron will continue to handle the reports."

'Rell looked around the room for any sign of discord before he continued.

"Darryl and Derek Mince are not to be contacted until further notice. I'm sure there's been talk, gossip, and rumors about the trial they are involved in. None of us know the length of the proceedings nor will we be disclosing information as it goes on. Please do not let this be a part of the breakroom gossip. We'll tell you what you need to know. It does not affect your employment unless you are one to spread the gossip. Also as you know, Tonya Mince has recuperated. She is seeking to find information on stocks she once held. I believe Alan Scott and Robert Franklin have been assisting her. If they can't provide her with the information Mitchell Carter will. If anyone is giving her any information without approval from them you will be fired. If anyone is providing any other business information to Tonya Mince, they too will be fired. Alright, unfortunately at this time I can't take questions but you know my door is open and I answer calls and emails."

"Thank you for the work you do people," Mitchell spoke as he did at the end of each meeting. "Robert, Alan, and Kenny we need to talk to you guys. Keith and Craig stand by."

'Rell watched his staff as they exited the conference room. He wondered if his father would have handled things differently. When he started at D.Q. Enterprises he doubted himself. Now that he proved he had been trained by D.Q. and could fill his shoes, he hoped he didn't sound too shrewd.

"Kenny, good morning man. Mr. Simpson said he spoke with you about Tonya. She was here this morning. Give us a call when she shows up."

Kenny, a plain-clothed officer, smiled and shook his head. "What's up? Did I say something wrong?"

"Man, your dad said the same thing before he started working from home. She has never been able to just show up. My guys called this morning and Mr. Franklin cleared it."

"See man I told you. Robert Franklin knew she was here."

"No Mitch, what I mean is he cleared her when he came in. We had the clearance before she got here."

"Rell man he's a problem."

"Let it play out Mitch. He'll go and so will she. Listen, tell Robert and Alan they can go to their office. Let's see where the loyalty lies."

'Rell waited until the room was cleared to continue his conversation with Kenny. He introduced him to Craig and Keith without telling either of them Kenny's real job. They knew as did everyone else that he was the head of the security team. Securing the Mince family had been his job for years. 'Rell promoted him to the head of the team. He respected his mannerism and his discretion.

"Rell man I'll meet you at the car. I've got to stop at my office." Mitch left with Keith and Craig following him. Byron told them he'd meet them at the court.

"Kenny, one more thing, my uncle and Derek."

"Mr. Simpson mentioned what you needed. I'll be floating in and out of the courtroom. I've got some feelers out. If the trial lasts longer than a week I'm sure we'll catch wind of who tried to kill your brother."

"And if it doesn't last longer?" 'Rell waited to be disappointed.

"Rell we started looking when your brother landed. We've got some people checking out a few things. They'll be alright."

"Thanks man."

The two shook hands and promised to talk later. 'Rell returned to his office.

Forty-Eight

Monique pulled into the parking lot at eleven. Later than she expected but making sure 'Rell was out of the building was her intention. She called ahead and found out he was there at nine. She waited until the secretary informed her he would be out of the office and she wasn't sure he would return. It would mean a later arrival but the stage was perfectly set.

She parked her Avalon in the staff parking lot and made her way to the entrance. Monique rolled her eyes as she opened the glass door with D.Q. Enterprises stenciled in gold. Preparing to give everyone an attitude she approached the security podium.

There were seats in the lobby, a small café' and signs for the restrooms. Monique looked around slowly. She was impressed with the décor as well as the presence of the man who watched her as she approached him. He was what she would describe as a "fine specimen of a man". He was well groomed and in a suit, not a uniform.

"Good morning, may I help you?"

"I certainly hope so," Monique answered using a soft sweet tone. "I'm so glad you didn't say, ma'am."

"Excuse me," Kenny replied.

"You know most use 'ma'am' when they address females they don't know."

"I see. Well what can I do for you this morning?"

"I need to speak with Mr. Darrell Mince. Is his office in this building? I noticed there are two other buildings in this complex."

"You're in the right building, however, Mr. Mince is currently unavailable."

"So do I talk with his secretary about my reason for stopping by? I'm sure I don't leave the message with you."

"Was Mr. Mince expecting you?"

"What is your position? I don't think you should be asking these questions?"

"Just doing my job. If you made an appointment Ms. Berry would be more than happy to assist you. Without an appointment, this is the procedure."

Monique turned to look for the elevators. There were no signs directing one to them and no one else to ask.

"I noticed you parked in the staff parking lot. However, this is not the entrance for staff. Just an assumption, you're not here for an interview, nor are you staff. What can I do for you Ms…?"

"Davis, Monique Davis. I need to talk to Mr. Mince or Ms. Berry if I can without an interrogation." Monique snapped.

Kenny picked up the phone on the wall next to him. While he made the call Monique walked to the café which was further down the hall. She went in and bought mints as a cover. She returned to the lobby slowly still looking for the elevators.

Kenny was writing her name on a visitors pass. He handed it to her without a word.

"Follow me, please. Keep the tag visible. If security can't see the tag they will escort you off any of the floors."

Monique's thoughts caused her to smile. "What is Mr. Mince protecting? Is the vault in this building?"

"No ma'am, this way."

As they walked the lobby hall in the opposite direction of the café, they approached another set of doors. Kenny scanned his ID on the wall mount and the doors opened to the six elevators.

"The elevator on the end goes straight to Mr. Mince's office. Ms Berry will take care of you there."

Monique waited for the elevator and expected she would see staff or someone on the way to the twelfth floor. The elevator door open to plush carpet and glass doors. The doors were stenciled again with D.Q. Enterprises, CEO Darrell Mince. There was a door to her left and to her right, but no staff was walking through. Monique wondered if she would benefit from telling the only person she would see, Ms. Berry. She found out quickly that Yvonne Berry's desk was behind yet another door. A receptionist met Monique at the glass door entrance.

"Good morning Ms. Davis. I understand you are here to see Mr. Mince. Ms. Berry will be available in a moment, won't you please have a seat."

Monique sat down. She looked around the office. It was obvious that the company spent their corporate dollars well. The reception area was welcoming, not like most offices. The chairs were comfortable plush seats with a matching leather couch. It reminded her of sitting in someone's home. There were end tables and lamps which added soft lighting to the area. There were no magazine racks, but there were two bookcases containing novels. Magazines and newspapers were on the top of each of them. The wall décor held canvas paintings and wall sconces. The colors weren't dark and the air held a pleasant scent.

The receptionist sat at a beautiful mahogany desk quite a difference from the metal framed desk one would expect in a reception area. There were video screens on the wall near the desk. Monique could see Kenny, the café, the parking lot and other areas of the building. She watched the screens as they changed to other buildings in the complex. There was also a forty-eight-inch television mounted on the wall across from the desk.

"Excuse me, what are the latest projects D.Q. Enterprises are involved with, I mean are they doing any new projects in the community?"

The receptionist paused from the paperwork she was shuffling through and pointed to the bookcase.

"There's information about the company in the magazine on the bookcase. It has everything about the company, new endeavors as well as future projects. There's also a Community Viewer newspaper there. That's actually done by our staff here so you may find that interesting as well. I'm sorry your wait is longer than expected. I'm sure Ms. Berry will be out in a moment."

Monique was pleased the receptionist was friendly. She got up and pretended to be reviewing the magazines and papers. Carrying both she walked over to the receptionist.

"Have you been here long?"

"About four years now."

"I see. So you don't know Mr. Mince's father."

"No, I started working here after the son became the CEO."

"I see. Wow, you missed all of the drama he went through becoming the man you know as a boss, huh?"

"Well, I guess. We don't get involved in the personal stuff here."

"That's good. It gives everyone a good environment to work in. But then there's the lies and secrets that no one knows about."

The receptionist didn't respond, Monique waited for her reply.

"Well, you know every job has its own gossip. Mr. Mince warns against it and it works. I don't know if everyone gets along outside of this building but its peace within these walls. I can guarantee you that."

Monique leaned over the desk and whispered. "I'm here to disturb the peace. Please let Ms. Berry know she will be a part of the disturbance if her ass doesn't come out here now."

Forty-Nine

Those who sat behind the prosecutor and plaintiff's table wore suits and ties. It was clear they worked for Carson's Web in some capacity. Darryl sat directly behind Derek and Mr. Simpson. The three talked quietly waiting for the proceedings to start. 'Rell and their friends sat with a few of the staff from Quintech and D.Q. Enterprises. The courtroom was small and there was no overflow, including the few reporters there may have been thirty people in attendance.

Judge Clayton entered and everyone stood as the court was called to order. A small, frail man whose robe seemed two sizes bigger then he needed put the gavel down and asked the clerk for the folder that sat before the court stenographer. Microphones were checked by each party and the judge waited attentively as the Prosecutor introduced himself and the members who were seated beside him.

The representatives from Carson's Web was unfamiliar to Derek. He let Mr. Simpson know immediately he didn't know the men, nor had he spoke to them at any time during the investigation. He pointed out his boss, a few co-workers and the man Carson's Web told him to correspond with after he took the offer to resign.

Kenny arrived in the courtroom after Mr. Simpson followed protocol and introduced himself and Derek. He remained in the back row where he could scan the entire audience. He was summoned to the court by

Mr. Simpson. He assumed Derek recognized someone or there was other business that would to be addressed. Mitchell asked him to be sure whoever covered the lobby was aware of the security they needed.

The Prosecutor, Kevin Leahy, called a few witnesses who would give a testimony to the financial reports. It was to include details of the sales, expenditures and profits. They showed spreadsheets and charts explaining the reports never showed a deficit. The company found no discrepancies until they received complaints from two or more clients regarding their trademarks and logos. Both were handled by Derek Mince.

It took most of the morning for everything to be put into evidence as well as shown to a jury. The prosecution took its time with questions and there were many that were answered during the cross-examination. They were thorough laying out a picture for those who wouldn't quite understand what Derek's charges were.

Although Judge Clayton explained to the jurors what their job was, and how to examine the testimonies, it seemed they were wide-eyed. The judge looked at their faces and the clock after two hours of testimony. It was the financial reports that bored him so he called for more than an hour break at twelve. The court was adjourned until one thirty.

Kenny walked through the crowd to the front of the courtroom. Sitting next to Darryl he waited until Mr. Simpson noticed his presence.

"Kenny, here's the plate numbers and check these addresses. Any trucking companies, or car services that may connect with this information we need to know immediately. Also, have two other men here for the afternoon session. Have you checked the prosecutor's team?"

"I've checked out all but the cars. I'll have that report this afternoon. I'll cross check them with this list. Mr. Mince, Monique Davis showed up shortly after you left. I haven't got a call yet so maybe she left the premises shortly after I did. I'll be heading back there once I leave here."

'Rell checked his phone. Ms. Berry had alerted him to Monique's arrival. He gave her the instruction to have her wait and not interact with her. She hadn't called him back.

"I'll call the office while we're on break. Are you guys getting lunch or what?"

On cue, Mitch, Craig, and Keith said they'd meet 'Rell across the street at the deli. Byron, Derek, Darryl, and Mr. Simpson decided to eat at the diner a few blocks away. The courtroom cleared and everyone agreed they'd be back in time.

The deli wasn't as crowded as they expected. They placed their orders and decided to sit away from the door and the foot traffic the lunch orders would create.

"Craig, so have you decided to take the offer? I understand you and Keith did a walk through this morning. I was premature with announcing that you and Keith would step in during the trial. I hope I didn't call it wrong." 'Rell took the seat between Craig and Keith.

Craig smiled. "I have to send in my resignation. I'll send it today. Keith and I have agreed to be roommates until I find a place of my own."

"You don't have to rush man. That condo can hold your stuff and mine comfortably. I was going to ask you to join me anyway. I'm single right now and you've been dismissed by Monique, so hey, as 'Rell would say, it is what it is."

Everyone laughed and looked at 'Rell. He shook his head and extended his hand to each of them as a welcoming shake.

"How many rooms are in that place? It looks pretty large."

Mitch waited for Keith to give him an answer. Keith pulled out the tri-fold with the information on it.

"I went there this morning and got the keys. The rooms are huge and it's close enough to jump on public transportation if we wanted to. I like the area. Three bedrooms, and the other norms. You know me I've got to have that extra room for my music. I think we'll be comfortable. I mean Craig, you can check out the other units there too."

"We'll see. 'Rell, so rough morning for visitors at the enterprises huh?"

"Craig man that's a daily thing. Somebody is going to show up and stir up. This week it's Tonya and Monique. It's always Darryl and Derek. We're dealing with it. If I don't sweat they don't. That's how I want you guys to be. We've got people watching our backs for the B.S. that goes down but otherwise, you'll find its easy man. Nothing you or Keith can't handle. Be careful you're the new meat in the building though. It ain't no different than when we worked together in Maryland."

"Whoa, there's a difference. Right Craig, there's a difference."

Craig gave Mitchell a questionable look. "Oh, oh yea, yea, c'mon man I messed up. You guys know it. It won't happen again."

"I'm sure it won't 'cause Mr. Simpson got spies everywhere, trust me. That old man knows more than anyone thinks he does. Your dad picked the right lawyer. Oh, and please answer his calls when he hits you up all times of the day or night. It could be personal or business. One thing though, he's got our back."

'Rell watched Keith and Craig as Mitch gave a few examples of Simpson and the boys clearing up issues or problems with contracts or people who wanted a meeting and got put out of the building.

'Rell added the true purpose for Mr. Simpson's staff. "They make sure our money is where it should be, without problems guys. The more we keep, the more everyone gets paid. That's what business is about. Taking care of those who share your passion and vision. This is what we talked about in school. Now we have it. My father left plans for this business for the next ten years. That doesn't even count what we can build on our own or Quintech's expansion."

"Well, I'm glad to be a part of it. Thank you Mr. Mince for including me and Craig. It is as we talked about years ago now let's make the bound unbreakable."

They raised their drinks to give a toast. Craig smiled as he looked around the table. His phone began to vibrate in his pocket. He turned it on vibrate shortly after entering the courtroom. He was sure it was Monique calling him.

Fifty

Monique turned to face the woman who had her waiting for more than twenty minutes. She expected her to be the prissy type. To her surprise, Ms. Yvonne Berry was well put together but her demeanor spoke before she did. Her pantsuit coordinated well with her blouse, shoes, and jewelry. She was fashion conscious. Her appearance distracted Monique for a moment. Her hair was braided in an up-do and her nails and make-up added a touch of class to her ensemble.

Monique's temper rose a notch. She couldn't complain about the building, the security or the two women that would become the only audience for her planned performance. It was the only opportunity she would have, she decided she'd give them the story and wait for 'Rell's reaction.

'Rell told Ms. Berry why Ms. Davis was there. After working for the man every woman wanted in their bed, getting rid of the gold-diggers had become her job. She understood Monique's type and most of them came with less fire than she would give them in return.

"Ms. Davis won't you step into my office?"

"Is Mr. Mince here or not?"

"He's not here. As I told you on the phone, if he comes in at all it will be late this afternoon. He didn't give us a definite time for his return. If you'd like to come back tomorrow or call first...."

"So he can be warned? I don't think so. His dead beat ass knew it would come to this."

Monique paused to see if the receptionist was paying attention to what she was saying. She tapped on the desk to get her attention.

"Well, I can try to reach him. If you just step this way."

"I said I ain't waiting for him. Listen either of you can deliver this message. I'm no longer going to see a therapist about this shit. What does that mean? It means I'll be here every day until he hears me out. I'm going to take his black ass to court. The two of you will be working for me when this is over."

"Ms. Davis I'm sure he's not avoiding you. I can leave him a message on his phone."

"Listen, sweetie that's been done, that's why I'm here. You see I was the one who was supposed to get that proposal, the ring, the house, and the children….well. You tell his ass I lost the damn baby when he decided to take a detour with the whore he married. Who fucks the man they think may be their brother?"

The receptionist turned from her computer with a look of astonishment on her face.

"Oh, you may not know as much as Ms. Thang here." Monique turned to face the receptionist. "You see your boss screwed around on me with his now wife. The problem is she started out as his sister. Derek Mince, you know who he is right? Well, his sister Dershai Mince is his sister. How did she become a Mince before the marriage? Same shit I asked. Your boss's daddy. He screwed around on their mother and your boss's mother at the same time. Now that makes them related right?"

"Ms. Davis! I must ask you not to discuss what you don't know as details."

"Discuss it with who? Y'all the only ones here and you didn't tell her. That's right she said 'Rell doesn't like gossip in the office. Well, this ain't gossip! He was screwing me and that wife of his at the same time. The problem, the reason I'm here…."

Monique changed the tone of her voice as though there was someone she didn't want to hear her.

"They claim there's proof that Derek and Shai are not related to the boss. How? For convenience, some man shows up, a blast from their mother's past and he's the dad? Bull…..the Mince family money pays well. So, Ms. Berry, you're right, you give his ass this message." Her voice rose an octave. "I had a miscarriage with his baby due to the Mince family chaos. I was dumped and my world was torn apart once I found out he was screwing his sister and then to marry her? I know he didn't want children out of wedlock so he married that bitch. You see, the loss of our love caused me to lose a child, my job and yes my damn mind. I've got a lawyer and I'm suing him. Let his ass know that. My life is ruined because of my loss."

The receptionist turned her body pretending to focus on the computer screen. Ms. Berry closed her office door and walked over to the receptionist desk where Monique stood her ground.

"Ms. Davis, I don't know where you got your information or even if it's true. What I do know is this is not the proper way to deal with this and I won't allow it to disrupt the business we handle here. Now I've offered you my office to discuss this, I asked if you want me to call Mr. Mince. What we're not going to do is entertain your complaint with sideline gossip, remarks or opinions. What you and Mr. Mince have to deal with is not business we handle here."

"You think your job description covers you dismissing me?"

"I know it does. Pam, call security and have them escort Ms. Davis to the parking lot. Also page Kenny, he's left the building and let him know Ms. Davis is not to return to any part of the grounds without the consent of Mr. Mince. Ms. Davis, you can wait until security comes or you can take the elevator down to the lobby."

"Oh, you the shit huh? I'll take the elevator. It will give me a chance to check out the other floors."

Monique turned and put the papers she held on the bookcase. She exited the same way she came in. Ms. Berry and Pam watched her exit and slam the door. They could see her impatiently tapping the call button for the elevator.

"Pam, lock the elevator when she gets on it. Set it for the main floor."

Pam looked at the video monitors. Monique could be seen pacing in front of the elevator door.

"Ms. Berry, if I lock it, can't she still push the other buttons?"

"The elevator will only take her to the main floor regardless. Let security know she's on her way to the lobby so they can walk her to her car."

Monique stood at the elevator tapping her foot. It didn't go as well as she planned but the seed was planted. She wondered why she didn't see any other staff. What was 'Rell hiding behind all of the wooden door entrances? She got on the elevator and pushed the number for the sixth floor. 'Rell's office was on the floor marked TF, she wondered what that meant. There was another button that read Penthouse. She'd get off on the sixth and then she'd check out the Penthouse.

The elevator passed the sixth floor and Monique pushed the button for the third floor. It passed that floor too. It stopped and opened slowly on the main floor. Kenny stood at the podium watching as another man approached her.

"Good morning ma'am. I'll be walking you to your car."

"Who asked you to walk me to my car? I know where I parked."

"It's a courtesy ma'am. Just doing my job."

"Something tells me you don't do this with everyone. Let your boss know I'm putting this shit in the lawsuit too. This is harassing."

The courteous security guard was in a dark color suit. Monique noticed he had a gun holstered on his waist. She looked back at Kenny and wondered if he too was carrying a weapon. When she approached her car she noticed a folded paper was left on her windshield. The guard handed it to her and waited for her to get in her car. He stepped back when she started the ignition. Before pulling off, she unfolded the paper and read the note.

"I won't be in the office most of the week. Call me on the phone. I'd love to hear what you thought was so urgent that you had to come my office."

It was signed, 'Rell. Monique's temper flared again. *"Thought was urgent my ass!"*

Fifty-One

"**N**ikki, why would a woman continue to put herself in these predicaments?"

Nikki couldn't answer the question with a straight face. She smiled and shook her head. She learned whenever Nana asked a leading question to let her answer it as well. Nikki and Sam stopped in to visit the Reverend and Nana on their way out. They stayed well beyond the start of the movie at the Cineplex and decided they'd just get something to eat and return home later. The plans changed again when Nana assured the couple she prepared plenty for dinner. She told them what she was cooking smothered chicken, with rice gravy and onions, steamed broccoli, and there was pie for dessert. They didn't think about leaving even after dessert was served.

"I'll tell you why. No one told either of them what they need to hear. D.Q. is dead and gone and that Tonya is still reading the writing that was clear at the reading of the will. Karlton has nursed that woman back to the wench she is. I'm sorry Wallace before you say anything. That woman ain't never had no good in her. She should have been dead and gone but she's here. Shai and Karlton took care of her for months and as soon as she can walk and talk on her own she shows up at that office building? What's wrong with these women?"

Reverend Wallace chuckled. It was a conversation he and Nana had many nights. Nikki shared with them the phone call she got from 'Rell earlier. He was on his way back to the office when Ms. Berry called him about Monique.

"It's sad Wallace, ain't no need for these women to be chasing what's obviously gone. D.Q. is dead and gone. Poor 'Rell got to deal with that other fool, what is wrong with them?"

"I don't know what to tell you. Simone is just as crazy as them."

"Nikki I forgot all about her and that dummy Darryl. D.Q. had all the senses when it came to business. Neither one of them had much sense when it came to love. Both of them, I'm sorry Sam. I know you and Nikki dating or you know what I mean, but it upsets me so. How could love blind both of them?"

"Well Jewels, they had their reasons. The problem is the women they stumbled upon accepted them the way they were, flawed. The women just didn't let go."

"Reverend Wallace it seems that 'Rell is in the same boat. He was with Monique for a few years and then he married Shai. So please you or Sam tell me he's not doomed to a life of being chased and harassed by Monique. It's terrible to live with the thought that the old love may ruin your future with someone you really care for."

"You're right Nikki. It's hard to move on with someone constantly tugging you from the past. They just won't let go, Wallace. I know one thing they've crossed enough lines."

Nana sat back in her chair as though she had said enough.

"So what did 'Rell say he intended on doing about either of them."

Nana raised her finger in the air to emphasize what she was about to say. Her gesture caused the reverend to laugh again.

"Jewels what does this mean?" He raised his finger teasingly mocking her motion.

"Aww, you don't want to hear the truth. Nikki tell my grandson to talk to Mr. Simpson. He'll put a stop to Tonya and her mess, that crazy Monique too. She's throwing around the fact that she's going to sue? Well, we got the right lawyer for that mess."

"Sounds like they got a lot of bark and no bite."

"Sam you're right. They can't get nothing from the Mince family but a good fight. I can't tell you how many have come for that business 'Rell is running now. D.Q. would be in court or here writing letters time and time again. Nikki can tell you. A black man can't have nothing without everyone, including family coming for him."

"Darryl is killing himself and dragging Derek with him. Seems like he is self-destructing." Nikki's thought was made aloud.

"I told Jewels that just the other day. Remember what I said Jewels?"

"You're right Nikki. Wallace and I prayed about that the other morning. I keep Darryl in prayer. I spoke with Francine, you know, and she said that's why she still calls. She's scared for him too."

"Wait, are you saying he might kill himself?" Sam waited for an answer.

"No Sam. It seems he puts himself in situations that he knows will fail. Business, love, family it doesn't matter he always chooses to get involved in failure."

"Nikki I don't think he can tell the difference. He has always wanted to make his own decisions. But as D.Q. would say, they're always the wrong choice. Lately, he's been worse at choosing. No offense Nikki, you know I love Simone but he shouldn't be with her. He should have separated and got himself together before living with another woman."

"That's so true Wallace, but women like Monique and Tonya don't want a man. They want the money. Look at Tonya, D.Q. is dead and that Monique, 'Rell is married."

"Mama Mince you might as well add Simone to that list. Darryl was married and I think she thought he had the money."

Nikki looked at Sam and smiled. For the first time since starting her business, she was glad she had her own.

Fifty-Two

Darryl wrapped his arms around Simone while she stood at the kitchen sink. It was close to the dinner hour and Darryl called home after the court was dismissed for the day to say he'd be in early. It was Wednesday and since the proceedings started he hadn't come in before Simone was preparing for bed.

Simone decided she wouldn't ask from day to day how the trial was going. The anxiety was too much and it didn't seem to be a topic that Darryl cared to discuss. He noticed she had become silent giving one-word answers or none at all.

"Hmm, you smell delicious, edible, is the fragrance new?"

"You're smelling the roast in the oven, I'm sure."

Simone answered moving away from his grasp.

"I'm glad you're home for dinner. I made enough for today and leftovers tomorrow. I'll be at Nikki's tomorrow night. We're flying to Philly to see a client. We'll be back Sunday."

"I see. A weekend trip?"

"A business trip. There's a few places to check out, prospects we hope."

"So I'm on my own for what… three days?"

"Shouldn't be that hard. I mean since Monday you've been, as you said, on your own. It's not that difficult. You've got your business to handle and so do I. Darryl, I just need to understand how or why you're wrapped up in a case where Derek clearly took a chance by himself. What does this case have to do with you?"

"It's the finances. They're looking for the money he made. I guess they think he hid it in Quintech finances. Some of my money funded Quintech and I am a partner in the business. So I guess it would have to do with me in some way or another. That's what Mr. Simpson and 'Rell said, plus, he's my nephew."

"So Carson's Web is looking for money they should have got and the money you gambled has others looking? What the hell were you and Derek thinking? I don't understand any of this."

"It's two different things. Derek was trying to make money to help pay the gambling debt. That's how he got caught up. It backfired, that and my attempt to put up what he did get at the card tables."

"Something just doesn't register for me. Sixty thousand is a lot of money to win back at a simple card game."

"It wasn't simple babe and that's why I can't talk about it. The less you know the better. I'm not trying to include family in this. I lost the money and I'm working on getting it back."

"Darryl, really sixty thousand? Do you have that hid somewhere?"

Simone looked at him and smiled. Even with the misunderstanding between them, he knew she loved him. He wanted to tell her it would be okay. He couldn't tell her he made a call to Francine or that he planned on seeing Darlene before the week was out.

He helped Simone set the table. He said a silent prayer of his own as they held hands to pray over the food. His phone rang and he excused himself as he went to answer it in the living room. Simone tried to ignore his rush to respond to the call.

"Hello." Darryl waited to hear the voice come through. He didn't recognize the number that showed on the phone. He sat down on the couch hoping it wasn't another call with a problem.

"Darryl?" He recognized the voice. Tonya never called him before and he readied himself knowing anything was possible coming from his brother's ex.

"Yes, it's me, what's up?"

"I wanted to talk to you away from the family circle, if you know what I mean. I tried talking to Derek but I don't think what I said sunk in."

"About what? What were you trying to tell him?"

"Can we meet? I'm sure you can't talk freely. I don't want to cause a disturbance."

"Tonya, this week is a bad week. I'm at court with Derek. I'm sure you know that. I'm free to talk. There's no problem. You called, so talk."

Darryl sat back and then thought about Simone sitting at the dining room table.

"On second thought, how's tomorrow morning. I've got another stop to make before court starts but if you can meet me earlier than that...."

"Oh, good. What time?" Tonya was glad he agreed. She didn't want Karlton to be suspicious about the call. She looked back at the office where Karlton found solace after their dinner.

"Say about eight at Starbucks. There's one near the mall."

"I know exactly where you're talking about. I'll see you in the morning. Thanks, Darryl, I think you'll want to hear what I have to say."

"No problem. Thanks for calling."

He disconnected the call and left the phone again on the end table. Simone hadn't started to eat. She waited until he sat before she spoke.

"What could she possibly want to talk to you about?"

"Wow, eavesdropping? I didn't know you had regained that skill."

"Now you know your mother alerted me to your whispering phone calls. I heard you say her name. I think your family has some ritual that must be performed before anyone talks to her."

"C'mon now she ain't that bad. I don't know what she wants but if we all act like she's a demon we won't know what she's up to. Besides, she owes me a favor or two."

"Darryl, no! I know you aren't thinking of involving her in the mess you're in."

"Listen, her son is in it too. If she cares about him maybe she'll help get him out of this mess."

"I don't know. Tonya has been a problem to you all in more ways than one. Don't give me that look. What are you thinking?"

"Her being a problem is great for my problem, our problem."

They ate their dinner without mentioning Tonya or the dilemma Derek and Darryl were facing. Simone could only think of the risk Darryl was taking. She was sure if he made an alliance with Tonya he would lose his family. The lost was the lesser of the two resolves. Without the money being paid, Simone was sure there would be another accident.

They cleaned the kitchen together, something they hadn't done in weeks.

"Can I interest you in a shower, my dear? You look tense. Besides, I am tense. If you're leaving me for the weekend, I'd love for us to spend tonight enjoying each other."

"Hmm, I thought you lost that with all this mess going on."

"Stop, stop. I'm not losing you or my love for you to this mess. I told you, it's just a matter of making some connections."

"Darryl, why didn't you make these connections earlier? I mean wouldn't that have made this drama in the courtroom easier?"

"I don't know. I'm still working through this mess. I didn't think about it and now… Let's just say I was wrong and I'm trying to fix it. C'mon join me in the shower."

The water was running when Simone entered the master bedroom. Darryl stood before her and opened his arms, inviting her to a loving hug and a passionate kiss. The couple began to disrobe each other. Once nude, the clothes lying at their feet, they held hands and walked to the shower.

Darryl allowed Simone to enter the shower first. The water glistened on her body and the lighting overhead set a glow on her breast.

Darryl stepped in and closed the door. He stood close gently touching her face and raising her chin for his kiss. As their bodies touched the passion rose. The warm water quickly brought steam to the glass that enclosed the shower. Darryl massaged Simone's butt as he kissed her neck. He gently moved her to the seat that was in the shower, an added touch for steamed baths.

Simone leaned back onto the shower wall and lifted her legs for Darryl to explore. He teased her nipples as he kissed her neck and continued down to her thighs. His lips found his pleasure below her navel. He lifted her enough to focus his attention on what he knew would give her a sensual rise.

As her clitoris stood waiting for his tongue to explore and tease her to a climax, his penis began to throb. He lifted her. She wrapped her legs around his waist and the water rained on them.

Darryl placed her gently on the seat facing him. He inserted himself knowing they both needed an explosive gratification. He took his time kissing her breast and teasing her nipples. Their movement was in sync to the beat of the water from the shower. The moment between them was paced yet electrifying.

Simone opened her mouth yet no sound escaped as she began to tingle. A response to the pulsating she felt between her legs. They both began to moan as their movement brought the heat. Simone began to massage Darryl's back as she kissed his neck. She teased him with small bites and kissing until she felt him enlarge again.

They separated and Simone reached for one of the bathing sponges. Using the shower gel and the sponge she washed his chest, back, and extremities. Darryl did the same for her. He let the sponge fall as they stood under the water, holding each other tightly.

Simone opened the door as Darryl cut off the water. The couple dried themselves and each other and went to the turned down bed. Darryl laid on the bed and invited Simone to join him.

Simone climbed on the bed and stopped at his erection. As she teasingly fondled him she gave him the thrill she knew he'd enjoy. As he grew under her kisses, she mounted him and found her own satisfaction. The movements between them caused a climax and they separated, silently thankful they hadn't lost the passion between them.

Fifty-Three

"He's doing what? Derek, you can't be serious."

Shai and Derek were up before anyone else. Shai was preparing breakfast and lunch for the twins while 'Rell was in the shower.

"Listen, I didn't tell Leeza. Keep it between us for now. He said she called him."

"Uncle Darryl knows better. Our mother can't possibly think he would know about stocks that D.Q. had."

"Shai, I don't know what she thinks. I know what his angle is and hey, let it play out."

"What angle?"

"We need the money. If she's got it, let her help us out of this mess. If she can't help, then done deal. I don't want to hear anything else from her. She's been no less than a bitch toward you and me. Let him milk her for what we need. And he can feed her some B.S. about the stocks in the meantime."

"Derek, did you come up with that mess by yourself or are the two of you just that crazy? She will be furious with false information. The other thing is, you can't believe she will just give you money like that."

"Not me, Uncle Darryl. Shai, we don't know what she owes him. They both have done some mess and I'm sure they covered each other."

"Mommy and Uncle Darryl? Really?"

"Why else would he think he could get money from her?"

"Because of the way she treated you!"

"And you. We don't know Shai, let's just wait and see."

"Damn. Will it ever end? Okay, what about what she may want in return?"

"We don't have the information she wants. Unless she thinks he does. Who knows?"

"Okay, forget them. How's the case going?"

"Mr. Simpson thinks it may be over by the middle of next week. I'll have to pay the money back. I've got it though. I've saved it up. Now the fines will have to be paid and I'm hoping they don't want to see me in jail. So if Mr. Simpson can work his magic and I just have to pay, I'm good."

"Do you have to stay here until you pay?"

"Ooo, I didn't think about that. That may be a condition they throw at me huh?"

"I would if you owed me."

"Gee thanks, sis."

"Seriously, if you leave the states how would I be ensured you'd pay up?"

"Yeah, or they'd take it out of my business."

"Yep. Bryce and Brianna let's go."

"They can get dressed by themselves?"

Shai looked at the clock. "Nope, by now, their father has been in their room; got them up and dressed. He works the morning here like a well-oiled machine, believe me. They'll come down and then he'll finish dressing."

The children entered the room smiling and hugged their uncle before they sat at the table. Eggs and bacon were served with juice. They recited their prayer and began to eat.

"I'm sending my children to you and 'Rell."

"Nah brother, you and Leeza got that. I walked in on her reading to them last night." 'Rell shook Derek's hand and kissed Shai. "I heard you, man. Shai and I may want to add one or two more to our home. Cousins should stay with parents until they're potty-trained."

"You got that." They laughed as Shai made the men their plates. They ate seated at the island.

"Did you hear Leeza stirring?"

"No, the door was still closed."

Derek excused himself to go check on her. He opened the door to the guestroom and found Leeza was still in the bed. He exited without disturbing her.

"She's still sleeping." He stated as he took his seat again. He looked at 'Rell and Shai who were smiling at him.

"Okay, what's up?" He paused and then looked back at the stairs that led upstairs. "Nah, she would have told me first."

"Okay, but girlfriend gets her sleep in. Her appetite is good too."

"Nah, she would know. She's a nurse."

"I would know too."

"Shai, you think so?"

"I know a way you'd be sure without asking her?"

"How?"

Shai and 'Rell answered in unison. "Nana!"

Fifty-Four

Darryl ordered two coffees and a breakfast sandwich before taking a seat nowhere near the entrance of Starbucks. He hoped Tonya wouldn't arrive after the coffee got cold. He waved his hand in the air when he saw her enter. He stood watching her excuse herself as she cut through the line that continued to grow.

"Good morning Sir. Whew, is it a lot cooler than the forecast predicted or is it just me? They've got a crowd this morning huh?"

Tonya was dressed in a pair of jeans, a sweatshirt, a short jacket, and sneakers. Her attire caused Derek to raise his eyebrows before he answered.

"You trying to be incognito? I've never seen you dressed like you are. A new look?" He smiled as he passed her the coffee and the sugar packets. "The temperature has been crazy lately."

"I'm dressed just as casual as you," Tonya replied looking beyond the end of the table at Derek's attire. "I'm on a breakfast run."

"Oh, I see. So whatever you've got to say shouldn't take more than a breakfast pick-up across town?"

"Hush. You're always the investigator. Now I know why Francine didn't catch you cheating earlier."

"My dear, anyone that gets caught wants to be caught. How have you been? We haven't really talked in a while. You cut me off from our little conversations. I can honestly say I miss them."

"Not you miss me? I thought we had more than conversations between us." Tonya reached for another sugar packet. "I'm glad the coffee is warm. They serve it and you have to wait to drink it. So how have you been since your….well did you get a divorce?"

"Yes. Francine asked for one. I gave it to her. I owed her and myself that much. She deserved the chance to move on. I had done it too many times in our marriage. I don't blame her and we still talk. About the kids, business and whatever, but it's over."

"So you're here permanently? I know you and Derek are in business together. Where are you staying?"

"I have a home. I bought it about two years ago. Not far from Darlene's, far enough from everyone else though. I'm at home here, nothing new, I was visiting enough anyway."

"You look well, so you must be doing something right."

"Yeah, if we can get this trial over with I'd feel better. I got a few things hanging while we're in court. You know the stress of the unknown."

"I can agree with that. That's what I wanted to talk to you about. Did you invest in any of the stock at D.Q. Enterprises?"

"Yes, still have a few. Nothing new though. I think I got them the first ten years that D.Q. was in business. It has helped me finance a few things."

"Do you still have it?"

"Yeah, I don't touch it though. I drained it with the divorce and giving Francine the construction business. You know you wives get to dig into that stuff."

"Some wives. That's my problem. I owned stock too and I believe I owned more than they gave me. They claim it was sold. Darryl, all of it wasn't sold. They owe me more than I got. I want to check on it but I'm getting the dial tone, closed-door, closed lips, you know what I mean. Nobody wants to tell me anything.

I know that they're hiding the returns on the investment somewhere. They may be hiding them in Quintech. I just want to know."

"I doubt that. The Quintech files, Carson's Web files, and even the construction company files have been pulled. They've checked the financial reports for the money they are questioning Derek about. That's why I've been in court every day."

"Really? Darryl is it just Carson's Web or is Derek in more trouble."

Darryl saw the opportunity but decided he'd wait.

"I don't know."

"Darryl it wasn't Carson's Web that tried to run him off the road."

"No, it wasn't. Tonya, there's a lot more that you probably don't know."

Tonya looked at him and thought about his relationship to 'Rell. *His alliance may be the door opener.*

"So what was it?"

Darryl told her about the money. How they tried to pay Carson's Web by gambling. He explained it became an addiction when they saw the money grow. Over the months they didn't bank it they played over and over again. He stopped talking when he told her the men they owed were willing to kill when he and Derek stopped playing and paying.

"I didn't know. I didn't know it was that serious. I thought Derek was getting high or something, you know. Oh my God, so he could wind up in jail and still be threatened?"

"We both are taking it day by day. I received two calls since he returned to the states. I wouldn't tell anyone about it."

"What about Mr. Simpson? Did you tell him? He's an undercover O.G."

They both laughed causing the people in line to look toward their table.

"You have lost it. An O.G?"

"Listen, D.Q. would be sweating about situations and then after talking to Simpson, it was like a breath of fresh air. If he finds them they will be done, believe me."

"Oh, well yes, he knows. In the meantime, I decided I couldn't keep trying to get the money by sitting at their gambling tables again."

"Yeah, that's a chance. So you said you have stock? Can you check into the one I have for me? I mean the portion I know about is lucrative but where did the rest go. I can't find any of my papers from the separation. I'm sure D.Q. got rid of them. The papers Simpson gave me only show the stock that was sold. Robert and Alan were handling things then. I'm not getting much out of them."

"Robert still the same? He had his eyes wide open for you or should I say on you. I'm sure those jeans could get some information from him."

"Yeah right, probably five minutes sooner than he'd give it to you. D.Q.'s brother has some pull, I'm sure."

"So you want me to talk to them about it?"

"Yes, and if there's something there maybe I can help you and my son. Don't tell him though."

Darryl smiled and took Tonya's hand. "I'll help you and thank you. I really appreciate any help you can give me, I mean us."

"How much do you owe them? I know it's got to be quite a bit if they're willing to hurt someone severely for it."

"Sixty grand maybe more if they're looking for interest. I know you may not have that much but anything will keep them at bay for the moment."

Tonya moved her hand. She sat back in the seat as tears welled in her eyes.

"Darryl, they weren't trying to just hurt Derek were they?"

"No. They were—"

Tonya finished the sentence. "...trying to kill him."

She wiped her eyes as she stood to exit.

"Call me after you talk to Robert and Alan. Oh, how long did they give you?"

"Until the end of the trial." Derek hung his head over his coffee cup. He hoped she wouldn't see his action as staged drama.

"Call me. Let's see what can be done. Darryl we can help each other, but I need to know about that stock."

"I'll talk to them today."

Fifty-Five

"Craig, please return my call. I'm not going to beg you and I guess you're right. I need to let this anger I have for your boy, go. I just want to talk a minute or two before you leave to go back to Maryland."

Monique hung up the phone. It was the middle of the week and Craig still hadn't called. She followed the news about the trial posted on the community page on the internet. It didn't give many details for the public to go on, and the proceedings were still in progress.

She hadn't called 'Rell again. His message was clear, he wouldn't be in the office for the rest of the week. She needed another angle. Leaving bits and pieces of her insanity with his secretary and the receptionist hadn't stirred his emotions. Maybe 'Rell had changed. Higher positions often give people another level of power, or so Monique thought.

She signed on to the website of D.Q. Enterprises on her computer as she had many times before. Keeping up with 'Rell's progress was a habit. She began following his father two years prior to his death. Understanding 'Rell would be at least one of his beneficiaries, she was expecting to be a part of 'Rell's prosperity.

Monique read over D.Q.'s biography. There was no mention of Nikki Robbins, 'Rell's mother. Tonya Mince was listed as his wife, but three children were listed. She wondered if that information had been or would be updated. She questioned how Tonya must have felt knowing that 'Rell was listed as his child for the public to see. There was information regarding the transition of the company after 'Rell became the President and CEO. All the records for stocks, transactions of property, as well as titles that changed within the company, were listed.

Monique went through the pages hoping to find Tonya's name as a stockholder or one who held vacation properties. There she found Nikki Robbins name as well as all of D.Q.'s children. She went back through the pages. Tonya Mince had been separated from D.Q. Enterprises totally. Monique wondered what Tonya received as the wife of wealth.

There were articles Monique found regarding D.Q.'s death. Most were about the son who was groomed to take over the company. There were a few regarding the business and the mention of Shai and Derek.

Monique googled Tonya's name. The information she was looking for was the first search result posted. There had been a legal separation, and then their divorce. The last two paragraphs of the article detailed what she shared in the company. She received nothing at the time of his death.

Monique smiled. *When one door closes......* She was sure there was a way to contact the real Ms. Mince.

Fifty-Six

Craig sat in the reception area waiting for Ms. Berry. Pam offered him coffee to make sure the well-dressed man who sat in her area would remember her gesture. Craig smiled but declined her offer. He noticed her coy attempt to get his attention.

"Is it always this quiet around here?"

Pam turned her attention away from the screensaver on her computer. She hadn't started any work, nor had the phones begun to be an annoyance.

"Not really, just this week. I think it's because everyone knows Mr. Mince is not in the office or that everyone is in court."

"I see. So you get all the calls here for the company?"

"No. Each unit has a receptionist. Some of the area directors or those with titles have their own secretaries. The calls here are for Mr. Mince."

"I see. So this is the office that runs it all."

Pam smiled without giving a response. Ms. Berry opened her door and invited Craig to come into her office.

"Good morning Mr. Masters. I don't know why I'm delivering this message but I do know that a job undone here will get you fired."

She smiled, letting him know she was teasing.

"I know that lesson well. So what is it that is totally out of your job title that you must do?"

"We need to talk about Monique Davis. She's been here and I would guess that she'll be back, either through phone calls or another visit. Mr. Masters, she may be arrested for trespassing if she returns. Harassment may be filed if she calls and behaves in the manner she did the other day. Any behavior determined to be a threat to any staff or the business won't be tolerated. I've drafted paperwork to protect you from any problems at Quintech. I will need your signature so that it can be on file. If you don't want to sign it, you'll have to take that up with Mr. Mince."

"I see." Craig took the papers and read through the two pages.

"This, of course, is if you are taking the position at Quintech."

"Oh, yes. I do have a question, Ms. Berry. What will be my title?"

"Derek Mince will have to discuss that with you. I'm sorry, I don't have access to your file yet. I'm sure Mr. Mince can tell you, Darrell Mince, I'm sorry."

"No, no problem. I wasn't sure." He signed the paper and placed it on her desk.

"Mr. Mince will see you now in his office. Do you know where that is?"

"Yes, thank you. I hope Ms. Davis didn't disturb the peace around here."

"Mr. Masters, she's one of many. We handle them like disgruntle clients. They come, get told what they need to know and go. It's just some can't return. She's one of those."

They both understood Monique would try again. Craig waved at Pam as he exited. He dialed Monique's number as he took a seat in the hall outside of 'Rell's office.

Craig was impressed with D.Q. Enterprises and though he hadn't been at Quintech for a full day he was satisfied. Monique would ruin his chances again. A call to warn her was his intent. He had joined 'Rell and the team at D.Q. Enterprises. She'd have to realize he was no longer a partner in her attempt to destroy 'Rell's life.

"Hello Craig?" Monique seemed surprised. He didn't know how to read her reactions any longer.

"Yes, listen, you've got to stop this plan of yours."

"Is that what you called to say? I'm doing this for you and me. He owes us Craig."

"Monique, that's between you and 'Rell. I must have been a fool to step between you and him from the beginning. I was wrong, but all that is in the past. What I did learn is if you are so intent on revenge, then you never loved me. I was your revenge. When 'Rell didn't pay attention to our so-called love, you went for more. It's always been about getting back at him for loving someone else. I woke up and it's time you did too. Find someone to love that will love you. I'm calling you to tell you to stop. Stop before you're hurt any more than you are today. Leave 'Rell, D.Q. Enterprises and me alone."

"Did he tell you to call me? What a weak ass! You and him both. You're scared of what he may do to you and that whack ass job you slave for in Maryland?"

"Monique, stop. I'm working here with 'Rell. Some things can't be broken. Don't call here or come here. It's a warning I'm sure you won't take but you can't say you weren't told. Get some help babe, you need it."

Craig didn't wait for her to respond. He ended the call. He knocked on the door and waited for 'Rell to tell him to enter.

"Man, I thought you got lost in the hall."

They shook hands before sitting across from each other at 'Rell's desk.

"No, I called Monique. Tried to talk to her one last time. I don't know how to get through to her."

"Listen, she's on her own path to destruction. Did you get a chance to go over to Quintech?"

"Not this morning, no. Are we going to court today?"

"No, we'll meet Mitch and Keith at Quintech. I want to be sure that you guys are set. I need you to be up to speed by the end of the court proceedings. We may have to get Derek out of here from the courts. He nor my uncle may be able to return right away."

"Wow, really." Craig took a deep breath as he realized how serious his position would be.

"I'll brief you as we walk over. Listen don't worry about Monique. We're on top of that too."

"Alright, let's get busy."

Fifty-Seven

Darlene didn't think any deeper into the conversation when Darryl called to say he needed to speak with her before the end of the week. They talked about the trial, its possible outcome, and his family in Detroit. At the end of the call he mentioned stopping by but she had no idea he meant the next morning or that there was an urgency for the visit.

The doorbell rang as she rolled over for a second time. Warren left at seven, an hour before she promised she would get up. It was now eight thirty and she still could have slept another two hours or more. Appointments were made for late in the day since she knew she'd have a late night.

She grabbed her robe from the foot of her bed and slipped her feet into her slippers. The bell rang again and she quickened her steps. As she got closer, hurrying down the staircase, she tried to make out the silhouette that stood at her front door.

She opened the door prepared to give the morning intruder an attitude. She really hated solicitors, especially those who pretended to be college students trying to pay their tuition by selling overpriced products.

"Hey, sis." Darryl smiled as though they hadn't talked the day before. "What's wrong? You're not up? Are you okay?"

"Yea, yea, yea, all that. This was to be my sleep in morning. C'mon in and ignore my tude."

"Really?" Darryl laughed and walked pass Darlene who closed the door slowly and let her feet sliding across the floor tell her story. She plopped on the couch next to her brother and buried her head in his chest.

"Damn, your chest is still the best ever. Do you remember me comparing you and D.Q.? I loved teasing the two of you, but really your chest is the best."

"Until you find that special someone. That's what brothers are for. Making sisters feel good, loving them unconditionally, giving those compliments, and whatever they need until… a man comes along who they may have to kill about their sister. Who is he, huh?"

Darlene sat up and smiled. Giggling, she teasingly hit Darryl.

"Look at you. You're acting like you're in love. Who is he?"

"Funny you always could tell when I was in a relationship."

"Yep my sister, another brotherly trait. You're avoiding the question. Don't get me wrong, I'm happy for you but I need to know who is he?"

"Warren Stykes. He's a sales rep for a beauty supply company I do business with. We've been dating for a minute now and I guess it's getting, you know, along well."

"Hmm, I'd say more than well. I'm glad my chest is still the best though. I'm sure Mr. Stykes wouldn't appreciate him being in second place."

"Funny." Darlene changed her position so she could face her brother. "So Mr. Mince, what's up? How do I rate to get this early morning visit?"

"I've got a few stops to make before going into the courtroom this morning. I don't know what the outcome will be when this is over."

"I thought this case was about Derek. Oh, are you worried about Quintech?"

"No our smart-ass nephew is handling that."

"Whoa, why are you upset with 'Rell?"

"I gave up my life and company in Detroit to go into business with Derek. I thought it would be ours, you know, one we would run and manage. Darlene, 'Rell is all over it. The finances, staffing, security, all of it. He's got people in place to report any discrepancies to him or those next to him on his golden ladder."

"Darryl, wait a minute. You left Detroit to do what? That's not how I remember it. I remember you cheating on your wife and when given an ultimatum you decided to leave your home and business for the woman you were bumping with. Let me say this bit too. This ain't the first time. So let's talk truth and not the fantasy."

Darryl took a deep breath. "I know what you're thinking."

"No, you don't. Let me finish. 'Rell had no intention of running things at Quintech. Derek was in no position to run it and you, you were ready to do the "Darryl" thing."

"What is the "Darryl" thing?"

"Take over, strip it for its worth and then cry broke. C'mon we know you have a gambling problem. D.Q. made it easy until he was fed up. 'Rell knew what you had done with your company in Detroit. Francine called him Darryl. She told him. We all know what you did with the assets on a regular and before the divorce. So no bashing 'Rell."

"Darlene, what did you think of D.Q. running your business? Do you remember when you first started? You were trying to grasp being the CEO, the owner. You wanted D.Q. to let go and give you a chance. Sure, we wanted his advice but not his 'hands on everything' approach. Do you remember that fight you had before opening your second then the third shop? Darlene, I admit I failed with my marriage, gambling, and business. I'm trying to get back on track without hurting Derek."

"So what, you think 'Rell gives you both what you need only to watch it be gambled away? The precautions he's set are there so he won't lose his investment in Quintech. His love is a permanent investment with you as his uncle and Derek as…"

"As what a charity case?"

"Darryl! Why would you say that?"

"Darlene why would he stick his neck out or his money out and then not give us the room we need to grow?"

"Darryl I don't know what you're thinking. You wanted him to give you the startup money but not monitor the growth or loss knowing you are a gambler?"

"Was a gambler, Darlene, was. Derek's accident affected me and my habit."

"Well I'm glad it did but that doesn't change the desperation you have Darryl."

"Darlene, I needed to try to save our lives. Losing the business before the accident wasn't real to me. Then they threatened our lives. So I tried to get the money. Derek's trial was another effort to pay. I gambled that money trying to double it."

"And you lost that and they went after Derek."

"Yes. I had to use the assets from the construction company to keep them away from my kids, the family and Derek's hospital bed. That's why he left for Brazil. Now, this case is going sour, I think. Mr. Simpson says it's looking like the money, a fine and maybe probation. But Darlene, the gambling debt is still there. We're right back where we started."

Darlene fell back on the couch and closed her eyes. She knew what Darryl wanted. She braced herself waiting to hear the total.

"They want it by the end of the trial. I thought I would be able to put money in Quintech from the contracts we've had so far. I made a little over thirty thousand over the past few years but our nephew has found the account. His accountant went over the records for the court proceeding and reported it to Mr. Simpson and 'Rell. They're hoping that Carson's Web doesn't think that this is the money Derek made from the trademarks."

"Even so, that money would pay the fine and the money owed to them."

"Right, that's what I'm saying, Darlene. I tried to fix the problem and again, I fell short. I would have had a way to pay them back from that account. I could have shown them that with the contracts slated for us to work over the next few months we would be able to pay them."

Tears began to roll down his face. He sat forward on the couch and clasped his hands together.

"I can't save Derek, my family or any of us. I don't have the money to give them and they want lives as collateral."

"Darryl being mad at 'Rell or any of us is not a way to solve this. You can't bully any of us into believing you won't gamble and lose our money away, again. D.Q. warned all of us this would happen. He was worried about jail time. Now you're talking about someone losing their life. How much Darryl? How much do you think Mama can take of this? She can't know. We can't tell her this time. You can't go to her and ask for anything. You have to talk to 'Rell and we have to work this out. She can't be included. Do you hear me? You have to include 'Rell. I won't be a part of this if you exclude him."

"Alright, I understand. But Darlene, it's sixty thousand."

A silence fell between them. Each had their own thoughts about the past, the present and what would happen if they didn't handle the situation. Darlene released her judgments realizing there was no time for condemnation.

"Darryl, let me talk to 'Rell. I think we can get around this. The contracts you took on are solid?"

"Yes, they're legitimate and ongoing. I'm working on others as well. There's a few investors looking to buy property here and some locations outside of Richmond as well. I've worked with them in the past. So yes they are solid."

"Good. I'll call later. Answer your phone please."

Darlene stood and indication their visit was over.

"You throwing me out?"

"Yes, you have disrupted my sleep and my day. I've got to make a few calls so see yourself out. Love you."

Darryl's emotions rose again. Darlene was special to the family. She was like their mother, the answer to disputes, disruptions, and any problems he or D.Q. had. The tears fell again. He heard Darlene stirring upstairs. He stood to his feet and wiped his face. Maybe she could save him. He wondered if that was possible.

Fifty-Eight

"Is he for real? We don't have a way to check it. I mean no one knows if the threats are still threats."

Darlene had a few people to call just to plant herself firmly in Darryl's story. Francine knew her husband, she was the first call.

"Darlene, no one has called here or our home. I know Darryl probably wouldn't call to warn me. He wouldn't want me to worry or be afraid to do what I do, you know. I've got the business, these kids and now this shit? I don't know, I don't think he'd be bluffing though. He's not that type of man."

"No he's not and they did try to kill Derek. But as you said we have no proof or any way to check it. Thanks, Francine, I'm just trying to save my family, my brother and my nephew. Who knows who will be next if it is true, that's all I thought about.

I'm not calling for money. I wanted to know if any threats had reached your family. If they reached Detroit they definitely would return to Virginia. They're sending a message and Darryl nor Derek can answer them."

"I can't either. I've answered a few times over the past years. I did it for your brother Darlene, because I loved him."

"I understand. Things have changed for us all. I'm sorry, thanks for the information though."

"No need for you to be sorry, it's your brother's doing."

"Yep, and as usual we all feel his mistakes."

Darlene hung up the phone unsure who she would call next. She decided to call 'Rell and tell him to meet her at his mother's home. She got dressed and called Mia letting her know their mother-daughter nail appointment would be canceled. Darlene tried not to sound anxious. She hoped Mia wouldn't have Marci call her asking questions. Her oldest called as Darlene suspected but her questions had nothing to do with why she canceled with Mia.

"Hey Mom, I was wondering if you would be taking off time when the baby is born?"

"Of course I would, why?"

"Mitch wants his Mom to come to be with us. I told him there was no reason for it. She's nice and all but you know, she's not my mom."

"Well, she'll be a grandmother too. I'm sure she's as excited as me. Listen, they live in another state. I'm here always. Let her have her time."

"Mom, I don't want her to be that intimate with me. I understand her grandmother time, but not… you know. I don't want her helping me bathe or learning to breastfeed. I don't want to push her off or make her feel uncomfortable but she's not my mother."

"Marci, honey, there's no reason for you to get upset. I'll be there. She and I will have that conversation and it will be fine. She won't be pushy. Is she that way now, I mean pushy?"

"No, she's sweet, a little too sweet. She doesn't mean it but Ma, she calls me every day. Same time, same questions, same warnings, too sweet, I can't deal with all of this new mommy business, new marriage, and new, I don't know. I don't want her to think I don't appreciate her and I don't want to be rude."

"Okay, it's going to be alright. How are you feeling?"

"Fat, too fat." Marci laughed and Darlene felt relieved.

"You'll be fine. Your sister will be more of a pain then Mitch's mother. You'll have enough people around you. You just need rest. We'll spoil the baby and you'll get the rest you need."

"Yes, I can fantasize about that. I take cat naps now. You didn't tell me that I wouldn't be able to sleep comfortably."

"You'll find comfort when your baby snuggles with you. When you take a deep breath and know your baby is near. When you feed your baby and watch as they fall off your breast asleep. Mothering will be new but you will be comfortable."

"I can only imagine. Thank you. Are you on your way to the shop?"

Marci asked as she smiled rubbing her stomach. The baby was moving slowly turning seeking comfort in her touch.

"No, I have to stop at Nikki's."

"No more surprises. Between you and Mitch the room is beautiful. Nikki has done a beautiful job already. I don't think there's much more to be done."

"Okay, if you say so. It's an impromptu meeting of the minds so you never know."

"Okay, I'm hanging up now. Please, we're good. Thanks, Grandma."

"Oh, that would be Ma-Lene."

"Okay, Ma-Lene."

Fifty-Nine

'Rell smiled as the voice from the dashboard announced, *"Call from Monique Davis."* He was ten minutes away from his mother's home. He answered prepared for her rant.

"Hello, Ms. Davis."

"Mr. Mince. Are you able to talk or should I call back?"

"No, I've been waiting for your call actually. I left that message a few days ago."

"I didn't think you'd be available until the afternoon. I took a chance thinking you'd be at lunch or something."

The small talk was annoying 'Rell. It was a game Monique played to soften the outcome of her conversation. He promised Shai he would hear her out. It would be the only way for them to find out her angle. The traffic was slow, another annoyance, 'Rell decided to pull over and park. He'd allow her to talk as long as she needed for what he hoped would be the last time.

"I ate a late breakfast. So what is this about? You've got my attention."

"What did Craig or the girls at the office tell you?"

"Nothing I wouldn't verify first. So you tell me what you want me to know."

"So I'm the verification?"

"No, it's just better to hear it from you. What's going on?"

"You're so calm about this."

"Why wouldn't I be?"

'Rell cut the car off. "Listen, I heard them and I'm listening to you now. What's up? Aren't you tired of this? It's time for both of us to drop the games."

"Yes, both of us. You and I 'Rell. You played a dangerous game and got caught. You love me 'Rell, I know you do. You married her playing the game. I know you were confused. What were you thinking about, dating your sister? How could you fall in love with your own sister? I know you got trapped. She was pregnant and you had to marry her. I know everything."

"What the hell are you talking about?"

"You. 'Rell! I understand why you did it. There's a way out of it. I'm your way out."

"Monique, I'm not looking for a way out."

"Rell you and I were to be one, married. I was pregnant and you were the father. I know you didn't know and that's my fault, but we can fix this."

"When were you pregnant? There's nothing to fix. There's no baby or is there? Where is it? Boy or girl? Monique, you do know that this is not going to pan out in your favor. You do know that right?"

"I had a miscarriage because of you and that bitch! You married her!"

"Monique, we didn't get married until the twins, our children, were two. You had two years to stop the marriage, stop what you claim was madness. You didn't try to tell me then that I was a father. You had two years to make me realize I was making a mistake; that our love was real and I was living a lie. Why didn't you Monique? Could it be that you're lying about being pregnant or that the baby was Craig's?"

"It was yours! You let me go through a miscarriage because of your jealousy. You were jealous of Craig. You wouldn't even hire him."

"That had nothing to do with you baby, it was about business. Listen, I loved you, no doubt. I saw that you were a gold digger. You proved it more when you thought about what I was inheriting. Shai and I were internet friends, acquaintances. The rest is history, a history that you didn't write. You weren't a part of the last five years of my life because you didn't fit. I learned you weren't who I wanted to be with, no I couldn't be with you. We hadn't had sex in weeks. The last two visits I pretended to be with the guys. You were happy with money or gifts and that's what I gave you. I made a choice to test the waters with Shai and I never swam back to your shore."

"Bullshit 'Rell, bullshit! You loved me I know it. You love me now you just can't see yourself beyond the embarrassment."

"Telling them at my office about a child, really Monique? Seems like you wanted me to be embarrassed. You can't touch me. But you're right, I did love you. Monique when my father died, I realized that I needed to be truthful about everything in my life. I wasn't truthful and I had been faithful but you hadn't. You aren't truthful now and you never were. You didn't love me. You loved the idea of what I was to inherit. Monique, what is it you really want? You wanted Craig to help you so you offered him a job. A job you couldn't give him. What do you want? Money, recognition, what?"

"I want you. I want the father of my dead child to recognize publicly who I am and what we lost together 'Rell. We lost what was supposed to be. Our happily ever after. You gave that to your damn sister!"

"We're not related Monique. She's not my father's child."

"That can be verified you know."

"Monique it has been. Like I said I have everything verified. I've had you verified. I knew about you and Craig."

"You can't verify the loss of our child. You need to know how I feel. You're the father. You should know the feeling of the loss needs no verifying."

"Everything you do and say needs verifying. Again, what do you want?"

"You to lose it all just like I did."

"And then what?"

"And then I'll walk away from you, just like you did me. You'll know what it feels like to be alone with no one. Don't make me prove it."

"Don't threaten me, you'll regret it."

"No 'Rell you will."

Sixty

Nikki and Darlene listened to 'Rell explain his apparent anger when he arrived at his mother's home. He hadn't responded to any of their attention-seeking antics prior to the explanation. He just kept nodding his head and smiling. Once he finished giving them the details of his conversation, they understood Monique had gone too far.

"Is she crazy?" Darlene asked looking from Nikki to 'Rell.

"She always has been. She's like that damn Tonya." Nikki looked at her son. "We'll just have to be prepared for her whatever. You said Mr. Simpson has someone checking her files. Just wait, that's all we can do."

"I'm not worried about her fantasy pregnancy. It was something about her telling me I would regret my choice. You know, me marrying Shai. I don't know what that really means but there's something about how she said it. I just hope she doesn't try something she'll regret."

"Rell, as your father would say, it is what it is." Darlene looked at Nikki who was still deep in thought. "What Nikki? What's your thought?"

"You know some women never get over losing their first. I remember 'Rell telling me about Monique. As time passed, there was something about her. She was clingy but so was I, with D.Q. Even as a grown woman I felt the need to be his everything. I felt that was the only way to keep him, you know show him that I was all he needed. Maybe in some small way Monique didn't know what she was doing. She doesn't know why, I didn't know why, but 'Rell her love for you was all she had. You lose yourself in that person. You give up your norms, your life, and your all. Now I didn't go through what she's going through but I understand. I was a grown woman, she was a student. She can be dangerous 'Rell and her threat can be serious."

"Ma I can't worry about her right now with all that's going on. I'll talk to Simpson about her threat and we're checking the records."

"Rell aren't medical records protected?"

"Auntie, there's a way around everything. I learned that working with Mr. Simpson there's a lot that can be uncovered and found out about anyone if you have the money to pay for it. We'll be okay. Now, what's this meeting of the minds about?"

Darlene told them about her visit with Darryl. 'Rell wasn't surprised. Nikki couldn't deny she was aware of Darryl's concerns through her conversations with Simone.

"What can we do? Are you guys thirsty? I've got tea. 'Rell do you need something stronger?"

"Wow, really Ma? I'll get the tea for all of us."

'Rell left his mother and aunt. He needed to text Simpson. It was close to two o'clock. He'd need to put security in place near his home.

"Darlene, what's your thought? What can we do?"

"Darryl guarantees the money will come back. I think between you, me, and I hate to say it, but Tonya maybe we'll get the total up and take it back from Quintech as they get paid."

"How long will it take for us to get paid in full?"

"I don't know. Nikki all I thought of was when they step out of court they wouldn't owe anyone. Carson's Web wouldn't be knocking at Quintech's door and the gamblers wouldn't be seeking to teach a lesson. I just want it to be a clean slate for Derek and Darryl. Let's end this mess if we can."

"What about Tonya and her mess? Do you think she'd stop?"

"Tonya's mess is always going to be a mess. She didn't love my brother. I guess she was the opposite of Monique or maybe they are the same and she's just as confused. Derek is her son and she's got to want to save him. I don't know, hell, it's Tonya."

"Rell? Are you lost son?"

"No, I got a call. Sorry."

'Rell brought out the glasses filled with the tea they loved. They took a pause to think and drink.

"Ma where's Simone? I thought you guys worked from here."

"We're leaving tomorrow night for the weekend. Business and pleasure, we haven't traveled in a few months. So I think she may be at the mall a habit of hers and mine but I postponed."

"Wow, Nikki did I keep you from going to the mall? We can go together and meet her. I mean when we're done."

"Yeah sure. Does 'Rell know what you're purposing we do?"

"What's that? Once you mentioned the mall I went into my own thoughts," he teased. "The mall for me means Shai has the cards and I'll know about it later."

The humor faded as they talked over the dilemma they faced. 'Rell understood his uncle's concerns and was grateful his aunt knew his point of view.

"Let's leave Tonya out. I'll have the company cut the check. I'll check the stocks and the properties. I'm sure we can pull it from there without touching either business. I'll have Byron work up the numbers."

"How will we be sure he won't gamble it away?"

"He'll have to tell us who it is or I'll have Kenny go with him."

"Cash or check?"

"Ma, maybe you're right, cash. That kind of transaction can't be traceable. So you ladies, go have fun at the mall. I'll get back to you guys about the funds. Aunt Darlene, you can talk to Uncle Darryl and let him know we got it worked out."

"Thanks 'Rell. Your father would be proud of you."

"I don't know. You know him and Nana would have a lot to say about this mess. I'm gonna use his saying more often though."

Nikki walked 'Rell to the door. They stood in silence gazing at each other. "I know Ma. It's going to be okay. We'll all be fine."

"Rell, I don't understand why."

"And we never will understand why. Tell Sam I still want to have a talk with him."

"Boy, don't." Nikki reached out her arms. 'Rell needed his mother's embrace. His cell phone rang. He kissed his mother and answered his phone while walking to his car.

Nikki watched him from the door. For the first time in years, she saw D.Q. getting into the car and not her son. She returned to the living room where Darlene sat apparently crying.

"He's so much like his father Nikki. How do you look at him and not see D.Q.? Everything about his appearance, his demeanor, even his sense of humor. God, he's his father all over again."

"That's what I'm afraid of."

"What does that mean?" Darlene wiped her tears with the tissue Nikki offered her.

"Monique Davis may be in trouble. Especially if she tries to harm Shai."

"Why would she try that?"

"Rell loves Shai, his family, and that business. Monique wants to see him lose. I hope she doesn't try him. That's what Karlton Harris tried years ago with D.Q. He tried to destroy what he thought would ruin D.Q."

"His business, family and Tonya?"

"Yes, that's how he found out Shai and Derek weren't his children. He verified the information and tried to kill Karlton."

"I never knew that."

"I was there the night of that fight Darlene. I was glad I was there. D.Q. may have killed him if I wasn't. The problem was D.Q. no longer cared about Tonya and that's what Karlton wanted the most. D.Q. wouldn't let go of the business or the children. That's why they never knew he wasn't their father. D.Q. wouldn't let them go. I hope that girl wasn't pregnant and didn't tell 'Rell."

"Wow, I hadn't thought about it that way. Secrets and lies your son is still digging up the past. When does it end?"

"Girl let me grab my purse. I'll call Simone from the car. You can leave your car here or I can ride with you. Let's try to turn the rest of the day around. Call Darryl so he can stop worrying."

Nikki went up the stairs leaving Darlene to a moment of random thoughts. She was tired of it all. D.Q. had been right, giving Darryl a way out would be something she would regret. But she loved him. She dialed her brother's number. His voice came across the phone with the prompted message. "Darryl call me. Don't do anything else until you call me."

Sixty-One

Darryl left the court at twelve-thirty hoping the traffic across the city wasn't heavy. His intention was to get back to the court before the proceedings ended that afternoon. Mr. Simpson told him don't worry about the statements made that morning regarding the assets that seemed to increase at the same time each month. The attorney for Carson's Web presented the dates for payment made by the clients. The dollar amounts were a close match but the dates didn't coincide, a point Mr. Simpson made when he cross-examined the young accountant who took the stand.

The case was dragging, the jurors and those who watched religiously each day were tired of the mundane readings from the prepared notes. Carson's Web's lawyer, another youngster compared to Mr. Simpson, was losing ground. The judge allowed explanations and assumptions which Derek would note by tapping his pen on the desk. He had been warned about any verbal outbursts. Simpson requested a short break which allowed Derek a chance to stretch his legs and say what he wanted Simpson to say or object to.

Darryl told Kenny he would try to make it back and there had been no sign that those they owed were present in the courtroom. The phone call he told everyone he received early in the week distinctly said they would meet at the conclusion of the case. Darryl explained to Kenny he wasn't sure how they would know what day it would be without having someone monitoring the case.

Leeza was with Derek and promised Darryl she'd call if he hadn't returned by the time they were dismissed for the day. Darryl drove to meet Robert and Alan at D.Q. Enterprises. He'd call Tonya while returning to the courthouse.

Robert and Alan shared a suite on the sixth floor. Darryl knew his way around the building and those who worked on each floor. He smiled as he passed the receptionist desk there was no need for him to be announced. He knocked on the closed door and gently pushed it open.

"Hey, man, c'mon in, c'mon in." Robert stood to his feet. "Let me call Alan. He stepped out to take a call while we were waiting. So how's it going? I hear you guys got some good things going on at Quintech. That Debonair project should put you guys in the forefront for construction."

Darryl took a seat across from his old friend as they continued to discuss upcoming projects. Robert, Alan, Darryl and D.Q. were friends long before there was a thought of D.Q. Enterprises. Similar to 'Rell and his friends, they had a vision. Darryl met Francine and although his brother begged him to stay in Virginia he married and moved to Detroit. D.Q. sent Robert to set up his financial profile as a gift. Robert and Alan were only a call away and never refused any requests Darryl made.

"Hey, there fella. You and your nephew are blowing up the town." Alan walked in and the two men greeted each other with a manly hug and hand shake.

"Yes indeed. You looking good Darryl. What's up? What brings you to the lower level?" Alan took his seat next to his old friend.

"Tell me. 'Rell didn't make y'all leave the upper-level office you had. What was it on the tenth floor?"

"No man. If you remember we weren't on the same floor. 'Rell wanted us together. This floor is all finance. It works a lot smoother too. That young man has a head on his shoulder. We don't have to go up and down with reports or meetings. All right here at our disposal."

"Damn Alan, that's what computers are for. You send that report through an e-mail or zip-file. Ain't nobody running paperwork around, are they?"

"Darryl don't start your mess man."

The three men talked about the past and how they watched the business grow. They spoke about the days when they rushed work past D.Q. and his nosey secretary.

"Yeah man, you know Simpson ain't changed none. And Robert can't stand that boy, what's his name Rob?"

"Byron. That boy is sharp. All of them are. They're going to make some money with that plan your brother left."

"Man, I guess we're lucky 'Rell didn't boot us out huh?"

"Alan, D.Q. left a plan and names. My brother wouldn't see either of you go. Hell, you helped start this business. It's getting rough though."

The silence was understood. Each had their own thoughts about their friend and brother. D.Q. told them they wouldn't have to ever worry about employment. Whenever they were ready to leave they could but they would be set for life for all they had done for him and his family.

"How's Shai? We don't see her much. Seen their children though. They come here whenever 'Rell is working half days."

"She's good. You know Marci is pregnant so she's been spending a lot of time with her. I guess she's got another month or two. I never was one to keep up with a pregnancy."

"Darryl, you ain't got to tell us. How's Francine and what, five children now?"

"We're divorced. I moved here permanently about five or six months ago. I was going back and forth before then."

Robert smiled and then laughed. Darryl and Alan gave him a questioning look.

"You know what I'm laughing at, don't act like you don't."

"Okay, I don't."

"Who is she? You know you don't let the bed sheets get cold."

"Oh hell, yeah Darryl. Rob is right. Who is she?"

"The two of you, boy, you're no different than my brother. It's Simone, Nikki Robinson's cousin. Have you met her?"

Robert raised his eyebrows. "Not a bad choice my friend. She's a looker."

"Wow, and you got a divorce?"

"C'mon Alan don't make the man feel bad about his choice. Look it's cool. But seriously how are Francine and the kids?"

"They're good. Everyone is good. But listen, we need to catch up and hang out, whatever. I do need something from either of you. I need to check my stocks or whatever I have with D.Q. Enterprises. I'm trying to stay on top of what's left after this divorce. If you show me how to check it on the system, I'll do it myself."

"Well, I've got that meeting with Mutual Benefits so Rob can help you with that. Man, don't be so long stopping by. You know those of us on the lower level have to work so I don't get to leave my desk much."

"Darryl don't listen to him. He's saying it as he walks out the door. That's that mess that D.Q. used to talk about. You say one thing and I got my eyes on you."

The men laughed together as Alan made his way out of the office.

"What is it that you need Darryl? You know your password and everything don't you?"

"I think so. Can we get in the system without it?"

"You can, well let me say that another way. I can. We'll find what you need."

Sixty-Two

Alan went over Darryl's personal accounts. The stocks he invested in during the initial stages of D.Q. Enterprises as well as his personal acquired stocks over the years. The amounts were no different than Byron and Mr. Simpson explained to him. He waited for Alan to stop his evaluation before asking what he really wanted to know.

"How long has Robert been working with Tonya?"

"Uh, what are you talking about? Man c'mon, how would I know that?"

"Alan, look man, how long do you think it will be before my nephew finds out. Listen, Rob is stringing her along. We both know why. If he tells her what she wants to know she'll stop talking. If he keeps meeting with her, feeding her bits and pieces of information he may be able to tag her. That's all he wants is a chance. I know Alan, that's all he wants."

"Man, I tried to stop him. I gave up. This job here is the savings for my grandbaby's college, you know. Just what D.Q. said, I'm putting mine through school, me and mine live well. I ain't trying to mess this up. Rob, well, he's a widower. His wife has been gone some years and so are his children. They left home after college and didn't return here. Look I told him a few times about 'Rell and him finding out. I don't know what they do or what she wants."

"Alan, I know my nephew. We need to find out what information Robert is feeding Tonya. If it's simple, give her what she wants. His love interest, well, he'll just have to step up his game."

"I think it's about her interest or lack thereof, you know what I mean?"

"No." Darryl tried to sound bewildered. Alan got up and went to the Barrister files in the office. The folders located in the up scaled cabinets were in individually locked cases. He retrieved the keys in another file drawer.

"These are Mince family files, kept separate of course. We have all of them here in the office as well as 'Rell's copies in his office. I guess Simpson has a copy too. This is what I've been trying to tell Rob. Tonya should have her own….."

"Tonya should have her own what?" Robert entered the office as Alan was returning to the desk where he and Darryl were working.

Alan stopped and began to stammer. "Listen, you've got us both caught up here. I told you, I told you, no good would come from messing with D.Q.'s ex."

"What? What's that you need Darryl?"

Robert stood over Darryl who remained seated watching the two men share a quick glance with each other. It seemed as though they were holding precious information.

"Look man, 'Rell is pissed about this court case and as you know the Tonya thing. Seems everything is causing underlying tension to rise. I was just telling Alan we can relieve some of the pressure if we just tell Tonya once and for all what she wants to know. Good, bad or indifferent, D.Q. didn't hold back when he wrote his will. If there's nothing else than let's push her on her way. I mean unless…"

Darryl smiled at his old friends and each returned an uncertain grin. Rob pulled up another chair. He reached for the file Alan was still holding tightly.

"There's nothing here. What Tonya wants existed on paper only when she and D.Q. were married. I'm afraid what she saw or remembers is the original investment papers we wrote up when she complained about being a part of the company. Before the separation D.Q. bought stock in her name and sold it a few days later. There is no record of him buying it, conveniently it disappeared. The only record is the purchase of the stocks that she now possesses. The sale was lucrative and there were stipulations that have been upheld. It's been years but I'm sure it's written they are not to discuss the small print, shall we say, of the deal."

"So Darryl, I think if I remember, Rob is right. If they mention the details of the sale other than the basics, they will pay D.Q. Enterprises the percentage over with interest they were paid to make the deal."

"Yeah, it was something like that. Now since you and Derek had to have the books pulled for the court case all records were reviewed and cleaned, if you know what I mean."

"I got you, Simpson and Byron went over the files before court."

"Yes, all Tonya has is what she holds in hand. I didn't want to tell her but, that's it."

"Rell won't like you telling her anything."

Alan took the folder from Rob and placed it back in the file under lock and key. "We won't need to review any of these right Rob?"

"What are those?"

"No man, leave it. Tonya isn't a part of any of them."

"What are those?" Darryl repeated his question now frowning since there was no reply.

"Other stock investments," Rob answered. "Most of them are the backbone of the company. Repeat investments that the brokers manage. We review them quarterly, check the sales and what they recommend we buy."

"So they are active exchanges?"

"Darryl, I know what you're thinking. They have nothing to do with any individuals. These are solely company stock. Profits are banked and pay for, uh, uh, things like the building of Quintech."

"Exactly! New ventures are paid through those accounts. That's how lawyers, immediate business and unusual things are paid." Alan chimed in hoping to suppress Darryl's curiosity.

The look of fear crossed Alan and Rob's face. They knew immediately they had divulged information unknown to Darryl.

"I see. So does Quintech have investments under its name?"

"I don't think so Darryl. Being a new company and the problems in court and all. 'Rell watches these accounts to be sure they make a profit."

"Well Rob, D.Q. did the same thing."

"Wait, these investments have always been here?" Darryl couldn't begin to count the money that must have been sitting in the accounts.

"Yes, that's what pays for the resort land, upkeep and wow, Rob wouldn't you agree?"

"Darryl, you need to talk to 'Rell about those accounts. I'm sure Tonya won't be a problem." Rob hoped Alan hadn't opened a door they couldn't close.

"No, unless she's a problem for you. But, Rob make your next date totally personal. I would hate for my nephew to think you told her about these accounts that have been profitable since her marriage."

"Darryl, man c'mon. Her money was totaled when they separated. It ain't about money for me. I had a thing for her and you know it. D.Q. is gone now."

"Like I said, keep it personal or you won't be working here. Thanks for the time. Catching up is always fun and informative. Rob, I'll handle that for you. I'll talk to Tonya. That way when the two of you get together D.Q. Enterprises won't stand between you. You'll be able to keep your job that way."

Darryl left the office. He had the leg he needed to stand on. Tonya lost another round and she'd never be able to prove he was ever in her corner.

Sixty-Three

Monique couldn't find the number she needed. Karma seemed to be working against her as she cussed between taking sips of the alcoholic drink that sat close by. She couldn't control her anger and the pills she took earlier gave her a two-hour slumber, a temporary relief, without a resolution.

During her erratic thought process, she concluded she would need to speak to someone who would agree with her methods. She needed Shai to understand the marriage had to be over. There was no one better to convince an unsuspecting wife of the necessity to face this matter other than a mother that had gone through the same humiliation.

Monique flipped through her contact list on her phone again. She took the number down when she checked the public information for properties owned by D.Q. Enterprises. She was surprised to see Nikki Robbins name in the listing but calling her would be useless until she had contacted all others.

"Ah, here it is." She sat back on the couch and dialed the number. While waiting for Tonya to answer, she topped her glass off with the remaining Martini Mixer. She seemed to be relaxing more now that she found the number. She propped her feet up on the coffee table and turned down the radio that she was listening to in the background.

"Hello, yes?" Tonya answered a little more cheerful than Monique expected. She had no idea that Tonya sat her drink down to answer what she thought would be an annoying call.

"Yes, Ms. Mince? This is Monique Davis."

"Monique who? I'm sorry sweetie, hold on a moment." Tonya sat up reaching for the remote to turn the television volume lower. She placed the call on speaker for clarity the drink no longer allowed. Karlton called to say he'd be bringing home their dinner which put a major dent in her plans for leaving the house.

"Yes, now that's better Monique Davis did you say?"

"Yes, I'm a friend of your daughter's husband. I was at their wedding."

"Oh, I see." Tonya frowned at the phone. "How or what can I do for you?"

"Well it's a sensitive matter and I believe the question is what we can do for each other."

"Go on, I'm listening, although I don't know who you are or what your intentions are."

"Ms. Mince when your husband passed he ruined my life and I'm sure he ruined yours again. I mean, I understand he had tampered with your emotions some years earlier."

Monique paused. She hoped she stung the former Ms. Mince. She took a slow drink waiting for a response. Tonya sat up on her couch and took a drink as well.

"Well you see Ms. Mince, I was 'Rell's love interest before he fell for his sister or whatever. During the time they were beginning to weave their tangled web, I was here in Virginia being the doting girlfriend in every way."

"Oh, now I know who you are. So what does your loss or whatever you think you've lost have to do with me?"

"I think we both are owed compensation for our loss. You financially, I'm sure. Me, I lost the man I loved, the child I was carrying that was his and yes, the inheritance as his rightful wife."

Tonya was silent. She sipped from her glass as Monique repeated the story she told at D.Q. Enterprises and to 'Rell.

"Ms. Mince, I've come to the conclusion that Shai should know. As should 'Rell's mother and grandmother. I thought it best to alert you to my intentions and let you know I understand your loss, as I am fighting for mine."

"Child, please, did that man ask you to marry him? Was he aware you were pregnant?"

"No, he didn't and I lost the child before their marriage. I couldn't bring myself out of my depression to tell him. I guess I felt in a way like you."

"Like me? How so?"

"You know. I felt guilty. I mean I understand your reasons for stepping outside of your marriage, but I only wanted him to want me. You do understand my actions don't you?"

Tonya shook her head and put down her glass. It wasn't the first time that someone blamed her for D.Q. falling in love with Nikki. By the time she realized 'Rell was their child, she and D.Q. were no longer sleeping together. She tried to lure him into their bed and despite the attempts, it never resulted in a pregnancy.

"Just what do you think you will gain? Shai won't fall for the nonsense and apparently, neither has 'Rell. I'm sure you've talked to him. Why would I help you with anything like this? It would ruin Shai."

"You help me and I'll help you. You didn't get what you deserved but if you can separate them or convince Shai the marriage isn't worth the shame….. Well I'll push for enough to leave them alone which will include monies for you. The shame alone is worth saving her don't you think, I mean you should know."

"Listen, I'm glad we had this time to talk. Is this a good number to reach you? I have to go, I'll think about this. Goodbye."

The phone went to the dial tone and Monique had no idea she had been placed on speaker. Tonya had no idea how much of the conversation Karlton heard.

Sixty-Four

Karlton ignored the look of shock on Tonya's face. It was obvious he walked in on a conversation she didn't want him to hear. He shook his head as he passed her sitting with the phone in hand.

"Alright babe, we've got your favorite salad and I thought you'd love salmon. I didn't know whether or not we had white wine."

Tonya joined him in the kitchen once she realized his conversation wasn't a prelude to questioning her about the phone call. She pushed the thoughts regarding the call out of her mind. She'd have to deal with Monique's fantasy at another time.

"Whatever you brought for me is fine I'm sure. Here's the wine and there's more in the cabinet. I'm waiting for a call from Darryl. He's talking to Rob regarding that stock I told you about."

Karlton didn't answer as he washed his hands. He turned and faced her and again shook his head. The gesture made Tonya a little nervous. For the first time in years she couldn't read his emotions.

"Say something, go ahead damn it. I know I was drinking the whole time you left and now you're annoyed right? I prefer my drink, not the white wine."

"Tonya I didn't say anything about you drinking. You're grown, you're home and obviously you feel that's what you need to do to cope with, whatever. Darryl can't help you and he'll call to say so. Why would Rob tell him anything different? Let it go."

He passed her a plate from the cabinet. "Go get your glass so we can eat, baby. I'm not entertaining it anymore. You have your way of dealing with it and when I get tired of it, well we won't talk about that now. I'm really trying here Tonya, can you try just a little. This is the life you said you wanted. Me, you, us, remember? Just us. No D.Q. Enterprises, no D.Q. and no hiding our love."

Karlton walked to where she was standing and kissed her forehead. "I love you Tonya and that's what matters to me."

"I love you too." Tonya did as he asked and went to get the glass she felt immediately needed a refill. She drank the remains of the glass and returned to her prepared plate.

Returning to the kitchen she asked, "So you think I should let it all go?"

"Tonya, what is there to gain? Money? You're not hurting for D.Q.'s money. I don't understand your need to remain attached to that business. Baby, with all you've been through, I just want to leave the past in the past. Let's enjoy life together, maybe get away a bit, spend some time with the grands. How about the weekend? They're supposed to be visiting this weekend. Plan an outing with them and let's focus on living again."

"Sounds good, but Darryl is going to call. I don't want you to be upset about me delving deeper if he gives me more information."

"That's okay. Tonya as long as it doesn't interfere with our relationship with our children or grandchildren. Agreed?"

"Agreed." Tonya thought about Monique's proposal. Shai would be shattered if she wasn't with 'Rell. Karlton was right after all they had been through Shai was there for her. She cared for her mother regardless. Shai was more like D.Q., more like Karlton, and Tonya could admit that. She just couldn't be like them.

The phone rang interrupting her thoughts. Karlton answered and just smiled. He handed her the phone and took his plate and drink with him leaving her alone to talk freely.

"Hello." Tonya answered unsure of who may be on the other end of the call.

"Hey, it's Darryl. Tell old boy that I hope I didn't disturb anything. Hell he can't possibly be mad at me, or can he?"

"Oh, I don't know. You tell me. Should we be mad at you?"

"No, I mean, I'm in this like you. Okay, I talked to both Rob and Alan, most of the afternoon I might add. I didn't even get back to the courtroom. Have you heard from your son?"

"No, why would he call me? I told you he said for me to reach out to him with any news. What did you find out?"

"Nothing, absolutely nothing. What they gave you, that's all they have. I looked in the system with them and the files. There's nothing there. You have it all. Do you have your copies?"

"Copies of what? The sale? Sure I do. Listen I thought you were going to look into other stocks as well. I told you I think it's buried in the company, maybe your company."

"Listen, they went over our books for the case with a fine tooth comb."

"You mean an eraser. Darryl, your brother had a vision. Everything he did was directed toward the future. Financial protection he called it. It's there somewhere."

"Okay, I know what you mean but here's the issue. Even if he did plan for it, it's not in your name. For that matter, it's not in anyone's name. So how do we get it?"

"We? What the hell is with the 'we' shit today?"

"Huh? Tonya, what are you talking about?"

"Listen, what you're saying is my sorry ass lawyer needs to subpoena financial records."

"Whatever. From what Rob said, there is no personal entitlement due to you or anyone else after 'Rell took over. The records for any money due was reviewed and handled before the reading of the will. I guess that's when it was determined what everyone would get."

"So you're saying you are satisfied. Oh, that's right, you're still a Mince and you have a business that will benefit."

"Hell Tonya, so does your son and daughter."

"Well, there goes your request for sixty g's. I ain't got it and you can't find it. Let me know if I have to save money for Derek's commissary."

Tonya pushed the end button on the receiver. She began to eat her salad without giving her words a second thought.

"Karlton, I think there's a children's play at the mall this weekend. I think it's a short performance at the Kids Main Stage. Brianna loved it when we took her and Bryce there for Christmas. Call Shai for me please? I'll call and get the tickets okay?"

Sixty-Five

Darryl checked the phone when he realized Tonya disconnected the called. He smiled, she had no idea what he knew. He wouldn't need her sixty thousand if she was entitled to anything. D.Q. was smarter than he thought. The money in the company would multiply year after year. There would always be a profit of some sort. Property, investments, consulting and then there were new ventures like Quintech. If 'Rell wouldn't release Quintech he'd have to pay for his father's secret. D.Q. hadn't relinquished all his assets, or had he? 'Rell inherited a gold mine. The gold mine that belonged to the family. They all bought in on his father's idea when the business started. Sure he paid them but his money continued and 'Rell was now the recipient.

Darlene had called again. She'd be after the next three calls. First Mr. Simpson, then Derek and 'Rell; they all needed to know he was on to his brother's secrets and he wanted in. The amount of money he wanted would be well above the figure he gave them earlier.

Simone left a message saying she would call when she got to Nikki's. They would be leaving early the next morning. There was one more day of testimony and Darryl needed to know how the trial would be ending. He needed Mr. Simpson and 'Rell to understand the payment had to be paid regardless to the fines that Derek would have to cover.

He went into his office and looked around. His home was smaller than any of the young men that sat in the top seats at D.Q. Enterprises. Knowing about the money that was being made pained him. D.Q. never offered him a position. Nana and Darlene put up equal shares when asked to invest in D.Q.'s venture. Darryl got the money from his company and Francine's savings to pay his share. He made a few stops before reaching Virginia leaving money along the way. His investment was ten thousand dollars shorter than his commitment. D.Q. covered it and gave him shares equal to his mother and sister.

Money never was an issue to his brother and it seemed his son felt the same way. 'Rell paid all debts owed with the exception of the gambling debt that grew each time Darryl told the story. The threat was pending and now that the trial was ending he needed the family to believe that without the payment someone would be hurt again. He opened the cigar box on the desk and twirled the wrapped tobacco between his fingers. Putting the Arturo to his nose and then his lips he lit it and inhaled slowly.

Mr. Simpson's phone rang twice before the lawyer answered. "Darryl, thought you would meet us here at the office. Is everything okay?"

Darryl frowned at the phone. "Everything's fine sir. Just had a lot of business to attend to. Are you alone?"

"Yes, everyone left about ten minutes ago. What can I help you with?"

"We need to talk. I mean I can do it over the phone if you like but I know how you love the face to face discussions."

"Is this about the case or some other business?"

"Humph, it ties in, I guess you can say that. D.Q. Enterprises is sitting on stock. I mean stock that is not recorded as owned by family or outside investors, right?"

"I'm not sure I'm following you. The Enterprise has titles that are not personally owned yes. They are owned by various boards within the company."

"I see. Who is on the boards?"

"Executives within the company."

"Rell, Mitch, Craig? Who?"

"Rell yes, the others no."

"Family members other than 'Rell?"

"No."

"You?"

"No."

"What the hell Simpson, who?"

"Sir, you'll have to speak with 'Rell."

"What is the big secret?"

"There is no secret. If 'Rell says I can talk with you about it, I'd be glad to discuss it. Without his approval, I can't discuss it."

"Okay, okay, what are the investments in."

"Property, gold, entertainment ventures, it varies Mr. Mince."

"Oh, it's Mr. Mince now. You've put on your lawyer's hat?"

"I don't know what information you're seeking. The investments at D.Q. Enterprises are public. Any that are not, well I'm not at liberty to discuss."

"Did D.Q. own them before his separation from Tonya or before he wrote the will?"

"No, oh no. None before the separation or the pending divorce. The money was invested at the time of his death. The instructions were clear. What to invest in and how much as well as when. Nothing was done until the will was read. It was one of the first assignments your nephew had. Investments were made immediately after the reading of your brother's will."

"So D.Q. trusted 'Rell to invest in property, gold, and other ventures? How much?"

"Darryl, I can't discuss that really. Talk to 'Rell. What is it you need to know?"

"Be honest with me. Did my brother ever mention me working in his business?"

"No. He supported you in yours. Whatever you or Francine chose he made sure to keep your business afloat."

"What?"

"D.Q. had his office monitoring debts, payoffs, loans, for you. Francine knew about the balances, the monies needed and he funded your business."

"There's no way D.Q. Enterprises is making that kind of money. What is really going on?"

"Talk to your nephew. He has made the same decision as your father. The family is not to be a part of the inner workings of the business. I'm sorry, I'm obligated to 'Rell and D.Q."

Sixty-Six

"Nana he sounded drunk. Yelling and screaming about how me and D.Q. snuck money behind his back. You know I tolerated his nasty attitude about money for years. If D.Q. hadn't stepped in the few times that he did, this business would have went under."

"Francine, only you baby, only you. Ain't nobody got time for Darryl crying years later. That's what his problem is, he woke up chile. D.Q. left everyone enough to get on with their lives, their business and build more if they wanted. Everyone is fine but him, now he got to stir up something?"

"Yea and I guess his woman ain't around, so it's me."

"No, she ain't. She ain't for that foolishness either. She got a business going with Nikki. I'm telling you he just wants someone to cry with him. He knows better than call here with that mess. Are the children okay, did he even ask about them?"

"No ma'am he didn't, but he never does. I just want to know what's got him so stirred up."

"Could be this case Francine. You know they been in court all week. I think Monday they'll be finished with the whole thing."

"How is Derek holding up?"

"Chile, you know as much as I do. Rev Wallace said he's going to the courthouse tomorrow. I ain't going. I can't sit there like that and don't ask my own questions. Wallace and Sam can go. That other mess is still overhead too. I know Derek will be glad when it's over."

"What other mess? Oh! You mean with the gambling and stuff. Nana, I'm gonna be honest with you. That ain't never gonna end. You know maybe that's what's got Darryl all tied in a knot. If Derek got to pay out money he won't have none to gamble away. You know they found that account he had hid. Taking money from the profits and peeling it off to gamble. Same thing he was doing here."

"Rell stopped that mess, honey. Got that young boy, his friend Byron, keeping them books. Darryl's gambling money is being watched."

"I know he mad about that. Nana, do you think someone would try to hurt Derek again about the money they still owe?"

"Still owe? I thought that was paid up?"

"I don't think so. Darlene called here about it the other day."

"Oh. Well, Derek is going back to Brazil. Darryl will just have to face that band."

"You think they'll hurt him?"

"Francine, people funny about their money. Specially when you owe them or they think you do."

"That's Darryl's problem right there. Calling me like I owe him something. No sir, I'm done with that mess."

"You better be baby. You got left with 'dem kids and a business. You blessed, 'Rell followed his father's footsteps and kept everything afloat. If Darryl can't see the blessing, well somebody will sure show him different. I pray not, but everyone has that one. Darryl has always been mine. Listen, I got supper on and Rev will be walking in the door soon. Kiss the kids for me, baby, y'all be good now."

Nana put the phone in the cradle. She looked at the clock on the wall. Jeopardy was coming on. She wouldn't be caught talking on the phone about Darryl and missing her favorite show. Rev. Wallace called to say he was on his way just as she took the meatloaf out the oven. The potatoes were done and she decided they would have a mixed salad.

The comforts of home kept her going and the thoughts of Derek's trial and Darryl's continued chaos kept her in prayer. She sighed at the thought of Darryl being involved with Derek in business. It was clearly a mistake even though 'Rell and Wallace told her it would work out. Now the business would be left in Darryl's hands. The hands that always moved money to the gambling tables. Nana picked up the phone and dialed her son's number.

"Hey Ma, how are you?"

"No, the question is, what's wrong with you?"

"What, did Francine call you already? I just called to ask her some questions that's all. What's the crime in that?"

"Darryl, really? Leave that woman alone. She's trying to hold herself together. You left her with that business, the children and a home."

"Hey, she's doing better than most divorced women."

"Darryl! You know there's no reason for you call her other than to upset her."

"Mama, listen, I just found out that D.Q. left more money than we thought. And you know what? He left it to 'Rell and that lawyer of his to handle it and invest it."

"What's wrong with that?"

"That money should have been divided among us."

"You can't be serious Darryl. You were left with plenty."

"Did you know about this?"

"Yes. I knew."

"Darlene knew."

"No, she didn't."

"Why, who told you?"

"Have you been drinking?"

"I'm home. I'm not going anywhere so yes, I can drink until I fall out."

"Darryl why you drinking like that?"

"Mama, why did he give all that money to that boy?"

"Who?"

"Rell, you said you knew about it."

"Rell put the money where D.Q. told him to put it. He followed everything his father told him to do. Listen you know I don't talk to people who can't remember their name until the morning. Jeopardy is on. I just wanted to tell you to stop worrying Francine with your nonsense. Ain't you with Simone now?"

"Why 'Rell, Mama?"

"D.Q. is dead and gone. Don't none of us know why. But here's something for you to remember. He lived his life his way and left what he wanted to who he wanted to have it. You're living Darryl, time for a change baby."

"You right Mama, and if I can't get what I know is mine, I'm going to take it. Go on, watch your show. Good night."

Nana looked at the phone. It would be a waste of time to call him back or call Darlene. She'd catch him after the trial.

"D.Q. you better tap your brother's shoulder, he headed for trouble. I just know he is." She smiled to herself as she looked up to talk to her departed son. The music to Jeopardy startled her. She hoped she didn't miss the start of the game.

Sixty-Seven

Shai couldn't believe how tired she was. Keeping up with her regular schedule and trying to entertain her brother and Leeza in the evening was wearing thin. Although they both would tell her to go to bed if she felt tired she remained up laughing and talking until midnight or later. Now two weeks later it was catching up with her. She entered her home early hoping to sneak in a nap before the evening rituals began.

'Rell told her he and Derek would pick up the kids. They were dropping off Leeza at the hospital. She was meeting a few of her friends. That was Shai's signal to leave work. It was just about seven when she finally began to relax with the remote in her hand. Although it had become her favorite position after dinner, baths and story time, she was enjoying the moment alone. She began to doze when she heard the squeals of the twins as they entered the front door.

Although she had no idea what they were trying to tell her between their giggles and shouts she was now smiling and telling them "yes" whenever they harmoniously asked. "Can we, can we?"

"What are they so excited about?"

"Karlton called and said he and your mother want to take them to Kid's Stage or something like that." Rell shrugged his shoulder. "I told him they could pick them up from school tomorrow. I did tell them if you had something else planned it wouldn't happen."

"No that's great, I mean wow. They haven't been on an overnight at my mother's in a while. Although she will scoop them up for shopping spree at Children's Place. They love that place."

"The best thing at the mall for children I guess. It's not there all the time though. Imagine if they had a permanent location."

"You're smoking 'Rell. No, we don't need to invest in a Kid's Stage location."

"You're good girl. Listen did you eat?"

The couple stared at each other.

"Where's my brother? Leeza hangs out and he disappears, what's that about?"

"He went to hang out with Aunt Darlene. Don't ask. She called and told him to stop by before tomorrow. That was yesterday, I think. Well anyway, our house is ours again for a minute."

"Wow, how are they getting back here?"

"He didn't say. Leeza won't be back until tomorrow. She's meeting us at court. Derek is slumming with Aunt Darlene."

"So we've got to get the tiny ones fed and in bed."

'Rell looked at Shai and smiled. It was more than obvious they both needed the time to unwind. Shai called the twins. There was no answer so she nodded her head and went to the stairs.

"They ate, please say yes?"

"They did and if you don't ask they won't say they're hungry."

'Rell took her place on the couch and roamed the channels on the television with the remote. The phone rang and Darryl's name appeared on the screen.

"Hey Unc what's up?"

It took a moment for Darryl to respond. "What's up with you?"

"Just getting in. You okay, you don't sound right."

"Cause you and I need to seriously talk. This court thing, the gambling debt, the money you and your father kept from the family, we need to talk about it all. Oh yeah and your business being mixed with mine, that too."

"Okay, when you want to have this talk."

"Now! Right now!"

"Okay, on the phone or do you need to see me."

"Humph, I asked your protecting lawyer the same thing. It's up to you. What you comfortable with?"

"The phone is good. I got time."

"Me too. Listen 'Rell I know your father thought it was best for you to take over, but you can't take over me. You can't just think you can run what is mine."

"What do you think I took over or I'm running?"

"Quintech, my construction company in Detroit, you took that over. Right from your father. He would do that you know, just step in; ain't nobody ask him for help, he just thought we needed it."

"Did you tell him that?"

"What you a psych now? You ain't gonna be analyzing me!"

"So what is it you want to talk to me about?" 'Rell realized his uncle was drunk, the question was how drunk. He didn't want to have the conversation twice. "Listen, how about we talk about this after the case is over."

"Nah, that ain't gonna work. I told you, the money needs to be paid by the end of the trial."

"No, you told Aunt Darlene that. You haven't talked to me."

"That's right because you need to tell me how much money you and your father were sitting on before the investment. You took that money and your father was dead. That wasn't your money to invest nowhere. We might have wanted our money back."

"We who? What money?"

"Boy don't play with me. Your father left money for you to invest. Simpson told me that much. Who is on this board that knows about this money? It ain't theirs."

"Listen, we need to have this conversation when you're sober."

"Why you can't lie to me cause' I been drinking?"

"No, you need to remember what I have to say about you approaching me like this. We need to have this talk so it won't have to be repeated."

"Oh, you big now?"

"What, look after the case; you said they want the money at the end of the trial, fine they'll wait."

"Oh so someone else can get hurt. You're just like your damn father. You don't care if I take the bruises for this."

"Derek took the last one, it's your turn if they see it that way. I'm not going to talk business with you now."

"Well Quintech is the bargaining chip. I want you out of my business."

"Yeah, you need to be sober." 'Rell laughed.

"What's funny? Do you hear me laughing?"

"No, I just thought that Derek should hear this too. I mean since Quintech is his company. Read your papers from the reading of my father's will. You weren't left any business, neither was Derek. Quintech was built at the request of Derek and you were asked to join at his request. Nothing to do with my father's money that he left for investments or my suggestions to Derek. I was left instructions. We do need to talk. You and a few others need to recognize who I am."

Sixty-Eight

"Nana I needed to talk to you. Are you going to be home on Saturday?"

"Rell if you need me here on Saturday tell me the time suggah. Wait, let me check this here calendar. You know since the Rev is here we've had to keep a calendar. I never kept one before, what was I thinking?"

The silence and then the mumbled words between them had 'Rell confused. *"Does she want me to answer about her thinking? Nah, I'll leave that alone."* He waited and as he suspected his grandmother didn't need him to answer.

"Now, it's just easier this way. Write it down when there's too much to remember. I know that's the way your father did things all the time. That's why there was so much for you to go through when he died. I told him I wouldn't remember the goings on in his life and live mine too. Anyway, 'Rell, I got a Seniors meeting at the church early that morning." Nana laughed. "You ain't coming here at no nine in the morning, I know."

"You right Nana, I'll be sleeping in. Karlton and Tonya have offered to keep the twins. They're taking them to Kid's Stage at the mall. You know that place that puts on shows for kids right?"

"Yes, I've seen that place. Sure is a lot of kids there all the time. Do they do that every day?"

"They have something there daily and special shows every month or so, I think. Anyway, they'll be with them until Sunday. A break for me and Shai."

"Derek and Leeza there with y'all ain't they?"

"Yes, ma'am. I don't know their plans. They're out tonight. As a matter of fact, Derek is staying at Aunt Darlene's tonight."

"Where is his girlfriend staying? What happened?"

"Nothing, she's visiting friends she has from the hospital. So what time will you be free, say, after twelve?"

"Lord boy, you could come here by eleven. This talk ain't got to take up the good part of the day."

"Nana that's what I need. A good day, all the parts need to be good."

"How is that trial going?"

"I think Derek will be fine. He'll have to pay for it of course but he won't do any jail time. They'll be done on Monday unless something else comes up. Mr. Simpson doesn't think it will be a large sum. I think they just want to teach Derek a lesson and of course stop any other employee that would attempt to try what he did."

"Hmm, I still don't understand what he did or why?"

"He sold a design another client bought as their own. He sold it to another company. The company is not in the United States. Derek didn't think they would do international promotions or correspondence using the design. He did it with two clients. One was totally upset, that's the one that sued Carson's Web. Since he represented Carson's Web in the deal his boss fired him and now they're suing him."

"What about the other client?"

"That's what Simpson is looking in to. He thinks it may be the one who tried to run him off the road."

"I thought that was the gambling thing. That's what your Uncle said."

"We can't find anyone who has tried to contact Derek after the accident or an attempt to contact him before. We got the team on it."

"They'll find it. Did Simpson call Kenny?"

"Yes, they're on it."

"They'll find out, that's for sure. Well until tomorrow baby, I've got some other calls to make I was just checking on you."

"Thank you, my sweet grandmother. What would I do without you?"

"I'll leave you the instructions like your dad did."

"Whew, please don't. I don't know if I could look through all of your things and find out the secrets that you have."

They both laughed. "We all have secrets my child, even you."

'Rell thought about his grandmother's words. He didn't want to think that his grandmother had envelopes and paperwork to sort through. He'd have to ask her again without the humor and pray she wasn't serious. Nana and D.Q. were close and from what he understood in reviewing the company's infrastructure, Nana's input was embedded in its foundation. She and D.Q. built the company from the start and when 'Rell's father proved his strength Nana gave him full reign.

If 'Rell was to deal with his uncle and the company's history, he and Nana would have to talk again. A talk he had avoided once he thought the dust surrounding the business had settled. Now the business was being tested. Their discussion about his father and D.Q. Enterprises would have to be serious.

Sixty-Nine

The blinding sun caused Derek to put on his shades as he drove to his uncle's home close to sunrise. After receiving his call late the night before, he promised he would see him before going to court in the morning. Derek could tell his uncle had been drinking heavily. The two had many nights together where he became the caregiver to a man, who after drinking more than he could handle, became the disheartened child. Darryl Mince told Derek things about his life, his mistakes, and the struggle to be noticed as a Mince. Derek understood his pain or could relate since Dershai had always been the favorite. The common factor was D.Q.

As an older brother, D.Q. led the way for Darryl but the younger brother couldn't follow the path. His success, he owed to D.Q. If he failed, D.Q. would fix the problem. This began years before they became men, years before D.Q. became successful. D.Q. cherished Shai and never hesitated to tell Derek to stay close to his sister. Derek would receive the pat on the back while Shai received the love. D.Q. would explain to both Darryl and Derek that a man needed to be able to stand tall in spite of his mistakes, his weakness or his ignorance. He had explained that standing was the first step to manhood.

Darryl and Derek felt they stood behind D.Q.'s image. They couldn't step into his shoes when he passed on as D.Q. groomed Darrell, his only true son to take his place. Derek never thought much about it until his uncle, though drunk, mentioned it should have been one of them. They should have been chosen and now just like D.Q., 'Rell was running their business.

Derek's thought about having his own had changed since his accident, the court case, and his conversation with the family. Each expressed their reason for him to become more involved, more serious, more dedicated to his own.

Leeza loved him and he loved her. It was her thoughts and opinions he appreciated more. Darryl was a hiccup in Derek's vision for the future of Quintech. He would have to have this conversation with him before leaving for Brazil. Darryl would have to stop gambling, lying about the money made, and allow the company to grow. It was the future for him, Leeza and their family that he now was working for. Watching his uncle move from wife to wife, woman to woman and leaving children wherever he laid his head was not the direction Derek wanted for himself. It was time for him to stand and the meeting this morning would make or break his relationship with his uncle.

Derek's overnight stay with Darlene reminded him that although D.Q. wasn't his father, he gave him and Shai what others work for all their lives. The freedom to be independent and stable. Darryl was enslaved by alcohol and gambling and wherever it called him he would follow. Darryl would take the business down with him and he would run without giving anyone a clue.

Derek parked the rental car in front of his uncle's home. He stood for a moment to take in the view of the neighborhood. He was comparing it to the homes in his uncle's past. Aunt Francine was still in Chicago, there was Aunt Carla in Philadelphia, and Aunt Maxine in New York, he smiled remembering Shai's list of aunts he hadn't married. *"Darryl made his rounds with the women, but that came with drinking and gambling",* Aunt Francine's words made Derek shake his head.

He rang the bell after stepping onto the porch that wrapped around the front and sides of the home. The white and red brick was an accent to the stucco structure. Derek rang the bell a second time and turned again to admire the homes on the lots next to and across from the porch where he stood. He tried the knob before attempting to ring the bell again. It was unlocked, so he entered without announcing his entrance.

Derek found Darryl sprawled out on the couch barely holding the remains of the Grey Goose Vodka bottle in his limp hand. Removing the bottle caused him to stir, Derek stood back allowing his uncle to sit up slowly. The room was in order with the exception of the area where his uncle obviously began his drinking binge.

"You got coffee? You need some."

"Yeah." Darryl took a deep breath. "What time is it?"

"About six, I guess. You got coffee or not?"

"Yea, I got coffee, damn."

"Look you said you wanted to talk. You should have been up. You know I have to be in court this morning. Get up, let's go to the kitchen. Let's go."

"Humph, you got a lot of nerve."

"No, I just got jolted into what can be my future if I don't change what's soon to be my past."

"What the hell are you talking about? Don't talk riddles boy."

"Uncle Darryl, if there's one thing I've learned through all of this, I ain't a boy. Now, let's go, get up."

Derek walked to the end of the living room and through the dining room. The kitchen light was on and revealed the mess from the night before.

"What the hell happened in here? Shit, what were you trying to do in here?"

"Just make the damn coffee."

"You right, that's about it." Derek put on the coffee and returned to the dining room. Darryl made his way to the chair sitting across from his nephew.

"So what's up? I thought you'd call after court today."

"No, I told you I'd be here this morning. I don't know what they have planned today. After this case, I'm out. Back to Brazil where Leeza can continue to work. That's where she plans to be and I plan to be there with her."

"Oh, so you running? Leaving the country falls in 'Rell's plans perfectly. You giving him the company?"

"Uncle Darryl, let's get real since you're predicting the future. We need the business to be clean, squeaky clean. You may ask why but you're not sitting where I am, with a judge and people trying to sue you. I don't need to relive this again. So can you run it clean? I don't think so after seeing you this morning. Have you been checking in on what's going on since neither of us is available?"

"Oh, it's about what I do now?"

"It's always been about what you do or didn't do. I need someone to run the company, remember? That's what I asked of you before I left. You promised me you would be happy to be a partner in this business. After seeing the books, c'mon I know what's going on. Everyone has had my ear about you and business. You can't think that I wouldn't find out."

"Find out what?"

"The money Uncle Darryl. You keep saying we owe the people from that backroom game. How long have you been stealing money to pay them?"

"You knew about the payment. Listen the money you gave me…"

"Yeah, the money I saved up should have paid the debt in full. Then you said you gambled it to double it and lost it. So now we still owe that with interest. Sixty g's? Uncle Darryl, we didn't owe that kind of money."

"Well, now they want more."

The coffee maker bell chimed before Derek could answer.

"Get the damn coffee. You wanted to talk, so get me some coffee. I'll be good and sober for this talk."

Darryl and Derek talked for more than an hour. Darryl went on to tell Derek about the stocks D.Q. had which was money left for 'Rell and none of the family got a fair share.

"Uncle Darryl, D.Q. left the money and business where he wanted it. To be honest I couldn't handle what he gave me. Hell, without 'Rell's help and the assistance from his friends Quintech wouldn't have been developed and running by now. You would have gambled yours away, I'm sure of it. So neither you nor I lost anything. But if we don't come to some understanding about the company's future, some things are going to have to change."

"What does that mean?"

"I'll give it back to D.Q. Enterprises. I can't manage it by myself living in Brazil. You can't manage it gambling and drinking. I won't see it fall under. I'll have D.Q. Enterprises staff it and run it. I'll still own it but I won't have it fall."

"Who the hell are you to tell me that I won't be running the company that I built?"

"Uncle Darryl you designed and built that beautiful building. The internal workings, the structure of the business component, the contracts, and clients....well they're mine. I give your business the construction contracts. I design the logos and you put them on their buildings or you reconstruct the offices. I'm sure you know your company and mine are two entities that could separate and exist independently. All I'm saying is my part won't fall because of you."

"Damn Derek. He got to you. You don't even hear me telling you that 'Rell has what should have belonged to the family first."

"My mother said something about other stocks. Funny you should be the one to find it. Listen, my father, D.Q. gave everyone a boost in life, financial stability. I can expand to Brazil, I can cash in and move on. What I won't do is fall! You want your brother's stocks, his money more than he gave you? Stand toe to toe with 'Rell and see how far you get with the family. We're not the favorites Uncle Darryl that's a reality. I learned that at the reading of the will. Once my mother lied about me being a Mince, I understood D.Q."

"Get a backbone, Derek! There's money that should be ours, the family, mine."

"You sound like Tonya Mince. It was about what was hers for years and she found out D.Q. was about business. 'Rell was groomed to take over and he's about the business that D.Q. left. If there was something left for family 'Rell wouldn't keep it. Did you talk to your mother, Nana? She wouldn't let 'Rell keep it."

Darrell gave Derek a questioning look.

"Oh, I guess you haven't talked with Aunt Darlene. Well I did, last night. Nana knows and knew all along about 'Rell taking over. If she knew that, I'm sure she knows about the stocks. So, uncle, no one is surprised except you and my mother. Two people, that have carried hate for a dead man, how many years? Get over it, talk to your real nephew, 'Rell. I don't give a damn about the stock. I got what the man who raised me wanted me to have. If I stand in it, I've got a fortune waiting to be made."

"Derek, you don't understand any of this do you?"

"I understand that I could lose it all if you only think of revenge. I almost lost my life because of your choice to continue to gamble. Pay them, Uncle Darryl, before someone else gets killed."

Seventy

"**G**ood morning 'Rell. I was hoping you had time to think about our conversation the other day."

'Rell looked at the console on his dashboard as though Monique was sitting before him.

"Why are you on my damn phone this early?"

"Oh, you feeling some kind of way Mr. Mince?"

"No but I'm just wondering do you still sleep with me on your mind?"

"Oh, we feeling spunky this morning?"

"Not at all but as an afterthought, you know, following our conversation, I began to wonder. This is a woman that I truly loved, I must have been insane. But nevertheless I loved her, so maybe, just maybe, I turned her out and she just can't get over it. You know my smell, my flirtatious ways, my smile, my laughter, my taste…..maybe you just want me once more and then we can move the fuck on!"

"Don't tease me baby, you know your wife wouldn't allow you to share what I allowed her to have. Besides, you weren't as good as I pretended you were. My moans and shrieks just kept you hard long enough for me to get mine."

"Well that's true 'cause I barely got mine. Other than your lips and sounds I barely shook or shivered. So if this is not a cry for a good bangin' what do you want on this perfect day?"

"I expected you to be angered by my call but hey, I'm loving your teasing."

"You always did Monique. What do you want?"

"You. You to recognize you left me without a choice or way to deal with the loss of our baby. I should reap what would have been mine if you walked off from me and the child."

"There is no child and there is no fee to walk away from a relationship. We weren't engaged, nor had I promised you anything. As it was, I left you before I inherited a dime. Please don't make these calls a habit. Each call will have the same ending. I don't want you in my life."

"I know. You have the "happily ever after" with Shai and your twins. Bryce and Brianna right? The baby was a boy if you're wondering. I remembered you liked the name, Deon."

"Why didn't you call when you found out Monique? Why didn't you call when you had the miscarriage, the abortion, the lie?"

"Oh, you think it's a lie?"

"Look baby, do you, whatever that is. If the only way to get over me is to fake a pregnancy, do you. It won't change reality. I'm happily married. We know your story and without proof, there will be no need to feed into the lie. I can't even hurt for you, I wish I could because at one time I did love you. My worst was seeing you with Craig. You hurt me deep then. Are you looking to hurt me again? Just remember what I did when you flaunted your relationship with Craig. I got married."

Monique couldn't believe her ears. *He got married because I was dating Craig, could that be true?* A sick feeling came over her. The silence on the phone was deafening.

"Monique, I've got to go to the office now. Have a good day baby. I hope you feel better. The queasy feeling in your stomach is how I've felt about you ever since that day I saw the two of you."

"But you gave him a job, another chance."

"Yea, I realized he was hypnotized by your beauty too. You showed him the ugly though. I take care of those I love. I watch out for those who want to do those I love harm. I'm watching you baby, just what you wanted. Me and my people watching you."

"You need to believe me. I won't let things end this way."

"As always Monique, do you."

Seventy-One

Kenny sat waiting in the reception area of Mr. Simpson's office. The court proceedings would conclude on Monday as both sides had given all documents and testimonies for the judge to make his final statement. After Monday's decision, Kenny would take Leeza and Derek to D.Q. Enterprises for immediate arrangements.

Kenny's assignment was easy since there didn't appear to be any threats made since Derek's return home. There were two men assigned to Leeza at all times as well as one man who followed Derek. Neither suspected they were being followed or protected. No one made an obvious attempt to threaten them in any way. The instructions were presented by Mr. Simpson but initiated by 'Rell. Mr. Simpson entered the office and led the way for the trained retired detective to follow.

"Hold my calls please." Mr. Simpson spoke into his phone as he settled himself behind his desk.

"Stan, we've got a few things that I just wanted to go over with you before Monday."

"What do you have? Is there an issue?"

"Just making sure sir, just making sure. First, we've got Tonya Mince…"

The meeting lasted about two hours. Mr. Simpson assured Kenny that 'Rell would be made aware of his concerns. He too didn't quite understand any of the family motives. Tonya, Monique nor Darryl wanted the problems that they brought on to cause 'Rell to react in anger. They wanted to be paid and they would simply go away, or so the lawyer hoped they would. The question and answer were obvious, Kenny may have to persuade them to back up. Nothing that he or his team hadn't done before, 'Rell would only have to give the okay. The alternative would leave them financially devastated. Monique would be facing harassment charges. Kenny understood as he had in the past, the alternatives were always the last resort.

There had been no one in attendance during the court proceedings that couldn't be identified. It was as though there was little to no outside interest in the proceedings or the results. If the proceedings were an interest of a gambling ring, they had other plans. The paperwork from the Monique's doctor's office was the most difficult to get, however, the doctor agreed they didn't want to be involved in a drawn-out case that may entail a testimony against distraught women claiming to be pregnant. Their law firm would be in touch with Mr. Simpson within the next two weeks or more. Lastly Tonya and Darryl seemed to be digging into the stocks and who the original investors were. Alan contacted Kenny once Darryl left the office. Robert was becoming a liability and it could cost him his job.

The report was thorough and 'Rell would receive what he needed to know later that day. The men shook hands as they had on many occasions. It was understood Kenny would follow any instructions given without question.

Mr. Simpson took a moment to sit back in his executive chair and close his eyes. He allowed his thoughts to go back to a time when there was no private office, no choice in the cases he covered and the start of a career that seemed to be heading nowhere fast. It was then he met D.Q. Mince a young businessman who needed a personal lawyer.

Stanley Simpson introduced himself after being referred to meet with D.Q. They met at Starbucks and laughed about it years later. D.Q. nor Mr. Simpson had an office. The lawyer was just five years older than the ambitious young man but they latched on to each other and grew together for more than thirty years.

D.Q. Enterprises' first contract landed enough money for them to get adjoined offices in the downtown district. They each grew their businesses and never parted ways. Simpson missed his friend dearly and kept his personal opinions about the family to himself.

'Rell was like his father in more ways than one. Simpson promised D.Q. he would stay with the company and his son. He promised him there would be no difference. The problems would come and go but if they kept things in order and followed his vision, no one would want for anything money could buy.

Simpson laughed each time his memory would remind him, money couldn't buy happiness. He hadn't remarried after his wife divorced him, he hadn't seen his children in years, and he didn't know if he had grandchildren. He only had the family D.Q. shared with him and that was 'Rell.

After D.Q.'s death, 'Rell stepped into his father's shoes and for the past two years he got to know the family more. He enjoyed the talks they shared, the dinners with Nana and the Reverend. He spent time on the phone with Shai and Nikki and 'Rell brought the twins to see him at his home.

He wanted to believe that his friend, D.Q., left a note for 'Rell somewhere that said take care of my friend Stanley Simpson. What he didn't know was that 'Rell understood his emptiness and knew his father wouldn't want him to be alone.

"Mr. Simpson, 'Rell on line one."

Seventy-Two

"Marci, it's just that easy." Shai and Leeza laughed at the confused look on Marci's face.

"I'm just not ready. I know I'm not."

"Your stomach says otherwise. Leeza, tell her, she's dropped. It's just a sign that everything is moving along as it should. It's nothing to worry about. Aunt Darlene will be there with you and Mitch."

"What about his mother, will she be there as well?"

Shai and Marci turned their heads slowly to face Leeza.

"Oh please no. Not the smirk face stare!" The three ladies laughed hysterically. The ringing of a cell phone broke up the laughter.

"Wait that could be Mia. She's been on her way since this morning."

It was Friday afternoon, the ladies agreed to spend the evening with Marci. The week had been long and tiring. They were glad the court proceedings would soon be over. Mr. Simpson advised Derek and Leeza there would be no motion for Derek to be sentenced to jail. They would wait to see what the fine would be. The men went out to celebrate knowing Derek would be leaving Virginia once the money was paid to the court. He and Leeza would be on an early flight to Brazil the next day.

"Hello." Marci shook her head when she heard the voice on the other end. She pushed the speaker button and sat the phone on the coffee table between them.

"I just wanted you to know that I'm not mad at you Marci."

"Why would be mad at me Monique? There's no reason for me to be involved in your antics in any way."

"Oh, so you don't care about your cousin or her feelings? I mean after she goes through this and finds out you knew first she'd be mad at you as well as her doting husband."

"I take it that 'Rell didn't fall for your story?"

"He will. You can be sure of that Marci, he will. He can't be stupid enough to think I am playing with my life in this manner."

"What do you mean in this manner? What do you think, Shai will just disappear?"

Marci looked at Shai who was watching the phone as though she could see Monique as she spoke.

"That's why I am calling you. I've tried talking to you, 'Rell, and Ms. Mince."

"Ms. Mince who?" Leeza, Shai, and Marci leaned into the phone as if they couldn't quite understand what she said.

"Who Monique?"

"Shai's mother. Tonya Mince. She knows about my situation and understands what I am going through."

Shai began to rock back and forth on the couch. Leeza tapped her legs to help calm her. Shai gestured for a pen. Marci pointed to the small table at the entrance of her home. Leeza quickly went to get the pen. Shai wrote her question on the paper.

"Her mother agrees with you? What did she say?" Marci asked and the women waited for the answer.

"Not much, she was very understanding. She said she wouldn't be able to talk to 'Rell of course but she would protect her daughter from the hurt she fell prey to. You see 'Rell has repeated what his father did. He fell for the other because I was like her mother, stupid in love."

"Monique you have lost your mind! Shai and 'Rell are not the same as my uncle and aunt in any way. You are not like my aunt, nor is this so-called love you profess to have the same. What the hell do you want?"

"What is mine!! 'Rell would have never married Shai if I had realized he needed more. I tried to give him all of me but the distance between us…" Monique got quiet. The sounds of her crying followed.

"Monique, seriously? Shai lived here too. If 'Rell truly wanted you in his life you would have been. My uncle and aunt are no comparison to the mess you made of your relationship with 'Rell. Aunt Tonya has been cruel, bitter and sick behind this lost love of hers, I guess that's what you're pretending to be. Post-traumatic lovesickness, is that it?"

"Marci, you can't see what you don't understand. Mitch is your first and you made sure you trapped him. Shai did the same thing to 'Rell, set the trap and after she got caught he married her."

"Monique, let me tell you one damn thing. If you think I'd leave my husband so your ass could be happy …… bitch check the history closely. My mother held on because she wanted a man that didn't want her. My mother ruined a love that should have been simply because she didn't know how to love. My mother is a miserable bitch just like you. Take heed, I love my life, my husband and my kids. Yes, bitch that's right, I have his children. His seed grew inside of me right where he placed it. If there's anything I am sure of it's our love. Give it your best shot bitch and know that I'll be the one coming for you! Marci hang up this damn phone on this stupid trick!"

Marci did as she was instructed without saying another word to Monique. The phone rang twice after the call was disconnected. They listened to the ranting Monique did after the second call.

"Keep that shit. I want 'Rell to hear her threats. She's really looking to be locked the hell up."

Leeza raised her brow causing Marci and Shai to laugh.

"A little too much drama? I told you, it ain't easy being a Mince."

Shai extended her arms to embrace Leeza who looked like she wanted to cry.

"Listen, we truly are a loving family. It's just darkness that comes overhead every now and then. We stick together and get through it. You and Derek will be fine, you hear me? It's not how you fight or what you look like fighting. For most, it's the fact that we will fight."

Leeza sat back and wiped her eyes. "I'm scared you guys. The trial is over Monday and what happens then? Will he be safe? Will any of us be safe?"

"Rell and Mitch will make sure we're safe. Shai you know they will right?"

"Marci, 'Rell said Mr. Simpson is checking into who it is that is behind this gambling threat. I don't think they found anyone. No one showed up in the courtroom."

"Would they be that dumb? I mean who shows up in the courtroom where everyone can see them and then attacks the defendant? They're smarter than that."

"Marci, that's what I thought. I told Derek that's more the reason for us to leave right after the case is settled."

"Leeza, they protected my father for years. Mr. Simpson and Kenny, who is a retired detective have a team. Believe me, you don't know what they do until it's done. The debt will be paid and you guys can go home safe and sound."

"Yes and start your family. You better invite us to do your wedding in Brazil. That would be fire! Shai tell her."

Leeza took a deep breath. She was sure she'd be a Mince, she just wasn't sure Derek would propose.

Seventy-Three

Another round was ordered. Mitch, 'Rell and Derek met at the Steakhouse. 'Rell took the twins to Karlton and Tonya after he left court. Shai thanked him knowing her mother could be more annoying than thankful that they allowed the children to visit for the weekend.

"So Tonya Mince, my mother, didn't give you any flak. Man, you've done the impossible."

"No Karlton did. He answered the door. That's what we do. Tonya can be a bit much, I mean I don't have to tell you about your mother, but man she loves those kids. She's a different person around them."

"You don't have to tell me about my mother. You and Karlton know her too, that's why he answered the door."

The men laughed and tapped the three beer bottles in agreement. Derek shook his head thinking about the chaos his mother could cause.

"Monique called Marci. Shai and Leeza became the audience while she tried to go off about this pregnancy mess."

"You've got to be kiddin' me. Marci don't need that shit."

"Hell, Derek Leeza don't either. Probably scared that little butterfly of yours." Mitch teased him with an imitation of Leeza's timid smile.

"What? Scared her? What did Monique do?"

'Rell started laughing. "Listen Shai was trying to tell me what she said and then Marci and Leeza cut in to tell me what she really said. They're fine, Shai explained herself to Leeza but told her she would need a backbone to be a Mince."

"To be a Mince? What does that mean, Derek man you proposing son?"

"Nah, no. Not even Mitch. We've got a few things to iron out with her family. You know they're traditional people. To them, I'm the patient that she brought home to heal. Like a puppy or something. I do love her though. Not now, but I hope in the future. Her father is the main one. Her mother is really quiet."

"Do they live by that thing where the woman is submissive to the man?"

"I don't know. I can't really tell much about how they live. Whenever she visits them, I don't go. They don't come to visit us much since we moved. The living arrangements didn't work. We had to move if we were to make it or if I was to heal. She told them she loved me and her father laughed."

"Wow, really? I guess that was enough for you."

"Mitch man, I held my tongue so much. Don't get me wrong they have a nice home, plenty of room. He does something with agriculture there. He works for the government so they're considered well off. Nothing like us. Can you imagine that? I'm lying in someone's home who thinks I'm so needy I had to come home with their daughter? If I didn't love her, I would have left."

"So now what? You're living near them in an apartment?"

"Rell you know it's just temporary. I wanted to be sure about this case and Quintech. I had to set Uncle Darryl straight about the business last night too. He was so damn drunk. I guess that's why he didn't show up in the courtroom today. Anyway, I want to buy some land and begin building that home. You know, something a Mince would live in. If all is well with us, then she'll be my Mrs. I want to be sure everything is in place. Her family has no idea what our family does or what we have."

"Man, you mean Leeza didn't tell them. She didn't show them the website? I don't know, seems like she would quiet them down. I mean she left home to become a nurse so they must know she's able to stand on her own."

"I guess, but being here has opened my eyes. I really want a family. I want to be that man that D.Q. would be proud of, you know. He was a man's man and I know living with Leeza's people that would never happen. If she wants to be near her family, okay but, we have to have our own home."

"Well, we can get that done. Like you said once the dust settles we can work that out."

"Mitch you like Brazil man?"

"Rell don't play with me. You know where I'll be for the next what, year?"

"Better practice getting sleep early in the evening man. At least you ain't like 'Rell here. Twins must have killed you guys, huh?"

"Ain't nothing better than feeding them and watch them doze off to sleep. That was one of my favorite times. We did things together and separate. I learned to be grateful all over again. We're blessed fellas. My father, our father Derek left us a blessing, a life. We've just got to live it. So with that my brother we'll buy the land, build the home and have a wedding they won't forget."

'Rell and Derek said their good-bye to Mitch as they left the restaurant. It was the ride home when they realized they had to come together and be one.

"He's really taking this thing too far."

"Listen Derek, you know that I did everything that dad asked to be done. Whatever plans he had, hell, I'm still following his blueprint."

"What stocks is he talking about?"

"D.Q. had money he invested from family, friends and those who started the company with him. You know, Robert, Alan, and Stanley were the main ones. I was instructed to keep them on because they were the foundation. Nana, Aunt Darlene, and Uncle Darryl put in, man I guess, their life savings at the time. He never mentioned my mother or your mother. Whatever funds or the people who he was told to invest in brought in a fortune. Man the money turned over and it keeps turning over. Simpson knows where it's invested. I know there's two or three spots out west, the others are overseas."

'Rell waited hoping Derek's questions would ease the anger he felt was between him and their uncle. Derek was silent.

"Listen, Derek, for some reason our uncle feels he deserved more. I don't know what he expected but what I do know is just like your mother, he has to find his place and stay in it. I have given them what dad instructed was theirs. I signed more than my share of paperwork, granted favors, gave loans and forgave those who sought to do me wrong. Derek, I am not the boy who woke up and found out my father had another family. I'm a man running a Fortune 500 company. We can do this the right way my brother, for the family. If we let family push us to do what they want every time they call or just throw money away, it all will be gone."

"You right man, I understand."

'Rell parked his black Escalade in front of his home. He turned off the engine but neither of them moved to get out.

"Rell man, D.Q. did what most black men want to do. He did it the right way and paid everyone more than what they put in. Uncle Darryl just fucked over his."

"And part of yours, that's the problem. He wants to have that access man to just blow it all. His gambling is an addiction, it's his drug."

"Along with that damn alcohol. I was trying not to yoke his ass up. Then he had the nerve to tell me Quintech was his. Listen, I told him if he can't handle the business then it should sit under the Enterprise. I know it will be too hard for me to manage from Brazil."

"Man squash that shit. Quintech is yours, that's what dad wanted. You know what I mean. Each of us was left our own. Uncle Darryl was bailed out more than once. His construction company here and in Chicago stands only because of D.Q. Enterprises money. Nah, we'll get you staff and they can interface with you to keep the business managed by you. Craig and Keith are on board they'll run it here. Now if Uncle Darryl wants to pull out we'll just hire another construction company to work with you. It ain't hard man. That's what he doesn't understand, ain't nobody losing no more."

"Thanks, man. I didn't want it to seem like I was undermining him but hell, he took it too far. Now he's saying that the money owed is more than sixty g's. 'Rell he's lying. We owed fifty when this thing first started. He said he was pulling a couple of thousand a month from Francine and then from Quintech. Something ain't right."

"Derek, did you ever go with him to drop the money to these guys?"

"No man, he did or didn't. He would get caught up in another game and lose more. I can't live looking over my shoulder like this and man, he could care less."

"Yeah, that's the problem with a drunk. They only care when they can't drink. Whether it's from the bottle or the money well."

Seventy-Four

'Rell turned the key and entered his grandmother's home. He called her, letting her know he was on his way. She told him she was just leaving the church. Rev. Wilcox was there with her. The aroma of their breakfast had gone but the smell of coffee was still in the air.

He proceeded to the kitchen where he found the coffee pot half full. The red light indicated it was still warm. Nana left the pot on as she had many mornings. He smiled thinking about her drinking coffee throughout the day. Some days it would be water for her tea. Nana was predictable. A coffee day was completely the opposite of a tea day, or comforting day, as she would call it. He wondered if she knew what his conversation entailed. After pouring himself a cup of coffee, he returned to the sitting room.

It wasn't long before the front door opened and he could hear his grandmother and uncle talking.

"Darryl, I'm not going to argue with you. You're not making any sense. Now you can stay if you want to but you know I ain't going for that cussing and arguing in my home. I told you today wasn't a good day and you still insisted on "stopping by" as you said. You had no intentions on coming here until I said I was expecting 'Rell to come by. 'Rell, you here baby?"

'Rell stepped out of the sitting room where they could see him. Darryl gave him a hardened stare.

"Do you want me to come back? I mean I'm not trying to be in the middle of you and Nana's talk."

"No, I think I'll stay and so will you. What, the two of you gonna discuss what I told you I found out?"

"What did you find out Darryl? 'Rell, what is he talking about?"

"Nana, maybe it is good he's here. Yes, stay. C'mon Nana have a seat, do you want coffee? You, Uncle Darryl, coffee or anything?"

"Cut the pleasantries. Mama, I'm gonna need you to tell the truth about this."

"What in the world?" She followed Darryl to the sitting room. 'Rell returned from the kitchen with Nana's cup of coffee.

"I guess this will be a coffee day Nana?" 'Rell smiled at his grandmother and sat on the couch across from the two of them.

'Rell started the conversation repeating the talk he had with Darryl. He told them the concerns Derek had about Quintech as well.

"The company needs to stand on a solid foundation. Derek agreed that if you couldn't manage and maintain the level of contracts and more, the Enterprise would manage it totally. He will be working from Brazil."

"He ain't never coming back here to live huh?" Nana took a deep breath.

"Not to work. He's thinking Leeza wants to be there and their future may be there as well."

"Oh, I see."

"Well, I don't think we need your company overseeing Quintech," Darryl stated as he sat back in his chair.

"To be honest it's not your decision. That's up to Derek."

"And it ain't for you to convince him otherwise."

"Uncle Darryl, he brought this to me. Just like you called the other night, he wanted to clarify a few things."

"Wait a minute, hold on here. I see you getting huffed up Darryl. I ain't having it, I said that already. Now Quintech and D.Q. Enterprises ain't your business. That there construction company or interior, whatever your company is; you make the decision for that company, don't you?" Nana didn't wait to make her next point. "You wouldn't let Derek make no decisions about it, I know you wouldn't. You wouldn't let Francine make no decisions about that company you had in Chicago, she made them 'cause you wouldn't. When have you ever run a company?"

"You right Mama, I couldn't cause your son was always putting his mouth in my business."

"It was a good thing he did."

'Rell interrupted, "Listen, Uncle Darryl, I can't have you digging into the paperwork or the funds that keep both companies in the green. You can either work with things the way that Derek and I agreed on or feel free to legally step away from the business."

"Listen man, I ain't going nowhere. D.Q. was my brother before he was your damn daddy. Whatever he left should have been my mother's, my sister's or mine. You would have got yours eventually."

"You gonna watch your mouth in my home, that's what you're going to do first. Second D.Q.'s wife and children come before siblings and mother as far as the law is concerned. What else did you want from him? I know you didn't think he'd leave you the company that he built from the ground up?"

"Why not Mama? Why not? We gave him the money that he's been investing in stocks over the years. Yea, he gave us a bone. What about the money that is building from the money we gave him?"

"Boy, that ain't ours, especially yours. You didn't even put in all of your shares. 'Rell you do what you need to do with Quintech. You and Derek make sure the company can stand on its own if necessary. Have Simpson draw up the papers for your uncle just in case he wants to withdraw his partnership at this time."

"Aw, ain't you the business... You on that board or committee that knows about the investments aren't you? Tell me the truth, Mama."

"You don't need to know that. Just know I'm watching you, the businesses and the expected growth. Run your business, that's enough for you. 'Cause you see son, when you can't have what you want, you leave everything for others to pick up the pieces. Throwing a temper tantrum ain't an attention getter when you're over forty."

"So that's it? That's what you came running to your grandmother for? You wanted her to put everything in place?"

"Uncle Darryl, listen man, you need a gambling debt paid and Quintech has to pay the court. The next thing for Quintech is getting back to business. I'm sorry you feel some sort of way about what my father did or how he did it. I followed his rules, it was his business."

"Mama, you can't possibly ignore the money that is being invested without us getting our fair share."

Darryl looked at his mother.

"Son, let's be honest, for real as you young folks would say. You didn't even have the money to invest. How much do you think D.Q. gave you over the years? Saving your company, paying your bail, taking care of the kids, time has run out Darryl. Ain't nobody looking for nothing more 'cept you. Why? What did you get yourself into now?"

"Rell, what are you going to do huh? Should I tell mama how much this is costing the family?"

"What are you talking about? How is D.Q. Enterprises costing the family Uncle Darryl?"

"Let's see, we all have needs. It seems that the family is paying the expenses for your staff, the infamous Mr. Simpson, that security team, need I go on?"

"Darryl, you sound foolish. What is it you want?"

"I want what's mine Mama. D.Q. made his off us and we got what for it."

"Uncle Darryl, how much is either of your companies worth? If you lost the one in Chicago, how would your family get by? You're paying child support in three states, you're running a company here and you owe a so-called gambling ring money. Could either of your companies collapse and keep you from drowning yourself in an alcoholic coma. Really, my father kept you from being on the short pier to your own death. I read page after page of payments made to you and for you. He told me to cut you off, period. There was never supposed to be a spot for you in Quintech. Derek suggested it, he said he'd love to work with you. Today, he said he regretted making that decision. What, how much? If I have to pay you, you'll sign papers and I will cut you off."

"Rell baby, he's just upset. Darryl, you understand what you're staring at right. Stop looking down the barrel of the shotgun son. Nobody wants you to fail or lose nothing but whatever you think you're supposed to get from 'Rell's business is a lie. Those stocks are what run the extra. Extra for us all. Emergency money for us. D.Q.'s instructions was not to touch the investments unless it was a necessary emergency. Derek's case and his hospital bills is what he meant. Situations you don't plan on."

"So Derek is the priority, that's what you saying, Mama?"

"Derek almost lost his life. You know that. He had to pay for those medical bills and he needed to get away from here."

"So you big Mama now, controlling 'Rell and still running D.Q. Enterprises from what, your sitting room?"

"Whoa man, you out of order now. I'm not going to sit here and listen to you talk to my grandmother like that."

Darryl stood to approach 'Rell who raised to his feet. Nana got between the two men.

"Enough! Darryl, you've said enough. Go home, go somewhere, just leave here. Don't you cross my threshold until you understand that I will always be your mother! If that were you who was lying in the hospital close to death, the money would have been there for you. I don't know what's come over you, but today ain't the day for it. Go on now, move toward that door boy!"

"This ain't over by a long shot 'Rell. Humph, D.Q. dies and leaves his stingy ass spirit in you. It's our money you building on and it all will crumble."

"She asked you to leave."

"What that mean? You gonna put me out of this house too? First the business and then my Mama's house?"

"It ain't the first time Darryl, now go on. You been drinking again and ain't no talking to you with that liquor swimming around your brain. Now go on, go on before it takes me longer to get over your disrespect in my home."

"You better call your lawyer and get ready for what's coming your way."

"If that's a threat, you won't be able to stand the repercussions. Watch your step, I ain't your brother." 'Rell didn't flinch and his stance spoke louder than his words.

Darryl paused in the doorway. There was no more to be said. He'd have to handle 'Rell and Derek at the same time.

Seventy-Five

Stanley Simpson listened as Nana repeated the scene that took place in her home. 'Rell left shortly after his uncle. They didn't discuss her son's antics. For the first time in years, Nana needed to be guided legally.

"Julie we've talked about this mess that Darryl gets into. 'Rell won't do anything that he won't discuss with you or me first. He's not a hot head."

"No, Darryl is. Stan, I just couldn't understand what he was getting at. He kept mentioning the stocks that we invested in that started the business. He didn't even have enough money to put in his share. You remember that?"

"Yea, I do." Stanley nodded his head yes. Remembering how frustrated D.Q. was when he brought the money to his office.

"D.Q. thought the deal would be off the table if he didn't have all of the money. We were able to convince the investors our business would be viable to them and the community. The call came in from the mayor's office and the deal was done."

"Darryl has no idea what we went through and if 'Rell lets him run Quintech I'm sure the money would vanish. Derek won't have no business if Darryl has his hands in it."

"And what's wrong with 'Rell's friends being there? I don't understand what he wants to do."

"Darryl has a problem with gambling. We're looking into Derek's accident. Did 'Rell tell you?"

"No, he left right after he was sure Darryl wasn't turning back here. He was here to talk though."

"Well, we can't find anything that points to a gambling debt. I've got someone on him, Julie. He's still trying to sit in on the big games and he's not winning. I don't know where the money is coming from. 'Rell has a lock on Quintech money both coming and going. Simone is out of town and he's been gambling heavy since Wednesday."

"During the day? I didn't know they gambled during the day."

"Whenever, wherever."

"What kind of trouble is this Stanley? I mean why? He doesn't need money like that. I mean he don't buy nothing for himself and that woman, poor Simone. She's working with Nikki you know. They've got a business together."

"We're trying to figure it out."

"Is it another family? You know he drops children every time he drops his pants seems like."

Stanley laughed as did Nana. It lightened the moment for her.

"So what do we do Stanley? You know, when D.Q. knew he was too sick to do anything else, he told me to call you. He said to call you for whatever. Well you know there was no man here other than him. I always wondered why he told me that. I thought to myself that the business would fall if God took D.Q. from me. Everything I had I gave to him for that business. He promised it would sustain our family for generations. I can't let Darryl destroy that."

"He won't. I promise. 'Rell won't let him, I'm sure of that. Julie, can you handle Darryl? What I mean is he's going to get a lot madder if 'Rell cuts him off."

"Do you think it will come to that? 'Rell won't have to ruin him, will he?"

"Darryl has his company. If he let's go of this idea that he's owed something, he'll be fine."

"And if not?"

"Your grandson is just like his father."

"I know, that's what I'm afraid of. Stop Darryl Stanley. Stop him before 'Rell asks you. I saw D.Q. in him today. I saw his spirit rise up in his son. Stop Darryl in whatever he thinks he can do. He can't win. You and I know that."

"Yes, ma'am I do. Let me know if you need anything else. Whatever it is don't hesitate to call."

"Did 'Rell speak to you about that girl, Monique Davis?"

"Yes, we spoke about her and Tonya. We're working on both problems, yes ma'am. The problems are being handled."

"Thank you. I'm going to get me something to eat. You have a good afternoon."

Nana sat with her eyes closed. After her silent prayer, she let the comfort of the chair take over. It was an hour later when she heard her husband close the front door. She had a full morning of family drama to share with him, she had to shake off the sleep that gave her a break in time.

Seventy-Six

Karlton and Tonya treated the twins to breakfast at IHop where they ate their favorite, waffles with strawberries. The show at Kids Main Stage was at three and they would spend the time before the show shopping at the mall. Brianna nor Bryce complained. The four-year-olds were acquainted with roaming the stores and behaving, as the adults shopped. Tonya loved the attention they received and the question, *"Are they, twins?"*

Bryce would stay with Karlton while Tonya and Brianna looked at shoes and other female items. Periodically they would wander through the men's display of ties and shirts. There was no doubt they were raised well, their mannerism showed it.

Tonya took the time to put the two in matching outfits. Both wore their denim jean outfits with lime green plaid shirts. Brianna's hair was braided neatly with beads that matched her shirt and sneakers. Bryce wore a lime green hat to match his sneakers. The two ran ahead of their grandparents to the carousel that sat in the center of the mall.

"Can we please?" They ran back to Tonya excited that she would allow them to ride the horses.

"Let me tell Poppa to get the change for the ride." She called Karlton back to where they stood watching the children get on the ride.

Karlton knew what she wanted and went to the ticket booth on his way to them. Brianna started to cry.

"What's wrong sweetie? Now, now you can't ride the horsey if you're crying. Horses don't understand tears." Tonya picked up her granddaughter to console her. "Poppa is getting the tickets for you and Bryce, see?"

Brianna stopped crying as she saw Karlton approaching them waving a few tickets in his hand. There were three rides in front of Kids Main Stage. Parents were scrambling with their children running from one ride to another. The area was filling quickly with families waiting for the doors to open. The show wouldn't start for another hour. The seating was first come first serve and many knew the doors would open only fifteen minutes before show time.

Monique spotted them as she stood in front of Janet's Fashions, a small boutique she frequented often. The crowd was increasing in size and caused many of the shoppers to pause as they navigated their way around the crowd. Monique watched Tonya and Karlton as they kept the twins from getting too far from their reach.

She recognized them from the wedding. It had been two years and the twins had grown a bit. She remembered how the guests chatted about their friendliness and how cute they were then. Brianna was busy, just as she was at the wedding. She was pulling her grandmother to look at things that interested her in the moment. She wasn't willing to sit patiently for the doors to open. Bryce stood to see where his sister was leading Tonya. Once he saw they weren't going far he sat again next to Karlton who held no interest in watching Tonya or Brianna.

Monique watched the little girl and allowed herself to imagine the child being hers. The twins favored 'Rell, thick curls and bronze skin. Their button eyes showed their innocence yet there was a gleam of excitement each time they spoke.

Karlton stood holding Bryce by his hand. He approached Tonya and pointed to the corridor of stores opposite Kids Main Stage. Tonya leaned in and spoke to Brianna who shook her head. Karlton leaned in to speak with her and again she replied shaking her head "no". Monique smiled slowly. She understood the question as Karlton and Bryce headed in the direction he pointed out to Tonya.

"The bathroom," Monique whispered.

Tonya and Brianna returned to the waiting crowd. Brianna found a seat on one of the benches that were near the carousel. She began to entertain herself watching the ride go around and around.

Suddenly she sneezed.

"Oh my, let me get a tissue. Let's see, I should have one here." Tonya began to dig in her bag she carried. "Oh dear Bree, wait let me go and get you a tissue. Sit still baby okay?"

Brianna nodded her head as Tonya stepped away quickly hurrying toward the pretzel stand across the mall floor. Brianna got up as she wiped her nose with her hand and wandered around the carousel.

Monique followed the child with her eyes until she noticed Brianna was walking toward the other stores in the opposite direction. Monique looked back at the pretzel stand where Tonya was talking with the lady in line. She excused herself as she pulled the napkins from the holder.

Hastily, Monique walked behind Brianna. "Brianna? Where you going, baby?"

"I want to see." The small child replied.

"Where are you going, baby? Bryce is over here?"

"Byce?"

Monique smiled at the little one's mispronunciation of her brother's name.

"Yes, let me take you to Bryce."

Brianna looked up at her and smiled. "Byce. I want Byce."

"We're going to Bryce baby. Then we'll call daddy okay?"

"Kay." Brianna gave Monique her hand.

Monique quickly picked the child up and went to through the nearest store to exit the mall.

Seventy-Seven

Darryl called Simone. She said she'd be home late she and Nikki had two new clients to visit before they left Washington. He pretended to be upset but the reality was it would give him enough time to work out the payment arrangements. He would need to know before Monday how the payment would be made. After talking to 'Rell and his mother they left him no choice but to go to the lawyer and tell him what the family was facing. He'd be the one to relay the information and wait for their response. It was simple. 'Rell would either give the family the money he felt was owed or pay it through the debt.

Sitting at his desk he pulled out a folder with receipts and the pictures of Derek's accident. He'd have a courier deliver the urgent package of the collected information to Mr. Simpson. He added a typed note with the demand for payment.

The debt owed has not been paid. We've been following the case and have been patient. The amount of eighty thousand dollars is what you are to tell your client is due. Sixty thousand for him and another twenty thousand for us not killing him during the trial. The Mince family is on notice. Payment is past due.

Darryl thought it best not to wait until the conclusion of the trial. It would soon be behind him and the family. This would prove there was a serious threat and once the payment was made he would convince

'Rell that as D.Q.'s brother he should have been given total control of Quintech. Especially since they wouldn't find the culprits. Derek could return safe to Brazil and he would have the company and access to the stocks.

The courier had instructions to deliver it to the law office by three. There would still be a doorman on duty. Darryl knew with the package marked urgent, Stanley Simpson would receive a call.

Chapter 1

Too Close for Comfort

Stanley answered the phone hoping it was Kenny. Once he got the call about an urgent package he called Kenny so they could meet at the office. He had been there for more than an hour and Kenny hadn't arrived. The phone ringing was a sign something was wrong.

"Hey, Simpson we've got a problem."

"Yes, I've been waiting for you here."

"Can't. The baby is missing. I'm here at the mall with the cops. 'Rell and Shai are talking to them now."

"What baby? Where in the mall?"

"Kids Stage. Tonya and Karlton had the twins out to see some performance. Brianna's gone."

"How? I'm on my way."

Simpson hung up the phone and grabbed the package he received from the security desk. 'Rell would have to know before Monday. The court proceedings would have to be held without Derek being present.

He thought about the content, the message and why he was chosen to receive the collected information. It seemed too close, too strange. Now with a possible kidnapping, maybe the package was the icing on the cake.

It took fifteen minutes for him to arrive at what was total chaos. Simpson had to weave his way through police and a panicked crowd to reach the Mince family. Police were keeping back the spectators and clearing the area near Kids Main Stage. There were a few couples who said they noticed the little girl with the woman who was standing with the family. No one remembered Brianna wandering off.

Tonya was with Karlton and an officer. Stanley looked for Kenny who was with 'Rell and Shai who were standing at the pretzel stand. Shai was obviously shaken but quiet. 'Rell was on his phone.

"Mr. Simpson, thank you for coming but they have no idea..." Shai began to cry.

'Rell turned to embrace her. "Yeah man call Aunt Darlene for me and ask her to come here. I'm going with Kenny to do something, I don't know just come. No, not Marci. Mia is fine. Yeah, yeah, I'll wait for you and Mia." He disconnected the call. "Stanley, thanks man you must have ESP or something. Listen baby, Mia and Mitch are on their way here. I'm going to find out what some of these people know so we can do our own search."

"Rell, that's for the police to do. Why can't you just be here?"

"Shai, I can't just stand here. I'm trying not to go off. Listen, I'm not leaving until they get here." He tapped Kenny and the lawyer on their arm. They moved a few feet from Shai. "Listen, nobody seems to know a damn thing. Including that sorry ass Tonya. Karlton and Bryce were in the bathroom. She was with Brianna. Brianna needed a tissue, she came here to get it and got back over there and my baby was gone."

There was an outburst from the crowd. Shai was confronting her mother.

"What the hell were you thinking leaving a four-year-old in a crowd like this? What the hell are you good for? Are you drunk again? Why Karlton? Why the hell would you leave my daughter with her? We let them go with you! Bryce let's go. Let my son go!"

The police rushed to the area to back up the crowd and come between them.

"Shai, wait honey. Let me explain. It wasn't like that I told you what happened, oh my God….." Tonya broke down in tears as Karlton let go of Bryce's hand to catch her before she fell.

"Great fuckin' performance. My child is missing and you fall the hell out. Take her ass out of here before I kick her in her ass. Where is my child?!"

'Rell pushed his way through the crowd. "Shai, c'mon baby, c'mon." He picked up Bryce and spoke to Kenny who was close. "Keep her away from us. I don't care how. She is not to come anywhere near us."

"No problem." Kenny talked into his watch and three men in the hall moved. "Mr. Simpson has a matter to discuss with you sir, I'll stay with the family."

'Rell left Bryce and Shai with Kenny and he walked outside of the mall. Stanley flashed his headlights once he saw 'Rell in front of the exit door.

"What the hell happened?"

"Shai went at her mother. This shit will be everlasting. There's no clues there. We're going to have to figure this shit out. Someone walked off with Brianna. They had to know who she was. All these damn kids running around and Brianna is the one that's picked up? I don't believe that."

"Don't."

"Don't what?"

"Look at this. It was an urgent delivery at my office at about three this afternoon. What time are they saying they think Brianna was missing?"

"The show was about two or three. I'm not sure."

Stanley handed 'Rell the envelope. He looked through the contents and read the typed note.

"This is from who? The gamblers sent a notice to the lawyer? Does that make sense?"

"No, not to you, me or Kenny. It tells me it's someone who does more than gamble with your uncle and brother."

"I'm not understanding why not send it to me? I mean you don't have the money."

"Exactly, but I guess they know I'm the family lawyer."

"Shit."

"What?

"We need protection for Nana. She will want to know what's going on."

"So you tell her. Believe me, she won't be surprised."

"Why do I think my father had his own mess going on?"

"Because he did Mr. Mince, he did. I just needed you to know what we have. Kenny is getting the team together to track a few things. We have to find Brianna, and find out who this gambler is."

"Keep me posted."

Chapter 2

Brianna cried herself to sleep. Monique covered her with a blanket in the backseat of the car. She was parked in the mall parking lot watching the police presence increase. After walking quickly through the mall with Brianna away from the frantic response from Tonya and the other mothers, Monique slowed her pace to a comfortable stroll. Brianna was quiet and didn't seemed disturbed that she was with a stranger. Monique entered a few stores as though she was shopping.

She made sure to stop at a kiosk that had children toys. She allowed Brianna to pick a toy of choice. It would keep her quiet as Monique watched the turmoil grow. Now seated in her car not far from the entrance where the police setup a makeshift reporting station, she waited for the Amber alert to sound on her phone. They had no clue who had the child and since Monique's actions weren't pre-planned she didn't know what to do next. It was obvious they hadn't seen her on any surveillance cameras. What was next, a ransom note? She didn't know.

Brianna wasn't a problem. She was a beautiful child. Her innocence kept her from understanding Monique actions as being vindictive. Monique wanted so much more. Having 'Rell's child with her was surreal. If they were together, he would still have contact with his children. She hadn't thought of that before. He wouldn't leave Shai and the children, they would be attached forever.

She needed to talk to him. He needed to understand she too would be attached to him. They shared an undying love and if he gave her a chance to make it all up to him, maybe. The thought ended without a way to make it right. The police would want to arrest her. Shai would see to that.

Monique would say she found the girl wandering. She stopped thinking about it. There would be so many questions. It didn't matter. It was a chance to get 'Rell to understand, she was serious. Maybe if she called Mr. Simpson, 'Rell's lawyer, he would be able to explain her temporary lapse of thought. It really was a lapse of concern. Monique didn't care what Shai thought or felt, after all no one was worried about her feelings.

It wasn't about Shai or the family she thought was secure. Monique felt her fantasy, her dream of being Mrs. Mince was stolen. Taking Brianna was just that simple, getting back her stolen dream. Now as she watched the crowd grow in size the Amber alert buzzed on her phone. It was then she heard 'Rell's voice, *"You're not her mother."* The police were standing at the entrance. They were emptying the theatre and directing parents and children to their cars. It seemed they were checking each child and parent as they exited the building.

The phone rang, startling her as she quickly answered before it rang again. She checked the small child in the backseat before speaking softly.

"Hello?"

"Monique, why didn't you answer you cell?"

It was Craig. Monique didn't want to sound rattled. She got out of the car and closed the door gently, hoping not to awaken Brianna.

"What? I don't know. I wasn't near my phone. What are you calling me for?"

"I think we both know why I'm calling."

"No, we don't. You told me to do me remember?"

"And just what did you decide to do Monique? I told you to be careful. You take things too far."

"Craig, what are you talking about?"

"Turn on the news Monique. I hope you aren't behind the kidnapping of 'Rell and Shai's child."

"Why would I kidnap a child Craig?"

"They're going to find that baby and I hope they don't find her with you."

"You've really lost your mind. I don't know what you're talking about."

"Good, you're at the top of my list of suspects."

"Well as long as it's your list it doesn't add up to much."

Monique disconnected the call. He knew. She didn't know how he knew, but if he did, so did 'Rell. Craig wasn't at the mall she was sure of that but he'd call 'Rell. She'd have to get away. She searched her car for a pad. A note to explain, no a note to let 'Rell know how close he came to losing. Once again she'd have to go with her instincts. She just wasn't sure where.

Brianna was sleeping soundly. Monique didn't want to startle her or cause her to panic. There was no way to sneak through the crowd. It was the crowd that would disguise her dastardly deed. There was an entrance two doors away from the police, parents and children. Other shoppers were using it to enter and exit the mall. Monique tapped Brianna gently. The angelic smile brought tears to Monique's eyes.

"C'mon baby. Let's find Bryce."

Brianna sat up and grabbed the doll. Monique stuffed the note in the pocket of the dolls dress. She carried the young Miss Mince in her arms until they got close to the chosen entrance. Monique thought about entering the mall pretending to be the hero. Proving how unfit Shai was to leave her child with her unstable mother would shed light on a front page story. The woman who was left, pregnant and in love would make great headlines. She'd call the journalist from the Tribune. Yes, the story would be her story how 'Rell's lost love found his child.

Just as quickly as the thought came, the doubt rose. Craig's phone call would destroy her account of what happened. He wouldn't allow her to win that easy. The crowd had grown but was contained to the area just outside of the theatre. The majority of the police were at the door helping parents and children as they exited. There were a few walking in and out of the theatre. Monique scanned the crowd for the Mince family.

The movement toward the food court was slow as was the foot traffic that was trying to avoid the entrance checkpoint. Monique spotted Karlton and Tonya sitting where Brianna left them.

Monique squatted to talk to Brianna.

"Baby can you see Bryce and your Pop-Pop over there?"

"No Byce. I don't see him."

"Look over there. Do you see him now?"

"No," Brianna replied as she moved a little further away from Monique.

Monique pushed her a little toward the crowd hoping the tiny child would see her grandparents. As she did, the group surrounding them began to move. Monique couldn't see Brianna and had let her hand go leaving the child to wander again.

Monique quickly backed up to the door where she made her entrance. She hoped the child would not be lost again as she blended in with those who were shopping and not pausing to see what the confusion at Kids Stage was.

The parking lot traffic was at a standstill. Monique returned to her car and watched the entrance where the police were. There was no indication they found the missing child. 'Rell was talking to an officer and shaking his hand. Monique smiled hoping his calm manner meant the baby was with her family.

Other Novels by Nanette M. Buchanan

Family Secrets Lies and Alibi's

A Different Kind of Love

Bruised Love

Skeletons Beyond The Closed Door

Gossip Line

Bonded Betrayal

Scattered Pieces

The Stranger Within

The Perfect Side Piece

The Hustler's Touch

The Corner Pew

Purchase Your Copy Today

www.NanetteMBuchanan.com

Books are available in Kindle, Nook and other ebook formats